THE WIND OFF THE SEA

"A blessed companion is a book"—JERROLD

THE WIND
OFF THE SEA

*

DAVID BEATY

THE COMPANION BOOK CLUB
LONDON

For B.

© David Beaty, 1962

*Made and printed in Great Britain
for The Companion Book Club (Odhams Press Ltd.)
by Odhams (Watford) Limited
Watford, Herts.*

S.963.UA.L.

NOTE

In this novel, I would like to make
it clear that all the characters are
fictitious. Inevitably, some ranks and
titles and the names and numbers
of organizations are used, but they
are in no way based on real-life
counterparts.

PROLOGUE

THEY met for the first time under the gaslight of the tiny booking-hall.

"Henderson," said the pear-shaped one, taking off a shabby glove.

"Bunting."

As they shook hands, they eyed each other warily. They had been the only passengers the London-Lincoln express had disgorged that night, and now they were the sole population of North Luddenham railway station. Even so, being English, it was unlikely they would have spoken, let alone introduced themselves, had they not also been officers of the Royal Air Force.

Both were Wing Commanders, both had rather pale faces, both were middle-aged—but there all similarity ceased. Where there was a certain amiably plump untidiness about Henderson, Bunting was tall, erect, and though his fair hair was at present turning a metallic silver, it was obvious at one time he might have been a considerable athlete. Under a small square moustache, his lips were smiling as he asked, "Is this your lot, too?"

"How d'you mean?"

"Posted to this dump . . . are you?"

"No. Just a visit."

"Lucky bastard! Just back from Aden . . . now they make me Wing Commander Admin at Luddenham." Bunting paused purposely to hear the other man's business, but all Henderson volunteered was that perhaps he should telephone for transport.

"There'll be a car out there for me somewhere. They know I'm coming." Bunting looked through the open door to the railway yard outside. "Ah, there it is!" He had caught sight of two smudgy sidelights. "I take it you're going up to the Station?"

"Yes."

"Then you better come with me."

"Thanks."

7

They walked out to the Humber, and settled themselves in the back seat while the airman-driver stowed their luggage in the boot. "Bad as the blackout!" Bunting complained, as the car set off through dark winding lanes. "God, how I hate this place!"

"You've been here before then?"

"Not round *here*. Farther south. But Lincolnshire's all the same."

"You never know . . . North Luddenham may be different."

"What makes you take that optimistic view?"

"Well, it's not exactly the usual sort of R.A.F. Station."

"Won't make any difference. Still be surrounded by fens and chapels." Bunting pointed through the side window. "Look . . . we're entering the metropolis!" The Humber hissed past rows of terraced brick houses, empty wet pavements, shuttered shops. "Lord . . . a ghost town! Whatever is there to do in the evenings?"

"The R.A.F. Station . . . I believe . . . is well equipped with entertainment."

"Who told you that?"

"Somebody at Air Ministry."

Bunting gave a snort. "Those Air Ministry characters tell you anything!"

"Thanks apparently," Henderson continued, "to the efforts of the Commanding Officer."

"Thanks to Gavin Gallagher, eh?"

"You sound as though you know the Group Captain?"

Though Henderson looked expectantly towards him, Bunting neither confirmed nor denied it. A silence fell between the two of them. Their new-born acquaintanceship seemed on the point of drying up completely, when Bunting suddenly said, "As a matter of a fact . . . I do. Same college at Oxford."

"So you're old friends?"

"Well . . . we *knew* each other. Sport was more my line. He was . . . arty."

"Have you known him in the Service?"

"We did our flying training together . . . twenty years ago. Haven't seen him since."

8

"He's done very well."

There was the slightest pause. "Rather . . . surprisingly . . . well."

"It'll be quite a reunion for you."

"I suppose so." Bunting turned his head away from his companion to gaze out at the black landscape outside. The last shadowy house had fallen behind them now, and the car was humming up a slight incline flanked by tall hedges. Rain was falling in fine silver needles, and on the road ahead scatterings of autumn leaves rose up in the wind like coveys of startled birds. Several times, Henderson made remarks about Gallagher, saying that though he did not know the Group Captain he had heard a great deal. But Bunting either had nothing further to offer on the subject, or he felt that it was now the other man's turn to produce some information about himself, for he countered such observations by indirect probings into Henderson's comings-and-goings in the Air Force, finally finishing up (for Henderson was evasive) in straightforward directness. "Not General Duties . . . are you?"

Pilots were General Duties. General Duties were the élite of the Air Force, providing the top brass. Henderson confessed that he was not.

"Technical?"

"No."

"Equipment?"

"No."

"Legal?" And taking the other's silence as an affirmative. "So you're a lawyer!"

"Not exactly," Henderson said reluctantly. "I'm on the Provost Marshal's staff."

"Oh . . . a policeman!" Bunting gave a jerk of surprise, conscious of having spoken openly as though to an ordinary man, and now trying to remember what he'd said. As always, he felt suddenly guilty, as though *he* was the one who was wanted, and the law in the shape of Henderson had finally caught up with him. The remark about Air Ministry was unfortunate, of course, but hardly illegal. He began to remember other occasions when he had met men of the same branch: in a court-martial for fraud in Cairo, a cowardice case, a sabotage inquiry, "a few questions" about a crashed aircraft. None, of course, had

9

anything to do with him. He was witness, spectator, officer-under-instruction, once member of the Court. All the same, one couldn't help feeling a little uncomfortable with them. "Well, I must say," he said, meaning it as a compliment, "you don't look like one."

Henderson laughed.

This time, silence fell fully and finally upon them. Obviously something had happened at North Luddenham: obviously Henderson would say nothing about it: obviously Bunting did not wish to appear curious. He was a correct officer, who did not like to put a foot wrong. All the same, within the privacy of his mind, he began to conjecture what the trouble could be: certainly something serious on account of North Luddenham being what it was, and because of the investigating officer's comparatively high rank.

One thing at least . . . and he basked in the balm of the perfect alibi . . . it could have nothing whatever to do with him. Never had he even laid his eyes on the place.

Here it came now, up over the horizon. That green glow on the brow of the hill would probably have something to do with it. A corrugated iron hangar showed up through the mist, then a Nissen, the squat shape of a Control Tower, the beginning of a runway—looking like the approach to any other aerodrome.

Until you saw glass missing in the windows of those buildings, and grass and weeds growing on the runway.

That must be the thing there, the rectangle of barbed wire right in the centre, bathed in the limelight of neons from concrete standards. Bunting was studying the blue steel huts and silver cylinders inside the enclosure, when his eye was caught by three phosphorescent shimmers, and following them upwards above the glare of the lamps, he could just make out the white silhouettes of three rockets against the darkness of the night.

He made no comment on what he saw. Neither did Henderson. In any case the scene had soon faded into the prosaic and the every day. The usual Married Quarters. Familiar barrack blocks, water tower, M.T. Section, Stores. As the Humber began turning left towards the Guard Room, its headlights picked out laurel bushes, the wire-netting of a hard tennis-court, and then the lettering on a painted noticeboard: R.A.F. STATION, NORTH LUDDENHAM. NO. 12 STRATEGIC MISSILE SQUADRON.

Commanding Officer . . . Group Captain A. G. Gallagher, D.S.O., D.F.C., A.F.C.

"Yes . . . what is it?"

Stripped to his shorts and singlet, Bunting was half way through the exercises he always did night and morning. To all intents and purposes, he was back home, for this bedroom was a replica of officers' bedrooms throughout the R.A.F.: the same iron-framed bed, the same blue and red rug, the same basin, the same washstand on which, scrupulously neat as always, he had arranged his razor, shaving brush, soap, toothbrush, toothpaste, After-Shave lotion as though they were on parade. The train journey, the meeting with the Wing Commander, the ride to the rocket station he had packed away into his compartmented mind when he had said good night to Henderson in the entrance hall downstairs. A little tired, he had been aware only of the white sheets invitingly opened at one corner, the striped flannel pyjamas waiting for him on the coverlet, and now his voice sounded irritable as he acknowledged the knock on the door.

It was the Duty Batman. "Sir . . . you're wanted."

"Who by? Where?"

"Sir . . . in the Group Captain's Office."

"At this time of night?" Bunting looked at the watch on his wrist. "It's half-past eleven!"

"Sir . . . there was a phone call and——"

"Oh, all right!"

He gestured the batman away, and again started dressing. As he put on his trousers and slipped into his uniform jacket, he began to wonder moodily what the hell all this was about anyway. It was most unlike the Gavin Gallagher he remembered to be working in his office at this hour. Surely the man couldn't be in all that much of a hurry to meet him again! Might of course have something to do with that Provost officer johnny. A niggle of conscience started to run round his brain. He gave a characteristic polish to his buttons and shoes, while he tried again to remember exactly what he *had* said in the Humber. Then grumbling to himself that this was a bit much, he let himself into the corridor, walked down the stairs, and pushed his way through the glass swing-doors out into the night.

No one was around. In the silence, his footsteps sounded loud on the tarmac. Though the station was new to him, he recognized the standardized buildings, caught sight beyond a group of black trees of the familiar shape of a shadowy Station Headquarters.

All quite dark and shuttered up, except on the extreme right hand side—one lighted rectangle.

Behind that window, Gavin Gallagher would be waiting.

Bunting was not looking forward to the reunion. He had not wanted the posting. He did not relish the idea of serving under Gallagher. But war was war—like all Air Force officers he was under no illusion that peace had broken out in 1945—the country had to be protected, and the self subordinated. Always the conscientious officer, specialist books and compulsory lectures had hammered home to him that cold though this war might be called, it was infinitely more dangerous than the hot one.

The doors of the S.H.Q. were open. Inside, all the way up the linoleumed corridor to the door marked *Commanding Officer*, he tried to think of a few conventional things to say. He knocked. A voice called out to him, "Come in!"

The figure seated at the desk looked up and acknowledged his salute. "Hello, Bunting."

At first glance, he thought that time had worked a miracle of transformation. This face was oval, and had amber eyes. Then he saw the thick ring and the two small rings round the blue uniform sleeves. With a sudden jolt of surprise, he recognized Air Marshal Sir John Ingleby, Commander of the Rocket Group.

Then surprise gave way to misgiving. Over by the window, he caught sight of the Provost Marshal's man, sitting beside a solemn pale-faced Squadron Leader. He had a quick unreasonable feeling that he was being got at, invited into some curious midnight Star Chamber. There was no sign whatever of Gallagher.

"Henderson here tells me you've met. Mumford is the Senior Launch Control Officer on the Station." Ingleby's voice as he made the introductions was brisk and matter of fact. It underlined rather than diminished Bunting's uneasiness.

Then the Air Marshal folded his arms and leaned over the desk. "Sorry to drag you out . . . but this won't wait. It is also confidential. More . . . top secret. Understand?"

"Yes, sir."

"You've arrived into a most puzzling situation. Henderson thinks you might be able to help.

Relief that it was nothing that concerned himself made Bunting say loudly, "I'll do all I can, sir."

The immediate surprise of seeing these three men, instead of Gallagher, diminished. He began to take time to look around. The whole of the top of the desk was strewn with files, documents, folders, and Confidential Reports, from which Ingleby produced a pile of photographs and passed them across to him.

"Take a look at these."

Bunting studied the top print, already yellowing at the edges. It was like being taken back twenty years in time. Five rows of airmen with white flashes in their caps, posed in front of a Nissen hut. Number Forty-Four Course at Service Flying Training School. He saw his own face—then face after face of boys now only half-remembered and most of them dead. Finally, standing at the back, a little away from everybody else, the only one smiling —there could be no doubt whatever who that was.

One by one, Bunting scrutinized each of the photographs. The same man appeared in them all: getting into a Blenheim bomber, standing on the steps of some Mess, Flight Lieutenant's stripes now on his battledress, sitting in a wheelchair outside a hospital, surrounded by nurses. An official investiture photograph showed him in his Best Blue. In the centre of a squadron now under the giant wings of a four-engined Hertford. Here he was on some staff college course, hair a bit grey over the ears, but otherwise much the same. The last photograph of all, taken on the Guided Missile Course at Tucson, Arizona, showed him unsmiling in the centre of a crowd of genial American airmen.

"Recognize anybody?"

"Gallagher."

"You know him well?"

"*Quite* well, sir. A long time ago."

"Look at that last photograph again. Has he changed?"

"Hardly at all." Bunting put the photographs back on the desk. In the silence, the eeriness of the men grouped round Gavin Gallagher's desk, in *his* office, looking at *his* files, *his* photographs, made him ask sharply, without waiting for the Air Marshal to give him a lead, "Why, sir? Has something happened to the Group Captain?"

13

In a neutral voice, Ingleby said, "That's what we're trying to find out." He glanced across at Henderson. "At present, we don't know."

He paused. Then as if that break was to give Bunting time to digest information, piece by piece, the Air Marshal went on, "You might as well hear the facts we *do* know." He cleared his throat. "At twenty-two thirty hours yesterday, Group Captain Gallagher passed the guard at the Main Gate. He was on his way to his house, a couple of hundred yards down the road." Ingleby arranged the photographs into a neat pile. Like someone beginning a long anecdote, who has suddenly forgotten the ending, he finished simply, "But he never arrived."

"Did he leave any message, sir?"

"No."

"So he's—" Bunting searched for the right word "—missing."

"Yes."

"But he can't just vanish!"

"Exactly what he *has* done." Ingleby spoke somewhat testily. "That is all the information we have. No trace, no clue. Nothing!" And then in a different tone. "Of course there *may* be a perfectly simple explanation. At this stage, we must not get unnecessarily alarmed."

"By now he could have gone quite a way, sir."

"Gone, Bunting? But why should he want to *go anywhere*? And even if he did, *how* did he go?"

"By car, sir?"

"His car's in the garage. No buses pass. The guards take the number of any car passing the station. Routine. They've all been checked. He didn't go to Luddenham railway station. The last person to see Gallagher was the guard who saluted him."

"There can't be many things that *can* have happened, sir."

"Exactly!" The Air Marshal sat back and put the tips of his fingers carefully together. "An accident, of course, is the first thing one thinks of." He shook his head. "We've contacted every hospital and police station in the area. Nothing there. Then," he tapped one finger against the other, "we try to decide. Is Gallagher *alive* or *dead*? If he didn't meet with some accident . . . what about . . . suicide? But his wife assures me he had no personal troubles. We know he had a great future in the Air Force."

"Murder?"

14

"A possibility. Anything's possible. But I know Gallagher. Known him for years. He got on well with everybody. Let's consider something else. Let's consider that Gallagher might be alive. And if he's alive, is he sick? A heart attack? Amnesia? A stroke? . . . yet a Group Captain in uniform doesn't wander around ill without *some*body noticing. Has he gone off then with free intent? Behind the Iron Curtain? Myself, I'd rule that out. But strange things do happen . . . nuclear scientists, Foreign Office officials, even pilots . . . so we *must* consider it. Or has he gone *against* his will? Was he politically kidnapped? Few people have more defence secrets." Ingleby rubbed his forehead. "We just don't know."

"He must be *somewhere*, sir."

"Exactly! But *where* is *somewhere*? Where do we *begin* to look?" Ingleby once more leaned forward across the desk, and gave Bunting a sudden penetrating stare. "You've realized the political complications? The very real danger? If this fact got out . . . say the Press got hold of it . . . you can imagine public reaction?"

Bunting nodded.

"Well then! We've got to find out! We must work quietly. Above all, we must work *fast*."

"But——" Almost to himself Bunting said it. "There must be a *reason*."

"Of course. That's where Henderson comes in." He nodded towards the Wing Commander. "His theory is our only hope is to piece together the *man*. His outlook . . . his make-up . . . what made him tick. Several of us here knew him at one time. Any *one* of us might have some clue . . . some small bit of information . . . that could point the way."

Doubtfully, Bunting said, "It's so many years since *I* knew him, sir. Difficult to remember."

The Air Marshal interrupted him with a wave of his hand. "Try, Bunting! Think back! You were at Oxford with him. What was he interested in then? Did he have friends? Who were they? What university societies did he go to? His politics . . . his outlook? You've *got* to give us a lead . . . understand? Tell us now, Bunting . . . what was Gallagher like as a young man?"

THE BUS TO BIBURY

I

HE came up into the High from Oriel Street—head down, hair in his eyes—scuffing at a pebble on the pavement with the crêpe-rubber soles of his sandals.

He moved as though in a dream, utterly absorbed. An air of invisible insulation surrounded him, as though the pebble had exercised some hypnotic effect. His face was pleasant enough—good features, wide-spread brown eyes—but it was his clothes that were remarkable. A double-breasted white coat, cotton check shirt, a cream tie ending in a silky bobble, with socks that might have matched when they were cleaner. In his button-hole was a small silver eagle, engraved with the letters *R.A.F.V.R.* Gavin Gallagher was his name—only child of a West Country solicitor, second year student in P.P.E., not very good at games, and now he was having trouble with the pebble. Round and smooth, it showed a deceptive turn of speed, rolled to the left and trickled through a grille in the gutter.

"Damn!"

He shook his head with chagrin, then lifting up his eyes, suddenly he became conscious of something unusual. There was no traffic on the road. Past St. Mary's, past the fifteenth-century façade of All Souls, the curve of the High was crowded. And people were not just walking up and down, looking in the shop windows and talking. They were standing still in dead silence—waiting for something.

Royalty? A procession? Or some military parade?

The last most likely—something to do with the war. That being so, he had not the slightest desire to watch. The effect of the news from France on Gallagher was to make him give up reading newspapers, pack up his books, and go and see Harpo Marx at the Classic cinema. Look where political philosophy landed us, he would point out when his tutor inquired why his essay contained neither middle nor end. Not that he didn't do his bit. He was waiting for the Air Force to call him up, and meanwhile he belonged to the Local Defence Volunteers.

That was quite enough military duty for Gallagher. He was too old—at twenty—to get a thrill from the sight of marching men. Because that was what all this was about. He had been right all along. Already as he pushed his way through the crowds, he could hear the sound of their feet. Any moment now, the band would blare out and everybody would start waving and cheering. It was bad enough as it was trying to get through, and that would slow him up even more. Though he had no idea of the time, he had a feeling already he wasn't exactly early for his rendezvous at Folly Bridge.

" 'Scuse me . . . do you mind? . . . sorry . . ."

People turned and looked at him in disapproval as he tried to slip by them. The marching had gone louder, the clanging of many men's boots echoed against the college buildings along the High. He heard a military order called out: now there was a rumble of gun carriages. But he could see nothing. Only slices of moving shadows that filtered through the standing crowd, and flickered against the sunshine on the pavement.

Yet nobody cheered. Nobody said anything. The silence of the watchers seemed only to have increased.

Sensitive to atmosphere, conscious of tension, now Gallagher became curious. There'd be time for a quick peep. He was coming up to Merton Street, and he walked up the steps of the Examination Schools to look over the heads of the crowd.

It was soldiers all right. But this was no parade. Nothing of the march-past about this lot—no band, no regimental colours here. In rough ranks of four, not in line, not in step. Only one man in ten carried a gun. Some wore tin hats, a few had packs on their backs. More had their arms in slings. All the uniforms were ragged and mud-covered. Between the companies, lorries rolled. Two ambulances went by. Then a field gun, towed by a Bren carrier, its barrel split like a greenstick fracture.

"The B.E.F.," he heard someone whisper. "Our Army . . . back from Dunkirk."

Nobody else on the pavement made a sound. No one showed any emotion. As column after column of troops went by, only the clang of their boots, the rubber tyres of the lorries, the rattle of the caterpillar tracks could be heard. Eyes glazed, heavy-lidded, the men marched on as though they were sleep-walking.

And then something caught the eye of one of the soldiers. Something in the crowd round the Examination Schools. This soldier pointed it out to his neighbour. A rustling went down the ranks, mutters, whispers. Awakening from their sleep, now the soldiers' heads were turning.

The whispers turned to hisses, cat-calls, boos.

Almost opposite Gallagher, a whole Company slowed. Someone lifted his rifle high above his head. "Christ! Look at 'em! The brilliantine Brigade! Nancy boys!"

Rank after rank wavered. And then suddenly, there were no ranks at all. Only a milling crowd of khaki. Leaning forward, Gallagher saw a group of Air Force men, neat and jaunty in their blue uniforms, standing on the pavement at Merton Street.

Led by a red-faced corporal with butcher's hands, the soldiers fell on the airmen. Above the heads of the intervening on-lookers, Gallagher had a vision of a sergeant-pilot putting up his hands to defend his face. Then a huge paw gripped him by the throat. Next moment, the pavement was littered with a squirming mass of blue and khaki uniforms.

An airgunner's knees collapsed under him. His whole body made a momentary arch, then the back of his head connected with the pavement.

"Where were *you* at Dunkirk, eh? You bloody bastard!"

A Flight Lieutenant's wings were clawed off his uniform. "Spitfire pilots, eh? *Fighter* pilots! Christ! Who were you fighting? The women? Glamour-pusses! Pansies! Left us to the Stukas, didn't you?"

The R.A.F. officer's head bobbed up again. Gallagher could see a trickle of blood oozing out of the corner of his mouth. But now that the initial surprise was over, the airmen were fighting back. Fighting the way the army had started off—pummelling, tripping, shoving, kicking, trying to push the soldiers back on to the road.

It had got too hard going for shouting. The only sounds now were the scraping of boots, grunts, heavy breathing, the smack of fists on flesh. There was a smell, too—a reek of sweat, blood, hate, sick.

Seemingly stunned, at first the crowd did nothing. Then a man right beside them tried to intervene, and got a fist in his face. A woman gabbled shrilly, "There's blood on my dress!

Oh . . . look!" Some disembodied voice said, "Hey, there! Steady on!"

Someone gave a sharp, suddenly cut-off cry of pain. "The flicking Air Force!" screamed the corporal. He shambled from the fight now, walking up and down the road. "Stayed at home!" he yelled as if trying to force the crowd over to his side. "Yes, they bloody well did!" He raised his clenched fists high above his head, running now, backwards and forwards like a madman searching for a victim. "Any more Raf bleeders? Just let me get at 'em!"

Nauseated yet fascinated, Gallagher saw the bloodstains on the man's knuckles, the blood-veined eyeballs staring out of his head. Then he remembered the R.A.F. badge in his lapel, and quickly put his hand over it. Discreetly removing it, he slipped it into his pocket.

These men were berserk. There was no point in getting involved with lunatics. He was too far to join up with the airmen, even if he'd wanted to. It was important, in any case that the fight should not spread. The only possible thing to do in a case like this was . . . to keep one's head.

"Kill 'em!" shouted the corporal. "Use your bayonets on 'em! Let the Air Force flickers know what war's like!"

He was just thumping his way towards a battling young pilot, when abruptly, the air was filled with hooting and whistles. Bells clanged. Now a new cry went up, "The redcaps! The redcaps! Look out . . . for Chrissake . . . the M.P.s!"

Motorcycles were rushing up, then ambulances. The scuffling started to slacken. The more belligerent battled with the military police, while the others began disappearing. The noise died down a little—but the fighting was still going on when behind two small tanks, a new Company began moving up the High.

Not very many of them, perhaps two hundred altogether. But these soldiers were on parade. All in step, a ruler could have been laid along their ranks. Every man had his gun, and on every gun was a glittering bayonet. Packs on their backs, webbing brass bright in the sun, boots shining black as a wet road. Hardly a hair out of place, though there were bandages under some of their caps. Led by a Regimental Sergeant-Major—the sort with the waxed moustaches that can be found in all the funny papers—they marched with their heads high past the slowly dying disturbance, not a flicker of interest on their faces, none of them batting an eyelid.

"The Guards," said a woman close beside him. "Cold-streamers. Thank God, anyway . . . we've got *some* men left!"

Weeping willows hid the boathouse at Folly Bridge. Gallagher began jumping down the stone steps three at a time, then paused as he saw the figure drenched in the freckles of light and shade, standing on the wooden quay, looking at his watch.

Bunting.

Half affectionately, half derisively, as if within himself there lurked a hidden companion, an understanding confidante, Gallagher smiled. If he were a photographer now, he'd take Bunting like that . . . neat and very clean in white flannels and blue blazer. He was nicely built, too. Broad shoulders, tall, his fair hair brushed back except for a nonchalant carefully cultivated lick hanging sportily over his bronzed brow. Handsome, rather small-featured face—pity about that, half an inch bigger all round and *there* would have been a man—frowning now because Gallagher, the slipshod, the slacker, the scruffy, was late.

Portrait of an Englishman circa 1940, Gallagher said to himself, jumping down the steps again . . . and hollowly came an echo of some one's remark . . . Vince most likely, because Vince was the only bright boy around . . . "A medium man, Bunting, a very *medium* man."

Aloud as he banged on to the landing, Gallagher said, "Hello, Bunting."

"Good evening, Gallagher."

They were not exactly friends. But they lived, along with Vince, on the same staircase in a sixteenth-century quadrangle at St. Jude's. They borrowed beer or tea from one another, and sometimes sat next to each other in Hall. They did not go to lectures together, for Geography was Bunting's subject, but now they were both bound for the R.A.F. And *that*, Bunting appeared to assume, made some special bond between them.

For in this un-especial friendship, it was Bunting who made the running. Bunting it was who made any arrangements, fixed dates, went out of his way to stop and talk. And yet at the same time, some peculiar attribute of his nature, which Gallagher had not the interest to pin down, precluded any real friendship.

"Not late, I hope," Gallagher said.

"On the contrary . . . the early bird as always." And then less affectedly, "Good God, man! Can't you *ever* be on time?"

"I was held up. Just now . . . in the High. Bunting, a most extraordinary thing——"

"What's extraordinary is that you came at all."

"Then listen to this!"

As the augmented and highly coloured account of the fight poured from Gallagher's lips, Bunting's expression grew more and more pained.

"And look!" Gallagher regarded with no small pride a stain on his white sock. "Blood! Bunting, I've been blooded!"

But Bunting didn't look. He was staring at the bright surface of the river, frowning. "Damned bad show!" he said. "Trust the army! Bloody awful bunch! So *they* reckon *we* let *them* down! That's pretty good irony!" Although he had never left the ground, he identified himself already with the airmen. Whenever he could, he picked up scraps of Air Force jargon. Unlike Gallagher, he was impatient to be gone.

Basically, he needs to belong. Vince had said. A shoulder-level man, Vince had called him. He needs someone with the head up above him.

"I hope you gave the bastards what for!" Bunting finished off indignantly.

"Oh . . . I——" Gallagher began. "Why . . . yes!" And without meaning to, his voice trailed, exploded suddenly into laughter.

Bunting's light eyes sharpened, half suspicious that Gallagher was laughing at *him*. And then remembering, again looked at his watch and whistled. "Christ, Gallagher, you talk like a bloody old washerwoman! Hurry! We should have been practically there by now. The girls will be furious."

Still grinning, Gallagher followed him across the quay to the punt, already drawn up alongside. He surveyed the almond-green cushions, the two paddles in the stern. "Bunting! No pole!"

"Hardly worth it. The Antelope's not far from Lady Margaret Hall." He regarded Gallagher's untidy figure with a faintly superior smile. "That is . . . unless you want to show your prowess?"

"Just a suggestion." Gallagher cheerfully untied the rope from the iron ring. "Actually I'd hoped *you* were going to do all the work."

"As usual."

Sitting side by side on the deck, they pushed off into midstream, and began slowly progressing up river, their paddles dipping into the sluggish water. The sunlight beat down on them, fusing their two shadows into black Siamese twins on the slatted floorboards. The blunt bows of the punt were well up from their weight at the back, and they were leaving behind them a slight bubbly wash, while Bunting did the talking.

As usual, he had made all arrangements for the outing. A double-date with the more attractive undergraduettes was difficult enough to achieve. They were late enough already, and he was determined Gallagher wasn't going to spoil it any further. They were picking up the girls at the Women's College garden which went down to the Cherwell. From there they were going to a riverside pub, where raspberry-and-cream teas were already ordered.

"Margaret is yours, Gallagher. She's the dark one."

"What, Bunting, is yours called?"

"Anne."

"Anne's the pretty one, I suppose?"

"They're both *exactly* the same."

"Bet Margaret's got glasses."

"She has . . . yes. Very nice ones."

"Bet she's bloody awful. Pretty girls always have plain friends. No competition. Very nice contrast. And the plain ones don't mind, because that way they go places."

"You'll like Margaret. She's your type."

"Oh, she is . . . is she?"

"Yes."

"Well, if you think so highly of her, let's swop."

"That would hardly be fair to Anne."

"Toss then! That's fair to everybody. The luck of the draw." Gallagher produced a penny from his trouser pocket, spun it in the air, and said, "Call, Bunting!"

"No."

Resignedly Gallagher pocketed the penny. "Thought you wouldn't. Well . . . that practically confirms it. Never did have any luck with women. Not with *pretty* women. Where *do* you find 'em, Bunting? Vince got me to join the Communist Club last Tuesday. *Swore* that all the prettiest girls went there." He turned his head round hopefully. "Is Margaret a Communist?"

"For Chrissake, Gallagher . . . she's a stockbroker's daughter!"

"Oh."

The river was narrow here. Not very steadily, they crept upstream, the punt continually wavering between hawthorn trees on either bank. Chickweed grew here in big green stains. From a mattress of leaves, the golden eyes of waterlilies winked at them. Mayblossom hung low over the water, coloured strawberry and vanilla. They reached at last the weir at Parsons' Pleasure, and hauled the punt up the rollers to the traditional sanctuary of naked bathers. A scattering of white bodies splashed around them as they set off again.

It was during this final stretch, the half mile before they reached Lady Margaret Hall, that Bunting became irritable, partly because their slow progress had now made them very late indeed, and partly because he had a shrewd suspicion that Gallagher wasn't paddling anything like hard enough.

"I'm having to backwater my side."

"Then don't, Bunting! Relax!"

"How can I? Now come *on*! We're hellish late as it is."

"I'm not going to make myself into a galley slave. Not for Margaret."

"God, you're a slacker, Gallagher! Christ knows what the Air Force'll make of you."

"A pilot."

"I *wonder*!"

"That's their worry."

A swirling trail of chickweed wound itself skilfully around Bunting's paddle. He had to raise the paddle and carefully and fastidiously peel it off. Under his breath he swore, and dashed the scummy stuff off his hands. "As a matter of interest, I've often wondered exactly why you decided to join the Air Force."

Judiciously Gallagher pursed his lips, shrugged his shoulders. "I like the uniform."

"Gallagher, you make me sick!"

"Bunting, you make me tired!"

Leaning back, his eyes crinkled up against the sun, Gallagher began, "If you seriously want to know my views——"

"Just so long as they're *your* views!"

Ignoring him, Gallagher continued airily, "Well then, in my opinion this war is one bloody nuisance. To me *personally*, coming at this time, *most* inconvenient. And could be highly dangerous. But war is primarily an extension of nature's hazards."

"That sounds like Vince."

"The last war caused this war. And this war will cause the next war. My tongue isn't hanging out to join the relay race."

"That's practically treason!"

"Treason, Bunting, is only a matter of timing."

"Vince *definitely*."

"Here am I," Gallagher went on. "Then out of nowhere comes the war towards me. What do I do, Bunting? Well, I'll tell you. I *adapt*."

Bunting snorted.

Warming to his theme Gallagher pointed to a reed, dead ahead in the path of the punt. "Look over there! To that reed, this punt must be like war."

"And you're like the reed?"

"I am, Bunting. I am."

"Well then!" Grinning, Bunting sent the punt shooting forward with a furiously energetic paddle. The blunt bows caught the reed fair and square. There was a rubbery squeaking and scraping along the bottom. "So much for you, Gallagher!"

"Ah-ha! But look behind! It's up again. Swaying, Bunting. But mark you . . . alive. *Undamaged*. Who knows? Stronger for its experience!"

"Vince! Vince *again*!" Irritably, Bunting mopped the beads of sweat off his forehead. His lick of hair clung now damply just above his eyebrows. His fine skin was shining and red, like perfectly cooked gammon, with a mixture of heat and exasperation.

The lawns of Lady Margaret Hall skimmed up towards them on their left. And distantly from up the bank came a faint reproachful hell-*ohoh*.

"Christ!" The combination of everything this afternoon had been altogether too much for Bunting. "I can't understand your attitude. You've just seen your country's defeated army. *Defeated*, mark you! The situation is *bloody* serious! Just about

25

as bloody serious as it could be . . . and here you are *idling* on the river, and talking a helluva lot of sheer bloody cock!"

"And what the hell are *you* doing, Bunting?"

But the boat was wobbling now into the bank. Under the willow tree, a slim girl in a red checked dirndl, and a tall intellectual creature waited disconsolately.

"We'd given you up. We thought you'd sunk. It must be past tea time now."

Bunting helped the girls in, still red faced, flustered, seething but painfully smiling. He apologized angrily for both of them.

Introductions were clumsily effected. Margaret sat down beside Gallagher. Always shy with girls, all Gallagher could think of to say to her was, "This'll probably be my last river party. I'm off to the war next week."

Bunting snorted, and pushed the punt off savagely from the bank. Margaret pretended to be interested. "Oh, really? Which service?"

"Can't you see?" Bunting leaned forward, thrusting a thumb under his own lapel to show his silver eagle. "This badge. He's got one, too."

He glanced across at Gallagher's jacket. Suddenly he saw that the R.A.F.V.R. badge was missing. His eyes first looked puzzled, then slowly understanding dawned. Outrage flitted across his face to give way to triumph.

"Beg pardon," he said loudly. "It *was* there. But Gallagher had to *adapt*." He smiled. The irritation smoothed away. He sat for a moment, letting the paddle trail. Pale green waves of reflected water shimmered up over his face. A trick of the tree-shaded river light made his eyes glint greenly. Now his face was incandescent with pleasure.

When he spoke, his voice was smooth, measured. "Gavin here's been in a fight. When? This afternoon. But he used *his* method and escaped unscathed. Tell them, Gavin, your wonderful method of winning the war!"

The slim girl's blue eyes and Margaret's round twinkling spectacles turned themselves upon him. Refusing to be drawn, Gallagher grinned. He had lost interest in the river, in the outing, in Margaret.

He had discovered something. What it was about Bunting. What it was that precluded friendship. Get him angry enough, flustered enough, irritated enough, and out inevitably came the little jet of pure malice. The flaw, Vince would have said, that's in all of us.

The particular flaw, varying with each individual, that *decides*.

"The flaws," Vince said, "the strains, the stresses, the strengths, the weaknesses . . . all add up." He paused in his peroration, hurrying ahead of Gallagher along the pavement, circumnavigating a courting couple with their noses glued to a furniture shop window. Then, as breathlessly Gallagher tried to catch up, he finished ringingly, "To the pattern of Life. Design. The mathematical precision of the Universe."

They were on their way, late as usual, to the local hop at the palais-de-danse. It was Gallagher's last Saturday night. They must celebrate it, Vince had said, in the traditional civilized manner of wine, women, song . . . and wise conversation.

They had already talked a great deal. They had drunk all their beer. Now the local sweat-box awaited them. They had their ninepence entrance fee ready. "But that sum buys more than freedom to dance with bosomy girls," Vince had said. "Being out of bounds, it's a gesture. Break a rule now and again, Gallagher. For by Christ, if you don't . . . rules will break you! Preserve the design that's *you*."

Though the evening's talking was technically over, Vince was still swaddled in trailing clouds of philosophical glory. Tall, long-legged he strode ahead, tossing behind him the last precious pearls which (who knew?) Gallagher might ever see. For pearls they certainly were, despite some who maintained that the brilliant Vince couldn't help scattering such glitters willy-nilly, leaving those who picked them up to distinguish between jewel and paste.

"For there's a design about *you*, Gallagher. Weakness, strength. A pattern that Nature will use. Your run probably already predestined." Vince glanced sideways to see if Gallagher was still with him. In profile, his face was bony, big-nosed, hawk-like. He had the thin lips and the bright fixing eyes of the young fanatic. He was the only person Gallagher knew to whom the expression "bending his glance" could accurately apply. For from under the rusty-coloured shaggy eyebrows, his eyes seemed to angle down an inescapable rod of compulsive communication.

"And of course," Vince added more reluctantly, "a design about *me*."

"Well, get that Vince design to de-celerate somewhat!" Gallagher suggested. "My legs aren't as long as yours!"

"Ah, you see! A fault! A fault in your genes!" Vince began making up for his slower pace by wider arm gestures. As he talked, he seemed to snatch at the air, as if invisibly all around him grew prolific trees of knowledge from which he could pluck unending supplies of rich and succulent fruit. "No doubt your maternal grandmother had short legs. Pity! Someone else gave you carelessness. Someone else . . . good humour. Sum total . . . Gavin Gallagher, healthy, house-trained, harmless . . ."

"You're pleased with your packet of genes, I take it."

"Very. A *good* packet. Six feet one with a tendency to stoop. First class brain. A physicist of no mean distinction. An intellectual leader of men."

"Cross here," Gallagher said. "The palais is the first turn on the left."

They waited silently for a couple of cars to go by. Reaching the other side of the road, Gallagher said with the self-satisfied smile of trumping Vince's ace. "What about your environment theory?"

"What theory was *that*?"

"You remember! Last month sometime. Up in Bunting's room."

"Oh, that! A month ago. I am three hundred thinking hours further on, dear boy." He sounded almost offended. As offended as Bunting might be should someone have accused him of not frequently changing his socks.

"Remember," Vince said, "the wood and the trees. Don't lose sight of former for latter. Environment, of course, comes in." He turned upon Gallagher his memory-rinsed exalted look. "Environment may modify. But a sunflower seed still produces a sunflower."

"And no sun, no water, no earth produces a no-sunflower!"

"All right. And manure produces a big sunflower. *All* sunflowers."

Now they had turned down the side road, and groups of girls and men in uniform littered the pavement as if drawn thus far by the booming jaunty music, but doubtful now as to whether they could bear to go in. Vince leading, Gallagher following the two of them threaded their way in and out of knots of people.

Gallagher's progress was somewhat slowed by the necessity to do a quick check-up on each group of females they passed. Eventually he caught up with Vince to ask solemnly, "What about education?"

"Education is part of fitting the individual into society. Making a big unit out of a lot of little misshapen ones. Society wants—" Vince squinted down from his superior height at a group of soldiers leaning against the dance-hall wall "—only the fitters-in. Good workers in peace. Good killers in war. The uniform man. Like you'll be, Gallagher. Unless you preserve *you*." He pulled his ninepence out of his pocket, and laid it on the worn ledge in front of the kiosk, as if it was the key of the intellectual kingdom. "If you don't, you'll be fitted into the war pattern. Uniform first. Body next. Mind finally." He waited for Gallagher to collect his ticket. "You'll look Air Force. You'll act Air Force. Then you'll *think* Air Force." Crossing the small foyer, Vince chanted, "You'll eat, drink, shit, march to numbers till you won't be able to function outside. What after all," he added loftily, "is the sovereign cure for constipation? Habit, Gallagher! Habit!"

They pushed open the swing-doors. A man seated behind a baize-topped card-table tore their tickets in half and said, "No pass-outs, mind!"

"And how the hell do you come into it, Vince?"

"Me? I don't. I shan't be in at all. I've decided against it. The Services are no place for the intelligent man of liberal education." In a wise and fatherly manner, he patted Gallagher's shoulder. "The biggest liability to any fighting man is *this*." He tapped his own magnificent forehead. "Beware not of pity, but of thought! The canker in the bloody bud. Take the issue philosophy with the issue uniform. It's part of the perks. But only for the time being!"

Yet even Vince's eye was losing something of its fanatic brightness now. Environment was already working something of a modification.

"Ah!" Vince said, as the warm moist air of the dance hall encompassed them. "It's like the embrace of an over-ripe blonde! Comfortable, nauseating, titillating."

He sniffed loudly, drawing in the smell of sweat, powder and cheap perfume as if it were mountain air. The harsh clatter of unthinking voices appeared to sound not unmusically in his ear.

"Good mammary development over there, Gallagher." He eyed a red-headed girl in a tight black dress. "Nice specimen!"

The good talk was over for the evening. Murmuring that Nature's happy compensation for the near-genocide of war was the marked enlivening of sexual stimulation, Vince made a bee-line for the bosomy girl.

From the distance, Gallagher raked his eyes over a bed of wall-flowers, hoping to pick up a similar above average specimen. Before making his choice he had a glass of warm lemonade, and a pale fawn bun with a round of jam in it that made him think it was like someone's heel pad with a corn cut out.

Then he ambled through a foxtrot with a girl who said she came from Cowley, and a quick step with another girl who didn't say anything at all, but relentlessly and tonelessly hummed the tune the band was thumping out.

"Of course," he said to each in turn, trying to cut a dash. "I shouldn't be here at all. If the Progs raid tonight . . . !" He cut his finger across his throat. But the first girl was eyeing the soldiers in the stag line. And the second girl had apparently drowned what he'd said in her humming.

And then, as though they'd heard him calling out to Them, obligingly They had arrived.

In the middle of a commotion round the door, there was the Proctor in his mortarboard and gown, flanked by the two Bullers in their bowler hats. They stood out among the mauves and pinks and yellows of girls in party dresses like ink-blots on a soiled water-colour.

As they thrust themselves forward, a girl giggled. Someone else squealed and said, "Do you mind?"

The Bullers' boots clod-hopped across the dance floor. Gallagher's eyes searched for Vince. The emergency exit door banged and there was the sound of running footsteps as some fool did a bolt for it. Contemptuously, a soldier laughed. So did a group of girls. The band shrugged, smiled, began to tune up again.

Suddenly he felt a fool, a small boy. He wondered why the

hell he'd allowed himself to get involved in a silly childish affair like this.

His only consolation was that Vince was in it, too. Being both involved—somehow it wasn't so bad. But where *was* the man? Surely it wasn't Vince who'd done a bolt for it?

No, there he was over by the door, talking to some character. He'd probably be the one who was caught first.

But it was towards himself that the Bullers came. The two bowler hats came off like a music-hall act. "Excuse me, sir . . . but are you an *under*graduate of this university?"

"I am."

"You will be aware, sir, that this dance hall is forbidden to *under*graduates?"

Again the man emphasized the word *under*graduate. And as Gallagher admitted the awareness, suddenly it struck him that Vince after all would *not* be progged. Dazzled by Vince's quick talk, he had forgotten that as a graduate, however new, Vince would escape. Rather like the war, he was outside again.

As he gave his name and college, he saw that although staring in his direction, Vince was quite sincerely unaware of him. There was no disloyalty, no abandonment. His mind had merely progressed. His eyes were bright, his lips were moving. And his hands plucked at the air, as if even in this barren atmosphere, he could pick succulent fruits of fresh intellectual nourishment for his new companion.

Gallagher was fined a pound by the proctors, and reported for disgraceful behaviour to the Warden of his college. It was the first time he had been progged. That Monday night, also for the first time, he went to war.

He and a classics don from Magdalen protected south-west Oxford against paratroopers. Their uniform was an armband with L.D.V. on it, and they were equipped with an air gun and a First World War Lee Enfield. In accordance with his seniority, Gallagher had taken the lesser weapon, which might perhaps have wounded a rabbit. Guns slung over their backs, they set off into the night together, reaching the patrol area at 22.00 hours precisely.

There the don thrust the Lee Enfield into Gallagher's hands. "You'd better have this."

31

"Oh, no, sir . . . no!"

"I insist."

"I'm not much good with a gun, sir."

"Wasn't bad once . . . but now I can't see more than a few yards. In the event of . . . er, trouble . . . I'm afraid of killing *you* with the thing."

"Well, of course . . . in that case, sir——"

They tramped the dark fields. A sweet smell came from the new mown grass. Towards dawn, it began to rain. The don quoted Thucydides, Gallagher yawned. At eight o'clock they tramped to headquarters, put in a Nil report, returned their guns and ammunition, and hurried back to their colleges for breakfast.

His last public appearance in Oxford was two days later. His train to the R.A.F. Receiving Wing left at midday, and one hour before that he walked into the sixteenth-century dining-hall for his don rag.

Sitting at the centre of an oak refectory table, surrounded by the college fellows in their caps and gowns, the Master of St. Jude's greeted him courteously.

His term's work was discussed. His tutor reported that his capacity for concentration was exceptional—when he wanted it to be. Of course, much must be forgiven on account of the war. Certainly he could not wish for a pleasanter pupil.

"Very satisfactory," the Master murmured, and then raised his mellow voice to announce, "Today Mr. Gallagher is off to join the Royal Air Force. We are quite sure he will make an excellent pilot. And now," he rose and took off his mortarboard and stretched out his hand, "the very best of luck, Mr. Gallagher!"

And after the Master, one by one the other dons rose, uncapped their heads, shook him by the hand and wished him *Godspeed.*

2

Hi diddle dee dee, an airman's life for me . . .

What appeared to be a crocodile of schoolboys was slowly covering the three miles between the town railway station and Cirencester aerodrome, singing a modified number from the

32

Walt Disney film *Pinocchio*. Dressed in blue uniform, with white flashes in their caps and propeller badges on their arms, these were the survivors of the June intake at the Newquay Receiving Wing. Four had failed the initial examinations. Seven more could not be coaxed solo off the ground in a Tiger Moth. There were thirty-nine of them left, all promoted L.A.C., and now they marched loosely in threes, shepherded by a pedagogic Warrant Officer, towards Number Six Service Flying Training School, whether they would either win or lose their wings.

The man in the middle of the rear rank was Leading Aircraftman A. G. Gallagher, 532.

Service life he had found different to what he had expected. Late on Oxford evenings, with the cakes finished and the empty toast plate pushed away, Gallagher had many times expounded with a kind of gloomy satisfaction on the iron hand of martial discipline that was about to descend on him, and how he intended to survive—physically, mentally and spiritually. So far, however, there had been little evidence of any soul-crushing philosophy. Elementary Flying School from which they had just passed out had been civilian run, and nobody there could have cared less what the pupils did, so long as they went solo. This Gallagher had succeeded in doing after twelve hours dual instruction—a thrilling experience in more ways than one—after which he had cautiously explored this new element on his own for a further two hours.

"Lep . . . lep! Lep—right—lep!"

Forty-Four Course, as the Warrant Officer had told them they were now called, was a mixed bunch of all ages from eighteen to thirty. Gallagher got on quite well with all of them. Better in fact than with the only other undergraduate. Leading left hand front rank man was Bunting.

"Lep . . . lep! Lep—right—lep!"

A bag of peppermints oscillated round the back row. He took one and began to suck. The song changed to *Shaibah Blues*, and afterwards another R.A.F. ballad, into which Gallagher joined with a discordant whole-heartedness.

I don't want to join the Air Force.
I don't want to go to war . . .

They were right out on their own in open country. Hawthorns with no leaves on them, just a mauve blur of autumn berries, lined the road. Evening was beginning to settle in, the mist was coming up like breath over the meadows.

I'd rather hang around
Piccadilly's underground,
Living off the earnings of a high-born lady . . .

Ahead of them now, Gallagher caught sight of the massive shadow of a hangar. Excitement rustled through the thirteen ranks.

"A permanent station . . . obviously," said someone.

"Anybody see any aircraft?"

"Maybe there aren't any. Maybe it's balloons."

There was laughter and some mutterings.

"Keep your fingers crossed it's fighters!"

The buildings on the aerodrome became gradually clearer. Brick barrack blocks, a water tower, a firing range revealed themselves, when suddenly there was a loud puttering and everybody's eyes went up to the sky. Down from the twilight sky, an aircraft was coming in to land—two engines, pointed wings, underbelly painted bright yellow.

"Christ . . . Henleys!"

"Not those bastards!"

"We're going to be bus drivers!"

So his lot was to be a bomber boy. Gallagher took the news with equanimity, crunching the last of his peppermint. It was the luck of the draw, and even if fighters were far easier to get out of when you were hit, two engines were certainly better than one.

The aerodrome was fast approaching, and the Warrant Officer urged them to quieten down and march properly. So Forty-Four Course swung through the main gates in silence, watched only by one bored S.P. from the guardroom.

They penetrated further—past the Stores, past S.H.Q. Just as they were coming up to the parade ground, a broad-beamed vehicle came bearing head-on down the road. They had to break ranks and wait on the grass verge for it to go by. Gallagher looked at it with interest. An ancient blue bus, endowed with the old-fashioned innocence that antiquity gives to everything. A big bonnet and a square body. A bus was something he remembered as taking him off to pleasant places—a sort of charabanc, on treats to the sea, as scorer or touchline man with the school team to away fixtures. This one rumbled past on its execrable springs. Twelve men were inside, dressed up in Sidcot flying suits. None of them took the slightest notice of the new arrivals, swarming disordered outside.

"What is it?" Gallagher asked the Warrant Officer. "Where's it going to?"

"That's Forty-Two course . . . in the bus to Bibury."

"Oh?"

"They call it the tumbril."

"Why?"

"You'll soon find *that* out . . . L.A.C.!"

"L.A.C.s! L.A.C.s!" Sergeant Dann held up both his hands to control this excruciating choir in his Signals' Section. "Where are your manners, L.A.C.s?"

Gone was all thought of the bus to Bibury. Under cover of an upturned exercise book, Gallagher was writing to Peter Vince, while around him Forty-Four Course buzzed happily away on their practice morse keys.

. . . less than a week here, and I haven't got over my surprise yet. We're still only airmen, and we were all expecting the usual barrack blocks. Not on your life! Luxury hotel isn't in it. Cirencester is a permanent training station, and all the pupils are lodged in the Officers' Mess. I've never been so comfortable. Thick carpets, two ante-rooms, and the food is out of this world. I've got a twin-bedded room straight out of a Maternity hospital which I share with Bunting. Our crest here is a young eagle over the motto Learn to Smite. Certainly I approve highly of the way they go about it . . .

"L.A.C.s!" The Signals Sergeant's right hand skidded over his perspiring brow. "I said only a short transmission for tuning purposes . . . didn't I, L.A.C.s?"

There was a chorus of "You did, Sergeant."

"Forty-Four Course isn't playing the game . . . is it, L.A.C.s?"

"No, it isn't, Sergeant!"

"Now I try to treat you chaps as gentlemen. But Forty-Four Course is making it difficult for me . . . isn't it, L.A.C.s?"

"Very difficult, Sergeant!"

"Now these S.O.S. procedures . . . you'll never know when you'll need them. Mayday . . . from the French m'aidez . . . repeated three times . . . make a note, L.A.C.s, of the R/T emergency call sign . . ."

35

. . . at present, we're doing lectures all the time and they're trying to impress on us that we'll have to work hard on the ground syllabus. But the instructors for the most part are simply schoolmasters dipped in blue uniform. Bomb-aiming consists of lying prone behind a contraption of wheels and wire, watching a roll of photographed landscape go by six feet below, and pressing the button like you'd throw a dart. Skeletons of neolithic aeroplanes attended by an ancient museum curator—that's Airframes, and everybody goes to sleep. In contrast, Signals is pandemonium . . .

"L.A.C.s, morse may one day—"

Dah dit, dit dah shrilled out the buzzers at him.

"—be the only way—"

Dit dah, dit dah, dit dah.

"—of saving *you!*"

. . . Cirencester is on the edge of the Cotswolds. It only wakes up on Mondays, when they sell sheep in the market. There's a cinema and a few good pubs, and a Y.M.C.A. where you can get a salmon roll and a cup of tea for fourpence. Because it's something to do, I go in most nights with one of the chaps on the Course. We're a mixed bunch—farmers, clerks, lawyers, office boys. There's a chap called Stephens who was a schoolmaster, and a policeman called Perriman. Bunting is the most conscientious of the lot of us. He's all right, of course, but he can't help being . . . well, Bunting.

The noise had now reached a crescendo, and Sergeant Dann decided to act. His fact turning from pale to pink, he stood up and banged the table. "L.A.C.s! . . . which L.A.C. is sending on his key?"

Everyone's hand shot up automatically.

Nonplussed, the sergeant's eyes stared hopelessly around the classroom. He was obviously wanting to do something impressive, but he couldn't see anybody to make an example of. Then he caught sight of a dark bent head and a pen moving.

"L.A.C. Gallagher . . . what are you writing?"

"Notes, Sergeant." Gallagher did not even look up. "Taking down every word you say."

Sergeant Dann hesitated, and then decided to look gratified. "Ah . . . a good keen L.A.C.! Now L.A.C.s," the note of his voice had turned to pleading, "if the Chief Ground Instructor should hear you . . . he'd think I was unable to control my class. And then he'd give me bullshit. Yes . . . bullshit! And you wouldn't want to get me into trouble, now would you, L.A.C.s?"

. . . the Signals Sergeant has just trod on the pity pedal, so at long last I can hear myself think. There used to be a master at school who couldn't keep order, but he's an absolute martinet compared to poor old Sergeant Dann. There's not a sign of war down here. As far as we can see, it doesn't even appear to be going on. Last Wednesday though, when I was Duty Pilot— doesn't mean a thing, you just sit in the Control Tower pretending to supervise the traffic—I did see two Hurricanes. They came in to refuel. Both pilots looked tired. They rang up what I suppose was their squadron, but spoke to nobody else. They lay down on the two beds in the Tower for three hours—asleep, I suppose. Then one fighter boy tapped the other's shoulder, and they both got up and as silently as they came, just slipped away and took off, side by side. Everybody said they'd been in a dog- fight—but I don't know. Hurricanes or Spitfires are of course, since the battle of Britain was won, what most of my Course want to go on, and now all singles are out, they want the next best thing. Yesterday, we were given forms to fill in for choice of aircraft. Generally speaking, the better you are, the bigger the aeroplane you're posted on to. I think it's something to do with economics: big aeroplanes cost a lot more and have bigger crews. Your own choice does come into it a bit, so I put down the biggest and safest—Sunderland flying boats. But d'you know, a lot of the others were putting down Blenheims? Small bombers that are used in really dangerous jobs like low-level attacks and ship-busting, so that Blenheim squadron casualties are terrific. We haven't started flying yet, so nobody really knows what will happen to them. We'll be meeting our instructors and starting our dicing, so the grapevine says, sometime next week . . . . ..

The afternoon wore on. Gallagher finished off his letter to Vince just before two hours Navigation. Standing above Mercator charts, Forty-Four Course drew Triangles of Velocities, interception courses to steer, points of no return—then rubbed them out and tried again. A cup of tea came round at four-thirty, and they were released at last round half past five.

It was cold outside. The autumn evening was beginning to

37

come down. Gallagher put up the collar of his greatcoat as he walked back towards the Officers' Mess with Bunting. On and on Bunting went, chuntering away about the things he'd learnt. Gallagher wasn't really listening. He was trying to remember what was on at Cirencester flick house, and whether it was worth going to, when suddenly a voice called out, "For Christ's sake, you two . . . stand to attention!"

At first he thought it was an officer he'd forgotten to salute or something. Then he saw it was only another L.A.C., a character from Forty-Three Course, and he was about to remonstrate when just across the way, he saw a small procession winding slowly down the hill.

A five-ton lorry led it, crawling along in bottom gear. Behind was an open trailer, on which was a coffin draped with the Union Jack. Six L.A.C. pupils followed, doing the slow march: and afterwards a sergeant and ten airmen, with rifles reversed. Bringing up the rear was half the Station band.

Gallagher stood there, watching it go by.

In the uncertain light, the wind came fitfully, ruffling the petals on the only wreath. There were no relatives, no civilians. Everybody was in uniform, even somehow the dead man whose hat was resting on the coffin. There was no sign of emotion—only minutely observed regulations: so much to be spent, so many men, the tombstone indented from Stores and signed for.

Down towards the side gate the procession wound, then up a slight slope. The Forty-Three Course pupil relaxed. Liking to air his little bits of knowledge, Bunting asked, "What was his rank, Gavin?"

"Like us, I suppose. An L.A.C."

"Full marks," said Bunting, slightly disappointed. "How could you tell?"

"I guessed."

"All you've got to do is to look at his escort. A sergeant and ten airmen. Got the idea?"

"Got it."

"And what about his escort if he'd been a Group Captain, Gavin?"

"I haven't the faintest idea."

"Three officers and fifty-five airmen."

They continued their walk to the Mess, the Forty-Three

38

Course pupil accompanying them. "That was Chesney . . . of our Course. I was nearly collared for the bearer party."

Gallagher said, "Where are they going?"

"To the village church. There's always a grave dug ready."

"What happened?"

"Night flying. Over at the satellite aerodrome . . . Bibury."

"Where the bus goes to . . . the bus to Bibury?"

"That's it."

"What went wrong?"

"Pulled up his flaps instead of his undercarriage. Stalled into a stone wall." The Forty-Three Course pupil had spent all his sympathy in standing to attention. "Clot!"

Just as they were pushing open the glass swing doors into the centrally-heated warmth of the Mess, an unfamiliar noise reached them from over the hill. Gallagher stopped to listen.

It was the first time he had ever heard the sound of muffled drums.

"Gallagher! You next! Come on! You're wanted! In Able. Get cracking!"

The owner of the voice disappeared around the corner of the Crew Room. The long wait was over. As he went outside, Gallagher felt the cool grass-scented air of the field rush into his throat. He tightened the harness of his parachute, and with it thudding like a satchel too low around his back, went waddling first across the tarmac, then across the grass to the waiting Henley.

It was close on twelve-thirty. Glancing back over his shoulder as he climbed into the aircraft, he saw the faces of the rest of the Course, a row of pale circles against the Crew Room window. Someone gave him a thumbs up, and he grinned back as if he didn't need it.

This was their first morning of flying instruction. The weather was none too good, and they'd had to kick their heels for hours before the day's programme even started. Gallagher had kept watching the lucky ones who got called out first coming back pink-faced, as if they'd been for a cold swim instead of their first take off and landing on twins—grinning, swearing that Henleys were cows to fly, and the instructors bastards . . . yet looking pleased with themselves, exhilarated by this minor

39

ordeal. Gallagher had smoked and tried to read, and found to his indignation that he'd had to trot round to the bogs a couple of times, and was just fancying a third when his name had been bawled out.

By then, he was thoroughly edgy. He was hungry, too. Never able to eat much before an ordeal of any kind, he had skipped breakfast, and now his stomach lurched and rumbled like a Henley's engine.

As he climbed into the aircraft, he was thinking of making some casual explanation of all this to his new instructor, when for the first time he saw him.

He was sitting in the left hand seat of Able—staring out dead ahead across the field, chumping a sandwich.

The back of his head was anonymous in the flying helmet, of course. It looked, as they all did, like a football. But the side of his cheek was pushed out by a knob of food, as if someone had just socked him on the jaw. On the sleeve just below the big left hand was the single stripe of a Flying Officer.

Hearing the slight sound of the aircraft door shutting, the instructor turned, and swallowing with some noise but with no embarrassment, said, "Hello, laddie! And what's *your* name?"

To add to the unfortunate opinion which Gallagher had already formed of his new instructor, he spoke with a slow rough voice in an almost consciously irritating Yorkshire accent.

"Gallagher, sir." And obeying the jerk of the man's head, sat himself down in the right hand seat and nervously eyed the instrument panel in front of him.

"Mine's Jim Tordoff."

Gallagher could feel the Flying Officer's eyes going slowly over him, as if Tordoff were some amateur psychologist trying to sum him up. They were extraordinary eyes: dark, bright, ugly. He had an ugly face, too, for that matter. But it was the eyes that Gallagher didn't like . . . greenish, slightly prominent, heavy-lidded, large-pupilled, *frog's* eyes.

They were set wide apart like a frog's too, though the rest of the face was human, or rather *simian,* enough. Big, firmly closed lips that opened in a sudden gap-toothed smile. A very ugly uncouth bastard, with a paper bag in his lap.

"Gallagher, eh? You Irish?"

"No, sir." And then loftily, "Are you Russian"

"Russian! Me? I'm not *that*." He laughed appreciatively, as if Gallagher had made a friendly joke. "Nay, lad. Yorkshire born and Yorkshire bred."

"Really?"

"I suppose it's a funny sounding name to you South Country blokes. But there's plenty of us lot in the Bradford Directory. That's where I come from. Where t'ducks fly backwards way . . . to keep t'muck out o' their eyes. Ever heard that one?" He laughed again, perhaps to make up for the fact that Gallagher did not.

"And how many hours of flying have *you* got, laddie?" The frog's eyes still looked him over, while deceptively the big mouth drawled and smiled. "Solo on Tigers, I mean?"

"Only two hours, sir."

"Tck . . . tck!" He sucked a mixture of sympathy and disgust through his teeth. "And how did you mek out?"

Gallagher had intended to say, "Oh, fine!" But there was something about the eyes that didn't let him. Instead he murmured stiffly, "I don't think I'm a born pilot."

Tordoff folded his horrid little paper bag down at the top. "I'd have said that missen'. But then, lad . . . there's few't are."

Gallagher glanced at his wrist watch. Tordoff seemed in no hurry to get on with the dual. Instead, he extracted an apple, and crunched it slowly and thoughtfully. "Saves time, you know," he said as if sensing Gallagher's near-nausea. "Don't bother missen to go back t'Mess for lunch. I can fit in three extra periods for time it takes to hang around till those Waaf waitresses pull their fingers out."

Gallagher sat there, watching him.

"And what were you doing before you joined up? Still at school?"

"I was at the university, sir. *Oxford* University."

"Teach you anything"

"I sincerely hope so, sir."

It could not, Gallagher thought, take even an amateur psychiatrist, such as Tordoff obviously set himself up to be, to appreciate that they were not the types to hit it off together. He cursed his bloody luck in drawing Tordoff out of the hat, and mentally (as often he did when he was exasperated) he composed a letter to Vince.

41

*. . . a real mechanic type, clumsy hands, slow-witted, straight
out of some reeking North Country back street . . .*

And as if he'd spoken aloud, and his instructor wanted to
confirm what he'd said, Tordoff began: "Now me, laddie . . .
I left school when I was fourteen . . . Alma Road Primary . . .
but I was lucky . . . you'll have heard of Yeadon airfield? Well,
it wasn't above a tuppeny bus-ride an' I used to tek missen off
there every Sat'day . . . help t'mechanics . . . mek tea for 'em . . .
fetch and carry. If I was lucky, they might think fit to let me
check the filters or the spark plugs. Once they let me swing the
prop. By gum, that was a day!"

The gist of it was that he had picked up a lot of flying gen,
got a job in a garage, gone to night-school, and then come into
the R.A.F. as a boy entrant. After that, he must have had a few
clues, for not more than a handful of the boy entrants in *those*
days made a pilot's course. *And* got commissioned. Though in
wartime, of course it would be different, because the R.A.F.
would be short of any trained men. . . .

With mixed apprehension and relief, Gallagher saw that the
apple core was being disposed of through the window, that
Flying Officer Tordoff was running his tongue round his teeth
to do the work of a toothbrush, and there was every appearance
that the lesson at last was about to begin.

"Well, right-ee-oh then, laddie! Let's tek a look at t'knobs
and tits!"

It was not often that Gallagher found it imperative to confide
in Bunting. In fact, knowing his propensity for storing little
barbs to be used at some future date, it was a practice that he
avoided like the plague. But after that first lesson with Tordoff,
it was that or getting drunk. And on seven shillings a day, he had
insufficient cash to get drunk adequately.

Besides, smelling out indignation with uncanny accuracy,
Bunting had taken the chair beside him for supper that night
and put the ball into play by saying "This flying's fun, isn't it?
How did *you* make out?"

"*Make out?*" With masterly under-statement, Gallagher just
said, "*I* had *Tordoff*."

Bunting minted a nice thick bit of lamb and chewed thoughtfully before saying, "They say he's all right. You're lucky."

"Who says"

"Well, whoever's had him. Smith, Plowright . . ."

"That's what I'd expect them to say."

"Why?" Bunting smiled. "Did you make a balls-up?"

"I did *not*."

"I saw some kite bounce six times. Was that you, Gavin?"

"It was not."

"I heard some type got a strip torn off for forgetting to put down his undercarriage." Hopefully, *"You?"*

"Sorry, no."

"Well then?"

Gallagher told him.

It was nothing, he said, to do with the actual flying. They'd merely taken off. He used the plural advisedly because Tordoff had had those ruddy red hands on the dual stick all the time, and the aircraft with his help had risen as sweet as a bird. He'd taken his hands off only when they were airborne, and then the Henley had plunged and bucketed around, while Gallagher had tried to get used to a largish aeroplane equipped with highly sensitive controls. Tordoff said nothing. Occasionally he'd whistled some flat tune through the gap in those front teeth, breaking off occasionally to say chidingly, "Think on, lad! Not so rough!" After fifteen minutes he'd said, "Now, d'you think you've got the feel of her? Well then, line her up, and I'll bring her in . . . to show you how it's done."

With difficulty, Gallagher had lined her up.

That was all. Tordoff had greased the Henley down on to the grass without any effort, with just a satisfied smile on that ugly face as if he liked flying for flying's sake. It had infuriated Gallagher somehow that those rough hands which he frankly despised had got . . . for the want of a better word . . . *expression*, a queer sort of music in them. If he hadn't been so bloody angry with himself and Tordoff, he could have got something out of that sweeping curve of descent, that ordered holding off of the aircraft till the exact second before raising the nose higher and higher, till the wheels met the earth so naturally that there was no real moment of contact, only a very gradual slowing down process . . . till suddenly the spell was broken, and the engines became clattering lumps of metal in an ancient protesting frame.

43

What he did *not* tell Bunting was that when the engines were off, Tordoff had turned to him and said, still drawling in that music-hall Yorkshire-tyke turn, "Aye lad, you've got a reet lot to learn. Happen one day you'll climb off that high horse . . . and learn it!"

He began to have an obsession about Tordoff. Even when they weren't flying and Gallagher was working at gunnery or engines, up floated a vision of Tordoff's ugly mug, or a phrase of Tordoff's stuck all day in his mind like a raspberry-seed in a hollow tooth, or the sound of a rough engine caught the same gruffness as the man's unmodulated voice. A disembodied airman's face would emerge from a squad marching, irons in hand, to dinner, and it would have the same tough coarse features as Tordoff's. A voice would shout, a figure cross the parade-ground, big, thick-set, walking with toes turned in . . . all Tordoff's. Like the camp walls did, his mind blossomed overnight with drawings of a man with a long nose, peering over a wall and nicknamed Chad.

Only it wasn't Chad with *him*. It was Tordoff.

And with the peculiar Freudian attraction of the hater for the hated, he did appear to see Tordoff in the flesh considerably more often. He always seemed to sit at the same table at mealtimes. He ran into him in the Mess corridor. If he went into the office to cash a cheque . . . there would be Tordoff. And always, the encounter would add some small fuel to his hatred. Tordoff crumbling his bread in his tomato soup and supping it down like a drain. Tordoff picking his nose at the table, Tordoff reading a notice on the board in the corridor, scratching his bottom at the same time, unhurriedly and with gusto. Tordoff emerging from the bogs, fastening his flies as he went.

It was as if there was some uncomfortable bond between them. The relationship betwen pupil and flying instructor at the best of times was an odd one . . . a blend of marriage, discipleship, the bond of father and son, with the prejudices and hates of all those relationships well on top. And hardly anything of the affection. And just to make the mixture bind, there was fear. Fear of failure, fear of a new element, and the honest-to-God fear of sudden death.

Occasionally, when he wasn't so tired that he went out like a light, Gallagher dreamed of him. Always, Tordoff was bigger than life-size. Always, it was his frog's eyes and his rough hands that threw everything else of the dream out of focus. And always, Gallagher was surprised when the next day, those same red hands took over the Henley and made her dance like a ballerina—soaring faultlessly through the breathless air.

Just once and very briefly, when Tordoff flew her like that, Gallagher lost all thought that this was a lesson, forgot all his troubles and tribulations. Dimly and distantly, out of the corners as it were, of the eyes of perception he glimpsed the sheer aesthetic beauty of flight. It was an odd sensation, physical and sensual as well as emotional, piercing his body like a spasm of desire.

He must have drawn his breath in sharply. For the frog's eyes turned towards him. Momentarily, he saw a gleam in them of understanding, a shy smile as if Gallagher had admired some secret treasure of whose high value Tordoff was somehow ashamed. For a second, Gallagher felt almost a kinship between the two of them, a possibility that he might actually one of these days *like* Tordoff.

Then Tordoff said, "Well, lad, don't sit there gawping! Try an' do it thissen!"

And he loathed Tordoff all the more for breaking the fragile, imagined spell.

Sometimes, Gallagher even got the idea that Tordoff *wanted* him to hate him. As if every instructor had to have a whipping boy, someone to get rid of their bile upon. One evening, coming along the Mess corridor to escape from it all to the Cirencester cinema, a great good-humoured laugh came out of the instructor's bar to speed him on his way. He stopped and peered through the glass door. He saw Tordoff wiping his mouth with the back of his hand. And immediately he was sure that Tordoff was laughing at *him*.

Telling them the latest about his least favourite pupil. That afternoon they had been up together, and Tordoff had been showing him steep turns. At the end of the exercise, Tordoff had said. "Right-ee-oh . . . take us home, lad . . . and think on . . . don't knock me teeth out when we touch t'ground!"

Tordoff had settled back in his seat, comfortably, contentedly. Glad that the tête-à-tête was over. Gallagher dipped the left wing and stared out of his side window. Not a sign of Cirencester

45

anywhere. A light fall of snow had camouflaged the countryside, and all he could see was a black and white carpet. Nothing that looked familiar, nothing that looked like home down there. He scanned the horizon till his eyes smarted. He searched Tordoff's profile to see if he'd allow him a hint as to where they were. Finally, furious and humiliated, he had to ask Tordoff, "Sir . . . where's the aerodrome?"

"Nay, laddie." Drawling and unhurried. "Don't ask me! Them as seeks . . . finds!"

At the end of twenty minutes searching, when the sweat was glueing Gallagher's helmet to his forehead, he discovered he'd been circling the airfield all the time.

He began to dread every flying lesson that he had. Like a kid at school, afraid of some unreasonable master, he wished the other lessons, the ground periods would go on all day. He hated the waiting in the Crew Room for the inevitable shout of *Gallagher*. He hated most of all the sinking feeling as he settled like a usurper into the left hand seat. Yet it wasn't fear of Tordoff that made him clumsy. That would have been bearable. It was worse than that. It was a genuine lack of aptitude. And it was a lack of which he knew Tordoff was aware.

During those early days, his take-offs were rarely straight. Once, he took off in a tremendous scimitar-like curve, finishing up practically skimming the Control Tower roof. Tordoff had said in a matter-of-fact voice, "Of course, there's openings for stunt pilots. But outside, laddie! Not with us!"

When he was flying, Gallagher was always conscious that his mind was trailing a long way outside—trying to catch up, to focus. And if his take-offs were shaky, his landings were worse. On the approach, he frequently had difficulty lining up with the aerodrome. The Henley was a delicately balanced aeroplane that responded instantly to every touch of the controls. She highlighted any mistake. She had all such little female habits as swinging, ground-looping, ballooning and wing-dropping. After a particularly bad landing, when Tordoff had said irritably, "What the hell d'you think you're laking at?" he would add, almost as if both he and Gallagher needed the solace of real flying, "Now get out of t'road. Watch me!" And he would bring the aircraft down as if he was putting an egg in a basket.

Yet when Gallagher managed at last to do the same, Tordoff's only comment was, "Come on with you, laddie, let's see you do that again!" And of course, that time he bounced. Tordoff's smile (for Gallagher was becoming well-versed in his horrid idiom) said, "Flash in t'pan, laddie!"

Four other pupils had Tordoff as their instructor. Diffidently Gallagher approached them and asked how they found him. "Fine!" they all said. "Always very fair. How do *you* find him?" Never one for confidences except in desperation, Gallagher repeated, "Fine! Yes, very fair."

Getting nothing from them, he would listen out for bits of information about Tordoff, trying to build up a picture of the man, as someone might build up a wax image, for the satisfaction of sticking in the pins. But Tordoff seemed to have no gossip about him, no scandal, no outstanding virtues or vices. He was married, he had a wife, and what would undoubtedly be two ugly brats, up in Yorkshire. He liked his pint of old and mild. But no more than a pint, for he boasted that he knew how to look after his bit of brass, and that he was saving up to buy a place up on the moors when all this was sorted out.

But right now, the big thing that must have been on Tordoff's mind to be sorted out was Gallagher. By the third week of flying, even Gallagher himself was seriously concerned. By now, the conversation among Forty-Four Course was invariably on going solo, and half of them had already done it. Bunting was among the first. Every day more of them were sent up on their own. Already Gallagher had had five hours dual, which was the average time for getting a pupil off. Still, Tordoff never even mentioned the word solo to *him*. Yet Gallagher did that week, get an insight into his instructor's thoughts on the subject.

It was a Thursday. For some reason Gallagher's mind had been rather more difficult to control than usual. It had waffled like the Henley's wing-tips under his hands, sailing off into airy unseen upcurrents, partly because his stomach was nervously upset, and partly because he had just had a letter from Vince. Vince was commenting on this inability of Gallagher's to concentrate on flying. *Of course*, he had written, *you must understand that your mind has been trained to think, to examine, to question, to throw a liberal net around the whole universe. It is difficult for it to be pinpointed within a narrow horizon. Mechanical jobs . . . and let's face it, flying is one of them, cause the higher intelligences*

*more difficulty than the lower mentalities E.G. your friend, the
mechanically-minded monster . . .*

That day Tordoff had waited till the throttles were shut off. He
hadn't raised his voice nor thickened his Yorkshire accent. Con-
versationally he said, "We've covered all t'syllabus now," and for
one wild hopeful moment, Gallagher thought he had under-
estimated his own prowess, that he was at last to be allowed to
go solo. "But what you need, laddie, isn't laid down in any
training manual." Tordoff didn't smile. He didn't make any
sort of joke. "A bloody good kick up the arse." He turned
his frog's eyes on to Gallagher, and finished in the same steady
tone. "And by gum, lad . . . I'd like to be t'chap to give it
thee!"

Only one thing gave Gallagher any comfort those days; the
rumour that was handed down the grapevine from Course to
Course. Tordoff had never had a failure. And on the Monday
morning of the fourth week, Tordoff himself confirmed it.
"Think on, laddie. I've never had a failure yet." He smacked his
lips with egotistical satisfaction. And then, as if deliberately
knocking *that* support from under Gallagher's feet, "Mind you,
they say there's a first time for all things."

Failure—there was an everlasting grotesque reminder of
failure in the Crew Room to keep him amused while he waited
for his lessons.

On the wall were pinned photographs of all the Courses. And
over the heads of some of the pupils were inked in either a halo
or a bowler hat. Gallagher knew now what the halo was, but he
began to be much more afraid of the bowler hat. It was a ridiculous thing, always too small for the head—so that there the pupil
stood, looking fearless and purposeful and warlike, with this
Chaplinesque article balanced on his head. Nothing could look
so humiliating; a perpetual laugh for all Courses to follow.
Already on the Forty-Four Course photograph there were two of
them, and there was speculation as to who the next would be.
For the first time in his life, Gallagher was conscious of real
ambition. The ludicrous disgrace of a bowler hat, the kicking
out of the Air Force to be called up again as an Army private,
the inability to do what Bunting had done—he simply could not
face all that.

He *had* to make it.

How exactly does one judge height above the ground, he had inquired of star pupils over a few beers under the guise of ordinary flying shop. Everybody however had a different answer: wait till you see the individual blades of grass: wait till the horizon is a foot above your head: take a sight on the height of the hedge: get a two bearing fix through the sides of your eyes. He got the impression that they simply did not know.

He even found the birds couldn't do it—not every time anyway, like Tordoff. Lying over the sill in his room, he would watch them in the tree opposite. A starling misjudged badly and had to go round again. A lark made a heavy landing on one leg. Sparrows were best—they did it in one hop. Sea birds, like the odd gull that had flown inland, being flying boat types, often made a balls-up.

So eventually he tackled Bunting, as the only one left. While the man was doing his endless evening cleaning chores at the basin, Gallagher inquired from his bed, "How do you judge height, Derek?"

"Oh, it's just instinct, Gavin. Like hitting a six." Vigorously he rubbed his face dry. "Why? Having trouble?"

"Not specially."

Bunting left the basin, and climbed into bed with a book. "Finding the slipping not so easy, eh?"

"Don't know what you mean."

"*Don't* you? Your theory. You were going to slip through the war. Bend, but not break. Like a reed . . . *you* remember!"

"Slipping's satisfactory, Bunting."

"Good." He was aware that Bunting's eyes were watching him. "Were you flying in Baker this afternoon?"

"I believe so."

"Then we watched you from the Crew Room coming in."

"Did you now?"

"You made a nice three point landing."

"Thank you."

"Pity it was a good six feet above the ground."

"You exaggerate, Bunting. You're always exaggerating."

"Everybody in the Crew Room went ker-*rump*."

"That would make a jolly chorus." Gallagher raised his hand to the switch above the twin beds, and turned out the light.

"Gallagher . . . I'm reading my navigation notes!"

49

"Not now you're not." Gallagher pulled the sheet up to his chin. "Sleep well, Bunting."

"I will if you don't snore, Gallagher. Sleep well yourself!"

"I will if you don't grind your teeth. Night, Bunting."

"Night, Gallagher."

Gallagher lay with his knees up, his hands clasped behind his head. It'll come, he said to himself, it'll come. No need to get in a panic about it. He'd evolve his own landing technique, and then it would seem as simple as falling off a log. One day soon he'd get the knack. The great thing was not to let Tordoff worry him too much . . .

Last Post sounded out, the notes crystal clear in the cold air outside. High above his head, a German bomber's desynchronized engines went aWhumm—aWhumm—aWhumm.

Presently, Bunting began to grind his teeth.

When he did get the idea, just as he'd hoped, it came suddenly. That next Monday, he went up again with Tordoff into a calm sunny sky. He took off and landed. He took off and landed. He took off and landed. Three good ones, all in a row.

"Right-ee-oh," Tordoff said. "Now I'll tek you upstairs and show you stalling."

Gallagher was actually smiling. For demonstrating the stall, he had found out from the more successful pupils, was always Tordoff's prelude to sending you off solo. Few instructors showed this manoeuvre—the majority telling their pupils the Henley's stall was too wicked and too dangerous, an attitude of mind that Tordoff poo-poohed. "You've *got* to show your lads every sort of scrape they're likely to get into . . . and how t'cope," Gallagher had once heard him say through the open door of the Instructors' Room.

"Now, laddie . . . I want you to watch me carefully!"

They were nearing five thousand feet, still in clear sunlit air. So close to his goal now, Gallagher was trying his best to be affable: bygones after all were bygones, and it was the future that mattered. As the aircraft climbed, he was making the odd polite remark, designed to show his keen interest and also his admiration for Tordoff's flying skill. "Isn't the Henley stall pretty tricky, sir?"

"No. I wouldn't say *that*. I'd say she's like a woman, laddie. You can do anything with her . . . so long as you let her know who's master."

Now they were straight and level at five thousand feet. Gallagher watched Tordoff's hands grasp both throttles, gradually pull off the power. Then he began easing back on the stick.

Up and up and up went the nose. The needle on the airspeed indicator flickered lower—90, 80, 65 . . .

Suddenly, the whole aeroplane juddered. For a split second only, the Henley shivered in a sick-making ague. Then the right wing flicked down. The left wing came up vertical. She started diving towards the earth.

"Nah . . . then . . . lass!"

The meaty hands opened up to full power and pushed the control column forward. Tordoff began bringing up the dropped wing with the rudder. Poised on her side, the Henley paused. And then rapidly the wings rotated. She was in a screaming dive, but at least now she was right side up. Tordoff began pulling back, and within a few moments the Henley was meekly flying straight and level again.

"Nothing to it, laddie . . . as you can see."

"Not much warning, though, sir."

"Don't be frightened of it, laddie! There's nothing you can't do with t'Henley. Get her out of any situation." He paused. "Got the idea?"

"I think so."

"It's the right wing drops . . . always the *right* wing. Get it up immediately with *left* rudder, because you'll start spiralling starboard. Push the nose down, and give her all the power you've got!"

"I see."

"Now *you* have a go. Remember . . . *left* rudder."

Gallagher took hold of the throttles. Rather more gingerly than Tordoff, he began closing them, easing back on the stick at the same time.

"Come on, lad! Get that nose up!"

Gallagher gave a sharp pull on the control column, till he felt he was falling backwards.

The Henley gave the expected momentary judder, the right

51

wing dropped, Gallagher put on full power, and then—it was an instinctive reflex action—jammed on *right* rudder.

Wings vertical, already beginning to turn right, now with the added impetus the spiral tightened. The left wing came swishing round the horizon. Next moment, the Henley was on her back, beginning to fall like a leaf in a slow upside-down spin, a fatal attitude, the death dance for a twin-engined aeroplane.

"Christ . . . !"

Gallagher was conscious that he was hanging by his straps. All he could see of the instrument panel was a blurred shimmy. Above the racing of the engines, he heard Tordoff shout, "Let go! I've got her!"

They were turning . . . still turning. Gallagher felt sick. He felt giddy. All through him, he could feel the Henley shaking and shuddering. The blood had run up to his head, and all his eyes could see was a red haze.

Clockwise, they were spiralling downwards.

And then the circular movement started to slow down. The juddering stopped. Next moment, they were right side up again and level.

It had probably all happened in five seconds—but it seemed an eternity.

Gallagher rubbed the sweat off his forehead. His hands were trembling so much he could hardly control them. He saw Tordoff's face, redder and uglier than ever. "You gormless bugger! What the bloody hell were you laking at?"

That was exactly the question Gallagher was gabbling at himself. Why? *Why?* He knew he had to put on left rudder. He was expecting to put on left rudder. He was intending to put on left rudder. Why in God's name then had he put on right? In that split second of time, what had made him do the exact opposite of what he intended?

Oddly enough, his bewilderment, his fear, his despair, made his brain think with crystal clarity. What to do? What to say? Cold-bloodedly, his mind examined possibilities. Confession was impossible.

"You put the bloody right rudder on! I told you left! *Left!* I said left. Christ! Are you deaf or daft? *Why* did you do it?"

Gallagher drew a deep breath. In a drawling voice, he said as steadily as he could, "To see what would . . . happen."

For a moment, except for the drone of the engines, there was silence.

"Just you say that again!"

"To see what would happen. You said you could get a Henley out of *any* situation."

The words seemed to take a very long time to sink into Tordoff's mind. For a full minute, Gallagher was conscious that as automatically Tordoff's hands guided the aeroplane, his eyes were examining his pupil with a single-minded absorption. Gallagher's only small hope of not being slung out was to make Tordoff believe he had coolly challenged something he'd said, despite the danger had deliberately called his bluff. He knew that he had to gaze back blankly. And he knew, almost with pity, that Tordoff was bedevilled by his own forthrightness and honesty. Nothing would have made Tordoff call a spade anything but a bloody shovel. If he ever did make a mistake, he would have said so. It was impossible for him to conceive a pupil lying cold bloodedly and flagrantly about his flying. Now almost visibly, Tordoff was balancing that against his own sizing up of Gallagher's character and flying.

Even when Tordoff took his eyes away, Gallagher did not know whether he'd been successful. He was aware that after that performance he would not be sent solo—but he no longer cared, so long as he avoided this new catastrophe. In dead silence, the instructor took the Henley down, made a circuit and landed.

Only when the engines were stopped and he was climbing out of his seat, did Tordoff speak. "Think on, laddie! Don't ever play such a bloody daft game on me again!"

After that awful show, he had to confide in someone, and it certainly wasn't going to be Bunting. He wrote in detail to Vince, and through the next three days, when there was little flying because the weather clamped down, awaited a sympathetic reply.

As usual, Vince took the scientific view—somewhat unhelpful in this context. . . . *do you remember our conversation about genes? The one on your last Saturday at Oxford? Along with the rest of the mixed bag, dear boy, you have undoubtedly inherited a tendency to mix your left with your right . . .*

"And a fat lot of good that is!" Gallagher muttered to himself.

. . . do you remember Anderson, medicine? He's doing some

interesting experiments under hypnosis. And he's found that many neurotics suffered in early childhood from suppressed left-handedness. Are you sure you're not spawning a neurosis?

But Vince ended on a hopeful note. Recognizing one's failings, he laid down, was ninety per cent of the battle. The other ten per cent was . . . could Gallagher guess? . . . of course, adapt.

Gallagher wrote his reply several mornings later in Signals.

. . . You may have the right idea about the Left Right tendency. Certainly I've known myself get a telephone number the wrong way round, mix up east and west. You'll be interested to know that I, too, have been doing some interesting experiments on this L-R business, using myself as a guinea pig. I'll let you know how I get on. For in spite of this damned Henley, in spite of Tordoff, I'll go off solo yet!

And five hours later, in a jubilant, almost illegible postscript: *Done it!*

Though he hadn't expected to do it that afternoon, some of his success was undoubtedly due to the simple experiments referred to in his letter. He knew it was only very rarely that he mixed his left and right. Only now and again out of his unconscious, suddenly the failing would pop out. If he could devise a mechanical safeguard against this occasional occurrence, that would be the answer. And suddenly he had a bright idea—so simple after Vince's high-falutin' theorizing. As soon as lessons were over he had gone round to the Naafi and bought two bottles of ink. One red, one green.

On the inside skin of the thumb of his left hand he had painted, a large red L for left, and on the corresponding part of his right thumb, the letter R in green.

"So much for the scientific approach!" he had said to himself, and heartened by the very childishness of his crib, he had climbed with something like confidence into the cockpit beside Tordoff.

The atmosphere between them was not exactly cordial. But by now, Gallagher was on his mettle. His back was truly against the bloody wall. Besides, he had begun dimly to perceive that everyone had their own methods of flying, their own memory aides (rhymes, good luck charms, and what-have-you). Everybody adapted themselves to flying in their own way, and this was his. In these early days while he tried out this new element, he would have to use every crutch he could. As well as on the panel, now on his thumbs he would have this crude additional instrument. On the circuit, he turned at a particular road junction, aimed for a particular point in the hedge, held off over a particular patch of grass. And in all these efforts, he was spurred on by his hatred of Tordoff. For that hatred, like some acid, ingrained everything Tordoff said deep in his memory. Years later, he would remember almost everything Tordoff had ever said or had ever taught him.

He knew that if it hadn't been for the stalling incident, by now he'd have gone solo. But the trouble was that his dual hours were now eleven—an unprecedented number, and every time a period ended, he was expecting to see the Chief Flying Instructor waiting to give him the test that was the equivalent of a public presentation of his bowler hat.

That Thursday was fortunately flat and calm—Gavin Gallagher's weather. He did three identical, mechanical circuits and landings. And then Tordoff said, "Whoa, there, laddie! This is where I get out!"

For such a big man, he walked lightly down the fuselage. He stopped at the door. "Think on, now! Behave!" He tapped the side of the aircraft. "This is an expensive lass. Don't bend her!" He jumped down. "Oh, and laddie! Don't bend thissen either!" But lest Gallagher should mistakenly believe Tordoff held him in any sort of affection, he added, "That'd count against me, laddie! Same as a failure, you know!"

Relieved of Tordoff's weight, relieved of Gallagher's anxiety, the Henley leapt into the air. For the first time, he was aware of the physical sensation of take-off, he felt the earth slip away from him gently, like a sleeping hand. With awe, he felt the majesty, the loneliness, the exaltation of solitary flight. Under instruction, his eyes had always been too busy squinting over too many dials to glance outside except to avoid collision, and he felt like a juggler trying to cope with too many balls, while the instructor waited beside him for one to drop. He had never been able to stare outside just for the pure pleasure of seeing. He had not known how beautiful Cirencester was from the air, hubbed round its Perpendicular church like a wheel round an axle. He saw the winter etching of the horizon, the march of the black-crested woods up the hillsides, the gunmetal curve of the river, with mist coming over the watermeadows like bloom on a greengage, a railway like a suture stitching up a patchwork of arable and heath. He saw his own shadow—a black moth flitting over parks, across rivers, through gardens.

Above all, he had never known the freedom and quietness that flying gave, the spiritual relief, the absolution from the small pint-sized earth below—his sense of Yogi-like elevation as he stilted over the sunlit winter earth. He spent thirty of the happiest and loneliest minutes of his life. Then reluctantly, he came back home and landed.

Before supper that night, in their bedroom Bunting was the first after Tordoff to congratulate him. "So you finally made it!"

"I knew you'd be pleased." Gallagher started off for the door. "And now, I suppose, I must go along and buy Tordoff the customary beer."

"He deserves a barrel, Gallagher."

"Well, he's getting a pint, Bunting."

In fact, Tordoff seemed no more disposed than Gallagher to make much of the long-overdue celebration. He let his pupil buy him a half. He bought him one back. When Gallagher suggested another round, he shook his head, and tapped his pocket. "Nay, laddie! Not me! I don't get missen mixed up in drinking sessions, thank you very much. Waste of brass! Besides, you'n me aren't finished yet, laddie. Are we?" He sucked his gap teeth with satisfaction. "You're not out of the wood yet, laddie. Not by a long chalk. You can still come a cropper. By gum, yes!"

Aware perhaps that he was not making the occasion as sociable as his pupil might have expected, he smiled with a curious genuine kindliness. "At this stage in the proceedings," he said ponderously, "some of the instructors like to give you youngsters a bit of good advice. Off the record advice. For free." Sharing some special joke with himself he smiled deeply, wickedly into his mug. A coarse finger momentarily stubbed Gallagher's arm. "Where *I* come from," he said, "they have a very fine motto, lad. One that I don't think any pilot could better. It sums up all *you* ever need to know, lad. Want to hear it?" And before Gallagher could say anything, "You'd better! Because you're going to!"

He set down his tankard, wiped his mouth with the back of his hand and with relish recited, "Hear all, see all, say nowt. Eat all, sup all, pay nowt. And if ever tha does owt for nowt, do it for thissen."

56

Then without any more sociability, he strode off to bed.

It was only a crude North Country translation of the good old Air Force motto *Blow you, Jack, I'm all right,* which people like Bunting found slightly repellent. But for all that, in the next few weeks, Gallagher found that it had a certain basic truth. In flying, you had to look out for Number One. For brother, if you didn't, nobody else *could.*

And as far as he was able, Gallagher did just that. He watched, he listened, he judged, he acted.

Number Forty-Five Course arrived that next week, so Gallagher didn't see so much of Tordoff. And though, like a creature that shed its skin, Tordoff seemed able to leave himself behind in his pupils' cockpits, it wasn't enough to make anything like the impression of reality.

Every day, Gallagher did what was set out for him in the flying detail. Sometimes well, sometimes indifferently, sometimes plain badly. At the end of every flying session, he entered in the Authorization book *Duty Carried Out.* Every day he counted as one day nearer. One day nearer exorcising failure. One day nearer telling Tordoff where he got off.

Every evening, he nattered with the rest of them in the bar and then over dinner. Later, if he felt inclined, he ambled along to the billiard room for a game. He began to feel confident. He began to think at last he could *really* fly.

The last Friday in December, after the usual routine, on the way up to his room for a wash, he saw a crowd round the notice board. It was probably the next day's flying detail, so he stopped to join them. Pushing his way forward, he ran his eyes over the usual typewritten words. His name didn't appear to be on it. No flying for him tomorrow. Then right at the bottom, just beneath a bullshit order about the wearing of gas masks, he saw that there had been an addition.

Night flying. Forty-Four Course. *The following Officers and Airmen will assemble at 19.00 hours outside the Main Entrance of the Officers' Mess for the bus to Bibury:*

Instructors: *Marshall, Bates, Tordoff.*

Pupils: *Perriman, Bunting, Machin, Rogers, Simpson, Smith, Stephens, King, Laker, Griffith, Atkins, Perkins, Gallagher.*

57

The instructors got in first, then came the pupils, all puffed up like green teddy-bears in their Sidcot flying suits. Gallagher got in last. The seats were hard and straight-backed, covered in thin leatherette with practically no padding—real penitential benches.

"All aboard?" asked the driver.

Tordoff turned his head and started counting. ". . . fifteen, sixteen. Right-ee-oh! We're all here. Let's go!"

Under Gallagher's feet, the vibration increased. They gave a sudden lurch forward. The ancient bus wound through the Station, through the main gate, and then plunged into the darkening Cotswold lanes on its way to Bibury.

Nobody spoke. Nobody seemed to feel like speaking—not even Perriman. In the seat opposite, the schoolmaster Stephens lit up a cigarette. Gallagher patted the parachute beside him.

He was not looking forward to it at all. Trying to analyse his feelings deeper, he came up with the disagreeable truth that he was dreading it. Twelve hours day solo wasn't very much. Though by sheer determined concentration, his flying had improved, he still didn't trust the Henley—or himself. Day flying was bad enough, but what happened when you couldn't see a thing?

Peering out of the window, he confirmed a suspicion that it was now as black as the ace of spades outside.

He had asked the pupils of the previous course what night flying was like. Various answers varying from "suffocating in a dark cupboard" to "being clasped in the arms of a negress, old chum" had not increased his confidence. Though some intakes were lucky, the average per course night flying lately had been two pupils killed, one pupil badly injured. An advertisement from *Flight* showing an aircraft silhouette beside a ghostly bowser over the caption *The Henley for Night Confidence* had anonymously been pinned on the noticeboard with the sole comment . . . !

"Gallagher." It was Bunting, tapping his shoulder from the seat behind. "At supper . . . weren't the Waafs silent?"

"Didn't specially notice."

"They say the girls hold a shilling sweepstake on who gets the chop."

"Do they?"

"What's that stuff on your hands? Ink? Christ, Gallagher . . . but you're a mucky pup!"

Gallagher said nothing. He had a pain, not exactly a bellyache, but a kind of hollow feeling as though his belly wasn't there. He was trying to go over his cockpit drill, imagining himself doing a circuit, taking care on the approach not to weave by correcting with wrong rudder. Silence returned to the back of the bus. Up at the front, now and again the instructors muttered among themselves.

It was ten miles altogether. Nothing to see except darkness, until they reached the village. There the hooded headlamps flickered over a row of gabled cottages, momentarily bringing out of the night the honey colour of the Cotswold stone. Then the bus turned right into what appeared to be a meadow, and started bumping along over the grass by the side of a loose stone wall till they reached two Nissen huts.

"Come on, lads! Everybody out!"

It was cold outside, and the wind was blowing. Airmen were laying out and lighting a flare path of glims—just ten tin pots of paraffin spaced a hundred yards apart. One after the other, they blossomed a bright yellow, glowing like braziers in the night and sending off wraiths of smoke over the three shadowy Henleys.

Gallagher shivered a little as he followed the others into the nearest of the Nissens. It was divided into two by a plywood partition: the near end for instructors, the far end for pupils. Concrete floor, five beds, a table and some chairs. A stove was smoking away in the centre. Pinned over the far door, a nude girl calendar flapped forlornly.

Gallagher took a bed and lay down on it. Perriman and Stephens started up a game of Vingt-et-Un with two others. King read a blood. Bunting sat studying his navigation notes.

Whatever they appeared to be doing, they were all really listening to what the instructors were saying next door.

"Cloud's too damn low at present." Marshall—Perriman's instructor—Gallagher could see him chewing the straggly moustaches that curved like thin tusks over his pale face. *Boy* he called every pupil, for the simple reason, Gallagher suspected, that he couldn't remember their names.

"What do you think, Jim?" Warrant Officer Bates—Bunting's instructor.

"Now look here!" The well-known Tordoff voice. "They're late enough as it is."

"You can't expect them, Jim, to go off night solo, after half an hour's dual in this sort of stuff."

Marshall sounded as anti as Gallagher was. Few instructors liked night flying. Most of them would agree with Gallagher that what was wanted was a flat calm, all the stars out and a nice round fat full moon.

"I'll have a look-see."

The sound of a door opening. Everybody in the pupils' section seemed to have turned momentarily to stone. Perriman paused half-way to laying down a card. King held on to a page he was just turning over.

"Two hundred bloody feet." Tordoff's voice again: a roar of frustration. "An' getting worse every minute!"

Immediately all the pupils became alive again. Perriman joyously snapped down twenty-one. King became re-immersed. Gallagher closed his eyes.

The hours of the night went slowly by.

The card players crooned to each other. Cigarette after cigarette was stamped out on the concrete floor. Now and again, a pupil would go through the door to piss on the nettles outside, returning with a staccato weather report.

"Mist's worse."

"No horizon."

"Sleeting now."

Finally, round five o'clock, Perriman came back triumphant, "Fog!"

And not long afterwards, Tordoff opened the dividing door between the two partitions and said brusquely, "All right, lads! Everyone into t'bus. We're off home!"

The bus to Bibury took Gallagher and the others night-flying the next night. Pretty much the same happened. Round dawn, it brought them back again.

December slid into January, and still the bus was taking them to Bibury and bringing them back again. There was now a regular nightly Vingt-et-Un school. Blood after blood was read and passed round. Gallagher even managed to sleep. Only

Tordoff—pacing up and down like a caged lion—could be heard on the other side of the partition roaring in frustration, "Christ . . . this bloody weather! When the hell are we going to get this damned Course off our hands"

There was sleet, snow, sometimes frost. Now and again "the Club", as Perriman called it, would be interrupted with Tordoff shouting, "All pupils out to give a hand with the covers!" and they would spend the next half hour fitting canvas over the tailplanes, rudders, wings, engines, everywhere. "Bloody things!" Perriman said, blowing into his cold hands. "Got more underclothes than a woman!"

Not that they did much good. The frost got under them, and then it would be "All pupils out! Get that ice off the wings!"

Underclothes off again. Scrubbing away in the darkness with brushes and alcohol.

Then back again to the hut to get on with the game, and hear Tordoff swearing away on the Instructors' side, till finally, with the first streaks of light turning the low overcast from grey to white, he would be forced to give up, and the bus would return them to Cirencester, with nothing accomplished.

On the thirteenth trip to Bibury, the atmosphere in the bus had relaxed so much, it was more like a Sunday School going off to the seaside.

The bus started off on the usual well-known route. Nobody really believed they would fly. Rain streamed down the windows, and outside the wind howled. Not that any of the pupils noticed. They chatted, smoked, sang Air Force songs, as the bus lurched onwards through the night countryside.

"Here we are again!" Perriman sang as they trooped once more into their side of the Nissen. "Happy as can be! All good pals and jolly good company. Never mind the weather, never mind the rain——"

The Vingt-et-Un school started up. The readers began reading. The sleepers lay down on the beds.

The rain, increasing now, hammered on the corrugated iron roof.

Gallagher lay on his back, watching the curve of the ceiling above his head. Tobacco smoke wreathed across it in long strings, staining the air a pale oily blue. His thoughts, relaxed and easy, wandered round in a comfortable confusion: it was as though he

61

had taken off the tight corset on his mind, so that now lazily his imagination wandered all over the place, one image coming up after the other, with no obvious sequence or reason: a sudden view of St. Jude's, his home in Cornwall, the chorus girls in the Ensa concert last Saturday.

He was not tired. He was not worried. The kaleidoscopic cinema show went on and he was enjoying it. What apprehension he once had over night flying was lost in the sheer routine of coming here and going home again. Sometime, he supposed, he would go off solo into the night—but not yet.

"Want to play Vingt-et-Un, Gallagher?" He was aware of Stephens' face spoiling his view of the ceiling.

"Not particularly, Stephens, old chap."

"What you thinking about, Gallagher? Women?"

"Life."

"Oh." Stephens move on to the next bed. "Want to play Vingt-et-Un, Smithy"

The night crawled by. The stove started smoking. Reports from urinators on the nettles outside continued unchanged: "Drizzle and rain."

And then suddenly, around twelve o'clock Perriman returned and announced dramatically: "Christ! It's clearing!"

"Sssh!" Stephens hissed at him crossly. "The instructors'll hear you!"

Everybody crowded to the door, and looked up into the sky.

"I don't call that clearing," Gallagher said, looking for *his* stars, *his* moon. "Black as bloody ink!"

Everybody went back inside. The card school resumed. "Somebody's paid twice!" Perriman irritably inspected the depleted kitty. "Come on . . . who's the bloody shyster?"

From the other side of the plywood came the sound of an opening door.

"What's that?"

"Tordoff . . . betcha," said a blood reader.

"Sticking," said a card player.

"Damn the man!" King said.

"Twist me one," said a card player.

"Won't the sod ever give up?" Stephens demanded.

"Give me another one," said a card player.

"Keen type," said the man trying to cope with the stove.

"Bust," said a card player.

There was a sudden burst of engines starting in the night outside. A hush fell over the hut. "Jesus!" Stephens said. "What a horrible noise!"

Perriman opened the door to investigate. "I see . . . I see . . . Christ, I see navigation lights!"

The note of the aircraft's engines rose: rose higher, shrieked up into a crescendo.

Perriman returned with the news. "Tordoff's taken off!"

"Looks like," Bunting observed in that pious tone of his, "tonight's the night . . . at last!"

The noise of the engines died away. The card players stopped their game. For minutes, nobody spoke. Then very faintly, back the sound came again: louder and louder, till it faded into the banging of wheels over rough grass.

"He's down," said the man at the stove. "Wonder who's going to be the lucky sod?"

A door opened on the other side of the hut. Everybody listened.

"How was it, Jim?"

"It'll do."

"Looks not so hot to me."

"It's two thousand feet!"

"We-ll . . . can't see the horizon."

"Now, Marshall, we're getting those lads solo tonight! They're weeks behind as it is. With this bloody weather . . . I tell you it'll be the last chance we'll get!"

There was the sound of heavy flying boots coming closer to the partition. The door was flung open. Tordoff with his helmet on stood framed in the lintel.

"Gallagher!"

With a feeling of disbelief, Gallagher raised himself and got off the bed. He was aware as he reached for his parachute that his mouth had gone dry. He tried to smile as Perriman sang, "Goodbye, Gavin . . . we're saying goodbye!"

Then he trailed through the instructors' room and out through the open door into the night.

He looked up. No moon, no stars, not even a horizon. Against the single line of yellow flares he could see Tordoff striding towards the red, white and green triangle of the taxiing post.

63

He struggled to catch him up.

"Laddie!" Tordoff had stopped and was shouting over his shoulder.

"Sir?"

"Able."

He had clambered into the Henley, and Tordoff was just getting in after him when the Aerodrome Control Pilot came along with his Aldis lamp. "Are you starting dual then, Jim?"

"What does it look like, lad?"

It was eerie inside. Like altar candles, the little lights made a halo, over the instruments. A black velvet mask covered the perspex of the windows. The cockpit looked strange: the throttle levers casting shadows, the control column sticking up frail and somehow inadequate, waiting for human hands.

"Now think on, laddie." Tordoff settled himself down in the right-hand seat. "You're getting two circuits. Two circuits, an' that's *that*. Hear me?"

"Yes, sir."

"Keep your eyes on the instruments. Follow the gyro on the usual square circuit."

"Yes, sir."

"An' I don't want any of your funny weaving on the approach, either."

The engines were started. Tapping out A in morse on the downward identification light, Gallagher received a green from the Aldis Lamp. Gingerly, he taxied forward. The ground, black like this, looked strange. It seemed that the flarepath, not the Henley, was moving—coming towards him like a procession of revellers carrying torches.

He stopped to do his Before Take Off Check, gave the throttle nut an extra special squeeze.

"Uncage your gyro on zero!"

Zero winked at him viscously, as though drowning in green water. He had opened his side window, and damp air came in to cool his hot face. Just beyond the port wing, the first glim sent up ragged yellow flames.

"Throttles open."

The engines roared reassurance to him.

"Right-ee-oh, laddie . . . off you go!"

Brakes off, the Henley seemed to charge at the night.

Gallagher felt the swing to starboard. Overcorrecting, he started to zigzag.

The speed built up. *Bump* went the wheels on the rough ground—then *bump* again, as the Henley tried to leap before her time. He felt Tordoff's hands pushing the control column, keeping the wheels on the ground.

The last flare rocketed past. And then, before he knew anything more about it, they were swallowed up into the night.

Lost—that was his first sensation. Blindfold in a circle game, he was being turned round and round. The sky was a black bottomless pit into which he was falling.

"Now then! Don't climb so steep!"

He had been climbing all the time, not diving. His body was lying to him. Trust your instruments, Tordoff had said. Whatever you feel, do what your artificial horizon tells you. Keeping his head down, he concentrated on its phosphorescent parallel lines.

"You're turning right . . . not left! You've pulled t'wrong wing up!"

This was a new world, nothing to do with the world they had left. The only inhabitants were Tordoff and himself. He was steering it madly through space, but what supported them, God only knew.

"Ackle yourself, lad! Time to turn!"

They were at 600 feet already. Cautiously he allowed the left wing to drop. The gyro trickled round to 270.

"Throttle back!"

The needle on the altimeter climbed rapidly to 1000, as he turned on to 180. Now they were on the downwind leg, and he should be able to see the aerodrome. Fearful of losing it, he lifted his head and looked outside.

Nothing but night.

"Stay on instruments!"

He jerked his head back into the cockpit, quite sure that he had already lost Bibury. No landing field could possibly be down there. England couldn't be down there. The earth had been taken away. His tongue came out of his mouth to moisten his dry lips.

"There's the flare path now."

It couldn't be. Not those disembodied orange blobs! Even as

he looked at them, they seemed to tilt up at a ridiculous angle.

"Watch your attitude!"

He became suddenly aware he had forty degrees of left bank on. Lifting up the wing, he tapped dit-dah—A Able, his call sign—on the downward identification light, received in return a glowing green.

"Not so near t'flarepath! It won't run away!"

But it was already too late. Bibury was practically underneath. Gruffly, Tordoff said, "You can't make an approach from here, lad. Go round again."

He made another square circuit, a wider one this time, and positioned himself so he could see that flaming line through his front windscreen.

But the Henley wouldn't keep straight. Descending, wheels down, he juggled with the stick to keep lined up with it. But off it went, over to the left at an angle.

"You're on the right hand side of the flarepath . . . and you're still turning *right*!"

He looked down at his thumbs. Under the phosphorescence, both of his marks looked green. All he could see were blurred smudges.

"*Get . . . lined . . . up!*"

Wretchedly, he started weaving the other way.

"Go round again! You can't make any sort of landing from here!"

Round they went for the second time. Beside him now, Tordoff kept an ominous silence. He made another approach. The flarepath didn't go over to quite such an angle, but still they weaved.

Lower and lower they came, till the lights were hurtling towards them like big yellow balls. He put his hand on the throttles and drew them back.

"Watch your speed!"

He put his hand back on the throttles. Preoccupied with pushing them forward, the ground sneaked up on him. He had the sudden sensation of being knocked under the jaw by a terrific right uppercut. The whole aeroplane shivered as though it was about to drop to bits.

And then, instead of having landed, he became conscious of being far higher than he had been two seconds before. He heard

66

the roaring of engines being slammed open, and Tordoff shouting, "I've got her!"

Then there was a hush. They were coming down. Next moment they were banging over the ground, and Tordoff was applying vicious brake.

As they taxied, the instructor said nothing till they stopped at the taxiing post. Then he swivelled right round in his seat and asked, "Laddie, what the bloody hell is up with you, eh?"

Gallagher looked into the eyes, more luminous and frog-like than ever. He swallowed, but could think of nothing.

"You've *had* your half-hour dual. There's others to think of. If you think I'm going on for ever-and-ever-amen with *you*, you've got another think coming! I'm not pouring good money after bad."

Visions of failure came swarming up at Gallagher. He went on staring at Tordoff as if indeed those frogs' eyes had some terrible hypnotic effect. Just in front of them, another Henley took off. How could he explain that the night seemed so strange? It didn't seem real. Without lights, without horizon, without the help of the ink on his fingers. There was an other-worldliness over everything, a disembodied farawayness, miles from reality.

"I'd swear," Tordoff went on, his voice full of a monstrous exasperation, "that you'd never touched a bloody Henley before. It's not going to *bite*! It's not a load of wet tripe! It's an aeroplane!" He gripped the stick in his own hands. "Tek hold on her, lad! *Mek* her do what you want!" The exasperation turned to a monstrous scorn, "You fly her like a bloody lass!"

Hearing Gallagher's sharp intake of anger, Tordoff paused in his wrath. As if his mind had suddenly hit on a possible explanation, more quietly, "You're not poorly, are you, lad?"

Thinly, hatefully, Gallagher smiled. "I'm *perfectly* all right, thank you." He drawled the words slowly.

"Well then?" Tordoff's anger was back at full blast again.

What seemed a long time ago, Gallagher had won a reprieve from Tordoff by a cool assumed insouciance. Perhaps it was hope of something similar, not only the hatred and rage which almost choked him, that made Gallagher say in his best, most irritating Oxford manner, "It's just that . . . I'm never exactly at my best . . . at one o'clock in the morning."

He attempted to yawn, but his lips were trembling. He was

67

aware of a tiny crackling silence. Neither of them seemed to
breathe. Then in the little light around them, Gallagher saw the
sudden flash of a heavy leather gauntlet. He was aware of a jolt,
a savage swishing noise and a burning pain in his cheek. His
right eye started to water where the empty thumb had caught it.
For a full minute, he couldn't accept that Tordoff had actually *hit*
him. His only thought was that he'd kill Tordoff if he thought
he'd made him cry.

"Get out!" Tordoff said. And then all in one deadly flat
sentence, "Get-out-of-my-bloody-sight-you-bloody-little-bastard-
before-I-brain-you!"

Clumsily, Gallagher got up. Dragging his parachute behind
him, he crawled down the fuselage to the door.

He saw Tordoff mop his brow. "Send Smith." He didn't even
turn to watch Gallagher go.

Wiping the sweat off his own face, Gallagher walked slowly
back to the Nissen, and pushed his way through the pupils' back
door.

"How was it?" they asked him.

He held his hand up to his face so they wouldn't see the mark.
"All . . . right."

"Been solo?"

He shook his head. He threw his parachute on to the nearest
bed and lay down. "Smith," he said thickly. "You're to go. Your
turn. He's waiting."

Nobody pressed him to say any more. It was as though they
understood. Already they saw the ridiculous inked-in bowler hat
on Gallagher's head. Purposely loudly, the card players continued. From outside came the continuous drone of Henleys
taking off and landing.

It was like being expelled, he thought. I'm out—finished. He
wasn't the right type: he mixed up things: he'd got too many
thumbs to fly. His cheek still smarted, but that was nothing. He
had failed. That being so, there didn't seem to be any point in
going on. What was he going to do now?

He curled himself up with his eyes tight shut, but he couldn't
keep out the sounds of the world around him.

The card players went on. Marshall popped his pale face
round to shout "Boy!" and a pupil would go out. Another pupil
would return to be greeted with the inevitable: "Been solo?"

"Yep."

"What's it like?"

"Nothing to it . . . once you get used to not seeing a sausage."

Through the hours of the night, the Henleys went droning on. Perriman soloed, so did Smith, Bunting, Stephens. Nobody else had failed.

Round four o'clock, Gallagher got off his bed, and went outside. For a while, he walked up and down, and then went into the ground staff Nissen next door. An erk was frying bacon over the stove, and the place reeked of burning fat. He accepted some on a plate, and winced at the sting of the salt as he ate it. He had no idea he had bitten his lip so hard. He was just finishing when suddenly he heard the wail of the sirens. He walked outside and saw the red stars of gun flashes.

"Cheltenham's getting it," said the erk beside him.

Back in the hut, the jubilation was considerable. Nearly everyone had gone solo. In came Atkins, Tordoff's last pupil, smiling and putting up his thumbs. "Gallagher . . . Tordoff wants you."

He thought it was just to finalize everything. Just categorically to state that he'd failed. And what would now happen to him.

"And . . . where's your bloody parachute?"

It took Gallagher several moments to realize he was being given another chance. His heart leapt. But when he came back, Marshall was remonstrating, "Jim . . . we really ought to call a halt."

"I don't see why!"

"We're sitting ducks with those damned glims!"

"Nay, lad. The raid's miles away. Twenty at least!"

"We've done an excellent night's work. Machin and Rogers are just going solo now. That makes thirteen solo tonight. Good going!"

"Twelve."

Marshall looked at Gallagher. "Well——"

"Then there's another twenty-odd on the Course to do, don't forget *that*. We're still weeks behind where we oughter be. An' with this weather . . . we strike while the iron's hot. Any lad in this lot who can't solo tonight has had it!"

Marshall spoke as if Gallagher simply wasn't there. "Come off it, Jim! The boy's had his dual. We want to go home."

"The squadrons are *screaming* for *every single* pilot we can

69

give 'em." Tordoff led the way to the door. "*Every* pilot!"

He didn't wait for Gallagher. He just went on ahead to the aeroplane. Over on the right now were the long fingers of searchlights, the intermittent flashes of anti-aircraft fire. Gallagher had the ridiculous wild hope that they might help him to navigate this horizonless, coastless black sea.

Inside the aircraft, under the phosphorescence of the instruments, Tordoff's face looked like a ghost. Tordoff was feeling the strain, Gallagher thought with pleasure. He felt not the slightest gratitude that Tordoff was giving him another chance. He understood the man too well for that. Tordoff too had *his* obsession. He couldn't bear to be defeated, to have to give up a pupil.

"And now, lad! Now you swanky little bugger! Do me two good circuits, or by Christ, I'll flatten you!"

And he thought he could do the trick by frightening him! Brute force and bloody ignorance!

If only Tordoff knew! Gallagher wasn't the slightest afraid of him. The only emotion he had right then was hate. He hated everything about Tordoff . . . his looks, his voice, his methods, his mercenary mechanic's mind.

The enemy wasn't some invisible German. The enemy was here right at hand. The enemy was Tordoff.

He taxied to the end of the runway. Hate took people many ways. With him, it was an adrenalin and benzedrine cocktail. It widened his vision, it steadied his hand, it cleared his head. It let him focus his whole being into one cold clear beam of concentration. It made him overcome his inadequacies, the left-right mix-up, his innate lack of mechanical aptitude. It made him reach up and beyond himself.

"We'll have the navigation lights off, lad." Tordoff leaned across to flick up a switch. "Don't want t'give ourselves away. Now off you go!"

Gallagher took off. He made his square circuit at a thousand feet. Descending in a straight approach, he levelled up at the first flare, flew horizontally for six seconds, till the wheels gently touched the grass, and then waited while the tail wheel connected before putting on brake.

Then he took off and did it again.

Tordoff kept silent while they were flying. Now, as they

returned to the taxiing post, he said "An' about time, too!" and started to get out of his seat. At the end of the flarepath, when the Henley was stopped, he clambered to the back and got out through the door. Just before he closed it, he called back quite softly, "Laddie!"

Gallagher turned.

"Only one circuit now, think on." He pointed to the flak and the searchlights. "Jerry's still at it!" He paused. "Now go steady, lad!"

Then the door slammed shut. Gallagher was alone.

"Thank God for that!" he muttered to himself.

The green that flashed at him now took on a new significance: permission not only to take off, but a green ticket to success, to wear his wings, to go forward into the future.

He opened up the engines. The Henley lunged forward and roared up into the night.

Purposely, to give himself plenty of time he climbed up to a thousand feet before turning left. The engines murmured sweetly beside him. In the pitch darkness, loneliness gave way to peace, and peace to exhilaration.

He turned downwind. Confident now, he did not immediately search the ground for the flarepath. He concentrated instead on the heading—180. Then, after he was steady, he glanced out of the window.

Yes, it was there! A line of warm yellow bonfires—though not so long as he had thought before. There seemed to be fewer, but that of course was his imagination. One by one, the glims slipped behind him and disappeared.

He counted sixty seconds out loud. Then he turned across wind, again keeping his head in the cockpit, concentrating on instruments.

His gear was down, all his checks complete. Cool and collected, he began to allow the aircraft to descend. Then he lifted his head to look out of the side window for the flarepath.

There was no sign of it. None. Not a light. Nothing.

He started to crane his neck this way and that. Then his eyes went down to the gyro. It read 090—just as it should have done. He checked it. Perfectly serviceable.

It'll be there now, he said to himself, lifting his head again. But again, there was nothing out there but the night.

Panic began to take hold of him—and as though it was catching, this fear communicated itself to the aircraft. The Henley began bucketing round—left wing going down, then the right wing. Unseen and unattended, as his eyes searched, the Henley climbed. When he looked back at the instruments again, he saw the gyro going round in circles, the altimeter reading 1500 feet.

In the few minutes since he had left it, the flarepath had dissolved. Just as in daytime he had lost the aerodrome, now he had done the same at night. Only this was far worse: he had lost the earth. He did not believe there was ground down there. How could there be? Above him, beside him, below him was one single sheet of uniform blackness.

He prayed for a light—a star even—to show that there was something else but himself. For this was like being dead, cut off from everywhere. Hell would be like this: just yourself drowned in billions of black years.

He began going in circles, round and round—not knowing which direction to take, his eyes now always outside.

His face was dewy with sweat. Against the rudder bars, his legs vibrated. Because he had also to fly, it was difficult to think. He was chained to the control column, trying to get some part of his mind to plan.

Bibury flarepath *must* be there, he told himself. It can't just vanish. He turned the Henley up on its left wing, and slowly revolved through a full circle.

Nothing.

Now he felt his heart thumping away under the heavy fabric of his flying suit. There was never a loneliness like this. Noiselessly, like black cottonwool, a cloud swept over him, cocooning him in this little green-lighted cell.

He pushed the nose down. The stuff came to pieces all round him as he dived into the clear black pit.

The clock on the instrument panel ticked calmly on. Now he flew aimlessly, letting the Henley fly anywhere. To the left, to the right, up, down—every direction was the same. Half an hour went by, as he tangled himself up in compass courses and circles till he was utterly, hopelessly lost. He began to give up. He would never find himself. And he couldn't stay up here in this dim prison much longer. He had only been sent up to do one circuit.

He pressed the fuel gauge. The needle flickered well back.

If the worst came to the worst he could abandon the aircraft. He tried it, getting up out of his seat and beginning the walk to the door at the rear. But immediately, left on her own in the uneven air, the delicately balanced aircraft turned on one wing, and she would have gone on her back if Gallagher hadn't grabbed the stick and returned to the seat. He would never be able to escape that way.

But was there another way?

By now, he might be over mountain, city, river, sea. When his fuel ran out, all he could do was to hang on and let her drop down and down and down into the black chasm below.

His whole body seemed to be drained of feeling. If fear this was, it showed itself as a paralysis of the mind, a kind of anaesthetic. Here he was chained to the aeroplane like a Siamese twin, each dependent on the other, each dead without the other.

And then he saw it. Suddenly written on the night in red morse: Dah, Dit Dah. TA—the Cirencester pundit.

He was saved! He began to breathe easier as he flew towards the aerial lighthouse as though to a lifebelt. Bibury landing ground was twelve miles due north of the beacon—that he knew. Say six minutes flying time. Circling the red light once, carefully timing himself, he set off on a northerly course.

But six minutes later, there was nothing down there. He looked all over, and then fearful of losing his only light, back he went to the warm glow of the pundit, and began circling it like a moth.

Round and round and round he went—every few minutes pressing the button on the fuel gauge.

The needle was falling farther and farther back.

Unless somebody helped him soon, he'd be crashing down on the beacon. With no other communication possible, he turned to the distress call-sign Sergeant Dann had drilled into him. On his downward identification light he slowly began tapping out dots and dashes. Dah dah, dit dah, dah dit dah dah . . . MAYDAY —*help me*.

TA in red came winking back at him.

MAYDAY . . . MAYDAY . . .

Mechanically, stupidly, mercilessly—TA.

Just a machine—not an individual, not a being with a human

73

heart. Appeal to it for all his worth—TA was his only answer.

Looking at his watch, he saw ten more minutes had passed. Again he pressed the button by the fuel gauge. The needle now indicated just about the Empty line.

In desperation, doubting his own sanity, doubting his belief in the compass, in morse, in flying, in everything about this topsy-turvy world—off he set again northwards, tapping out MAY-DAY all over the dark countryside.

Nothing, of course. Not the ghost of a light. And he was just returning to the pundit, when suddenly he saw what looked like a yellow pimple come up on the black skin of the night. Then another one, and another. Before his eyes, a flarepath was being created out of what seemed to be nothing. He turned towards it, breathless with relief.

And then it struck him what must have happened. The German bombers must have got closer, so the bastards had doused the flarepath. Tordoff had kicked him up into the air—and then left him to it.

Typical! He gave the rudder a savage kick, pulled the throttles back, and descended in a wide curve down to a thousand feet.

Then he began a very correct square circuit.

He was quite calm now. His heart had stopped thundering. In the fury of finding out the probable cause of the agony of the last hour and a half, his hate of Tordoff increased.

There were only six flares visible when he turned in on approach, but that was enough, and he was damned well coming down on them.

The needle on the altimeter ticked past 400, 300, 200 . . .

He could see quite clearly now the guttering bonfire of the first glim.

Then up came the grass—damp and dark. He slammed the throttles shut. Pulling back on the stick, he felt all three wheels touch together. Jabbing away at the brake, gradually he slowed to a stop.

He'd made it. In spite of them dousing the flarepath, in spite of an air raid, in spite of Tordoff, he had survived. He felt a tremendous exhilaration surge through him. In the end *he* had won.

He had turned right round a hundred and eighty degrees to go back to the taxiing post, when he saw all the glims had gone out again. Stopping the Henley, he was just swearing aloud about this bloody vanishing flarepath, when the door was flung open and the Warrant Officer instructor yelled, "Lights and engines off! Quick, for Christ's sake . . . follow me!"

Surprised, Gallagher did what he was told. He was just climbing out, saying "What the . . . ?" when there was a sudden rattle of machine guns. Jumping on to the ground, he saw a stream of silver tracer.

He started running. Warrant Officer Bates was already ahead of him. One after the other, they leapt over the stone wall into the next field and threw themselves flat, as the earth around them started to *put-put-put* with exploding cannon shells.

Lying there, listening to the desynchronized droning of German engines overhead, he heard in snatches what had happened. Just after he had taken off, three JU 88s had swept low over the field, and then began circling. The glims had been immediately doused, but the enemy aircraft had apparently pinpointed them as their target, and they began circling at not more than five hundred feet, waiting. All personnel had been ordered to disperse themselves in the fields around. Tordoff had champed away about Gallagher. He calmed down when he heard that his pupil was circling the pundit; the JUs couldn't stay for ever, and Tordoff had calculated Gallagher was for the time being still all right for fuel. Then over the sky ahead had come the Henley like a lost sheep, flashing out brightly for all the world to see *Mayday . . . Mayday.*

"Mayday! Those JUs'll give him Mayday! Unless we get him in . . . they'll shoot that bloody little swank-pot down!"

Alone, Tordoff had insisted on returning. He started to light up the glims. Minutes later, there had been the screaming noise of diving aircraft, then the whistle of bombs. After the blast had subsided, Bates had gone racing out. Tordoff had been caught in the centre of the stick.

The Warrant Officer's voice stopped.

"Was he hurt?" Gallagher said.

The German engines had faded. The countryside seemed suddenly still and silent. A pre-dawn wind lightly stirred the grass. Gallagher could smell the bitter dusty smell of blasted earth.

Bates crossed his fore-finger over his throat.

"He can't be!" Gallagher said indignantly, loudly. "Tordoff? He can't be!"

Of everything about this monstrous night, that one small gesture of the Warrant Officer's was the most monstrous thing of all. Gallagher scrambled to his feet. He looked around as if expecting to see Tordoff's big indestructible frame stalking towards them. He half expected to hear a shout "Nah then! . . . Come on there, lads! Get a move on!" To contradict this manifest, unnatural absurdity.

The Warrant Officer dusted the grass from his knees. Even before he spoke, Gallagher's certainty had done an abrupt somersault. Tordoff *was dead*. He could feel it in the morning twilight, in the smell of the earth, in the terrible shrunken smallness inside himself.

Reasonably, as if ending all argument, Bates said, "Well, you can't live without a head."

He began to shamble across the field and Gallagher followed. The huts were standing out now in the pale grey light. It was beginning to dawn. They could hear the sound of people who had dispersed themselves returning from the fields. Some of the ground crew were trailing shovels to fill in the bomb holes at the side of the flarepath.

The old bus was waiting for them where they had left it, quite unscathed. Just as Gallagher was climbing inside to go home, an ambulance arrived.

INTERLUDE ONE

Bunting had no idea while he was talking that he was going to formulate a theory. All he could remember thinking as he told his story was how deeply those memories had bitten in. How clearly it all came back! The clock behind Air Marshal Ingleby's head said five past two. Bunting stubbed out his cigarette. For a moment, no one spoke.

"The way you've told it," Henderson said, studying his policeman's notebook. "Gallagher was a great deal different when *you* knew him, to what he was later on."

"Different?" Ingleby said, *"Unrecognizable!* That was not the man *I* knew." Sir John's smooth pink skin was sweating. "Quite the *reverse.*"

"Reverse." Henderson appeared to muse over the word. "The reverse. Interesting! Why?" Henderson looked at Bunting. "Why did he reverse?"

"He got pretty steamed up over Tordoff's death. Felt it was his fault." Bunting could not help adding, "So it was!"

He was just getting interested in this theory of his, working out the pros and cons in his mind when the shrill sound of the telephone interrupted. He's been found, Bunting thought. He was glad now that he hadn't said too much.

"If you'll excuse me, sir," Henderson said, reaching out a plump hand. "It'll be for me, I imagine."

He lifted the receiver and said, "Yes, Henderson here." He listened quietly, doodling with his pencil, giving a brief shake of his head to the others to tell them there was no news.

"All right." He put down the receiver. "Keep trying."

He shrugged his shoulders. "A blank from all Eastern Counties hospitals. Nothing so far from the police."

"London?" Bunting said eagerly. "The airports?"

Ingleby shot him a calculating glance. Henderson smiled. "They *have* been notified. Nothing so far."

"What," Ingleby said, "would he be doing at an airport?"

"Yes, what?" repeated Henderson.

"Catching a plane."

"Where to?"

Bunting shrugged.

"In his uniform? He'd be spotted right away." Ingleby narrowed his eyes.

"He could have had civilian clothes somewhere."

"Just *what* are you getting at, Bunting?"

"I'm trying to help, sir. A man in uniform . . . especially a Group Captain's uniform is *easy* to find. A civilian is *not*."

"That," Ingleby said, "argues intent to leave."

"But he *did* leave."

"That we are aware of. What I'm *not* aware of is . . . what have you in mind?"

Bunting hesitated. "Could I ask Wing Commander Henderson a question before I answer?"

"Go ahead," Henderson said, leaning forward.

"Why don't you broadcast a wireless appeal? A television description? Get the press to help?"

"I thought you would have realized. For reasons of national security."

"Quite!" Bunting said. "Because everyone would jump to that one conclusion. There have been too many spies, too many disappearances recently. Everyone would say, he's gone to Russia. Or somewhere behind the Iron Curtain. That he's had a change of heart."

"Is that what *you* say, Wing Commander Bunting?" Henderson asked.

Having made his point, Bunting shook his head. He went on reasonably. "Not quite. I'd say a man who changes once . . . can change twice. And it's easier changing *back*."

"You've said absolutely the same thing." Ingleby got up and walked around the room. "You're giving *far* too much weight to what happened to him as a youth. Far too much attention to what happened at Oxford. Most boys have their bit of nonsense. He joined a Communist Club. He probably put a chamber pot on top of All Souls, too. It's all part of growing up!"

"That," Henderson said, "is exactly what the Foreign Office thought about Burgess and Maclean."

"Maybe. But if you must have your Communist theories, I think I can prove that he did *not* go willingly. You, Bunting, are not aware of one little point. Places like North Luddenham are under enemy observation. Perhaps he was kidnapped. You see, what has happened . . . even our *theories* . . . depend on the *character* of the man. You knew him as a youth. I got to know him later on. He was far too intelligent to get himself mixed up in anything like that. He wrote papers on all sorts of subjects. Fuel saving, tactics, Red-on-Blue accidents . . . that's setting the compass the wrong way round . . . mixing up north and south. Got the A.F.C. for those papers and his researches. He was very much the loyal Air Force officer."

There was a silence for a while. Then Bunting asked, "Exactly when was he missed, sir?"

All this time, the only person who had not uttered a word was the Senior Launch Control Officer. Sitting there beside Ingleby, Squadron Leader Mumford gave the impression of being a little overawed by the company. Now he gave a sudden nervous cough. "Ah, that's just it——"

"His absence was discovered," Ingleby said, "at 10 a.m. this morning."

"Not for nearly twelve hours."

"That is so, Bunting."

"But, sir . . . didn't his wife give the alarm when he didn't come home?"

"Mrs. Gallagher says she thought he was at the rocket site."

"And we thought he was standing by at home." Mumford put in. "So when it was necessary to lower Missile 199 for check and refuelling, we phoned. You see, we had to have the key."

"The key?" Bunting asked.

"The WAR-PEACE key," Henderson said. "The key that fires the Zeus rockets. Not only is the Group Captain missing. The key's missing too."

"And the Group Captain was the last person with it," Mumford murmured. "Which perhaps lends support to Wing Commander Bunting's theory . . ."

His words trailed away. In the silence that followed, slowly the implications dawned on Bunting. "In fact," he said, "those Zeus out there are immobilized? And the key itself would be valuable to an enemy?"

"It's a special key. They could get information from it . . . yes."

"Well then . . . sir——" The reception given to his theory

had not altogether pleased Bunting. Now it seemed as though it was the true one. "Hasn't he already committed sabotage, by leaving the Station with the key. Surely some rendezvous is the most obvious thing?"

"Now wait a minute!" Sir John Ingleby held up both his hands. "I can't believe that of him. If he did go . . . he went by force. I met him . . . how many years ago? Been with me on 720 squadron . . . at 81 Group . . . then with 777. Believe me, it's war that finds out the true worth of a man . . ."

THE DAZZLE-PAINTED SHIP

I

GALLAGHER lifted up his left arm, and began wiping the mist off the Blenheim windscreen with his uniform sleeve.

Once blue barathea, the cloth was now worn nearer grey with oilstains, dust and use. Two parallel stripes across it signified the rank of Flight Lieutenant, and through a thin ragged tear could be seen a white woollen sweater underneath. A yellow Mae West was round his neck, but his face, framed by his leather helmet, looked much the same as it had done at Cirencester. Leaning forward, he screwed up his eyes, peering ahead through the patch of cleared perspex.

Now they were approaching the Skagerrak, the overcast was getting lower. Skimming between grey sea and grey sky, the other three bombers looked like low flying wraiths accompanying him —one to port, one to starboard, one in front. A sudden tremor shivered through the metal plates as Victor was caught in the slipstream of Flight Lieutenant Scarfe in U Uncle, who was leading the attack. As Gallagher slid to the right to get out of it, long strings of raindrops started trickling over the windscreen, and he thought . . . Christ, if this stuff gets any worse, we'll not even get a sight of the bloody ship.

It was over a year now since he had left Cirencester. After a navigation course, he had gone to an Operational Training Unit, where to his surprise he had found Blenheims simpler and more forgiving than Henleys. Finally, he had come to this medium bomber Squadron, based at Wragton in Norfolk. In actual technical skill, he would always be a "rough" pilot—but because he knew his faults and limitations exactly, he was also a safe one. He was never, even yet, exactly sure where the ground was, but like a person coping with a physical deformity, he had worked out a compensation technique which now and then would produce bad landings, but would never produce dangerous ones. By sheer concentration and effort, he found he could discipline his deficiencies, so that even his tendency to mix his left and his right had now gone right underground, only showing up occasionally in harmless ways like getting a number the wrong way round, or by trying to tighten a nut anti-clockwise. With determination, he found he could do almost anything. As an operational pilot, he was the most press-on, by far the most knowledgeable in bombing, gunnery, tactics and ship-recognition.

Guilt drives harder than ambition, but it also drives unseen. The people with their eyes on gongs, gold-leaves and glory can easily be identified. But if anyone on 720 squadron had been asked what made Gallagher tick so hard, they would have shrugged their shoulders, and said "Keen type". The two pilots who were posted with him from Cirencester might have had an inkling. But Perriman and King had soon got the hammer—both shot down by flak-ships.

Solidifying out of the gloom ahead came four jagged rocks, which Traill, his navigator, pushed up to the front to point out.

"Vigso Bay, Skipper. Not bad navigation, eh?"

Gallagher shook his head. This was their landfall, the place to turn northwards. Anticipation tightened the muscles of his stomach. He tilted Victor's port wing.

"Right-ee-oh." The familiar expression of Tordoff's came up naturally, as it always did in times of tension.

For Tordoff never really seemed far away. Perhaps it was because one cockpit was very like another, because the changing seasonal sky they flew through conjured up the same nostalgic scenery, because fear and nervousness whether at Cirencester or the Skagerrak was of an unbroken continuity, that together they all combined to set the stage for Tordoff's Hamlet. Or maybe, as Gallagher had learned before, hatred was a fine engraver of the memory. Whatever it was, he flew as if Tordoff sat there. He even anticipated Tordoff's comments, not in his own mode of speech, but in Tordoff's coarse bellicose idiom. At first he had tried to stop himself. Then he found it gave him confidence, and from confidence came skill. For it wasn't what was near the surface of his mind that troubled him. It was the dangerous eight-ninths of the iceberg—that sailed stealthily underneath. And that eight-ninths was compounded of the single certainty that he had killed Tordoff.

Not in anger or by any violent means. But by his own hidden inadequacies. A man, they say, keeps his love, like his courage, dark. But even darker does he keep his weaknesses. Once or twice he dreamed of it. He dreamed that awful dream of the inadequate. That the disaster under which his mind cowered had not yet happened, that a second chance was there for the taking. Always, the sudden leap of mental relief waking him. Always, the dream, and the second chance dissolved. And then he would lie curled up in his bed, unwilling to get up with this dead-weight inside him. For guilt was bad enough, but guilt and hatred made an intolerable mixture—infinitely more binding than guilt and love.

Yet even a mind as muddled as his had been had found some sort of way out. Vince would have said he'd not rationalized it, but sublimated it. That he had turned to the age-old wisdom of the totem-pole, already inscribed with one dead hero's image.

In exchange for a superb, loyal and experienced pilot, the Air Force had got an unblooded reluctant, half-competent boy, whose flying ability was a question mark—the *Average* Assessment in his Log Book being no more than the pity of a Chief Instructor who could never bear to send boys off to almost certain death with the stigma of a *Below Average*. Without consciously substituting himself, Gallagher found his inclination taking him along the road that Tordoff would have travelled. And the Air Force, which in turn had slit open his inadequacies and failings like a surgeon, which had brought him to an emotional catharsis like a Pavlovian psychiatrist and had by discipline set him up again, which gave him rules to obey and an end to strive for, was slowly becoming, as it had naturally been for Tordoff—the object of his profoundest love and loyalty. And by the same token, the successful waging of his part of this war had become his most immediate obsession.

"Course 021, Skipper!"

Sergeant Traill was putting the course on the compass for him. Now right down on the water, they were sweeping up along the reciprocal course on which the convoy was expected. U Uncle was still leading a couple of hundred yards ahead, but K King and L London were now tucked up close, almost touching Gallagher's wings.

Traill stared into the weeping visibility ahead. "Think we'll see her this time, sir?"

"Your guess is as good as mine."

"Queer the way she's so elusive. Proper Scarlet Pimpernel, isn't she?"

"We'll get her one day."

"Course we will! Might even get her today."

"Might." Gallagher edged forward the throttles. "How's Paget?"

Traill ducked his head and looked aft, towards the gunner in his turret. "Happy as a sandboy, sir. Chewing a corn-beef sandwich."

"Tell him to forget his bloody stomach for once . . . and keep his eye skinned! She'll have a fighter escort."

U Uncle climbed a little, and started to slow down. Beginning to overtake him, Gallagher cursed Scarfe as he throttled back himself. Obviously the man thought he'd missed the convoy, and was going up a bit to get a better view. That was the way to give yourself away: a silhouette of a Blenheim against this streaming cloud . . .

"There they are! Skipper . . . *ships!* Look at 'em!"

Two miles over to port, blown by the wind into a curve, the curtain of rain had parted. Mixed in with the damp grey of sea and sky was a darker grey now: almost black, sharp-edged, underlined by a spume of white. A Wolf class German destroyer, and beyond, indistinct in the damp half light, the still bigger moving shadows of merchantmen. Gallagher saw Scarfe turn, and as he followed him a great silver stream of tracer sparked out of the mist and came lazily towards them.

"They've seen us! They're shooting!" Scarfe's masterly understatement over the R/T. "Quick, chaps! Bunch up!"

With all hope of surprise now gone, the four Blenheims huddled together and swept down to the sea.

"Now she'll be in the middle. We'll shoot to one side of this leading destroyer. Then we should easily spot her in the centre of the convoy."

The flak was coming at them from all sides now: big orange bursts of heavy stuff mixing with tinsel of tracer and the red and green cannon patterns. They were so low that Gallagher could see the tops of the waves, flapping over like great white tongues. They shot past the stern of a destroyer, and now ahead of them the greyness was lit up like the inside of a dark cave with yellow flashes.

"On the port bow! See her! See her!" In his excitement, Scarfe skidded to the left. "The dazzle-painted ship!"

No one on the squadron, no one in the R.A.F., no known person in England had yet seen that elusive vessel. The Norwegian underground gave her as an armed merchantman of 12,000 tons, recently completed at Hamburg and capable of the unprecedented speed of 28 knots. To disguise this fact, she had been camouflaged in a way more common in the First World War— dazzle-painting, a modernistic arrangement in black and white and grey and green, expressly designed to disguise her course and speed. It followed that such a ship would be given the most valuable cargoes, and certainly her trips between Norway and the North German ports were highly important. *Elisabeth* was her name, but to all 81 Group, from the lowest W.A.A.F. plotter to the Officer Commanding, she was known as "the dazzle-painted ship"—the ghost ship, for she flitted unseen from port to port, loading in one place one day, unloading in another the next. She moved silently, usually at night or in bad weather, and always accompanied by a destroyer screen worthy of a battle-fleet. Again and again 720 Squadron had gone out after her with their low-level 12-second delay bombs, but never had they managed to find her. Today there had been an Intelligence Report she was leaving Oslo under escort: that was why B Flight had scrambled.

"Bomb doors open . . . everybody!"

Even as he opened his bomb doors to Scarfe's command, almost under the cliff of the hull, Gallagher was hearing at the back of his mind that North Country scepticism: "Steady, lad . . . think on! Is *yon* t'dazzle-painted ship?"

A heavy hull and high superstructure, certainly. One funnel, fast clipper bows—all that. But the size wasn't there: this one was half the tonnage: and there was a thinner character to her. Gallagher had seen P.R.U. photographs showing the vessel like a fat seed, together with Intelligence reconstructions of what she must look like. In this pouring rain, all colours looked the same, so the camouflage would not be apparent anyway—but she appeared dark grey, the same colour as the escorting destroyers.

"Get ready to drop your bombs!"

The intention was to sweep over, all about the same time, dropping pilot release. Now the flak had intensified. Criss-cross

85

electric patterns seemed to illuminate even the rain. Gallagher was just hearing the rip-rip-rip of cannon tearing into his own fabric when exactly at the same time, as though they were doing an aerobatic act, K and L on either side of him simply turned upside down, and he saw the exploding petrol light up his whole cockpit. Then he kicked on rudder, and seeing the superstructure looming just ahead, he pressed the button.

"Bombs gone! Climbing!"

He began jinking from side to side, pulling out from the flak at full throttle. He was conscious of the spattering of gunfire from the rear turret as Paget sprayed the decks. He saw U Uncle streaking westwards, making for a gap in the destroyer screen, and now he raced just above the waves, following her.

Looking over his shoulder, he saw a great mountain of white water—but the bows of the ship still sticking horizontal through them, and close by an eerie yellow glow. Traill reported a straddle as Gallagher made for a thick patch of cloud and slid into even denser rain, the streams of tracer dying away behind him.

Fifty miles out he caught up U Uncle. The weather was clearer here, and when he closed up, he noticed Scarfe's jubilant face and saw him put up his thumbs. A few minutes later, on the wireless Paget picked up Scarfe's signal to base: *Mission completed.*

Scarfe had already landed when Victor touched down at Wragton, and was already giving his report in the Intelligence Office when Gallagher and his crew came in. He was sitting at the table, a white scarf round his neck, his hat pushed to the back of his head, drawing in deeply on a cigarette. "Well . . . that's one bastard less, eh Gavin? Finis . . . curtains . . . bonkers to the dazzle-painted ship."

Today, beside the Intelligence Officer another man was sitting. Partly because of the atmosphere of deference, and partly by the thick black bar and the thin one, Gallagher recognized him as the new Air Officer Commanding 81 Group. It was an added underlining of the importance of the dazzle-painted ship, an extra voltage to the air which now crackled with the electricity of success.

Gallagher was aware that Ingleby had transferred his bright, alert amber-eyed stare to him. He saw a plump middle-sized man with a boardroom manner. The Air Vice-Marshal was leaning slightly forward towards him, his small well-manicured hands clasped on his knee. He was waiting to be given the confirmation that would make him smile.

Eighteen months ago, in similar circumstances, Gallagher would have felt there was sufficient excuse to give it to him. Now he didn't. Now he'd learned that in flying and war, fact was fact, truth was truth. Compromise spelled someone's death, now or in the future.

"I wouldn't be too sure."

"What the hell d'you mean?"

"We didn't hit the ship. Don't think we even damaged her."

"Balls!" Scarfe said. "My gunner——"

Acutely aware of the lowering spirits around him, of Scarfe's wounded disappointment, of a general feeling of let-down, Gallagher had to force himself to say. "It was a straddle."

"It was a *hit* . . . I tell you!"

"Hits don't send up waterspouts."

"Christ!" Scarfe's cheeks were red and his face was sweating. "I saw fires. *Big* fires."

"K and L," Gallagher said slowly. "Burning on the water."

Scarfe went on and on. God knew, Gallagher understood why. It was bloody to come back after leading a sortie, two aircraft short and nothing achieved. As they argued, the face of the A.O.C. subtly altered. The quick smile faded, leaving the thin-lipped mouth oddly bleak. But the amber eyes remained as alert as if they were assessing the range, accuracy and effect of every remark.

In the end, as tired and irritated and sad and disappointed as Scarfe, Gallagher got up and said, "If you *really* want my opinion . . . I don't think we attacked the dazzle-painted ship. It was too damned misty to see properly . . . but she was *small*. She hadn't half the tonnage!"

And he left the lot of them, Air Vice-Marshal and all, to stump off back to the Mess and go to bed.

That, he thought, was the end of the matter. But three days later, he was summoned to 81 Group Headquarters at Avonmead. When he arrived, he was told that the A.O.C. wanted to see him. Gallagher could guess what for. No doubt a strip was to be torn off him for surly behaviour at de-briefing.

He had a shrewd suspicion that Ingleby was a very ambitious man. 81 Group was really a Bomber Command Group, but

Ingleby horned his aircraft in on any juicy target that happened to be kicking around. A peace-time officer, this was his ladder of success. Help him up it, and nothing was too good for his excellent chaps. Balk him of it, and some poor sod found out that those pearly teeth had other uses than just smiles.

But once inside the A.O.C.'s office, there appeared to be no question of strip-tearing-off.

"Hello, Gallagher! Come in! Sit down!"

He waved Gallagher to a chair opposite his own in front of a leather-topped desk, facing a long window. On the desk was a silver-framed photograph of a middle-aged woman with a wilted smile. On the wall behind the A.O.C., flanking a full-length picture of the King in Marshal of the Royal Air Force uniform were three mottoes. The first said *Nothing succeeds like success*. The second said *The impossible we do every day. Miracles take one week longer*. The third was a quotation: *Love the men under your command, but do not let them know it*.

"Gallagher." The A.O.C. opened a small drawer on the top right-hand corner of his desk. "There's something I want you to see."

He passed over a reconnaissance photograph taken at thirty thousand feet, and a magnifying glass.

Aware all the time that he was being scrutinized with much the same thoroughness as he now studied the photograph, Gallagher wrinkled up his eyes. It was a harbour. There drawn up against a wharf, alongside two other merchantmen, was a pip-shaped object which as he stared at it, revealed certain familiarities.

"I would very much like your interpretation."

Slowly as he usually spoke when something was expected of him, Gallagher said, "It's of Bremerhaven."

"What about the ships?"

"They're very small."

"Of course they're small! But haven't you made quite a study of ship recognition?"

"I'm interested in it."

"Good . . . good! Well, see how you can apply it, eh?" He pointed out the pip. "Give me your theories on *that one*."

"You can't be sure." Gallagher examined the photograph once more. "Such a small scale."

88

Still with a smile, but in a voice edged with irritation, Ingleby said, "I just want your interpretation."

Gallagher took the plunge. "She's the dazzle-painted ship."

The A.O.C.'s smile broadened. He held out his hand for the photograph, and turned it round and round in his well-manicured fingers. "The dazzle-painted ship," he repeated. "The whole convoy got safely in . . . without a scratch."

He appeared to wait for Gallagher to make some comment. Just as Gallagher was about to murmur commiseratingly, Ingleby smiled a prompting, congratulatory smile. "Gallagher, this proves you were . . . *absolutely right!*"

"I've ordered China tea," Vince said. "They still have some in this place. That's why I come here."

They were sitting in one of those tea places off the Corn with shepherdesses in big hats painted on the creamy walls. On leave now for a fortnight, Gallagher was spending the last two days in Oxford. He had hung his hat and greatcoat on the oak stand, and was now sitting at this table for two in uniform. He made a completely different picture now to the one that had previously haunted these streets less than two years ago. The two and a half stripes of a Squadron Leader were now on his sleeve.

Nearly all the faces were new. Only a few people remembered him. Outside Blackwell's bookshop, he met Margaret, the undergraduate he had taken on the river. "Hello, Gavin," she said. "I see they've made you cut your hair!"

In the High, he saw Cox who had been at school with him. "Didn't know you'd left, Gallagher."

On Folly Bridge, he saw Rogers with whom he had gone to lectures. "You look fatter, Gallagher. The military snaffle all the best grub. You should see what they give us now in Hall!"

He looked up all his old acquaintances. "That uniform is a fearful fit. You should have gone to my tailors in the Turl," "Are you one of those characters who fly low over the Radder and *shatter* my concentration?", "They must be pretty punk shots not to have got *you* yet, Gallagher." The porter at the college lodge asked, "Is the war going to be over by Christmas, sir?" And his tutor, beaming through his spectacles, shook his hand warmly, and said, "Keeping up with your reading, I hope?

Carlyle is the man to take with you to war. Those sonorous world-shattering sentences . . ."

By the end of his first day back, he was conscious of a certain disappointment. That feeling had started the moment he arrived at Oxford Station, to be met by Vince's welcome: "So you turned into a blue butterfly after all! Who'd have thought it possible out of such a chrysalis. Isn't Nature wonderful?" It had continued as they walked past the Castle, with Gallagher lugging his bag. Arriving at college, people were to-ing and fro-ing across the quad as much as they always did, and nobody recognized him. They climbed Vince's staircase, and Peter said, "I've got my scout to rig a bed up for you on the sofa. Dump your bag anywhere. And look, dear boy, if you'll excuse me . . . now I've got to dash. I'm half way through a terribly important experiment at the lab. Why don't you brew yourself up some tea on the ring? And there's some bread in the cupboard, if you feel like any toast . . ."

The second day was no better. Vince was again busy, and Gallagher just wandered around, peeping into familiar places that now seemed faintly alien. The war appeared to have made not the slightest difference to Oxford, and he felt somewhat resentful. Of course, Schools were on, and that was the reason, he told himself, watching the crowds of boys and girls in their white shirts and black ties and mortarboards chattering excitedly over the papers on the pavement after the examinations. He recognized Billings and called out, "How was it?"

"Bloody! An absolute stinker! Look at it!"

Gallagher studied *Political Economy I. Compare the philosophies of Hobbes and Locke* was the first question. Even in such a short time, the political wisdom of these gentlemen within his mind had faded. He handed the paper back. "Not too good. I sympathize."

He walked in Merton fields, following the banks of the Cherwell and the Isis. Then since Vince had said he was determined to tear himself away for tea, he had met him in this café.

"There is nothing," Vince said straightaway, "more tiring than brain work. You may feel tired. But Christ, I'm exhausted!"

He stretched his long legs in front of him so that the dainty table wobbled and the crockery rattled. Then he took a piece of toast and nibbled it with his eyes half-closed.

"What sort of brain work are you doing?"

"Me? *Intense* brain work. *Unrewarding* brain work. The tale of the snail. Up one inch, down two."

"In precisely what field? On what?"

"*There* you have me. That, I can't say." He covered his mouth and ears, and then with a theatrical gesture, lifted the edge of the tablecloth. "Careless talk costs lives . . . isn't that what they tell you? *You* should know." He smiled. "Pompous, I know you'll say. But it's secret. *Top* secret."

Gallagher was unimpressed. "Something to do with the war then?"

"Christ, what logic! Of course! What else? That's why I'm indispensable. Reserved. What have you."

"So *you* won't be called up?" Gallagher couldn't help smiling slightly derisively. All the same he wasn't sure if his predominant feeling was of resentment or admiration.

"Certainly not! I thought I told you." Vince gave a sudden jerk of his head as he did when he was put out.

"You always said you had no intention of going."

"Did I? I don't remember. If I did, I'm more psychic than I thought."

"How did you manage it?"

"I didn't. One doesn't. It's merely that *my* ideas and the government's coincide. For *once*. *They* decided they needed me. But *not* to fire a gun *or* swallow sea water, *or* break a bomber. The military machine has fallen in love with physicists. Didn't you know?"

"I didn't, actually."

"Well, now you do! Straight from the loved one's mouth. The courtship is intense. They work us like hell. In teams. We're even working with the *other* place. Pains in the arse-hole for the most part. *They* think they're king-pins because Rutherford started it."

"Rutherford?" In the hazy recesses of Gallagher's memory, the name had some association. "Didn't he smash the atom?"

Vince gave him a brief bemused glance, as if he was already miles away down a strange and different road from him. He smiled forbearingly. "He did, yes. He did a lot of other things, *too*. But let's not talk about it. *You* should know. An officer of the Crown. A holder of the King's commission! God, who'd have thought it. I wouldn't personally have trusted you with a bicycle. Don't you ever wake up in the night and laugh out loud?"

"No."

"You must have!" He counted the stripes on Gallagher's sleeve. "Not *just* an officer either. A *senior* officer. Christ, Gallagher! How *did* you do it? Dead men's shoes?"

"More or less."

Vince drained his cup. "They've done something to you, of course. You're quieter. Now I can get the odd word in. But tell me, what really *does* go on behind the scenes?"

Gallagher gave a brief and expurgated sketch of his training. He mentioned Bunting. He explained something of Blenheims and attacking ships.

"Do they use a scientific approach?"

"It isn't quite hit or miss . . . if that's what you mean. We've navigation and bombing aids. Our trouble is getting close enough to drop them."

"You use coming out of the sun?"

"Yes." It was Gallagher's turn to smile the forbearing smile of one who has moved a long way down a different path, who has reached some state of separate knowledge.

"Mist? Cloud cover? Night?"

"The lot."

"Everything Nature supplies, in fact?"

Gallagher nodded.

Vince stroked his long bony chin. "Pity you don't have more scientists on *your* job. There should be a *simple* solution. There's another of Nature's tricks though. Camouflage. Tried that?"

"*Both* sides try it."

"The Syrphidae, now. *They* always attract me. Harmless flies dressed up like wasps. The *volucella inanis*—marvellous name— actually lays its eggs and brings up its young in a hornet's nest. Nature is always at war of course. One forgets." The problem obviously attracted him. He appeared to find this mechanical teaser an amusing antidote, like a crossword puzzle to the complications of his laboratory day. He began arranging the sugar bowl and the cream jug and teapot in a convoy on the cloth. He dive-bombed with a spoon.

To himself, he murmured, "Extreme deflection? Camouflage?

Changed direction? Simulated invisibility?" And then to Gallagher, "Remember that delightful story of Chesterton's? Nobody saw the postman because they were expecting him."

Vince's whole posture suddenly stiffened. He snatched at his own words. He seemed on the verge of an idea, holding himself still, his bright eyes wrinkled up, like someone about to sneeze.

"They're *always* expecting us. And they *always* see us," Gallagher said grimly. He felt resentful, irritated at Vince playing at war with the teashop crockery.

For a second, Vince went on staring into space.

Then he seemed to sense Gallagher's impatience. He stood up. "Well, I don't suppose you want to talk about the war. What's a war, anyway? Oxford's seen dozens."

After lunch next day, Gallagher left. The train took five hours, and it was evening by the time he arrived at the aerodrome. The Mess was deserted. He parked his bag in his room, then went along to the bar for a beer. Only Grant stood by the counter, nursing a silver tankard. He raised his free hand in a limp welcome. "What's yours?"

"Beer. A half."

"Good leave?"

"Yes."

"Do much?"

"Not a great deal. Went to the flicks twice."

"Worth going to?"

"Not bad."

"Go to any dances?"

"One. A local hop."

"Meet any popsies?"

"Danced with a couple."

"Pretty?"

"Quite." Gallagher lifted up his glass. "Bit empty tonight, isn't it?"

"Bit."

"How's things been?"

"Much the same."

"Any sinkings?"

"Mullins got one."

"How big?"

"Just a trawler."

"Any big shows?"

"B Flight took off yesterday."

"How many?"

"Seven."

"Who led them?"

"Since you weren't here . . . Aylwin."

"What was it?"

"Shipping strike."

"Where?"

"Skagerrak."

"Target?"

"The dazzle-painted ship."

"How did they get on?"

"We don't know. Nobody came back to tell us."

Two weeks after Gallagher returned from leave, on a warm July morning, the hunt for the dazzle-painted ship assumed a new and alarming urgency.

Just before dawn, a message relayed from a Norwegian fishing boat twenty miles west of Stavanger was picked up and decoded in London. It contained three vital pieces of information.

The *Elisabeth* was now loading in Bokn fjord. From there, she would proceed under escort of sixteen destroyers and two heavy cruisers to Bremerhaven.

Those two pieces of information were sufficient to put the Air Ministry on its toes. But the third piece, its significance not readily appreciable, was sufficient to reach the Prime Minister, to bring about an immediate discussion between Naval and Air Force Chiefs of Staff.

By the time the sun was clear of the Thames mist, and glinting on the silver of the barrage balloons, a clear picture had been presented in that secret conference as to *why* the Germans had so fostered and cared for their *Elisabeth*. The trips she had so far made, against which 81 Group had thrown their Blenheims, were important enough, but they were also in the nature of proving trials. Satisfied now that she was unsinkable, the Germans were making her ready to assume her real task: the transportation of machinery, plant and materials from the Norwegian heavy water establishment for proper and immediate development in the Ruhr.

This last intelligence was cloaked in secrecy. A condensation was made in a five word directive. *Sink the dazzle-painted ship* echoed through the halls of command, gathering operational detail as it went. At twelve-thirty it reached Air Vice-Marshal Ingleby, then in 81 Group Operations.

It gave him three days in which to do it.

After the address, time of origin and top-secret prefix, the signal read: *Elisabeth with full escort leaves Bokn fjord 18.00 hrs Saturday, July 4th. Arrives Bremerhaven 10.00 a.m. Sunday. Sink repeat sink Elisabeth after loading but before repeat before unloading takes place.*

By thirteen hundred hours that same day, there had been three telephone calls from Command on the scrambler to the A.O.C. of 81 Group. And by fifteen hundred hours, though many of the Stations were scattered over Lincolnshire and Norfolk, he had assembled in Operations, his Wing Commander Operations, his Signals Chief, his Bombing, Navigation and Radio leaders, and the C.O.s of all his light bomber squadrons, each with their two flight commanders—most of them now equipped with Boston aircraft, except for 720 and 722.

Pacing up and down the small dais in front of the pitifully depleted squadron readiness map, he put them, as he called it, "briefly in the picture".

Already on the table round which they all gathered was a relief map of the Skagerrak, with the models of the *Elisabeth*, her naval escort, and on long pins *above* the map the probable strength of her fighter cover. In front, a thin red ribbon across the flat blue of the map, stretched the dazzle-painted ship's route, daintily picking its way through German and British minefields from Bokn to Bremerhaven.

"I've brought you all here," Ingleby said, "because we're determined to lay on the best possible show. Command has given us our heads."

A Flight Commander from Long Sutton whispered to Gallagher, "They've done that all right! In the bloody basket!"

"So that it's up to us," Ingleby finished, "to find that ship and send her smartly to the bottom."

If the little speech was meant as a rabble-rouser, it could

hardly have fallen on more battle-hardened hearts. Unconsciously, all their eyes turned from the relief map clustered with German defences to the chewed-up aircraft readiness map on the wall behind.

Swiftly, smoothly, Ingleby went on, "Four Group and Five Group are providing high level bombers . . . but Command have little hope they will hit her. Coastal are laying mines . . . but she'll have minesweepers in front of her. A low level attack, pressed home, is what Air Ministry are really pinning their faith in. They've promised us everything they can muster. The best torpedo squadrons are in the Med or the Far East, but we'll get extra Bostons . . . a dozen if we're lucky."

The C.O. of 742 Squadron asked who was going to take care of the fighter escort. Too far away for our fighters, Ingleby replied. What about the Navy, someone else suggested. Too close to the enemy coast for a large force, Ingleby said, and the *Elisabeth* was too fast for any submarine.

By sixteen-thirty, it was hot and sticky in the Ops Room. The conference had become a free-for-all. Here and there went the models . . . the *Elisabeth*, the destroyers, the heavy cruisers, the fighter escort. Down from the wall came the depleted squadrons. They attacked from the north, from the south, from the east. They came out of the sun. They came in over the North Sea, over the Skagerrak, over land. They clustered just outside Bremerhaven. Sweating hands left moist fingermarks on the map. Ingleby gave permission for officers to remove their jackets. His brown hair clung to his temples as if he'd been swimming, and there were dark stains in the armpits of his shirt.

But his eyes didn't lose their brightness. He examined every suggestion, found the holes in it, and threw it out. Increasingly it was becoming apparent, that even at full muster his aircraft hadn't the range, the speed or the armament to take on the escort and the fighters, let alone sink the dazzle-painted ship into the bargain. Increasingly, Ingleby's quick smile became more down-pointed, sharp and shark-like.

It was just as he was about to call a quick break for tea and a smoke, for this conference was going on till they dreamed up something, that Gallagher, the new B Flight Commander of 720 Squadron, shifted in his seat, and said, "I've got one rough idea, sir. But I don't know how it'd work out."

Ingleby had an inkling even then that it might be a good one. He prided himself that he'd got where he was because he was a good judge of men. He had already promoted this man above Scarfe, his senior. Men, by and large, were very like machines. Far from being equal or alike, they were as different in their capabilities and worth as a bent Henley from a brand new Beaufighter. He'd already ear-marked Gallagher as a useful leader, forcefully propelled by some deep bellyache, which Ingleby for one didn't want to know about.

"Well, let's have it," Ingleby said. "We won't see the holes till we give it an airing."

All the same, Gallagher hesitated. He wanted to marshal his strength before he was shot down and ridiculed at the outset.

Vince's idea, tossed off undeveloped at Oxford, had borne in Gallagher's mind a curious fruit. That fruit nurtured by the loss of B Flight, hastened still further by the urgency of this conference, might well be immature and valueless.

"If it's good, you can have as many aircraft as we've got," Ingleby promised. "How many did you have in mind, Gallagher?"

Gallagher could never remember whether the hush began before he said it or afterwards. "One Blenheim, sir."

Whenever it was, Gallagher knew he had to take advantage of that silence quickly while it lasted. Ingleby, apart from an almost audible start, as if briefly afraid Gallagher had dared to be funny, said nothing. But the once smiling mouth was now thin and threatening, the amber eyes wide with a quick calculation.

Briefly, suddenly lucid, Gallagher outlined his plan. The essence of the attack was that it should take place *after* the dazzle-painted ship reached Bremerhaven.

It was the story of Vince's fly, the other way round. Not a fly like a wasp, but a wasp like a fly. The expected harmless aircraft that everyone knew they'd see. In short, the plan hinged upon the remarkable similarity in silhouette of a Blenheim to a Junkers 88.

The silence stretched on for seconds and seconds after Gallagher had outlined his idea. Then Ingleby said, "And *you* feel quite confident that you could do this successfully, Gallagher?"

"I think so, sir. Given certain information."

Thoughtfully, the A.O.C. took two steps forward, till his stocky head and shoulders cast a humpy black shadow on the relief map. He appeared to be accurately summing up the arguments for and against the sortie. But in fact his quick mind was already ahead of such considerations. The plan was excellent. It was daring, imaginative, original, suicidal. He'd already summed up the chances of success as Gallagher was talking. Given faultless planning, the chances were as good as one in five of actually sinking the ship, as high as one in three of severely damaging her. And, of course, about four hundred to one that Gallagher would get the chop.

Well worth the risk.

His silence now was while he overcame his dislike of leaving the attack so late, while he pondered how they could lay on a massed effort with all his aircraft if Gallagher totally failed, and to expunge the impression that he was snatching at Gallagher's offer.

At length he said, "Well, Gallagher, I'm going to let you give it a try. Let me know exactly what you want and we'll lay it on."

Gallagher asked for a lot. A scale model of Bremerhaven was rushed up. Fighter airfields were marked. The German colours of the day for July 5th were already known from coded information found in an aircraft shot down over Kent. Every available moment he spent in memorizing landmarks, going over tactics with his crew. The weather was carefully watched, and though it couldn't be really accurately forecast, noon in July gave a reasonable chance of bright sunshine.

At nine a.m. every day, a JU 88 took off from Bremerhaven aerodrome, and carried out a normal meteorological flight collecting weather data, temperatures and pressures on a northwesterly course into the North Sea, finishing up with a climb to 18,000 feet, afterwards returning in a slow glide to cross the sands near Bremerhaven always close on noon. Fighter Command was generally too busy to worry itself about the regular milk-runs of the enemy met aircraft, but on this July Sunday they went to the unprecedented lengths of sending six Spitfires over the North Sea at 20,000 feet. And an hour later, in the cockpit of Blenheim O Orange, Paget pushed up from the wireless table the message he had just received—the one word *successful,* which was more than the high level bombing attack had been.

"Means they got it." Gallagher screwed up the paper and dropped it beside his seat. "Traill . . . course to Bremerhaven. *And* quick! Don't want to be late!"

The Blenheim, flying in the clear at five thousand feet, headed south-east. Gallagher, with his jacket off and his shirt sleeves rolled up, sat behind the stick, and felt, now they were committed to it, a curious relief. The sun beat down on the surface of the sea, sending off thousands of sparks, appearing and disappearing like an immense guttering firework: it beat through the glasshouse of the cockpit, making the sweat rise from his reddened skin and hotting up the throttle box, so that it stung his hand to touch. Not a cloud in the sky, and the sea calm. Normally, as he got nearer to the enemy coast in weather like this, he would have been more and more tensed up. Not today. This was how he had planned it: he had wanted a bright glare. As slowly O Orange descended towards the German coastline, the round bright disk of the sun rose up more and more overhead in the heat-haze blue of the sky.

"Paget . . . leave the wireless now. Test the turret."

The Wop/Ag went aft. Gallagher felt the Blenheim skid as the gunner swung the turret, and heard the chatter of a short burst.

"Guns O.K.," Paget reported.

"Estimate the German coast . . . 11.56," the navigator said. "That's in twelve minutes time."

"I can see it already."

The coastline ahead, which had been a grey scribble dizzily shimmering in the sun, began to come up in greater detail as though the windscreen was a microscope and he was using more and more powerful lenses. He saw a long flat strand of yellow sand, laced by creamy foam.

"Got the double-red cartridge ready, Traill?"

"Already in the Very pistol, Skipper."

Opening his side window slightly, Gallagher felt the draught of cool air on his face. Then he wiped the sweat off his hands meticulously with a handkerchief, before throttling back the engines. Speed was dangerous on this trip—a lazy return from a routine job, that's what he was simulating.

Out of the corner of his left eye, he could see the big block-house that controlled the beach, built like a huge fort. Deliberately he turned, and as he did so, put down his undercarriage. At 100 knots, O Orange crawled across the enemy coast.

From behind the barbed wire on the beach, on the hummocky sand-dunes, three soldiers looked up and waved. There was no other sign of war, till a Very light lit up the sky a bright phosphorescent green.

"They're challenging us. Go on! Give 'em their colours of the day."

"Hope they haven't changed 'em!"

Two reds went up. For a moment, everyone in the aircraft held their breath. They could clearly make out the muzzles of the anti-aircraft guns in the fort. But the barrels stayed still, pointing out to sea. Directly below him, Gallagher caught sight of a small white blob: a gunner shading his eyes against the sun dead overhead, seeing only a black shadow etched against the hot blue sky—the usual met. JU 88 coming back from its North Sea patrol.

The fort slipped underneath their wings. There ahead was the city, with its vast harbour. But purposely Gallagher turned away, steering towards the double white cross of the runways on the airport.

Nothing was taking off. Nothing was even moving.

Still keeping his undercarriage down, he went into a slow descending turn as though making a circuit to land.

"Paget . . . see any fighters back there?"

"Nothing, skipper. Got the sky to ourselves."

Silently, Gallagher started counting—something he always did when he wanted the time to pass quickly. Twenty, twenty-five, twenty-six—expecting at each second to hear the bursts of flak and the stutter of guns. But the sweet murmur of the engines and the light whistling from the open side window were the only sounds that accompanied the wheeling jigsaw of fields and farms below.

Now he was east of the airfield. Down to five hundred feet, he straightened up as though on final approach to the main runway. But as O Orange descended, all the time his eyes were on the city beyond, searching for landmarks he had memorized from the model: the church there, that red brick factory building, those chimneys standing by themselves. Almost on the edge of the aerodrome, he called out, "Raising the undercarriage!" And a few moments later, pushing the nose hard down: "Hang on! Diving!"

At full power, the Blenheim streaked across the field. Gallagher saw a tram trundling along a cobbled street: the glitter of a glass roof: white concrete walls. Ahead now were warehouses. Cranes, tugs, barges, wharves, silver balloons on thin stalks came hurtling towards the windscreen, as the bomber slipped down lower.

220 knots. Gallagher flattened out over the water, and began weaving through the balloon barrage to the other side of the harbour.

Still nobody fired. Though the red and blue roundels on his wings shrieked like targets to be shot at, and his engines roared louder than any air-raid warning, not a gun in that stunned city seemed even to be aimed at him.

"Look out for her!" he shouted. "Yell when you see her!"

He was conscious of the oily surface of the water, floating debris, seaweed, orange-peel, broken boxes, a wobbling buoy He turned to avoid the masts of two trawlers. A rowing boat scudded under his wing, the man in it lying prone, not wanting to see. They must be practically across the harbour now. His attention fully occupied with avoiding cables, ships, and keeping above the water, Gallagher was just worrying that he was going to miss the thing when Traill suddenly pointed. "Left, Skipper! Left! There she is . . . Christ, *there*!"

Gallagher skidded on left rudder. Then he lifted up his eyes and saw her—dead ahead.

She was huge—far larger than he had expected. Her length lay beam on to him. Black, white, grey, green—the whole of his windscreen was a whirl of jazzing colours. Angles, lines, stripes, were kaleidoscoped all over her hull and superstructure, so that at first he could hardly make out the one funnel, and that distinctive clipper bow. Then he saw king-posts, an open hold, three strings of portholes, a crane in the very action of unloading, tier upon tier of decks, now towering above him.

"Bomb doors open!"

Stuck on the side rails, white gargoyle faces looked up at him. Out of the corner of his right eye, he glimpsed multiple pom-

pom platforms, the gun muzzles still turned skyward. He braced himself, feeling the hypnotic fascination of intense excitement, as adrenalin poured into his blood. And then suddenly, she wasn't a ship at all. She was just a blinding daub of dizzy colours, and he felt for the bomb-release button on the stick.

He pressed.

There was a bump as the Blenheim skimmed the ship. Gallagher's only reaction was one of immense lightness. The Blenheim soared. Exhilaration came as he pulled back hard on the control column. Then he went into a screaming turn to starboard to get the hell out the way he had come.

Behind him, he heard the sharp clattering of Paget's gun. But he did not look back. He did not want to look back. Now the twelve-second delay bombs had gone, all he was interested in was escaping alive. Straightening up again over the city, he was almost surprised to hear Paget shouting exultantly from his gun-turret, "Got her, Skipper! Bang on! She's going up! She's going up!" A pause, and then in an awesome voice: "She's gone!"

All the time he was over the roof tops, Paget was saying, "A big white cloud first . . . fire . . . bits and pieces next, like someone throwing things . . . then nothing, Skipper, *nothing*! She's simply disappeared!"

But Gallagher was only half listening. Shooting across a factory, he tried to hide himself among some elms in a park beyond. Now he'd been seen, and every gun was firing. Bead curtains of red tracer were being weaved around him, and the horizon ahead was patterned with the big brown blots of heavy flak.

Here was the airfield, and this time he rimmed it, keeping low, flying along a straight road to the sea. Every moment, the Blenheim was getting farther and farther away from the city.

The light flak here wasn't so bad. All he had in his mind now was the hope that he could get away. He held his breath, started counting again, began cursing the way the ground seemed to flow so slowly. A railway bridge came up, an engine puffing placidly across it. And then, stretching out from pole to pole, here at last was the beach. He streaked across the sand, passed the line of foam that was like a winner's tape, and comfortably conscious of the grey-green camouflage on the topside of the wings which would blend into the water, tucked himself right down close to the sea.

The Blenheim was still at full throttle. Every fifteen seconds that he counted was another mile. He was conscious that the coast was rapidly diminishing behind him. On his left were the low lying sandflats of Dutch islands. Another ten minutes on this westerly course and they'd be quite safe, lost in the green wastes of the North Sea.

He wiped his face with his handkerchief, allowing himself now to think back over the last few minutes. "Well . . . it worked!"

Beside him, Traill turned his head. "What was that, Skipper?"

He smiled. "Oh, nothing . . ."

Five more minutes went by. All sight of land had disappeared now, and all the time below them the calm sea went racing by. Helped on by the hot sun and the empty sky, an atmosphere of relaxation was just beginning to creep through the aircraft, when over the R/T, Paget's voice suddenly said, "Me 109 . . . eight o'clock low."

"Has he seen us?"

"Don't think so. Just a moment . . . yes, he has. *He has!* Skipper . . . turn port!"

But before he could get the Blenheim up on her wing-tip, Gallagher felt a great jolt, and heard the sound of cannon shells ripping into metal. Both engines started to shiver in their mountings, sending vibrations through the whole fuselage. Then Paget's gun started firing behind him, and his nostrils were filled with the reek of cordite. The black shadow of the fighter flashed just overhead.

"Paget . . . you all right?"

"Yes . . . all right. He's hit us, though. Starboard wing." And then in a higher voice, yelling his head off: "He's coming back! Standby to turn left!"

Never run away from danger. Always turn towards it, try to get as close as you can. In came the Me 109, and up went the Blenheim on her port wing, as though Gallagher was trying to collide. The fighter shot overhead again, this time his cannon shells going wild.

"Attacking from behind now!"

He won't be able to go on much longer, Gallagher was thinking. He'll be running out of range. Another five minutes on this westerly course . . .

"Turn, Skipper . . . left, *left!*"

All over the deserted calmness of that sunlit sea, the two aircraft performed their macabre two-some, drawing away from each other, closing with each other in a kind of love-lock, interrupted by the spattering of their guns. And still the fighter hung on, so that Gallagher knew the only way to shake him off was to kill him.

"This time, Paget . . . get him!"

But as Gallagher automatically turned towards the diving fighter, there was a shattering noise of ripping duralumin throughout the aircraft, and Paget was yelling from the turret, "The starboard engine, Skipper! Smoke . . . there's black smoke!"

Gallagher knew the engine had gone by the aircraft's quick flick to the right. By an already trained conscious control of his subconscious, he had deliberately restrained himself from adding to the turn by putting on starboard rudder. Now he held the yaw by jamming his left leg hard down. They were straight and steady—but the speed was falling off. Now they were showing blood so blatantly, Gallagher knew in the nature of things their end was close.

"Coming in, Skipper! Dead behind us!"

To finish us off, Gallagher thought, struggling now to keep flying speed, the sweat going cold on his face. But all he said was, "Makes a sitter for you! No deflection, so you'll——"

The whole aircraft reeled. He felt the controls go slack. The cockpit filled with black blinding smoke. Out of the corner of his right eye, he could see the starboard engine streaming yellow fangs of flame. And above all the noise and confusion, Paget's exultant voice, "Got him! Whole pieces off his wing! He's on fire! Skipper, he's——"

Gallagher interrupted to snap, "Paget . . . get on the W/T. Send S.O.S. . . . d'you hear me? S.O.S.!"

"Right, Skipper!"

The speed dropped back to less than a hundred knots. Sluggishly wallowing from side to side just above the water, the Blenheim was close to stalling. Gallagher called out, "Can't keep her up much longer! Paget . . . screw down the key, so they can get a fix . . . and then the two of you, get ready, we're ditching . . . I'll——"

The sea interrupted him. Water came pouring over the glass-house. His head banged against the dashboard. Slewing right round, the cockpit began to concertina under the immense pressure, and he felt a sudden stabbing pain all the way up his stiffened left leg. He struggled up, loosening his straps, opening the escape flap, his eyes stinging from salt water and his mouth full of sea.

He felt himself falling. Darkness covered him. He began flailing around with his arms. In his throat was a choking sensation, and his lungs seemed to be just about to burst. Yet through it all, he could feel the pounding of his heart, and throughout the time, he fought back the unconsciousness that was the beginnings of death.

He would *not* close his eyes. Panting and struggling, he fought his way up. Gradually the darkness lightened, then became bright sunshine. He broke the surface of the sea, and painfully treading water, for the blood was pounding in his head and his leg was aching, for five minutes he did nothing but gulp in the air.

Then he looked around for the others.

Not a sign. All that remained of the Blenheim or of his crew was the dinghy, released and inflated by the immersion switch from its stowage. It sat riding gently on the waves, big and fat and yellow. He struggled towards it, managed to heave himself aboard. Then he called out, "Paget . . . Traill . . .", and began looking round for the bobbing circles of their heads.

"Paget . . . Traill!"

There was not even an echo back from that circular sea horizon that showed no trace of land. Sitting in the dinghy, his eyes traversed the water, studying each little wrinkle and ripple. A few patches of oil, that was all—and he was just about to lie back and rest, for now his leg was throbbing like mad and his eyes were sore from the sea, when suddenly he saw a black blob a hundred yards away, bobbing up and down in the water—and excited now, he grasped hold of the canvas paddle and began feverishly rowing towards it.

At least one of them would be safe.

And then as gradually he drew nearer, he was not so sure. That black head seemed to loll so much, seemed half under the water anyway. He quickened his strokes, urging the dinghy forward. And arriving at last, he put out both his arms, and from behind grasped the body round the waist.

The head in the black helmet turned, fell a little to one side on the shoulder. Gallagher saw an unfamiliar, rather white face. Through half closed lids, light blue eyes were looking at him.

A spiel of German came out in a weak rather husky voice. Then the one word he could understand. "Danke."

So Paget had done it, after all. The Me 109 must have crashed close beside them—both aircraft coming down in that last attack.

With difficulty, lurching from side to side, he managed to haul the German inside the dinghy. The man was wearing a life-jacket, but it had been punctured by bullet-holes and the rubberized fabric was stained with blood. Gallagher made him as comfortable as he could, propping him up against the round dinghy sides, but it was obvious he was in a bad way. He must have suffered a bad concussion, for he seemed dazed, his eyes stayed large and unblinking, and there was a huge blue bruise on his forehead. Gallagher unstrapped his own water-bottle, and tried to get him to drink. But beyond wetting the man's lips, the water did little else, though he appeared to be making an effort to drink, for his throat contracted convulsively.

Gallagher loosened his life jacket and tunic, pulled the black helmet off his head, exposing a mass of very fair hair, and a bleeding gash on the left-hand side of his scalp, which he did his best to staunch with strips of handkerchief and shirt.

"Danke," the man said again.

The hours of the afternoon went by. Neither of them spoke any more. Both hugged their pain privately to themselves. The only sound was the small waves lapping along the bottom of the dinghy, the same sort of sound that river water makes against a punt. The German seemed to be only half conscious. He was unable to keep still, wriggling around perhaps from pain, but saying nothing. Twice he fell out of the dinghy, and with difficulty Gallagher hauled him back again to safety.

Each time the German murmured, "Danke."

The pain in Gallagher's leg had increased. His head throbbed as though an iron bar was beating on his skull. He tried to stave it off, to keep it out of his mind by calculating his chances of being picked up. Not very great, though he tried to pretend they were. If Paget had managed to screw down his key, it couldn't have transmitted for long, and they were very low—not much hope of the wave being picked up in England which must be over a hundred miles away. So that round about eight in the evening, he was surprised and delighted to see an aircraft flying low over the water to the north—until it got nearer, and he recognized the big floats and two engines of a Blohm and Voss seaplane, the black crosses on the wings.

He bent his head down, and pushed the German's head forward, too—for faces above all else showed up to search planes. And this one was obviously searching, for it began flying definite legs, going up and down and then round, not very far away from them.

Off it went, almost out of sight to the west, and then came easterly, bearing down on them.

It was then that Gallagher saw it. At first he couldn't believe his eyes. It was an accident, a coincidence. It must be so. Wounded as he was, only half conscious, sitting beside one of his country's enemies, no man would dare do that.

His eyes watched the German pilot, the man's face not a foot away from him, his left arm touching Gallagher's right arm. The head was still bowed, but the man was looking up through the corners of his eyes. His right hand was hidden in the divide of his tunic.

Suddenly, there was a bright glint—no more than a momentary flash, that was all. Then seconds later, another flash. Then another shortly afterwards—always in the direction the Blohm and Voss was flying.

The man had a mirror in his right hand. He was using it as a heliograph, catching the rays of the setting sun to signal their position to the German floatplane.

Gallagher was just about to reach out his hand to snatch it away, when the man had another spasm. His face became contorted with pain, and his legs started convulsively kicking. His head lolled forward. Then with a sudden jerk, he fell out of the dinghy again.

Still acting automatically, Gallagher put out his hand. It had got within a few inches of the German's fingers, now making scrabbling slippery noises against the rubber sides of the dinghy.

And then it went no farther. It lay there, inert, on the rim of the dinghy. Withered and whitened by the water, palm upper-

most, the nails a little blue from the cold, it stayed quite still
while inches below, the German's head bobbed up and down,
his yellow hair strung out like seaweed over the surface of the
sea.

The minutes passed. The seaplane got farther away, flying off
now towards the south. In a blaze of pink, the sun began to set.
The scrabbling noise on the side of the dinghy got weaker and
stopped.

Gallagher never moved. As darkness came, it was as though
time, too, had frozen. Gone from his mind now were the fears,
the griefs, the exhilarations. Gone were his struggles, his
strengths, his weaknesses. Gone was Vince and his plans, Ingleby
and his ambitions. Gone was the dazzle-painted ship. All that
remained was . . . *this*.

2

"Is he alive?"

Through layer after layer of suffocating veils, Gallagher heard
the words as four syllables of sound. It was enough that a human
being had spoken them. The language, the meaning, what this
man would do to him, whether he was friend or enemy—all that
was immaterial. It did not matter because now he was no longer
alone. No longer was the circle of the horizon, the vast empty
saucer of sea his kingdom and prison combined. He was aware
of hands lifting him up from the dinghy, now half awash, where
he had been lying wet through for an eternity, curled up with
his head on his knees, his arms clasped round his legs. Blinking
his eyes, as though through a mist he saw the sharp bows of the
Air-Sea-Rescue launch rising and falling above him. And then
he had been lifted aboard, and they were giving him rum, and
with all the salt water inside him, he was being violently sick,
and that was the last thing he remembered before finally being
drowned in unconsciousness.

How long he was out of this world he did not know. It was
afternoon when he woke, that he could tell from the slanting
beams of sun patterning the highly polished brown linoleum
floor. Through the chinks in the screens round his bed, he could

see a trolley with a tin teapot on it and a plate piled high with bread-and-butter. Though he could see no one, all round him he could hear the murmur of voices. Down at the bottom of his bed, there was a big hump under the bed-clothes, a kind of little hangar over his legs. Cautiously, he moved the toes on his right foot. They worked all right: he could feel them scraping against the bedclothes. Then he tried the same thing with his left foot, and immediately winced with pain.

He must have made some noise, for round the corner of the screen peeped a pretty pink face with a starched cap floating on black wavy hair. "Oh . . . hello!"

"Hello."

"How d'you feel?"

"Bloody!"

"Oooh!" The voice was more like a nervous giggle. "Can I give you a cup of tea?"

"You can give me something to put me out."

"I'm only a V.A.D. I can't do that."

"Then go and get some flicking quack who can."

"Oh, I don't think——"

"Go on! Don't stand there blinking!" He was almost beside himself with pain. "*Do* something for me!"

Off she went then, eventually returning with a big young doctor fiddling with a syringe in the palm of his right hand, whose cheerful greeting Gallagher cut short with a curt, "Get on with it!"

Two minutes later he had got what he asked for.

It was his first indication that in this place he had apparently only to intimate a desire for something—and it was his. Because they kept the screens round him, because he seemed the focus of the doctors' attention, because he frequently heard the nurses warn the unseen others in the ward to keep quiet, he began to think that he might be dying. Sometimes the pain was so bad, spreading from his leg upwards till his whole body was throbbing with it, that he bit his lips so hard with his teeth that blood poured out into his mouth. When the pain was that bad, his immense will to live, his hatred of death as Nature's ultimate victory became so weakened that he started thinking lovingly of complete oblivion, as a man frozen in the snow thinks of a warm fire. He continually demanded drugs. Ingleby and the dazzle-painted ship he no longer thought of, though in an affectionate haze he remembered Traill and Paget. But the real ache came when he was most off guard, the sudden memory of the German's fair hair floating on the surface of the sea. Sometimes in the middle of the night, again he thought he heard the scratching of those fingers against the rubber dinghy, and this time he would sit up and reach out both his hands, only to sink back on his pillows when he found out it was someone slip-slopping in bedroom slippers to the bathroom. It was at those times rather than when the pain was bad that he asked for morphia.

There came a time, however, when it was refused. While he was still going on about it, they took away the screens, and he became aware of eight pairs of eyes from eight beds focused upon him as though on a statue that has just been unveiled.

He stopped binding and looked across at the boy in the next bed. Brown, neatly brushed hair, sitting up with pillows behind his head, self-consciously looking over the red cover of a novel at him. Catching his eye, Gallagher winked.

"Feeling better, sir?"

"For Chrissake don't call me sir!"

"Sorry."

"For Chrissake don't say sorry! Everyone in this damned hospital is always saying sorry! How did you get into the bloody dump, anyway?"

"Night flying. First solo."

He became aware that the boy was no longer looking at him. He said quickly, "I was never keen on night flying either."

A sister, coming through the swing doors, saw him and beamed. "Oh, you've had your screens taken away, Mr. Gallagher! Matron will be pleased." She fussed round him, tucking in the bedclothes. "Now you're quite comfortable?"

From just above the sheet Gallagher's eyes glowered at her.

"What's happened to your tongue? Lost it?"

Gallagher put it out as far as it would go.

"No, it's still there," she said placidly and reassuringly. "My, what a long one! Bit furry. Remind nurse to give you a dose of liquid paraffin tonight." She straightened, still smiling at him. "Now I must get Dr. Somers to come and have a look at you!"

For the rest of the afternoon, there was a succession of doctors and specialists coming in and standing round his bed, examining and grinning at him. The parts of his anatomy that appeared most to interest them were his left leg, completely encased in plaster, and his head. Little grunts of approval, mutual congratulatory nods, remarks like "Well . . . you're a lucky character, aren't you?" began to make Gallagher again suspicious of his condition. He tackled the last doctor about it. "Don't worry!" the man said. "You'll survive."

"What about flying?"

"Don't worry about that either." The doctor grinned encouragement at him. "We'll get you back flying."

Back in society again, he found that the officers in the ward treated him with such deference, at first he was uncomfortable and then he began to feel isolated. Even when at last they allowed his parents to come and visit him, they were so self-consciously remote from him that it didn't seem possible that he *could* be their son. He felt sorry for them: their awkward shyness in this bustling hospital, his father's "Mustn't tire you. Quite sure you're in good hands. Very proud . . . your mother and I," their quiet disappearance, shepherded by a sister as though from an audience, served only to depress him. Matron came always to his bed first. He was the first customer of the little old paperman in the mornings. And he was the last victim to be wakened by the nurses for the five-thirty wash. That all this must have something to do with the attack on the dazzle-painted ship he was aware, though it was never mentioned, until a week after he was allowed to get up. Then he was told he was going to Group —"something to do with your successful attack"—and up came the Air Vice-Marshal's Humber for him.

When he arrived at Avonmead, Ingleby was in the hall to meet him. "How's the leg? Manage all right? Here, lean on me!"

In the same office where the attack had first been prepared now they discussed the results. "All hush hush, of course, Gallagher . . . but I want you of all people to know . . . couldn't have been more of a triumph! Ship, cargo, secret machinery, a consignment of some stuff they call 'heavy water' . . . all down at the bottom! Air Ministry are cock-a-hoop, of course. We've even had a telegram from the Navy."

"What about 720 Squadron, sir?"

"Doing splendidly! Two sinkings last week." And then, with

a kind of heavy-handed casualness: "Oh, by the way . . . you've got the D.S.O. Confirmed yesterday. Congratulations." He patted Gallagher on the back and went on, "And now, are you up to having a word with Intelligence?"

"Don't mind, sir. Though doubt if I can add much."

All he could give them that they did not know, was the battle with the Me 109. He elaborated the shooting down of the fighter, emphasizing Paget's skill, but he said nothing whatever about the German pilot. That brief struggle for survival in the round yellow dinghy was his own private memory.

After the interrogation, he was taken round Group. Holding on to his stick for dear life, his plaster foot with its spike thudding on the linoleum, he felt like some exhibition prize turkey as he limped from room to room. The A.O.C. called it a triumphal journey round the sections—"Does them good, you know, when they're stuck here, to see someone who's actually *done* something"—but to Gallagher, now painfully self-conscious about the whole thing, it was a clown's performance he ached to escape from.

Wherever they went—Operations, Navigation, Armaments, Signals, Maintenance—there were smiles and congratulations. Everyone wanted to write on his leg, and obligingly he propped it up—at least it gave his aching lip muscles a rest from making inane remarks—while the S.A.S.O., the Controller, the Cypher Queen, the W.A.A.F. plotters signed their names on the plaster. After an hour of going in and out of Sections, the pain started to get worse in his leg, and Gallagher was just praying that this long corridor they were nearing the end of would be the last one, when Ingleby suddenly said, "Well now . . . don't suppose you want to miss the Radio side, eh?"

"Been there already, haven't we?"

"The D/F side I mean, Gavin. They did a fine job of work on you."

"On me?" He frowned. "You mean they actually picked up Paget's signal?"

"Certainly they did!"

Gallagher rubbed the back of his head thoughtfully. "But we were so damned low . . . I didn't think there was a hope. Not a chance in hell."

The A.O.C. smiled, at once imperturbable and triumphant.

"The signal *was* faint. *Very* faint. But they got a bearing. Surprised, eh?" Pleasure rounded the already bland contours of his face. "We're not *quite* so dim at Group as people like to make out, eh?"

Humping along on his foot, Gallagher said nothing. He had not realized until then that there had been anything but chance in the way he had been picked up. When he had allowed himself to think about those hours, lying back on his pillows in the hospital, he'd assumed that the Air Sea Rescue launch had been on one of its regular patrols. He knew they undertook them along the paths of missing aircraft. And he'd presumed that he'd been lucky. That other people had been involved had not somehow struck him . . . nor that Paget's last act, his fragmentary moment of communication with an unknown Group radio operator, had started the whole thing off.

Bang, *thud*, bang *thud* . . . like Captain Ahab's leg went Gallagher's plaster cast on the linoleum. "They must have got their fingers out smartly."

"Certainly! A pretty good show. You were miles off track. Without our bearing, nobody would have known where to *start* looking."

"I realize that now." In a diffident, almost reluctant voice, Gallagher added. "I've got a lot to thank you for."

"Well——" The A.O.C. spread out his plump left hand to indicate they would turn port. "Let's put it *this* way. I wouldn't be having the pleasure of *your* company . . . if *our* operator hadn't worked fast."

Having turned, they began to descend a flight of stone steps that seemed to lead to the bowels of the earth. Grey concrete lined the walls here, and it would have had the appearance of a megalithic cave except that every few yards there was a bright neon light, shining on line after line of wires and circuits. Above them, Gallagher knew, would be the tall radio masts and Adcock system aerials. As a background to the clanging echo of their footsteps was the continuous hum of electric motors.

"Well, here we are!" Ingleby pushed forward a heavy metal door, the other side of which was green felt. "What's happened to Robinson?"

The Chief Signals' Officer kept them waiting less than two seconds before appearing. In spite of the weird underground surroundings, the procedure, the smiles, the congratulations, were exactly as before. There was a queue to sign his plaster until there was hardly any room for another name. While all the time he balanced his leg obligingly on a chair, morse keys chattered, the teleprinters tapped.

"But these are the people Gallagher *really* wants to see." The A.O.C. pushed open a door marked MF/DF SECTION. DISTRESS FREQUENCY WATCH. NO ADMITTANCE. He stood back for Gallagher to lead the way, dotting and carrying on his gammy leg over the linoleum.

There was less light here than in the other rooms. Thick felt covered the ceiling and all four walls. Instead of whole rows of operators with earphones clamped over their heads and the background of morse and clicking keys, here there was only silence, and one girl seated at a radio with her blue-uniformed back to them.

He saw her hand first. It was small and square, with short nails and rough school-girlish skin. It stretched over the tiny table, tuning the frequency dial to and fro, with absorbed and somehow incongruous delicacy. She listened with her head on one side, while the green eye of a tuning indicator winked and blinked. Her hair was in a thick brown roll, carefully arranged so that it didn't touch the collar of her shirt. He could see the long pins with which it was secured, and a small wisp that had freed itself behind her left ear.

But it wasn't her hair, or the glimpsed profile, or the set of her head that fascinated him. It was her hand. Ordinarily it wouldn't have affected him. But there was something about this room that made him feel odd . . . something in its felted padded-cell-like quality, added to what the A.O.C. had just told him, added to fatigue and general weakness, that made a queer unbalanced hysteria seem to bubble in his brain. He became suddenly convinced that he was caught in some pocket of time. In a little while that schoolgirlish hand would move, tune with its exact precision, till it caught up again that message from Paget. But this time, beneath its guidance events would subtly alter.

Into the sudden shuffling silence, the Signals Officer said, "This is L.A.C.W. Corrie." And the girl turned round, saw the distinguished company, took off her earphones, and stood beside her seat.

Gallagher reminded himself that this feeling of déja vue, according to Vince, was nothing more than a shortage of blood to the left lobe of the brain . . . most emotional states had, after all, physical explanations . . . then he looked down with relief at a face of refreshingly ordinary prettiness.

The kind you see a dozen of on any R.A.F. Station . . . the kind of face that blended well with the slate blue of the uniform . . . with a nice enough figure to match, which quite against the R.A.F.'s intention, was highlighted by the snugly waisted battle-dress blouse, the tightly bottomed trousers.

The hands, which a second ago had seemed so poised and meaningful, were dangling at her sides, and she had a nervous habit of scratching her forefinger nail against the quick of each thumb. A small gesture that he found somehow disproportionately touching and endearing.

"L.A.C.W. Corrie was on duty that particular afternoon," prompted the Signals Officer.

And as if he'd noticed Gallagher's apparent lack of concentration, Ingleby butted in with, "She got the bearing, Gallagher." And to the girl, roughly as if she didn't exist as a person. "Good show! Keep that standard up!"

"Oh." Gallagher stepped forward and held out his hand. "Thank you, Miss Corrie. Thank you . . . I'm terribly grateful . . . I've a lot to thank you for . . . I don't know quite . . ." The trite ordinary words, muffled by a mixture of emotions, shrivelled by their patent inadequacy, seemed now unnecessary. He smiled down at her with a curious spontaneous pleasure.

He was wrong about the ordinary prettiness. Her oval face, with its wide smooth brow, short nose, and lipsticked mouth was ordinary enough. Until she looked up. Then her eyes, pointed at the corners the shape of alder leaves, opened wide. Large and green, their lightness in striking contrast to their thick brown lashes, they had the curious changing colour and quality of a winter sea.

The texture of her hand was rough, as he'd seen it would be, her clasp firm and friendly. She smiled, and the faint laughter lines round her mouth deepened. Her eyes lost their distant sombre quality. She looked immensely young, gay, guiltless. He suddenly wanted to sit down, not because his leg ached or he felt tired. But because he'd liked to have stayed with her, talked to her, somehow rested in her. Then just as suddenly, he didn't want to stay. He didn't want anything to do with her at all.

Here came someone else who had helped him. And superstitiously, he was afraid.

He wanted her to speak now, so that that red mouth would spill out a whole mass of simpering platitudes. And he waited for her voice to destroy the illusion.

But it didn't. It was gentle, hesitant, low-pitched, warm. It mumbled platitudes, certainly. Just as he had done. "It was nothing . . . just one of those things that sometimes happens . . . it was very exciting really . . . and . . ." While all the time, the expression of her face seemed to expect his understanding, to make those words only sounds necessary to keep the others happy. Just as a few seconds ago, his words to her had been.

"You must have worked fast."

"The note was very clear."

"But short."

"About five seconds," the Chief Signals Officer broke in. "And not strong. It isn't often we can get a bearing on a signal like that."

"Glad you made an exception *this* time," Gallagher said, and the girl and he both laughed, grateful that this stilted exchange would soon be over. "Lucky for me *you* were on. Thank you."

"I'm glad it worked out."

"For me . . . yes."

"I'm sorry about your crew," she said quietly. Any previous shyness was gone, as if her sympathy gave gravity and poise to her.

And then schoolgirlishly slangy, her small comforting tribute. "Your wireless operator was spot on frequency."

"Paget was always pretty good."

And then, as if all just honours and dues had now been done, the Chief Signals Officer steered the course of conversation away from personalities. He launched into a long description of Direction Finding. Dim fragments of Sergeant Dann's radio lectures from Cirencester days echoed in Gallagher's mind . . . the similarity in an aircraft loop between the two minimum signals . . . how fatally easy to read a bearing in the opposite direction . . . to arrive at the reciprocal or opposite of true.

Conversation by-passed the girl. Gallagher made no effort to include her. "Good thing I'm not on this job," he said. "I'm always getting things the wrong way round." He squeaked his caliper a step over the linoleum in the direction of the door. He wanted to be out of here now. The room was having a claustrophobic effect on him. For no reason that he could think of, he was annoyed with the girl.

The A.O.C. looked at his watch, picked up the headphones and handed them to the W.A.A.F. Operator. "Here," he said. "We can't disturb you any longer. You've your work to do. Thank you."

Leading the entourage, he moved towards the door. Half way across the room Gallagher stopped and turned round. "It's usual," he said, "if a bod gets you out of the drink . . . to throw a party. What d'you think? Would you like that?"

And smiling, still holding the earphones in one hand, she said without hesitation, "Yes."

The MF/DF Station turned out to be the last port of call.

Back again in the A.O.C.'s office, Ingleby dismissed the hangers-on, and ordering two cups of tea, pushed up the most comfortable chair close to his desk, and helped Gallagher settle into it.

"Tired, eh"

"Not specially."

The A.O.C. produced a packet of cigarettes, and when Gallagher took one, a box of matches to light it. "Well, now, you've seen for yourself this afternoon . . . the effect on us all of that fine job of work you did on the ship. Puts a new press on spirit into everyone. Thanks," he tapped Gallagher's shoulder, as he passed the ashtray, "to *you*."

Gallagher felt desperately uncomfortable. "What about the W.A.A.F. wireless op? I've got to thank *her*."

"A good girl, yes. Certainly. She did her job. Did it excellently. But then *they* do. They're a splendid bunch really. But even *you* can't say she sank the ship, eh?" He smiled merrily, almost michievously. "Nice gesture on your part . . . suggesting a party. Very nice. It'll give her something to tell her Waaf other-rank friends."

It was obvious that to Ingleby, the gesture had been sufficient. Now he waved his hand as though dismissing the whole thing.

"More tea, Gavin? No? Well then, let me take your cup."
He put it with his on the tray which he pushed to the far corner
of the desk. Then he leaned forward confidentially towards
Gallagher. "Before you go back to hospital, Gavin, there's something I want to have a natter about."

Gallagher regarded the end of his cigarette and said nothing.
All his instincts told him to concentrate hard on whatever
Ingleby was going to lead up to. But his mind refused to be
canalized. It had gone mushy on him. It was surfeited with com-
pliments and conventionalities, stale as the underground air
which had made his head ache. Right now, his brain seemed able
to cope with only two alternating pictures and these obsessed
him to the exclusion of all else. The first picture was the white
blank envelope of the hospital bed. The vision of it made his
eyes prick with fatigue. The other picture was the MF/DF room.
Its shrouded quiet, the winking green eye, and the small hand
poised over the tuning dials.

"I had intended to wait. To hold my horses before letting you
in on it. But today, I said to myself, what the hell? My mind's
made up." Ingleby slapped the palms of his hands down on the
desk. He waited while Gallagher expressed polite interest by
nodding his head and raising his brows. Then Ingleby leaned
back in his chair, crossed one leg over the other, and stared up
at the ceiling, smiling. As he spoke, he tapped the forefinger of
one hand lightly against the forefinger of the other. "Now! The
point is . . . *this*. We can't use your body. Right now that is.
Oh, we'll work the guts out of you when we can . . . don't worry!
But I'm *damned* if I'll let you rot your brain out in some stupid
admin job."

Gallagher wasn't listening, though his ears registered every
word. An *admin job,* almost as a reflex he pulled down the
corners of his mouth, and the A.O.C. laughed approvingly. "I
knew you'd feel like *that,* old boy!"

The leg was beginning to throb, great aching beats that
seemed to surge and die away with the pulse of his heart. Gallagher could imagine the bed, slipping down in between those sheets
. . . he could feel the coolness of them, the pillow against his
face . . . he'd ask for morphia again tonight . . . already he felt
the sharp prick as sister gave him a shot to soothe him away . . .
his mind and body swamped in dark waves, not of pain this

time, but of ever-softening, ever-deepening sleep. The white rectangular envelope of the bed seemed synonymous with Nirvana—a clean-smelling, pure white death. In his mind the other picture, fainter now . . . the winking green eye, the listening hand seemed its true opposite.

Gallagher shrugged and frowned to clear his brain, as the A.O.C. went bouncing on. "No, *ask* is the wrong word. *I* didn't *ask*. I *insisted*. I said what the hell . . . don't post me in some stooge from Command for my new Wing Commander Operations——"

He paused to let the last three words sink into Gallagher's mind. Then: "I've the man for the job right here. One of my own chaps. Absolutely first class." Again he paused. "What d'you say, Gavin?"

"Me, sir?"

"Why not?" He sat up straight again and regarded Gallagher directly. "Oh," he shrugged. "I know what you chaps are like. You want to get airborne again. Back to an operational squadron. Who can blame you? You look down on the staff jobs. The chairborne brigade. *I* know. You forget *someone* has to do them."

He was sweating a little with the heat of the room and the effort of convincing Gallagher. His fine silky red skin, all cleanliness and health, glistened moistly around the grey-brown hair line. It pleased Gallagher to discover that very slightly, but nonetheless distinctly, he could smell him. It took his mind momentarily off his leg and his general feeling of bloody-mindedness.

The A.O.C. spread his arms wide, magnanimously. "You all like to have a big belly laugh at Group's expense. *I* know. Never mind. What the hell? I've done it myself. The point is we *need* you *here*. Your *experience*. It's experience that counts. Having *done* the job. Oh, I know exactly what you're going to say . . ." When Gallagher made no effort to say anything at all ". . . you'll be *stuck* here. But that's *just not true*. Absolutely not! I give you my word."

Neatly-cropped head held sideways, amber eyes bright and alert as a foraging squirrel's, he regarded Gallagher from the shelter of his desk. Very slightly he changed his tactics. He smiled deprecatingly, and in a quieter, more man-to-man voice added. "Besides, cutting out all the nonsense . . . there comes a time when, hell, a character has to swallow down his own feelings and do what job's best for the war effort." He cleared his throat at the end, as if *that* had cost him some embarrassment. "Sermon over, Gavin," he smiled engagingly. "What d'you say eh? Will you take it on?"

But the A.O.C.'s rhetoric was wasted on Gallagher. He had already made up his mind. Not without some queer uncanny feeling that he was wrong, he stubbed out his cigarette, and as the girl had done just half an hour ago said the one word, "Yes."

Quite what attracted him to the L.A.C.W. wireless operator, Gallagher did not attempt to analyse. Instead, he lay back in his bed, comparatively comfortable, for his leg was paining him less these days, and tried to think up ways and means of seeing her again.

Away from her, away from the stuffy atmosphere of Group, he was able to push right down to the bottom of his mind all superstitious maunderings, and healthily and single-mindedly concentrate on the pursuit in hand. Being, when he tried, of a methodical and thorough disposition, he had worked out that she would be working the three-watch system, and if she was on during Tuesday afternoon when he went up to Group, she might well have next Thursday and Saturday evenings free.

"Hey, Gavin!" A piece of bread and butter thudded on to his blue bedjacket shoulder. Bainbridge's voice from across the ward said, "Wake up! Nurse McNulty's waiting to take your temperature!"

"Sure, and I wonder now what happened on your grand visit to Group . . . you've been so far away ever since! Come on now, open up, and keep that tongue still. Give me your wrist . . . your *wrist* . . . it's not *my* hand you want to hold!"

"Sure and it is," Gallagher mimicked her gently, as soon as she whipped the thermometer out of his mouth. "That's what keeps our temperatures up."

"Well, it's normal." She popped the thermometer into the meat paste jar filled with formaldehyde on the locker top, and then pulled back the bedclothes. "Come on! You can stop your dirty dreaming! Get up and help me make the bed!"

"Tut-tut, Kathleen *McNulty* . . . an' me with the same sweet Irish blood in my veins as yoursel'!"

"Tut tut not'ing, Mr. Gallagher . . . for the only t'ing Irish about you is your Blarney!"

Sighing, Gallagher began rooting round for his slippers. "And all the time me thinking it was time we had a party!"

The enthusiasm from everybody was immediate. During the last few days, the atmosphere around Gallagher had become considerably less reverent. Now it was he who led the talking, the laughing, the general boisterous behaviour that made Matron baptise Ward IV *the Beargarden*. Anywhere else in the hospital, a private party would have been unthinkable. But because the ward was a hut beyond the boilerhouse, well on the other side of the hospital, and communicated with it only by a long narrow corridor, there was every chance of a party being successful. The nurses had got used to the somewhat unorthodox ways of the Air Force and were only too willing to co-operate. The black-out was useful, Matron was no danger. The only problem was Night Sister who made her rounds at 8.30 and midnight. All that was needed was careful organization.

F/Lt. Pollard who was convalescent and allowed out, was put in charge of the bar. After a collection had been made, he would return from the local at night with a bottle in each of his great-coat pockets. Denise, the youngest of the V.A.D.s, was providing the gramophone and records. Isobel, whose father kept a grocery, had promised soft drinks and biscuits. An escape route had been devised. A roster for guards had been drawn up. Emergency drill was practised every night after lights out. Most important of all, the date was fixed for the following Saturday. And on an ordinary invitation card, Gallagher wrote to the girl, requesting the pleasure of the company of L.A.C.W. Corrie 20.45 to 23.45. At Home, Ward IV. On the back he wrote, "There isn't a bus back late enough. Have arranged for you to be put up in the Nurses' Home. Get an S.O.P."

And equally simply, she wrote back that she had done so.

That Saturday, there was a bustle of suppressed excitement. Had Gallagher wanted to give himself an explanation of his own odd moods, that Saturday would have supplied it. Emotion, pleasure, anticipation were all heightened in a curious beam of childish excitement. The world had shrunk to the dormitory-like ward. The day's programme unfolded with the precision and timing of a bombing raid. They sought carefully to please and to allay suspicions. So much so that Day Sister asked suspiciously, "What are you lot up to, eh?" and though from neat beds or orderly wheelchairs they chorused, "Nothing, Sister," she gave them a remarkably old-fashioned look. No one in the ward now was seriously ill, though there were still two in bed. The others for a change when evening came, helped the orderly to tidy the ward instead of the usual, "Christ, do we have to?" The liquor was hidden in Gallagher's bed, alongside his gammy leg under the cage.

Everything was so peaceful when Night Sister came on her round, she remarked on the pleasant change—to come into Ward IV and be able to hear herself speak.

"And *you*, S/Ldr. Gallagher . . . are you feeling all right?"

"Fine, Sister."

Aware perhaps of a forced smile, and a rigidity of pose, she said sympathetically, "Is your leg troubling you? Shall I take a look at it?"

"Never felt better. Honestly! Bang on!"

"Then why so quiet?"

"It's *you*, Sister. It's your beautiful face. I just can't help staring at it."

"You must try that line, Mr. Gallagher," Night Sister said, nevertheless beaming, "on someone younger . . . and *greener* than me."

Gallagher watched her make a brisk smiling round of the ward, her starched apron rustling, till she stood satisfactorily by the door. The time was twenty thirty-seven.

"Now keep this up! Don't give night nurse any trouble! No talking, mind now!"

"No, Sister."

She switched off the main lights, one by one. The blue-lit gloaming smelled of clean linen, ether-meth and floor polish. Sister was a black sentinel-straight silhouette against the lighted corridor behind her. "Good night everyone! Sleep well!"

"Good night, Sister! We will!"

They listened to the sound of her feet down the corridor, the slamming of the door at the far end that led to the hospital proper. Three minutes later, they heard the same door open. When Isobel, the night nurse on duty, reported that all was clear, cautiously they got out of bed and put on their dressing-gowns. Lockhart who was first on guard roster, took up his position just outside the ward kitchen, with a view down the length of the corridor.

Ten minutes later, the party began. One by one, the nurses and V.A.D.s arrived. Standing by the stove like a bunch of dressing-gowned wallflowers, the men heard the sounds of their heels click-clacking cautiously down the corridor, breathy whispers, shshs and giggles. When the ward door opened, they let in a delicious hotch-potch of scents, all frozen and preserved in the little auras of cool night air that clung to their clothes. L.A.C.W. Corrie was not among the first ten minutes' arrivals, and it somewhat marred Gallagher's enjoyment, as he helped the girls off with their coats, and like the rest of them feasted his hospital-starved eyes, on cocktail dresses, bare shoulders and nylon-stockinged legs.

"Where do you girls get the coupons?" he said, piling the coats on Evans' bed, and they all giggled and said "Ah-ha!"

He took them over to the stove, and Bainbridge handed round tooth-mugs half filled with gin, and plates of biscuits with daubs of some weird mauve-coloured savoury on them. Everyone knew everyone else, but the slight constraint of being in party dresses, and whispering in the semi-darkness added gaiety and piquancy. Glancing back at them, listening to the chatter and the laughter, watching their shadows, crumpled and elongated on the ward ceiling, Gallagher thought the whole scene had overtones of a dormitory beanfeast.

He walked to the door, and then took a step or two down the corridor—partly because he wanted to be the first to welcome her, partly because suddenly he wasn't at all sure that he would recognize her. He had told them all briefly who she was: attached, he had said to Group D/F, the people who had picked up his wireless operator's signal and got a bearing. They hadn't pressed him. He had a tendency to be irritated when pressed, as though he didn't want to think about anything in the past, especially this last flight. And that attitude was common enough for them to understand. He hadn't told them that it was she alone who had picked up the signal, because in his own mind he didn't like to think about it himself. Somehow, it made her too like Tordoff. In his weak moments, he seemed to have dreamed up this idea that if anyone helped him, he'd get them the chop in return. At night, earlier on, he used to shout out in his sleep, and the nurse, thinking he was in pain, would rustle over and straighten his bedclothes, wipe his brow, offer him a cool drink —but it was some nightmare he had woken out of, not the pain at all. And now that he was fit and strong again, this queer superstitious feeling couldn't be quite exorcized. It would pop up only occasionally, but it seemed to pick the moments of special anxiety or excitement—or as now, when he seemed to stand at some heightened threshold of happiness.

There was a slight clicking sound. He watched the blackout over the outside corridor door being drawn aside. Deirdre, the Staff Nurse, had brought her over. With a tact he wouldn't have credited her with, Deirdre walked past him with a smile and into the Ward on her own.

Miss Corrie stood for a moment staring at him almost in surprise. And at first he thought that it was because when she had seen him before, he was in uniform and he must look awfully different now. Then he realized that he was looking at her in much the same way himself—in that curious surprise, not of *absence* of recognition but of astonishment at some deeper, unlooked for quality. And at the back of his mind the old superstition again stirred uneasily. To placate it, he destroyed the moment by laughing out loud, and saying in his heartiest voice, "You didn't recognize me in my party clothes!" He took her arm. "I didn't recognize *you*, either!"

He stepped back a pace, letting his eyes travel over her. She was wearing her dark hair loosely, and it hung in waves to just short of her shoulder. Her dress was of some stiff red stuff, with a silky sheen that caught the light. It had a full skirt and a tight waist with thin straps that left her shoulders bare. "You look marvellous! Wizard!"

She frowned slightly at his heartiness, and then falling into step with his mood, smiled. "Thank you. So do you."

"Oh, this old thing." He fingered the lapel of his pyjama jacket. "Just some little thing my dressmaker ran up. Had it for ages." And pulling down the corners of his mouth. "Too many damned ages." He began guiding her down the corridor.

"I can hear the party all right," she said. "I hope no one else can."

"Amen to that!"

124

Deliberately he was dragging his foot, walking slowly.

"Is it hurting you?"

"Not in the slightest. I just don't want to hand you over to the mob straightaway. Besides, we haven't been introduced ourselves properly yet. I don't even know your name. Mine's Gavin."

"I knew that," she said. "And mine's Edwina."

He had just made the decision that he would enjoy a pleasant little flirtation with her, a healthily extravert pick-you-up-or-set-you-down affair with no strings either side. But the sight of her face, her half shy, half friendly manner made it slightly more difficult.

Again heartily he said, "I once knew a girl called Edwina . . . pretty girl . . . no flies on *her* . . . a Wren she was . . ." although he had hardly ever heard the name before.

"I expect you knew lots," she said.

He put his arm round her as they reached the ward door, and hearing it open, Deirdre came over. "Now then! Edwina . . . what's *he* been up to? I warn you about this character! If he gives any trouble . . . just let me know . . . and I'll put him to bed!"

"Nurses!" Gallagher sighed. "*Jolly* girls! Perfumed with ether-meth. Can't you smell it?"

"That's Chanel Number Five," Edwina smiled. "You've forgotten the difference." And after a pause. "They've made me very comfortable."

"That's because they're scared of me."

"They told me that," she said demurely.

From over by the stove someone shouted. "Gallagher . . . for Chrissake! Bring the girl over here . . . at least give her a drink . . . don't start snogging in the corridor straightaway!"

"These ropey types," he said, and led her across to the group by the stove and introduced her.

The others made room in the little ring of chairs round the fire. There were fifteen of them altogether—the nine inhabitants of the ward—Lockhart had temporarily deserted from guard—three nurses, two V.A.D.s and Edwina. Pollard poured some gin and some hospital orange juice into a tooth-mug and handed it to her.

"To your bonny blue eyes!"

Someone put on the gramophone. It was a record of some

early thirties vintage, with a booming rhythm of tropical drums. It made a soothing background to their conversation. Edwina whom he had expected to be shy and somewhat gauche talked well. She had been to the hospital once before to see some W.A.A.F. or other who was having her tonsils out. She knew two friends of Deirdre's. She'd been on a couple of Stations before her posting to 81 Group, and she'd run into several of Pollard's squadron. She had, too, a few amusing stories about the Waafery. And she had a breathless, slightly blushing, very charming way of telling them. Gallagher felt contented just sitting there beside her, now and again making some remark when he was pushed into it. The only time he raised his voice was when, putting his arm around Edwina's shoulders, ostensibly to support himself, he found one of Lockhart's plastered arms had beaten him to it, and he gave it a sharp shove.

"Take that gangrenous ruin away, Lockhart! Put it round Bainbridge, if you must."

"Coward, Gallagher . . . hitting a cripple!"

"Bastard, Lockhart . . . depriving a lame man of his only support!"

After a couple more tooth-mug rounds, the party got louder and more hilarious. Pollard started singing Air Force songs . . . strains of *Bless 'em all* drowned the muffled gramophone . . . with the rhythm stamped out on the ward floor by as many good feet as there were. *The end of my old cigar* was heralding in a more lurid vintage which Gallagher promptly stopped. Balked of that, Lockhart and Pollard started everyone on a furious game of sardines round the beds and the lockers. Denise tripped and fell. The men insisted on giving her drastic first aid, and tucking her up in Pollard's bed with a thermometer in her mouth. Every now and again, the guard on duty hissed, "Make more bloody row, can't you?"

Denise giggling said, "It's rather like having a party in the middle of a prison."

"Hmm. All right for you. You girls can escape."

"No, we can't," Deirdre put in. "We've got you. For better or worse. Mainly worse."

"Now you know you like it!"

"Like it! Like washing and bed making and changing dressings and being sworn at for it?"

"Who swears at you, Deirdre? I'll fix the bastard!"

"You do, Gallagher."

"Now isn't that just like a woman ..."

Over on the other side of the stove, there were spluttering sounds and then Kathleen McNulty's Irish brogue shouting, "And you're to stop it this minute I keep tellin' you ... damn you, this minute!"

"Now you know ladies and gentlemen ... *who* swears at *who!*"

At ten o'clock it was considered safe enough to start the dancing. The beds were pushed sideways along to the wall, and the main lights switched on. Everyone blinked in the unaccustomed light, their eyes seeming large as owls. The first record was a quickstep. Due to the shortage of girls, Lockhart got Edwina first, then Treece, then Bainbridge, then Evans. Next was a waltz, and Gallagher left the stove to give Pollard the push, just as he was bowing in front of her and opening his arms. "Not on your life! This is mine!"

Regardless of Pollard's remarks of "Watch that spike ... you'll crucify the girl!" and "Make way for Long John Silver!" he led her on to the floor.

They had only got twice round the Ward, when Treece cut in with mock regret, "Sorry, old chap ... your turn on guard!"

Swearing, Gallagher looked at his watch. Five past eleven.

"I'll come with you for a while if you like," Edwina said shyly, and smiling apologetically to Treece, "If you don't mind."

As they walked to the spy-post just through the open inner ward door, Pollard caught sight of them and wolf-whistled. He began saying something till Deirdre pulled him on to the floor, and then the dancing, the noise, the laughter went on and everyone seemed to have forgotten about them.

Coming out of the forced determined gaiety of the party, into their own isolation, he didn't know what to say to her. Their knowledge of one another seemed like the ragged incoming of a spring tide, so that in some ways he seemed to know her like himself. And yet he was unaware of the most ordinary things about her ... where she was born ... how old she was ... if she had parents, sisters, brothers, boy friends ...

It was unlikely that anyone would disturb them for the next fifteen minutes. He could ask her anything he wanted. Yet when he spoke, he found himself struggling to express that queer mood of his when first he saw her at Group. "It was odd," he said without any preamble, "but when I went into your Section . . . when I stood behind you, I felt . . . I don't know . . . an odd *sort* of sensation . . . as if I was looking down . . . from a distance on something that had all happened before. Silly, it was the heat or something . . ." his voice trailed.

She didn't for the moment say anything. She stood beside him, leaning against the cold green tiles of the corridor wall, her eyes half closed. "I must have felt the heat then, too."

He let that moment hang between them, like some fragile bubble. Then he said in a matter of fact voice. "D'you know anything about me?"

"Not very much." She laughed. "I know your name, your rank, your age."

"I know *your* name and rank only," he said.

"I'm twenty."

"Any brothers or sisters?"

"Two brothers. Not at home. They're both in the Navy. Charles is on corvettes . . . convoy work . . . and——"

"Yes, well," he cut her short. "It's not *actually* Charles that I'm interested in. D'you go home very often?"

"On seven-day leaves. It's not worth it, otherwise . . . we live in a small place . . . Rathlin, a market town . . . it's in Berwick-shire . . . about ten miles outside Berwick itself . . . Daddy's the local G.P. . . . he has an enormously wide practice . . . miles sometimes between patients . . . and in the winter . . ."

He levered himself away from the wall, stood upright, and turned her round so that she was facing him. With both his hands on her shoulders he pulled her close to him. Looking down into her wide, curiously-shaped eyes, he said "And it's not actually Daddy that I'm interested in *either*."

She was half smiling, her lips parted a little.

She knew he was going to kiss her, and she didn't draw away from him. She tilted her head back a little, and so poised, the meagre light made beautiful austere planes of her high cheek-bones. It also cast their blurred bent shadows on the wall beside him.

Over and above her head, through the glass door he could see the festivities in the ward. He seemed suddenly transfixed by the scene. He watched the men in blue hospital dressing gowns over vivid pyjamas, their heads bandaged, plaster on their arms and legs. Treece from the Desert Air Force who'd had a leg amputated, hopping up and down like a hopscotcher. Lockhart, his two arms in plaster, held his partner with a robot's white stumps. Pollard, with the left side of his face burned away after his Spitfire had been shot down, dancing with Denise. Laughing and joking, the couples rotated round the floor, the click of high heels blending with the shuffle of bedroom slippers, while all the time a wheedling little clockwork driven gramophone wheezed out *Jeepers Creepers* through a couple of pairs of Gallagher's socks stuffed into its old fashioned horn loudspeaker.

Uneasiness, like some wild animal dormant this last hour or so, stirred in its sleep. He looked down at her face. Now the blue light made it white and ghostlike. Now the narrow shape of the walls served not only to bend but to distort their shadows. His leg, his whole body for that matter, became enormous and elephantine. It loomed over her small shadow, and by one small involuntary movement of his obliterated it.

"Then what *are* you interested in?" she asked softly, her voice with its attempted lightness coming through, as if to drag him out of himself, at once pitiful and pleading.

A minute ago he would have said simply, "*You*. I'm interested in *you*." But now it became imperative, for *her* good, more than his own, to escape from her. Roughly, he pulled her against him, so that she gave a sudden breathy "Oh." He saw the pupils of her eyes widen, her brows draw together in a slight frown. Then he covered her mouth with his, kissing her hard and as cruelly as he could. She tried to take a step back, but he held on tightly to her shoulders. When he let her go, he looked down at her, smiling unpleasantly. "What am I interested in? I'll tell you! Those forty-eight hour passes. Sometime, you might spend one with me."

He saw her lips tremble slightly, her chin go up. He put his hand up to his head. He felt immeasurably tired, infinitely sad. He was about to say he was sorry, to tell her there and then about this wretched feeling of guilt and fear and superstition.

But at that moment Deirdre called "Pack up now . . . it's time!" The gramophone was cut short half way through a bar of *Begin the Beguine*. "Come on, nurses . . . *scarper*! And everyone else . . . *bed*!" She walked up and down, pumping at the antiseptic spray which was part of the plan to keep any smells of perfume, alcohol or other festivities from Night Sister's observant nose.

Pollard was handing Edwina her handbag. The men clustered around her saying good night. Over their heads she called to him, "Good night, Gavin! Thanks for the lovely party," in a voice that was quiet, even, and without sarcasm.

Then she was walking down the corridor with the V.A.D.s, her shoes clipping firmly, her head held high. The outer door opened, the blackout shuffled back, the door clicked behind them. And there was nothing but the empty blue-lit corridor, and the smell of the damp night air outside, and the dead quietness in the Ward as everyone waited for Night Sister to arrive on her round.

3

In the car from the Station, Gallagher decided there was a hell of a difference between coming to a place like Group for a visit, and coming to it—knowing you had to stay.

Arriving by train and car, you got a different perspective. You got a view of the less salubrious parts of this ancient, slightly shabby, slightly smug looking market-town . . . the cottages, the rows of quite fine Georgian houses, the shopping square, the High Street. Apart from these, the town boasted a shallow river, flanked on one side by a grain warehouse, a tolerable stone bridge, a couple of churches with spires, an A.A. hotel called the *Blue Boar*, several pubs, one large store, a Woolworth's and a tiny cinema called the Roxy.

Whenever he'd come to Avonmead before, it was always the Operations block he had visited. He had never been to the Officers' Mess, which was a requisitioned big house called Avonmead Grange, standing at the other end of the parkland on which all the Group buildings were built. This time, he went between stone pillars flanked by boars' heads, and up the drive.

Now, moving in as it were, Gallagher sat forward, pinpointing his new landscape. The leaves had begun to turn. Bright reds and browns were creeping over the green leaves. Somewhat sardonically, he saw that the lawns had been freshly mown, and he made a mental note to find out whose job it was to waste their time on that. Far away on the right, he could just make out the massive square structure of Operations, and the tangle of radio masts above it. Then to the left, in the valley of the parkland, beyond its razored ornamental undulations was the straggle of Nissens that was the Waafery. Down there was the only reason so far that made him glad he was coming to Group. *I'm sorry,* he had written to Edwina the day after the party, *I behaved like a bastard.* And later on in the letter, deliberately casual, something he had not yet told her . . . *I'm coming up to Group, so I'll see you then.*

The car swept him out of range, turned in front of a massive Queen Anne mansion, and stopped in front of a flight of shallow stone steps.

A batman in a white mess jacket came out and took his bag. He might have been arriving at a four-star hotel or a country club, except that at the top of the steps, he was smartly saluted by an S.P., who emerged from a glass-screened office that did duty as a guard room, the evening sunlight glittering on his buttons and blancoed belt. Bags of bullshit, Gallagher thought, watching the S.P. examine his Identity Card.

"You've seen one before, I take it," Gallagher said sharply, feeling a sod when he saw the laddie go red above his immaculate collar. Not the poor devil's fault that he didn't like this country house atmosphere of playing at soldiers. He stood for a moment staring around him.

The hall was vast and dark. From polished floor to corniced ceiling, it was panelled in oak. There were two large fireplaces surmounted by antlers. And at the far end were long glass doors through which Gallagher could see a portion of the stone balustraded terrace.

To the left an archway had been carved out when the house was requisitioned, and this led to additional rooms, newly built of breeze-blocks.

But despite these odd additions, through the house there seemed to linger an atmosphere of privileged living . . . flowers in brass bowls caught Gallagher's eye . . . high polish on antique furniture . . . muted voices floating in from the terrace. A portrait of Lord Trenchard did no discredit to a row of Lords of the Manor of Avonmead, and even the Squadron crests on their oak plaques joined the shields of the family's ancestors and marriage partners as to the manor born. The R.A.F. had apparently taken over the traditions as well as the house from its previous owners.

This wing of the mansion, the batman told Gallagher as he conducted him up the carved oak staircase, was mostly given over to officers' sleeping accommodation. Part of the east wing was used for Waaf officer accommodation, the gymnasium was the church and Padre's office. Being few in number, the Sergeants' Mess was in the servants' quarters, while such added amenities as squash and tennis courts remained for what they had been intended.

Gallagher's bedroom overlooked the west side of the parkland. It was half a large room, divided into two by plaster-board, so that he had half a corniced ceiling and half one long window through which to admire the lawns. The usual R.A.F. mess furniture, the white cotton-covered bed, the blue and red patterned rug, the brown dressing-table and wardrobe mated oddly with the large green hand-basin, the silk papered walls, the white marble fireplace.

"I'll come and adjust the black-out for you later, sir," the batman said, as Gallagher stood staring out, as if enjoying the last of the evening sunlight. In fact, he was enjoying nothing at all. Curiously enough, he was suddenly experiencing a bad attack of something like home-sickness . . . a real ache at the back of his throat, a sense of being in alien surroundings. Though naturally it wasn't for his home he longed. It was for a real operational station. As different from this set-up as the smell of high octane fuel from lavender water.

He wanted the sight of flat lands, fen-lands preferably, with a slight mist coming up in the distance, and the impressive watchful waiting of an airfield . . . nostalgic and austerely beautiful. He wanted barbed wire, not clipped hedges, rough grass between the runways with the sea-gulls and the damned peewits rising up off it. He wanted gaunt corrugated hangars, the harsh whine of metal on metal, and the roaring pulsing sound as an aircraft took off. He wanted the sight of an operational field riding the green of the countryside like a battleship the sea.

Disgusted with himself for taking on the job, but getting some sort of satisfaction from thinking that anyway he'd leave his steely caliper mark on the razored lawns or know the reason why, Gallagher washed and tidied, and descended the ancestral staircase.

On the extreme right of the hall, he found an ante-room carpeted in the usual R.A.F. pattern with the usual R.A.F. issue arm-chairs, and a few antiques that went with the place thrown in for good measure. Like the hall, this room was oak panelled and dark, and standing disconsolately in the doorway, at first Gallagher thought that it was empty.

Then in the far corner by the window, he noticed a Squadron Leader reading a paper, with one leg over another showing a great expanse of bare leg, and an Argyle sock straggling suspenderless over the ankle. It was such an untidy human touch in this stultifying place that Gallagher felt immediately cheered. He had the impression that here was a similar soul to himself, and picking up *Punch* from the table just in case he was wrong, he thumped his way over and sitting down in one of the chairs, said, "God, is it always as gay as this?"

The other man looked up. He had a square, pleasant face, fresh complexioned, with level sandy brows and a long upper lip. His light brown hair stood up in a stiff cockscomb from his forehead, but the line of it was receding slightly. He was older than Gallagher, probably about thirty, but at least he had pilot's wings up. He removed the pipe from his mouth, and without any expression on his face and in a dead-pan voice he said, "Tonight's rather more hectic than usual."

"How?" Gallagher smiled.

"Normally, it's empty. I'm only here because we don't have the *Mirror* at home. My wife prefers the *Telegraph*. But of course, I have to keep up with Jane."

"Of course. What *has* happened to her today?"

"She's just getting into another bath."

"God . . . but that girl's clean!" Gallagher peered over the other man's shoulder to look at the strip cartoon. "Nice to know that whatever else happens to the rest of the world . . . the same old thing happens to Jane. That's the attraction, I suppose."

"Well, *part* of the attraction." The other man smiled, and

then put out his hand. "My name's Ash. Ken Ash. Stooge Controller."

"I'm Gavin Gallagher."

"I know you by reputation." Ash looked him over in a placid unhurried manner. "Heard you were coming as Ops One."

"Yes. Not that I know what the hell I'm supposed to do."

"Everything. The lot. The pivot of Group, old chap. Hinge pin."

"Christ." Gallagher said, suddenly conscious of being only twenty-three years old. "And how long have you been here?"

"Too long." Ash puffed at his pipe and then added equably, "No, that's not really true. I've been let's see . . . seven, nearly eight months. Now I'm waiting to do another tour."

"Where did you do your first?"

"Dishforth. Ever get there?"

"No. I was never so far north."

"Wise chap! But I liked it. We had fun."

"How d'you find Group?"

"So-so. The job's a bit of a bind. But the place itself is pleasant. We like it very much. Rosalie and I . . . Rosalie's my wife." The Squadron Leader's face softened. "I live out and that makes a hell of a difference. Rosalie managed to get us a flat . . . the lease, too, by God. We were lucky."

"You must know this set-up pretty well by now, then."

"Like the back of my hand." Ash smiled. "Anything you want to know . . . just ask Uncle Ash!"

Cheered by having found some decent type among the inevitable deadbeats of Group, soothed by Ash's relaxed friendliness, and his obvious contentment, it crossed Gallagher's mind to make some enquiry about Edwina. Though she was in a different Section, there was a good deal of communication between the Operations Room and Signals. Ash might well know her, if he asked . . .

But the mantle of 81 Group must have already lightly touched his shoulders. He dismissed that inquiry as hardly the thing, and said, "Yes, there is something you can tell me. And right now. The bar! For God's sake, where is it?"

At 8.55 next morning, Gallagher turned up on the steps with the S.A.S.O., the rest of the Air Staff, the Intelligence and Met

Officers. Five minutes later, staff cars arrived and on to the Operations Room went the whole caravan. "Good morning, everyone," Ingleby said. "And what's our target for tonight?"

"Duisberg, sir."

It was a routine that was to be repeated every duty day he was with 81 Group, only varied by the target . . . Cologne, Essen, Bremen, Hamburg . . . or a stand-off for rest or weather.

Bomber Command—the whole of Britain for that matter—was at a very low ebb. The sinkings of ships by U-boats had reached a new high. The Far Eastern Fleet had been shattered, Singapore and the most of S.E. Asia had been lost. Japan stood at the gates of India. So little damage was being inflicted on Germany by British bombers that there had been Cabinet discussions about disbanding Bomber Command. Experienced captains continually reported bull's-eyes with bombs later shown to have dropped eighty *miles* from the target. Many in the Air Ministry simply refused to believe what the photographs showed. R.A.F. squadrons had been left largely to their own devices as to route, height flown, method of dealing with the defences, and way of finding the target. Often it was left to the decisions of the crews how to go about the job—and their results were as highly individualistic as their methods. To counteract this, the Pathfinders had just been formed, specialized crews equipped with the latest aids available, who would find and mark the target for the Main Force. Fortunately for 81 Group, due to Ingleby's successful forages into the provinces of Fighter and Coastal Commands, they came off better than the others, and were among the first to be re-equipped with four-engined aircraft. No light or medium bombers were now contained in the Group. 720 Squadron and three others had Lancasters, and there were two squadrons of Hertfords.

The Order of Battle of these 140 aircraft was on a big blackboard, immediately opposite the door, and the sight of it would bring the first frown of the day to Ingleby's forehead.

"Only 99 serviceable! Command are calling for 110." He would turn to the Group Engineering Officer. "And we're giving them 110!"

He would then look at the vast map of Europe on the left-hand wall, giving the main targets, the searchlight and flak belts marked with different coloured pins, the night-fighter patrols in red wool. Then he would look at the state of the moon chart, and he would then have a chat over the weather map with the meteorological officers. Afterwards he would talk to the Armament Officer about the bomb load, the percentage of incendiaries to H.E., and the need for bigger and better bombs.

The morning's conference would then start. This would commence with details of the previous night's results. Photographs would be shown, which Ingleby would study either with pleasure or disappointment. The number of aircraft sent, the number lost or damaged in action or in accident were then considered, and rockets or bouquets were distributed round the table accordingly. New tactics and security measures were discussed: and afterwards, general Group policy, new ideas that Ingleby could send up to the C. in C.

Tea and the plan of attack, the first via a W.A.A.F. and the second via teleprinter from Bomber Command, would arrive together.

Sipping slowly, Ingleby would criticize the Pathfinders' route through the defences, and the type of illuminations they intended to use on the target. He would have much preferred to have had his own Pathfinders, and would often remark on the indignity of being "made to follow like a string of sheep". Last minute suggestions and theories were aired, and then Ingleby and the S.A.S.O. would retire into conclave together, while the other Air Staff, under the co-ordination of Gallagher, would go into action. The Group Navigation Officer would liaise with the Squadron Navigation Officers on take-off times, speed, and times of arrival on target. Gallagher would get on to the squadron commanders, hear their excuses for aircraft or crew unserviceability, listen to their requests for spares or replacements and any other moan they had. They would talk to him much more easily and frankly, expecting him as a recent operational pilot to understand their difficulties, and Gallagher was, in fact, the hinge-pin between them and the A.O.C.

After lunch, he would be dealing with Group future requirements, chasing spares, trying to get more equipment. And as the afternoon wore on, there would be a continued watch on the weather, serviceability and squadron troubles as they bombed up and prepared—till by the evening, things quietened down.

From the first day, Gallagher found there were far too many

officers milling round. Hoping for big expansion, Ingleby had allowed a large staff to build up, many of them clueless hangers on, and they simply fell over one another in their efforts to prove their indispensability. Gallagher proceeded to hack away this deadwood ruthlessly, and he laid down a set of duties he expected the Air Staff to do. Chief among these was to attend in turn the briefing, waiting and de-briefing on every Station. He himself took his share. And on that first night, naturally he went back to 720 Squadron at Wragton.

In the half-light, propped up on his stick, he watched these new huge bombers thunder off. Then there were the hours of restless waiting, smoking endless cigarettes, before counting them back.

That night, all 720 Squadron returned. There were other times when things did not work out quite so happily.

For the first few days, while he was settling down, his life was hectic. And then bad weather intervened. In the lull, he resumed his search for Edwina. His second day at Group, he had snatched a minute to walk into the MF/DF section, expecting to see her there. But in her place was an airwoman with red hair and freckles who stood up, embarrassed, and asked, "Can I help you, sir?"

He tried again two days later, but though Edwina was on duty all right, so was a rather over zealous Radio Officer who insisted on accompanying him, and talking intelligently. In the end, Gallagher decided that the best and most dignified thing was to write to her, and suggest that they meet in the lounge of the *Blue Boar* two evenings later. He didn't get any reply to his letter, and he was undecided all day as to whether she would be there or not.

The *Blue Boar* was at the R.A.F. end of the town. Once down the long drive, it was only half a mile along the Basingworth to Avonmead road. It was a fine late summer evening, and all around him as he went slowly down the drive was the scent of the fresh-cut grass, the red and white and pink roses from the still abundant rose garden. It was impossible here to envisage any war anywhere. The evening sky was empty of aircraft. The road, as he passed through the open gates, served only for a few shabby lorries, the local bus, a handcart and the odd tractor.

And the *Blue Boar* itself had managed to keep at bay any signs of shortage or bombing. The plaster between the Elizabethan oak lathes was freshly painted. There were geraniums in a splash of red all along the small garden beneath the dining-room and lounge-bar windows. Already the car park contained a few cars whose owners could still manage to fiddle the petrol. And from the kitchens (for which it was famous) came the savoury smell of dinner being prepared.

As his caliper kicked up the gravel, Gallagher felt a surge of sudden almost hilarious excitement. He couldn't wait now to see her on her own, to explain away that fiasco at the end of the Ward party, to apologize properly, to come near to her again. He climbed the two steps to the main door, and paused, staring at his own reflection in the glass panels. He was afraid now that she wouldn't be there. He began to tell himself that he actually had a *feeling* that she wasn't. That from here he could be sure that the lounge was empty.

This lounge at the *Blue Boar* was really part of the hall. Only a few antique oak uprights, joined together by a carved moulding, separated it from the entrance. It was furnished with old oak and polished brass, and deep armchairs covered in blocked Jacobean-pattern linen.

Edwina was sitting on the arm of one of the armchairs, facing the door, one leg crossed over the other, swinging her free foot backwards and forwards. "Hello," she smiled, as he came in somewhat sheepishly, "I thought you were having second thoughts!"

"I thought *you'd* already had them. At least, *I* thought you'd decided against it in the first place. In fact, I thought you weren't going to *be* here."

He hung his cap on the stand just behind her, pulled at his tie, and said, "Well, now we're *both* here without second thoughts . . . what are you going to have?" He jingled the money in his trouser pockets, smiling down at her.

As if she had suddenly remembered something which his arrival had made her momentarily forget, she stood up. "Gavin," she said, going slightly red. "I'm terribly sorry but we can't stay . . . at least *I* can't."

"Why ever not?"

She laughed. "*You* should know. It's out of bounds. For me

138

that is. The *Blue Boar* is Officers Only. Out of bounds to other ranks."

She stood there smiling, half scornfully, half apologetically, while Gallagher said, "How bloody stupid! What the hell is all that in aid of? Christ, what damned nonsense!"

"Groups are usually different from operational Stations," she said tolerantly. "There's more bull."

"But hell . . . the only decent place to go for miles!"

"They'd hardly pick the worst," she said drily.

"Well, we're not going without a drink . . . I promise you!"

But she had picked up her purse, and was tucking it in the pocket of her uniform skirt. "It's no use. They're not supposed to serve. Come on! It'll only cause a scene."

He allowed her to persuade him out into the evening quiet of the pub garden. All the same, he had the curious feeling that, having succeeded, she was disappointed.

"Where now?" he said, "*You're* the expert. Where *can* we go?"

"There's a pub about a mile up the road. *Away* from Avonmead. It's not bad really. Quite fun. Lots of the farmers and locals drop in there."

"O.K.," he said. "Let's go."

"Can you walk as far as that? Is it all right with your leg?"

"Do it good. It's not that. I wanted to take you to a decent place. Give you a good time."

"This *is* a good time," she said. "Besides, some other time maybe . . . we can go to one of those splendid places for Officers Only." She laughed up at him, gently teasing.

"And I wanted a good place to tell you how sorry I am about last time," he said softly.

But with a shrug, she waved his apology away. "Of course," she said smiling. "You'd get a much better dinner if you stayed in the Mess."

"But think of the company I'd eat it in!" He took her hand and they walked along in step. Suddenly he didn't care where they went or what they did. He was content to walk along beside her, feeling the last rays of the sun warm on his face.

"As a matter of fact," he said, "I'd rather do this than anything."

She pointed out a farmhouse where some of the girls bought

eggs to send home, a flight of peewits rising up from a ploughed field. She told him how the A.O.C. insisted that they came down this road once a month for a route march, and that once the W.A.A.F. Queen Bee had ordered them out for a paper-chase across the fields.

"That was when we first found this pub. It was a wet cold day, and they gave us tea in the kitchen."

Gradually all trace of the town fell away behind them. They climbed a slight rise and at the top of it, the setting sun seemed to hold their two figures in a golden spotlight. The rounded hills cut off all signs of any other habitation. They seemed to be quite alone, walking along hand in hand.

Quite suddenly it reminded Gallagher of a photograph he'd seen in his mother's album. It was of herself, sitting on a hillside, taken no doubt in their courting days by his father. She had her hands clasped round her knees, with the sun full on her face. And underneath, sentimentally she had written in her big rounded handwriting . . . *if only this could last for ever!*

But all the evenings were not fine summer evenings. Inexorably, the fading year telescoped the few hours of light, when they could walk alone round the country lanes. As the weeks went by Gallagher and Edwina spent more and more time in the saloon bar of the little pub she had first taken him to. Although he didn't tell her so, he began to dread the moments when he would push open the brown painted door of the *Marquis of Salisbury,* and hear the landlord's welcoming, "Good evening, sir . . . good evening, miss! I've kept your seats warm for you!"

For however much he reasoned himself out of it, already it was beginning to appear slightly incongruous for him, the Wing Commander Ops, the new broom by day that was sweeping Group clean, to be by evening the tame attentive boy friend paying court to a twenty-year-old W.A.A.F. It was nonsense when he reasoned it out, of course. And he would have denied the feeling wholeheartedly, had she accused him of it.

But it was there, all the same. Gallagher had begun to discover that a certain sort of behaviour was expected in 81 Group, differing in accordance with the rank, not the man. Opinions, views, actions—these were almost as firmly laid down as if they had been written in Air Ministry Orders. Operational pilots, of course, were expected to be wild: and even at Avonmead some latitude was allowed to "junior" officers (regardless of middle-age), but none was admitted for "senior" officers (regardless of youth). Ingleby led the way with his daily performance of the efficient A.O.C.: the S.A.S.O. behaved like his perfect right-hand man. Everybody kept everybody else up to the mark, and certainly for Ops One to be taking out W.A.A.F. other ranks was stepping out of character.

Besides, although it was well out of the town, several junior officers and airmen had begun to frequent the *Marquis of Salisbury* and Gallagher's presence cast an obvious blight upon their pleasures. Not only that—they gossiped. He was not unaware of the occasional nudges and smiles exchanged in groups up at the bar, as Edwina and he sat in their favourite corner by the fire.

But perhaps, although she said nothing about it, Edwina knew what he felt. Twice when he arranged to meet her, she reminded him that there was a good flick on in the town, and suggested that instead of sitting in the *Marquis of Salisbury*, they spend the evening at the cinema. But when they got there, they had to queue up with a host of others from Group, before they could get into the dark anonymity of the circle and hold hands.

Shortly afterwards, Edwina had made some excuse for not seeing him. But that had been worse than any embarrassment he might feel. And in his bumbling inadequate way, he had told her that anything was better than not seeing her at all.

Not that he wasn't happy. Perhaps he had some sadistic streak deep down in him, for he actually enjoyed his pruning and tidy-up of Group. He had a scheme now, a picture in his head of the ideal of maximum efficiency, and he followed it through with single-minded undeviating purposefulness.

When he pushed himself, he had intense powers of concentra-tion, which now he applied to his work. His Air Staff were young and keen. Though seasonal bad weather made operations fewer, they were carried out far more efficiently. There was a better spirit of mutual trust between the Stations and Group than there had been, and a better understanding of each others' difficulties. Gallagher's insistence on constant liaison visits was beginning to pay off. Ingleby was pleased.

He knew that the rest of the officers, especially those who

suffered from him, said that he slaved like someone possessed. But it wasn't the possession of a demon. It was as if the knowledge of Edwina's presence . . . the thought that he could lift a phone, walk along a corridor, send for her if necessary, and hear her voice . . . gave him some power of complete refreshment.

Of course he could, if he chose, have solved the problem of seeing Edwina without being too much seen, by meeting her late and going for a walk after dark. For all around any R.A.F. station, a new form of night sounds could be heard: the squeaking and scuffling of airmen and airwomen in the seclusion of the woods. But he was quite honestly afraid of what might happen if they did. Not that it was a question of might. Of what *would* most certainly happen. For increasingly, he was aware when he kissed her good night, of her body warm and soft under the blue serge and the damnable buckle and brass buttons. He reminded himself, in his weaker moments, that an affair such as this must sooner or later move to its natural conclusion.

And while at times he felt, so what? . . . why not? . . . the sooner the better! . . . the old superstitious dread wouldn't allow him to for long. For he'd worked out in his mind the way he was liable to hurt her. It would begin by his sleeping with her. He knew just how it would happen, and God knew he'd known it happen to other people often enough. He'd give her a baby and before he'd time to do anything about it, he'd get the chop. The thought of that haunted him a good deal more than the gossip.

So that when quite unexpectedly the solution was offered him, he literally grasped it with both hands. It began quite simply with Gallagher taking up Ken Ash's often repeated invitation to come and take pot-luck. At the time he took it, he was feeling particularly brassed off. 791 Squadron had lost four aircraft for the second night running, and though he'd had to harden his heart to losses, he still got an uncomfortable twist in his guts when they were lost on a particular strategy which he had suggested at the combined monthly Bomber Command Conference. Normally he would have met Edwina, and if not directly talked about it, at least eased some of it off indirectly on to her.

But this Tuesday night was W.A.A.F. domestic evening, when they had to stay in and wash their undies and mend their socks and listen to a hygiene lecture or a travel talk. To console himself, he went earlier than usual into the bar, and there—as if waiting for him—was Ash.

In the course of his work, he'd seen Ash fairly frequently, boxed up in his glass Controller's cage in Operations. In the evening, they would often swop the odd beer.

"Drink?" Gallagher asked.

"Got one, thanks."

Gallagher ordered a pint and stared moodily down at the evening paper on the bar counter.

"Doing anything tonight?" Ash said.

"I thought I'd take in a couple of cabarets," Gallagher said, still scowling. "Why?"

"It's just that Rosalie's wangled a chicken. And it seems a waste to eat it all on our own."

Gallagher hesitated for a moment or two while he allowed Ash to twist his arm. "Come on, Gallagher . . . it's boiled fish in the Mess tonight . . . Rosalie's dying to meet you."

Gallagher was not altogether in the mood for meeting anyone new. But neither was he in the mood for his own company. He'd have preferred to stay and natter with Ash for a while. Next to Edwina, he was the easiest person he could relax with. The sort of character you could talk or not talk to, as the spirit moved you. Once or twice, Edwina's name had cropped up, and taking the pipe from his mouth, smiling, Ken Ash said, "*You* should get married. I can recommend it."

But meeting Ken's wife might be a sing-for-your-supper proposition. It was obvious that Ash was devoted to her. They'd been married just over a year, and Gallagher imagined that the gilt or what-have-you hadn't yet worn off the ginger-bread. He still brought her name into the conversation whenever it was humanly possible, and sometimes when Gallagher would have sworn that it wasn't.

In fact, some days when he was feeling particularly benevolent, he'd give him a lead. "What's Rosalie been up to today?" For she was always finding a bargain, buying a rare antique or designing a fabulous dress. He hoped that he wouldn't be compelled to engage actively in the Rosalie-Ash-Admiration-Society tonight.

"You'll come?" Ash said with genuine delight. "Good show! . . . I'll go and give Rosalie a tinkle."

Ash fumbled in his pockets and produced a couple of pennies, and went whistling out into the hall towards the coin box. As a gesture, Gallagher bought a bottle of gin and a bottle of Scotch from the barman . . . being single, he rarely took up his ration of spirits . . . and going out into the hall, stuffed them in his greatcoat pockets.

"All set," Ash came hurrying back beaming. "Rosalie's pleased as Punch. She's been nagging me to bring you over for ages. She says we're to hurry. The chicken's done to a turn."

Mentally pulling down the corners of his mouth, Gallagher followed Ash across the hall, and limped down the flight of stone steps that led to the car park in the courtyard.

There, Ash opened the door of his battered old black Austin. "Not much to look at, old man. But can she go!"

Apparently he viewed this old bone-shaker with the same indulgence with which he viewed his wife. And Gallagher was prepared for them to have much in common.

As they bowled along down the drive, turning right in a loose tyre-wobbling turn towards the town, Ken Ash sang any snatch of song that came into his head, out of sheer joie-de-vivre. They drove over the level crossing, past the square, past the long line of airmen and their girls patiently waiting outside the cinema. They looked exactly the same queue as he and Edwina had joined, so that almost he looked for themselves among it.

Smiling at the cinema queue with indulgence, Ash said, "We saw *you* there the other night. Rosalie wanted to ask you back for a drink . . . but I thought you mightn't like it."

Gallagher murmured something non-committal. Ash went on, "If ever you *are* in the big city and want a cuppa or a drink, just drop in . . . you don't have to wait to be asked. Look . . . you turn left here by the Co-op! It's a small street . . . Richmond Row. You'd miss it, if you weren't looking."

They came to the backs of some tall, once white-painted Georgian houses, and parking the Austin in front of an old stable block, Ash gave a long blast on the horn. "That tells Rosalie she can put the ice in the Martinis," he said.

Before leaving the car, he covered the bonnet with a rug. Then he opened a back-garden gate and led the way up a crazy-paved path to the side door. Here was a collection of bells, and beside the second one up was a printed card which said *Ash.*

"We're on the first floor," Ken said, giving the V in Morse on his bell as they walked into the side hall. From here an imposing staircase of wide shallow steps with a wrought-iron balustrade led up to a landing lit by a tall semi-circular window. There was an air of gently mouldering elegance about the place that certainly wasn't shared by the figure waiting for them at the head of the stairs.

For Rosalie Ash was young and tall and very slim, with dark gold hair, and she wore a dress that was expensively casual. It was of a creamy material with a tight skirt, and a scarf effect round the throat. The cut of the dress, and her position above them on the landing, highlighted her slender well-shaped legs.

She leaned forward and gave Ken a quick kiss when they were one step down from her.

"Well . . . *well,* so *this* is *Wing Commander* Gallagher!" she said. "Welcome to our humble home, Gavin!"

She smiled sweetly, taking his hand and holding it a little longer than a single girl of her age would have done. "It would be *quite* unnecessary to say I've heard a lot about you." She began walking towards the door of their flat, which they had obviously painted themselves a cheerful buttercup yellow, and which had an incongruous little wall vase beside it, filled with freesias. As she walked, she turned her feet at an angle, like a model would, and she studied them as if even to herself they were a fresh and beautiful discovery.

She led the way into a large room, with long windows that showed the bottom of the garden, and beyond that, the church tower and chimneys and roofs of the southern part of Avonmead. The windows were hung with crimson silk curtains, the walls distempered in pale apple green.

"D'you like it?" she said, smiling as he looked around. "Ken and I *love* dabbling with colour. We did it mainly ourselves. With the help of a few bits and pieces from home."

"That means *Rosalie* did it. She's too modest to say."

Ken put his arm round her shoulders, and she rubbed her cheek against his hand.

"Nonsense! Now let me take your coat, Gavin! And Ken shall get us a drink." She came up behind him, and he could smell her expensive perfume. He watched her long fingers with their pointed coral-painted nails against his blue crombie greatcoat. A dress ring sparkled on one finger. It had a dark golden stone like a cairngorm. It was huge and square cut and it seemed to weigh down her thin finger.

"A penny for them!" she demanded, hugging his coat against her.

And without thinking Gallagher said, "That ring matches your hair."

The effect on them both was immediate. They laughed with approval and delight. "Now you *never* told me *that* about Gavin," Rosalie said. "You never told me he could make pretty speeches, too, darling!"

"That's because *I* didn't know," Ken smiled at them both. "He certainly never made any to *me*!"

As she walked across the room, Rosalie called over her shoulder, "What on earth have you got it weighted down with, Gavin? Depth charges?"

And he remembered the bottles.

"Oh, I forgot," he said, following her and pulling them out, and unwrapping them. "I brought these along. Present from 81 Group."

"Bless you, Gavin! Darling, isn't he *sweet*?" She stood in the middle of the room, one foot at an angle to the other. When she laughed, she seemed to have a habit of raising her brows and half closing her eyes, as if the effect of a laugh was like smelling salts, or as if it was brittle enough to splinter in her eyes. Despite this affectation, despite her too heavy make-up, she was perhaps the most *femininely* beautiful woman Gallagher had ever seen.

"I shall give you a kiss for that!" she said, putting her hands on his shoulder and planting on his forehead a small peck of passionless rectitude.

"Don't take a penny for 'em this time, Gavin." Ken said with a peculiar understanding. "They're worth a helluva lot more!"

It struck Gallagher that so sure of his wife was Ken that he actually *liked* his friends to admire and feel attracted towards her.

"And now, my sweets!" She came back from hanging up his coat. "Let's have a drink and a natter . . . and then I promise I'll serve dinner."

She sat down on the edge of a long sofa, upholstered in faded brocade, which she had endeavoured to renovate by stretching over it a long swathe of multi-coloured Indian silk. She patted the place beside her and said, "Come over here, Gavin! You can stretch your leg out better here."

"What's it to be, Gavin?" Ken called, standing behind a low mahogany table by the window, laden with bottles, a silver ice-dish and all kinds of glasses. "What say you we open your bottle of Scotch?"

"Fine."

"Water with it?"

"Please."

"Rosalie? Martini?"

"The same as Gavin's, darling."

"That makes triplets."

While he busied himself pouring out the drinks, Rosalie turned to Gallagher. "You won't laugh at me, will you?" she said prettily. "But there is a superstition . . . if a newcomer brings spirits to your home . . . he brings you luck."

And as Ken brought over the glasses, she clinked hers first with Gallagher's and then with her husband's. "Not that we actually need it! We mustn't be greedy, must we, darling? But let's have a toast! May we *all* bring luck to *one another!*"

While Rosalie Ash was serving dinner, Gallagher had ample opportunity of studying her. The polished Regency table with its silver and crystal was fit for an Emperor, and he watched her, as she busied herself around it. A waterfall of light from a chandelier above them ("Mummy gave it to us, *wasn't* she a poppet?") caught the glints of gold in her hair. She wore it drawn back from her perfectly-featured face, and then piled in a long loose chignon at the nape of her neck. As the ring did to her finger, so the size and weight of the chignon made her neck seem white and fragile. Her skin was pale, fine and flawless. Feeling his eyes on her, she looked across the table at him. Her full lips curved in a smile of childish and uncomplicated satisfaction.

"Look at these roses!" she said, as if to stop Gallagher staring at her, and yet in some odd way, *underlining* the fact that he was. She pushed over a crystal bowl filled with red hothouse blooms. "Ken *still* brings me a bunch every sixteenth of the month," she said, as Gallagher admired them. "We were married on the sixteenth."

When Rosalie had wheeled in a trolley from the kitchen laden with hot dishes, Ken insisted on opening a bottle of Sauterne as this was an occasion. There was a good deal of fussing around with the carving. "You've given Gavin scarcely a *fragment*," Rosalie said, when Ken passed him over a plate filled to the rims. There was bread sauce to be passed, and game chips, and peas, and beans, and roast potatoes.

"Don't know how you do it," Gallagher said, tucking in to the best meal he'd had in months. "Haven't eaten like this for donkey's years."

"It's Rosalie," Ash pressed his thumb down on the table. "She has all the local tradesmen just like *that*!"

"Fibber! Besides, you don't know what I give them in exchange, do you?" She winked at Gallagher.

"What beats me is how she can slave over a stove all day, and serve a meal looking like that," Ken said, his eyes almost lambent with admiration. "What do you say, Gallagher?"

Certainly she sat at the head of the table looking like some glossy magazine advertisement for gracious living . . . something of a collector's piece . . . beautiful, fragile, expensive.

"Now will you please stop talking about *me!* Fill Gavin's glass, darling, like a good host! I want to hear what you two boys have been up to."

But when Ken Ash began an account of his afternoon watch, and Gallagher asked him about a planner called Burnett, and what the hell he thought he was playing at, Rosalie clapped her hands together, and said, "Not *shop*, my loves! Please! Close the hangar doors, for *goodness* sake!"

It was not until they were drinking coffee out of little gilt cups, that Rosalie appeared to find a subject of conversation that whole-heartedly pleased her. The two men were sitting on the sofa, and Rosalie had insisted on occupying a small footstool near their feet. Behind the drawn blackout curtains, the windows were open, and in from the garden drifted the smell of earth and cut grass mixed with the pungency of exhausts from the nearby roads. Distant lorries hummed. A disembodied voice laughed and shouted on the High Street. The only light was from a small pink-shaded reading lamp over by the marble fireplace, and the soft glow of the dying fire.

It was the time, the light, the atmosphere for confidences.

Rosalie put down her coffee cup, took a cigarette and when Gallagher leaned forward to light it for her, she put her hand over his to keep steady the flame. She kept it there.

Looking into his face, she said, "Ken tells me you're in love with a pretty little Waaf. *When* are you going to let us meet her?"

It was, Gallagher later discovered, part of her party repertoire to toss these playful little stones into the conversation. But this time he was thoroughly embarrassed. So was Ken. "Now, now Rosalie! Hey there! *That's* not quite fair . . ."

"Why ever not?" She glanced from one to the other pertly, provocatively. "*I* didn't make it up."

"Come . . . come! I said . . ." Ken began going very red. "That he was *interested* in Edwina Corrie." She concentrated her stare now on her husband, blinking her heavily-mascaraed eyelashes . . . until, as if he were under cross-examination, Ash's voice faltered. "Might have said *liked* . . . believe I did . . . well, maybe I *mentioned* the word love . . ."

"There! What did I tell you!" And clasping her hands round her knees, giving all her attention now to Gavin, "*Are* you in love with her?"

It was on the tip of Gallagher's tongue to tell her there and then to mind her own damned business. But it wasn't near enough being said to be of any use. Instead, he went as red as Ash had done. "I hadn't thought about it . . . we're . . ."

"Good heavens! Don't tell me! You're just *good* friends." She laughed. "No, never mind! It's awfully naughty of me to tease you. I'll promise to stop. If you have to *think* whether you're in love . . . take it from me, *you're not*." She smiled with sudden engaging simplicity. "You must forgive an old matron like me being interested."

"She's all of twenty-two," Ash said.

Ignoring him, she went on talking softly to Gallagher. "It's that *we're* so terribly happy! I want people *I* like to be just as happy, too!"

Ash leaned forward at that and touched her shoulder, and she covered his hand with hers. They both smiled almost in unison at Gallagher. He felt a wave of tenderness towards them both. His momentary irritation faded. He was trying to think of something particularly nice to say to her in return, the nicer perhaps in proportion to his irritation, when she went on, staring now at the carpet. "I suppose I didn't begin it very well, but I had a *reason* for asking. You see it struck me . . . the other night when we saw the pair of you huddled in the cinema queue . . . it must be simply *hell* . . . to find anywhere to go . . . especially when there's so much red tape about officers and airwomen."

She looked up to give Gallagher a gentle friendly smile. "It quite *worried* me that night, and I began thinking——"

"A great planner, Rosalie!" said Ash. "They don't know what they're missing at Air Ministry!"

"Don't interrupt, darling! I thought . . . why doesn't he *bring her here*? Oh, not *just* for a meal. Though we'd *love* her to come. But it won't be *us* she's interested *in*. She won't want to spend her valuable time nattering to an old pair of turtle-doves like us! If she comes, Ken and I will go out. We'll go to the cinema. We'll hold hands in the back row, won't we, darling? You can help yourself to drinks. There'll be cold supper in the fridge. Or if she wants to impress you, she can cook something herself."

It seemed to Gallagher too good to be true. The only slight fly in the ointment was that Rosalie seemed to have got Edwina a little wrong. It wasn't *she* who wanted to impress *him*. But the implication was so nebulous that it wasn't worth pointing out. And to be honest, he couldn't help being flattered by it.

"It's terribly kind of you, Rosalie," he said. "I don't know how to thank you . . . we couldn't possibly do it, of course . . ."

"Ken, *order* him to! Oh, no, beg pardon . . . *you* can't. It's the other way round. Please, Gavin. I shall be furious if you don't!"

"But we couldn't turn you out."

She laughed gaily. "Gavin darling, you'd be doing me a favour! I'm just dying to prise old man Ash out in the evening. He's such a pipe-and-carpet-slippers bod. I can't get him mobile."

"Homebound as an egg," Ash said. "Who's to blame me? No, the girl's serious, Gallagher. It's no use arguing. Give in. Do as Rosalie tells you. Look at me! I *thrive* on it."

"Well, if you're sure?" Gallagher smiled a little shyly. It did seem a splendid solution. "I can't tell you how grateful——"

"Don't! *I'm* grateful to *you*! I believe there's a terrific film at the Roxy on Thursday. All about monsters . . . a real spine-chiller. I shall make Ken buy me ice-cream and play footie in the back row. Ken shall give you the flat key. And we'll promise to make a fearful din as we come upstairs . . . and knock three times!"

"Thursday then," Ash said, lighting his pipe and throwing Gallagher a cigarette. "Is Edwina off duty?"

"Oh, she'll fix it." Rosalie laughed. "If she's keen."

"The *Marquis of Salisbury* has *had* it for tonight!" They had met at their usual place—the third oak past the gates. Gallagher kissed Edwina's cheek, and slipped his hand through her arm. He always felt elated when he met her. But tonight— especially so.

She smiled expectantly. "Where then?"

"You'll never guess."

She shook her head. "I know I won't. So tell me. Can't be the flicks, for it's Frankenstein . . ."

"You don't *have* to go to the flicks to see Frankenstein," he said flapping his hands and exaggerating his limp. "He's *right beside you.*"

And smiling, she said "I know."

With great éclat, Gallagher brought out of his pocket Ash's key, and tossed it in the air and caught it again.

"We're invited out."

"Where to?"

"Ken and Rosalie Ash's place. Squadron Leader Ash. *You* know. The Controller. She's nice, too."

Edwina stopped, turned to him, and said, "We're not going though, are we?"

"Of *course* we are!"

"Oh, Gavin! . . . you should have warned me."

"*Warned you?*"

"Yes."

"Whatever for?"

She laughed shyly. "I don't really know. Silly, I suppose. It's just that I'm not *prepared.*"

"Prepared! In what way? It's uniform or uniform! So how *could* you prepare?"

"In . . . well, mood . . . somehow."

He snorted loudly.

"Gavin, you know what I mean."

He did know vaguely what she meant, but he was disappointed in her reaction and he was damned if he was going to say he understood. "Frankly, Edwina . . . I haven't the faintest idea."

"I just don't feel like going."

"Why not?"

"I'd rather be just on our own."

"Well, we *will* be. They're going out."

"That," she said softly, "somehow makes it worse."

He began walking along the road towards the town, and with a shrug she fell into step beside him.

"Damned nice of them, I thought! But obviously . . . you don't."

"No."

"Well, I do."

She drew a deep breath. "It's so contrived . . . arranged . . ." She was trying to pick her words and she spoke slowly and carefully. She made a gesture with both her hands. "If you don't understand, I can't explain."

"I don't see the *difference*. After all, it's the same as sitting in the *Marquis of Salisbury* . . . except that it's a damned sight more comfortable, and we don't have half the station goggling at us."

"I see," she said. "I'm sorry." Her voice trembled half with tears, half with a rising, but still suppressed anger. "I *thought* you were beginning to find it a bit much."

All at once, they were on the edge of their first quarrel. And instead of finding it the last thing in the world that he wanted to happen, the idea became immediately exciting. He *wanted* to be angry with Edwina. He wanted some satisfying reason for hurting her physically. All the restraints and frustrations of their relationship were behind his next words.

"Well, *now* you *know!*" he said loudly. "Now you bloody well know!"

Immediately, she did a quick right-about-turn, and without any noise, ran like a shadow the way they had come—back towards the camp.

He caught her up, but it took him a hell of a while. And his laboured hobbling run drained all the anger and excitement out of him. He took hold of her arm, and said gently, softly . . .

knowing that for both of them the quarrel was already over, "That's a bloody awful thing to do to a cripple!"

She began laughing in a sobbing way. "And that's a bloody awful thing to say to a girl!"

"Then we're quits, aren't we?"

"Quits."

He knew she'd been crying as she ran, but he pretended when he kissed her not to notice.

"I didn't mean it, Edwina . . . you know that. Don't care *who* goggles at us . . . I couldn't stop seeing you. It's just that I'm a bloody awful bastard sometimes."

"No, you're not. It was silly of me not to want to go."

"No, it wasn't. I only wanted to . . . so we'd be together. But I know what you mean. It's other people's *interest* that's difficult. It's like being specimens arranged in a jar."

"And other people's places are so . . . well, so *personal*."

"Their's is, I'll admit."

"And I suppose," Edwina said, "habit comes into it, too. I've got fond of the *Marquis of Salisbury*."

"I'll kill the bastard!" Walking along, they laughed immoderately.

"Well," Gallagher said as they passed the cinema. "At least it's better than watching Frankenstein. And at least we can sit on our own. In peace and quiet."

But whether because there *was* something, after all, in what Edwina had said about people's homes being so personal, or whether because the memory of his previous mood of angry desire imposed a greater restraint on him, something marred their usual effortless communication. They smoked a little. They drank a little. They talked a little. But the elegant room seemed more perceptive and intruding than the airmen's stares. Gallagher was careful not to spill cigarette ash on the pale carpet, or pour too stiff a peg from the bottles . . . most conscious of all *not* to sit too close to Edwina on the waiting, expectant sofa.

And when Rosalie and Ken returned—early, but making enough noise to waken the dead, there was nothing that they couldn't have stayed for and heard or seen. And their teasing, their laughter, their jolly understanding served only to emphasize that, though only briefly, something had gone wrong.

153

More than ever now, Gallagher inclined to Vince's assertion that the physical law of compensation could be applied just as well to human relationships as it could to inanimate matter. In other words, you got nothing in this life for nothing.

And whereas he was happy to have Edwina at 81 Group, her presence also brought with it a proportionate amount of inconvenience. Because she didn't want to, and he wasn't very keen, when they met now, they very rarely went to the Ashes' flat.

The gossip continued.

No one who had not lived at Group could appreciate the amount of it. Maybe because there was so much in everyday life that one wanted to, or *had* to, keep one's mouth shut about, personal lives became not only fair, but in some instances the *only* game.

All the same, Gallagher hadn't expected the circles to widen over the months *quite* so far.

It was a Saturday morning in December, when they held an extra long version of the weekly operational conference. They'd spent an hour over the manning of light guns on the perimeters at 81 Group's airfields. Pyrotechnic methods of marking targets were argued over. Gallagher had had a long bind with the Armament Officer on the apparent inability of 81 Group to get the new block-buster bombs. And a rather shorter but somewhat stormier argument with the Wingco Equipment about spares which didn't exist. He was therefore in no mood to be buttonholed by Ingleby, just as the conference broke up.

"Ah, Gavin . . . don't rush off! I've got something I want to have a natter with you about." And when Gallagher put down his brief case, and folded his arms over his chest and waited: "Oh, not here . . ." He looked around at all the people in the Operations Room. "Tell you what, though," his eyes brightened with a splendid idea. "Come along to my office. We'll have a coffee. I need a drink after all that nattering." He clapped Gallagher on the shoulder. "You made your points splendidly, Gavin! You've got quite the conference technique." He kept his hand on Gallagher's shoulder while they walked the few paces into his office, and then he waved him into the same chair that he'd done when Gallagher came that first day from hospital.

He'd sat in it often enough since, of course. But for Gallagher that day still seemed to mark where many things began.

"There's a little bit of bumph I want to show you," Ingleby said when an airman had brought the coffee, and they both had a cup at their elbow.

He produced a file, and out of that a letter from the Admiralty, congratulating 81 Group on their recent successes in bombing U-boat building yards. "That's a feather in *your* cap, Gavin. It isn't often our friends at the Admiralty see fit to say good show, chaps, and thanks."

At first Gallagher thought that the letter was Ingleby's sole reason for having him in. He made a few remarks about publishing the gist of the letter in D.R.O.s,* so as to let all personnel get a kick out of it.

"And not a kick *up* the usual place either, eh, Gavin?" Ingleby said, his eyes twinkling, laughing more than the small joke merited. Gallagher finished his coffee, and because he was always in a hurry, reached for his cap.

"Which is exactly where, dammit, *I've* got to plant the next kick, Gavin. Right up the usual place!" Ingleby chuckled good-humouredly to show it was all one big joke. If you took it the right way.

Then in a-man-to-man, I've-done-it-myself voice, "Now what's all this nonsense I hear about you and that little L.A.C.W. whats-her-name in Signals?"

"So you see," Gallagher said to Edwina two days later, "we don't have much choice in the matter."

They were standing in front of Avonmead's one department store, watching two assistants put up the last of the Christmas decorations. "The less we're seen around in public . . . the better."

Edwina watched the girls arrange wads of cotton wool around a papier-mâché chimney pot, and said slowly, "I suppose so."

"Oh, the old man was decent enough. He's not such a bastard, really. He told me it was mainly *your* Queen Bee. She'd had a bind and a half at him. About discipline and what-have-you."

"She's a bitch, of course," Edwina said sadly and matter-of-factedly. "What did *you* say?"

"What *could* I say? I said nothing. Oh, he treated it all as a joke."

* Daily Routine Orders.

"*He* would."

"And he emphasized that it would be *you* who suffered. Not me."

"And shed a bitter tear, *I* bet." Edwina laughed, and squeezed his hand, "I bet you *both* wept at that!"

Gallagher rested his hand on her shoulder. "At least I'm glad we've got the Ashes. I'd feel a helluva lot worse . . . if we hadn't *them* to go to."

The assistants had finished the Father Christmas scene, and they had tied red and green streamers across the window. Now they were hanging the silver and gold baubles on ribbons down the pane.

"I know you don't like going there much. But any port in a storm."

"It doesn't seem like a storm out here. And I'm not awfully sure I feel in port *there*."

The two of them were, as a matter of fact, on their way to the Ashes' for tea. Edwina had a five-hour spell off duty before she went on watch at eight.

It was the last Thursday before Christmas. And it was one of those afternoons when the sky itself seemed to huddle for warmth over the chimney pots. Night and the black-out would soon squeeze the light and life out of the little town. The very commercial gaiety of the decorated shops emphasized the dampness and shabbiness of the streets outside. Gallagher was quite honestly looking forward to the comfortable room, the warm fire, and being (for Ash was Duty Controller that afternoon) looked after by two pretty girls.

"I know what you mean," he said, turning up the collar of his overcoat, and stamping his feet because now he wanted to move on.

"It's," Edwina said carefully, "like a sort of concentrated gossip with Rosalie. She wants to find out everything . . . to *own* it, to handle it . . . to touch what she hasn't any right to."

"She means well, you know. She's always asking after you."

"Asking you about *us*, you mean. And what we get up to."

"Perhaps."

Gallagher squeezed her arm. Staring into the shop window, trying to think of how to show that he understood, he noticed their two heads reflected, in miniature, in an enormous silver glass Christmas ball. Their earnest faces under the uniform caps caught in a silver bubble.

"Look at us," he said, pointing.

"Yes, look at us."

The sudden sadness in her voice pierced him as nothing in his life seemed ever to have done.

Staring at the silver decoration with an almost hypnotized concentration, he said slowly, "I don't have to say . . . what you are to me . . . do I?"

"No." Edwina was staring straight ahead, too.

"And . . . you *know* that whatever our future is . . . it's together . . . don't you?"

"Yes."

He gave a long sigh. "Well, then . . . who do we care about?"

She turned round to face him then, her eyes wide and shining. "Who indeed?"

"Let's go then!"

Their reflections left the silver ball as, still smiling, arm in arm, they walked up the road and turned left towards the Ashes' flat.

Rosalie was waiting for them in the lounge. She had left the door open, and as she heard their feet on the stairs she called out, "Come on, darlings, you're late!"

There was a good smell of toast and pastry, and there were the inevitable hot-house roses in a bowl on the mantelpiece.

"We'll let Gavin sit by the fire because he's tired," she said. "Edwina, *you* come in and help me with the sandwiches."

As the kitchen door closed behind them, Gallagher heard her say, "What, my dear! No engagement ring *yet*?"

4

1943 was Bomber Command's year. Amongst the begonias and the orange groves of Casablanca, the decision was taken by allied politicians and military leaders to obliterate Germany's industrial power.

The technique of the Pathfinders had now been perfected. A new radio device *Oboe*—called because it sang like that musical instrument—had revolutionized target finding. A fast Mosquito aircraft would fly along a "beam" which sounded as a continuous note in the pilot's earphones. If he deviated to the left he was advised by dots. Dashes told him he was on the right. When the target was close, via another station the observer heard *abcd*, dah-dah-dah, dit-dit-dit—after which he pressed the button to release the Target Indicator.

Accuracy was now measured not in miles but in yards. Thousand pound Target Indicators of intense brilliance were dropped—orange, green, red, blue, yellow, white, the colour varying every night lest the Germans copy them over dummy targets. The track in was marked by lines of flares. In the event of thick medium cloud muffling the T.I.s, sky markers were used —showers of sparks at high altitude. Bomber crews, arriving to a strict quick timetable, were simply told to bomb the markers.

Now, instead of the bombers' winter off-season, came the Battle of the Ruhr. That home of Germany's iron and steel industry was protected by a thick self-made smoke-screen from its belching chimneys. Individual cities previously could not be sorted out. Now they were pinpointed by Oboe. Krefeld, Wuppertal, Essen, Dusseldorf, Cologne were attacked in bad weather with such accuracy that the German High Command told Hitler that a blind bombing technique was being used—one more truth he refused to believe.

Night after night, Bomber Command operated. As many as 700 heavy bombers operated against a single city, saturating it with three thousand tons of high explosive. Morning after morning, ten, fifteen, twenty, fifty bombers failed to return.

81 Group was working at an almost unbearable pitch. Inevitably, Gallagher saw less of Edwina: when they did meet, inevitably it had to be at the Ashes'. Far from hindering his work, he found in her his only help in it. Only on her could he relieve the burden of his feelings. He poured out to her his fights with other people, the sickness he felt over the losses, his frustrations in dealing with authority and red-tape, the things he might have done but didn't. Those last few months of winter seemed to take their toll on everyone. All the old names seemed to have disappeared from the bomber squadrons, to be replaced by young boys, their faces as strange and as untouched by experience as their names.

The ordinary cracks that might appear in any set up that had been on the go for some time began to appear. Rationing was tightened, leave was harder to get . . . there were less buckshee forty-eights. Spares for the aircraft got to be like gold, so that it was nothing to have to ring almost every M.U. in the country to stop three or four aircraft being on the Q form—which meant they couldn't go on Ops for the one good reason that they were short of a part . . . a tighter watch was kept on petrol, and the liberty buses at 81 Group Stations were being cut by half.

The Group Padre reported an increased number of marital difficulties being laid before his brethren on the Stations. And the W.A.A.F. Senior Officer, when she filled in her share of the operational report, namely the number of airwomen in her command discharged under Clause II for pregnancy, found it to be double that of the same time six months ago—a black for 81 Group which would cause much eyebrow-raising at Command.

Increasingly, Gallagher lay awake at night, trying to keep the balance between what Command wanted and the morale of his squadrons. And when he did doze off, it wasn't darkness or sleep that seemed to come over him, but the grey-green of the Channel, the uneasy darkness just before dawn after a raid.

Now Gallagher's main concern was to get 81 Group to devise tactics to cope with the four hundred night fighters that lay underneath the main stream, watching for a bomber to be silhouetted against the sky, before climbing up to do its deadly dive from six o'clock high. He tried corkscrewing, the use of cloud cover, put in an urgent demand for 20 mm cannon instead of .303 machine guns in aircraft turrets. He visited every Station in the Group with what he knew was regarded as monotonous and dreaded regularity. He made snap checks, too, which were condemned as unfair. He tested crews. He was annoyed when they didn't get photographs. Now and again they bombed the wrong city. Sometimes they returned early with ice or mechanical trouble—not pressing on to the target. None of the crews these days seemed to have any sixth sense, as *his* contemporaries had. He had the leaders in for a bind after every inspection he did. But it began to dawn on Gallagher that his criticism wasn't altogether fair. It wasn't borne out by the figures. And as he said to Edwina, in fact it all boiled down to *him*. He was tired of watching.

"That's what you *really* want, isn't it?" she said. "You won't be really happy till you're airborne again."

"It's hard standing by," he admitted. "Telling other people to do it."

It seemed to him then . . . they were walking back to camp from the Ashes' again . . . that somehow in those few words an invisible screw of unhappiness had tightened.

Already guilty, he glanced down at Edwina. Her face was pale and her eyes dark-shadowed. These last few months had affected her too . . . every watch she did seemed to hold the possibility of rescue or tragedy. The sight of her pale face seemed to add to all his other trials and tribulations. And now their relationship was cramped by the Group's restrictions on seeing each other. They had to go more often to the Ashes. When they met, it was furtively. However much he might despise petty regulations, Gallagher always had the idea that Ingleby's eyes were on them, and they would have to go carefully.

And then, as winter turned slowly to spring, suddenly he had had enough. Enough of the war, enough of Group, enough of Ingleby. For the moment, he could take no more of work, of frustration, of bottled up emotion. He wanted only one thing and that was to get away from here.

One day in the middle of April, he said to Edwina, "You've never had a forty-eight hour pass since I've known you."

"It isn't worth while. It's too far to go home."

"It *is* worth while. And you're *not* going home."

She said nothing for a moment. She seemed to hold her breath. He smiled down at her. "Don't worry! I'm not asking you to go for a dirty week-end. It's just that I want to get to hell out of here. And I want to be with you. On our own."

"I wouldn't mind if you were," she said. "I *wish* you were. I'd like to." And then quietly, as if in fairness she must warn him against something towards which she would like to persuade him, she added, "People will notice if we get passes at the same time."

"Let them," he said. "This time I don't give a damn what anyone thinks."

It was another fortnight before Edwina could get a pass. And then, because they were short-handed, it was only for thirty-six hours.

"Maybe it's as well," Gallagher said. "Maybe it's your guardian angel looking out for you. I don't think my will power is good for a forty-eight." He squeezed her hand as they sat side by side in the railway compartment. The train, the one-thirty from Avonmead, gently rocked them sideways as rhythmically, a light plume of steam flying past the window, they puffed out of the station and began to gain speed.

Closing her eyes, leaning her head back against the dusty upholstery, she said, "I wish I *had* got a forty-eight then. I told you I *want* to, didn't I?" She turned her face to him. "D'you want me to tell you again?"

He kissed her mouth, sighed contentedly, and said, "No. It's unladylike. It might even be rude." He pulled her head against his shoulder, running his fingers over her short dark hair, "Sit still. Enjoy the countryside. The tickets cost twelve and six each. So let's get my money's-worth."

Already he felt two years of life and twenty years' worth of experience younger. Since they'd caught this ancient train, they seemed to have steamed out of all the complications of life. He felt as young and excited as a seven-year-old off for a holiday by the sea.

"Why the sea?" he'd asked Edwina, when almost simultaneously making the past fortnight's plans, they'd pointed to this place on the map lent them by the Avonmead stationmaster.

"You'll probably," she had laughed affectionately, "find some deep psychological reason . . . but *I* . . . I just want to go there, because I'm always happy by the sea."

"Are you happy now?" He leaned towards her, and saw their reflection in the carriage window as he kissed her. Watching it, he thought that surely the first pre-requisite of happiness must be its finiteness . . . that it must always be contained like liquid, by opposing substance. Love might be eternal, but happiness never.

"*Too* happy, I think."

Take what you want said God . . . and *pay* for it.

He began listening again to the clacking of the wheels. The inevitable rhythm. Night and day. Light and shade. Pain and pleasure.

"I don't think *I* can ever be too happy." It was the first time he had come near to telling her about his guilt and superstitions. "I have my own built-in set of happiness destroyers."

"I think most people have," she said.

They rattled across a bridge, over a canal. The water was glossy and grey in the centre, velvety green with weed at the edges. All along its banks as though it was a High Street, the village houses stood shoulder to shoulder, the pub . . . the eternal *Marquis of Salisbury*.

"Give a cheer," Gallagher said, pointing out the sign, and they shouted till the village fell behind them, the coffee-brown ploughed fields and acres of sprouting wheat and turnip fields moved at a stately pace to take its place, and then in their turn fell away. They passed a windmill, its sails still and unmoving as a feathered propeller. A church with a spire like some Guy Fawkes rocket, a field of sheep, some lambs.

"I'd forgotten it was May," Gallagher said, pointing out the lambs. "Just look at that greedy bastard. Give your brothers a chance!"

There were primroses on the embankments, and by one dark tarnished pool, a few daffodils. Slowly the soft glimmering of the horizon turned to a glittering sheen. When Gallagher pulled down the window, they could smell the sea.

Edwina stood up, and arranged her hair in the mirror between an old fashioned picture of the Lake District, and a red painted sign which said *Is your journey really necessary?*

"We're here! Get your bits and pieces." He helped her on with her coat. It was of light-coloured camel-hair, and underneath she was wearing a tweed dress of green and white checks. She looked younger and infinitely prettier. "They'll think we're a honeymoon couple," he said. "The beautiful bride!"

"What!" she said. "With two separate rooms?"

"I forgot."

"You're so used to booking a double, *that's* why." She smiled. "Anyway, I wonder what the hotel will be like."

"Frightful! If it was any good, it'd be requisitioned."

He picked up their two cases, and held the door open for her. Only about four other passengers alighted at Brinton-on-Sea. There were no place names up these days, and an old porter went hobbling up and down shouting, "Bri-inton . . . Brin-ton-on-Sea!"

"He walks like I do," Gallagher said. "Dot and carry."

Edwina laughed. "But he shouts better!"

They walked down the sloping road from the station. "Breathe in deeply!" Gallagher said. "Feed those light-starved lungs of yours with ozone!"

"Heavenly!" she said. "Absolute heaven! Oh, and *do* look. It's a sandy beach. With dunes. You can see it over there. There's sand all over."

"Probably in the food too, I shouldn't wonder," Gallagher said. "We'll go and book in. Then I'll take you for a walk."

The hotel itself was a small one with ten rooms, and a somewhat gloomy grey stone exterior. Inside however, it was clean and shabbily comfortable and, as Edwina remarked, there was a nice homely beer-smelling saloon bar.

"Shades of the *Marquis* again," Gallagher said, signing the register and producing his identity card, and then pushing the book over to Edwina.

Gallagher's room was large and draughty, but Edwina's had a view of the sea. At the moment, it was overcast, and there was nothing to see from her window but the scarcely discernible line where sea and sky joined, and the white curl and wash as the waves broke over the sand.

The front itself was deserted. "I meant to take you for a walk on the beach," Gallagher said, "and leave our foot-prints on the sands of time. But I'd forgotten about all that."

All that was the rolls of barbed wire, the gun emplacements, bored-looking soldiers pacing up and down on sentry-duty. The promenade was empty, swept clean as a whistle, it seemed, by a light wind blowing in from the east. It brought with it tiny droplets of sea-spray that tingled in their faces.

All the monstrous ugly hotels, that in peace-time glowered out to sea, had been requisitioned by the army. Green lorries and trucks trundled up and down, a despatch rider zoomed past. The old seaside signs . . . *Pavilion* . . . *to the children's paddling pool* . . . *Bathing huts* . . . *deck chairs* . . . had been replaced by Fire Hydrant . . . No. 6 Company . . . an archer in red paint . . . Bat H.Q. . . . Gunnery School.

Leaning out of an upstairs window of a once luxury hotel, a khaki-clad figure in shirt sleeves waved at Edwina and wolf-whistled.

"These bloody brown jobs!" Gallagher sighed.

"You should slap him down," Edwina said.

"He's too high up. Besides you like it. It's made your day."

"It'd make it even more if you did."

"Perhaps." He smoothed down a lock of her hair that was being blown about by the wind. "But right now, we're going to explore the big city. I might buy you a cuppa *and* a bun."

They turned to the right down a narrow road full of small shops. Gallagher stopped in front of one which still had a brave display of fading rude postcards, and Edwina could only drag him away when he'd bought one to send to Ken Ash.

They had tea and toasted teacakes in a snack bar, and then Edwina found a depressed-looking photographer's shop where, Gallagher said, the display of bathing belles was far funnier than the card he'd bought, and he wondered if they'd swop.

"Let's go in and see what they make of us," Edwina said. "Come on! Let's!"

They sat stiffly on a brown corduroy-covered sofa while a middle-aged woman said, "Look at each other, love . . . that's better! Ready in the morning . . . nine sharp!"

She had no need to tell them to smile. Everything seemed amusing, happy, inconsequential. Coming out of the photographer's, Gallagher said, "Christ! I'm damp! Some brat had wet that blasted sofa. Still, not to worry."

They walked to the end of the street, and turned right again, where the road paralleled the shore. Square red bungalow by square red bungalow, Brinton petered out, and all that remained was a straight tarmac road beside the dunes.

As they left the town, the sun came out, and on the flat unbroken surface of the sea, struck one huge blaze of light. So that in their eyes, there seemed only one bright dazzle, as their whole horizon ahead was filled by the shimmer of the sea.

Their path was bordered on the one hand by the fertile dark fields, and on the other by the roll of barbed wire with its concrete gun-posts, strung like ugly beads on a giant necklace. They walked on until they found a grass-covered dune on the right side of the wire.

"Look," Edwina said. "One that got away!"

"Let's sit on him, then. Over there. We'll be out of the wind."

The sun was warm on their faces. And here the smell of the

sea prickled like sand in their nostrils. There was no sound but the hush and sigh as the light waves broke, gently flooded, and receded against the soft sand. He waited for Edwina to rest her head against his shoulder, as if her touch was the fourth dimension of some indelible picture.

Stroking her hair, he said aloud, "When we're married, Edwina, we shall come here every year. I shall insist."

She smiled and said nothing.

"And we'll bring our children. To this very spot."

"Where shall we come from?"

"Oh, I don't know. *Anywhere*, I don't really mind. We can live wherever *you* want to."

"But where will you work? You'll have to have a job."

"I never thought much about a job. Perhaps because I never know if I'll be needing one. But if I do, I want to get away from all this . . . out of the Air Force . . . out of all this organization and what-not . . . away from characters like Ingleby . . . and just have a house and maybe a car . . . and a family . . . and of course *you*."

"Then we'll live by the sea," she said. "We'll think up some job. You could be a school-teacher. Or go into an airline."

"No, I don't want to be organized. I want to do something on my own. To think for myself." He gave a short laugh. "I've been lucky," he said. "Bloody lucky. I've found *you*. But in some odd way, I never seem to have found *me*."

It was sitting like that, on the sand dunes, without ever meaning to tell her, that he began talking about this stupid superstition he had. He told her about Tordoff, and for the first time that he'd ever told anyone . . . about the German.

"I get this funny feeling . . . this obsession . . . what-have-you . . . that I go on living because others die. I *want* to protect people . . . everybody . . . and yet I hurt them. D'you know what I mean?"

"I know what you mean," she said. "But it's yourself you hurt, that's all. And somehow," she went on, "the more afraid you are of a thing . . . the more you get drawn towards it."

"And that's why," he said, "I'm afraid that if we marry . . . I shall hurt *you*."

"But that's so silly," she said vehemently. "You couldn't hurt me at all. Not in any way. Except by not loving me." There was a short silence. Then in a small voice she asked, "Gavin . . . when *shall* we marry?"

"I ought to ask *you*!"

"Then *ask* me." And when he said nothing. "*You daren't*, you see. For you wouldn't take my answer."

"Why?" he tilted her face round to him. "Would your answer be never?"

"Now . . . not never."

But the breeze and the waves seemed to blur her words. So that they echoed over the dunes and the bare sand like *Now . . . or Never*. And the sound became some howl of utter desolation.

Gallagher shivered. The sun had gone in. The long dark clouds of evening began filling the western sky. The bright glitter beyond the sand had gone. The sea remained. Grey, smooth, but menacing. Grey as the concrete gun-posts, the big commandeered hotels that faced it, grim as the barbed wire, and the pointed guns.

He stared for a moment straight ahead. They seemed caught between two armour-plated giants. There seemed nothing human, nothing alive, nothing normal—except each other, and this one day together.

He turned, stretched down on the sand dunes, and pulled Edwina close to him. She knew what he was going to do, for she kissed him with an almost desperate passion. She put her arms round him as if protecting him as well as loving him. And she pressed her warm body as close as she could to him. He considered neither that this was what he had always feared, nor that he would probably regret it later.

She was part of him, as he of her. In a stupid, crazy, monstrous world, it seemed the only thing he had ever done that was truly right.

Afterwards, they hardly ever spoke of that day—not because it hadn't been happy, but because it had been perfect. And though neither Edwina nor certainly Gallagher would have actually said it, they both knew that it had deepened their relationship, so that—come what might—they were united. Though all that outwardly remained was a photograph which they each carried: the two of them sitting on the brown corduroy-covered sofa, beaming at each other.

After they returned from Brinton, Gallagher was even busier. A new radar known as H2S produced a complete map of the countryside on an airborne cathode ray tube: unlike Oboe, with its maximum range of 200 miles, this target finder could be used at any distance from Britain. Faraway targets like Mannheim, Stuttgart and Berlin could now be attacked accurately, and most nights a maximum effort was required. Losses went up to as high as 7% as the bombers slogged through hundreds of miles of defences. Seeing it all from the safety of 81 Group, Gallagher began to feel even more urgently the need to return. Though he would always have a slight limp, his leg was out of plaster and far better. And his conversation with Edwina would now and again turn on old Squadron doings. He still saw his return to ops as a possible way of hurting her—but at least on an operational squadron there would be none of this other-rank nonsense.

Once when they were having tea together in a café, he had asked her point-blank, "Edwina . . . about me going back on ops . . . what would you say?"

But she had lowered her eyes to the table-cloth and said nothing."

"I'll *have* to go back sometime. This won't go on for ever, you know."

She looked up. "Then let's pretend it will."

Now that the light nights had returned, they went for walks quite openly. Edwina still only went to the Ashes reluctantly, and that June anyway it was hot and sunny, so that it seemed a shame to stay hiding indoors. Ingleby and his friendly warning had retreated into the past. Gallagher's private life was his own, a fact that the Air Force would just have to realize. The A.O.C. had said nothing more about it—the gossip seemed to have died down, anyway.

So he wasn't prepared, just towards the end of the month, for what Edwina had to tell him. He'd had a day full of alarms and excursions: a trip over to a Station where casualties had been consistently far too high, a series of orders and counter-orders from Command, a contradictory meteorological forecast, a change of bomb-load for a raid on Kassel.

The Ashes had gone out for drinks to some friends, and the flat was empty but for the two of them.

Edwina always tried to break unpleasant news to him gently. "I heard a rumour today," she said casually, leaning forward a little, her hands clasped on her knee.

"Oh?" Gallagher lit a cigarette. "It'd be funny if you didn't. Nothing else *but* rumours in 81 Group these days."

"Well, I hope this is duff," she said, turning towards him. "It was about *me*. Margaret Parkes . . . she's in our hut and she works in the Orderly Room . . . says I'm up for a posting."

Gallagher frowned. "What made her say that?"

"I don't know. I suppose she wanted to warn me."

"Was she sure?"

"Not absolutely."

Gallagher thought for a moment. Then, with the remarkable facility he had developed for disregarding things that were either emotionally or mentally threatening, he found a dozen good reasons for not believing it.

He took a couple of long draws at his cigarette. Having weighed the matter somewhat briefly, he did at that time feel he could honestly dismiss it. "Look . . . you don't get a rumour *before* you're posted, Edwina darling. It just *happens*. You either *are* . . . or you're *not*. It's like getting the chop."

"That's what it *would* be like."

"Besides," he said, "if a *named* posting came in, we'd know by now. If it's unnamed, they wouldn't send *you*."

"I'm not sure."

"*I am!* Our star operator. Not on your life! Besides, we're bloody short of radio-ops. I doubt if they'd let the greenest sprog leave these days."

"I suppose not." She smiled, brightening, almost reassured. "Then you think it's all nonsense?"

"I'm damned sure of it."

"What about Ingleby?"

"What about him?"

"He did warn you . . ."

"Oh, he's forgotten all about that now. He's got too many other things on his mind."

"But posting me is what he *would* do."

"Let him try . . . that's all. I'll go and see him. I'll go and see everybody. I'm still Wing Commander Ops, after all. I won't *let* them post you."

A week later, she took the unprecedented step of phoning him at Operations.

When he lifted the receiver she said briefly, "This is Edwina . . . I'm sorry, but I *had* to phone you." Her voice was gentle. "I'm posted."

"Posted! Oh, Christ, surely not!"

"It's true."

"Where?"

"92 Group Headquarters."

"Where's that?"

"Stanbridge. About twenty miles north of London."

"When?"

"Forthwith."

"No!"

"'Fraid so."

"Can't they send someone else?"

"Apparently not. And . . . I'm on watch now till midnight. Tomorrow morning I'll be getting my clearance chit filled in."

"Look . . . they can't *do* this. I'll fix something. At least I'll have a good try . . . we're not having this . . ." Yet though he spoke with studied vehemence, anger and sadness refused to come to grips with him. He was like a man who couldn't believe something because he simply didn't want to.

"I don't think you'll be able to."

Around him, phones rang, voices called, typewriters clacked. Behind him, the scrambler telephone from Command buzzed. It blotted out, removed one stage further from him, the reality of Edwina's voice saying, "I'm routed on the 18.35 from Avonmead tomorrow. Shall you be there?"

"Oh, of course. Except that . . . maybe there won't be *any* need. For I'll bloody well do something in the meantime!"

It was only a dozen steps down to Ingleby's office. Must be the old bastard's doing. He'd have it out with him . . . by Christ, he would! But instead he lifted the now urgently buzzing scrambler from Command and said, "Gallagher here."

It was the usual complications.

766 and 732 Squadrons could only muster half the required serviceable aircraft for a low level pinpoint attack that night on Ostend. Gallagher sat down for a moment at his desk, before calling the inevitable ops conference. When finally he saw

169

Ingleby, Edwina was pushed far to the back of his mind.

In fact, he hardly had time to think about her posting again, until almost by force Ash carried him off for a hellishly late supper—almost ten-thirty—at the flat. Even then the fact of Edwina leaving wasn't a reality. It was more like a dull ache ... the sort of ache, Treece had told him in hospital, you got in a leg that wasn't there. And in some peculiar way, his mind wouldn't grapple with it at all.

It was probably for that very reason he told the Ashes about it. As soon as he'd got a bowlful of Rosalie's hot soup inside him, and he felt slightly more normal, he said, "I had a bit of bad news today."

Immediately large-eyed and sympathetic, Rosalie said, "Oh, Gavin darling! I *am* sorry!"

Ken Ash stolidly went on eating.

"D'you want to tell us about it?" Rosalie asked.

"Yes I suppose so. It's about Edwina. She's posted."

Most unexpectedly Rosalie threw back her head and laughed. "Gavin darling!" she said. "You gave me such a fright! I thought something had happened to your parents. I thought they were ill or blitzed. Or something truly *frightful*."

"This is," Gallagher said, and to Ken, "I thought I might try to do something about it."

Ken just raised his brows and in a wise old-owl manner, shook his head and shrugged.

"Well?" Gallagher said.

"Are you asking me what I think?" Ken said. "Or telling me that you're going to?"

"*Asking* you."

"Then *don't* . . . repeat *don't*."

Rosalie cleared the soup plates, and then served them with slices of cold ham. "Far be it from me to interfere," she said, passing Gallagher some sweet pickle. "But Ken is *absolutely* right. Besides," she reached over the table and took Gallagher's hand, "I may be a dumb blonde . . . but *is* a posting all *that* of a *disaster*?"

"I think so. Stanbridge is quite a way."

"But, sweetie, it's near London and there's a *marvellous* train service. You can see her on leaves and whatnot. Go up to town for a spree."

"You'll only make it worse, old boy, if you start sticking your neck out. They'll post her to Timbuctoo. Besides, the set-up at the moment isn't going to last for ever. What if *you* go, and *she* stays?"

"I suppose you're right."

"Ken's always right . . . aren't you, my love? Though I don't often tell him." Rosalie smiled. She played thoughtfully with her charm bracelet. "You know," she went on, "I don't *think*, if I were in Edwina's place, that I'd *want* you to interfere. I'd *hate* you to pull your rank just for me . . ."

"Rosalie knows the woman's angle, you see," Ken explained. "Puts it far better than me."

"And," Rosalie went on, "Edwina's in the Services after all. She's obviously *needed* in Stanbridge . . . they're probably frightfully short of whatever she does. And," she smiled at them in turn, "you're *not* to laugh if I go all patriotic on you, but there *is* a war on, and Edwina's got to do her bit, the same as everyone else."

After that, it was as if the scene at Avonmead station came to blot out everything else he remembered. The train was late. They stood side by side in front of the usual posters. *Careless talk costs lives. Remember to switch it off, Watch that black out, Save for Peace.* The sooty glass canopy allowed in very little of the late afternoon light. Already to each other, their faces were shadowy.

There were only a few other people waiting on the platform for this train: a sailor, two airmen who saluted him, and four or five soldiers.

Edwina had her own luggage beside her. Her white kit-bag with her name and initials and number on it in big blue letters, and a dark leather suitcase. In her free hand, for regardless of who might be looking she held his with the other, she carried her purse and railway warrant. In front of them on the platform was a pile of chip baskets filled with tomatoes. It seemed important to him that he should read the name of the grower three times before the train came in. When he had finished, he looked at Edwina to see she was staring at the baskets with much the same concentrated expression.

With an effort, he said, "And don't forget . . . write just as soon as you get your billet!"

"I will, I promise."

"I'll come up as soon as I can, and we'll give London a thrash."

"You bet we will!"

"And anyway, you'll *like* being near London, won't you?"

"Oh, yes, it'll be fun. And Gavin . . . ?"

"Yes, darling?"

"If you *do* go back flying . . . let me know . . . before . . . if you can, won't you?"

"I promise. And this time, I'll keep my feet dry."

"That's a promise too, isn't it?"

"It's a promise."

There was nothing more to say. The up signal dropped with a clatter, and Gallagher jumped as if it were a guillotine.

She was smiling when she said, "This is it, darling. Here she comes!"

And then everything seemed to dissolve in a flurry of steam, of noise, of pounding pistons, doors opening and shutting, humping the kit-bag over the step, pushing in the case, a quick miserable kiss on her cheek, and then . . . *stand back please*, the last slam of the last door, the whistle, the dropping of the flag, the slow measured pull of the train out of the platform, a wave, blotted out by a cloud of smoke . . .

And she was gone.

He stood for a long time staring at the steel curve of the track, the shunting yard, the shrubs beyond, the houses and the pale mauve rectangle of the evening sky.

When he did at last leave the station, feeling the way he did, it was natural that he should call in Rosalie and Ken's.

Ken was off-duty and mucking around at the back with the car. "We expected you," he said taking the pipe out of his mouth. "At least, Rosalie did. Go along in! I'll be up there myself, as soon as I've cleaned up a bit."

Gallagher had intended to stay only for a drink. But he didn't look forward to the walk back home without Edwina. He stayed till close on midnight, boring them he felt sure, because Rosalie yawned a couple of times, with talk about Edwina.

He could imagine, as they went to bed that night, Rosalie brushing her hair, and saying indulgently to Ken, "Oh, *he*'ll get over it. Give him time."

And if she *did* say that, she was probably right. For once he had got Edwina's first letter, he began to feel better. She wrote well. She sounded happy, and at the same time she managed to convey that she both loved him and missed him. The other girls were friendly and nice to work with. They worked similar shifts to the ones at 81 Group, and they had quite reasonable types in charge of them. The Wingco Ops was known as a bastard, but Edwina said with heavy exclamation marks that she'd been assured he was better than most. Stanbridge had once been a market town. Now it was half in, half out of London. It still had a few ancient cottages and a village cross where the buses started for Hyde Park Corner. She was living in billets in a road called Grange Court Crescent. Wasn't it an elegant address? Although when he saw it, he might not think it such an elegant establishment. Actually it was a Victorian house in a terrace, near the factory end of Stanbridge, and her landlady was a dyed-in-the-wool old Cockney who was extremely kind. She had already been up to town—the fast trains did it in less than half an hour —and it had been nice to see big shops again. One of these evenings, she was going to take herself to the theatre. She ended the letter with all her love, and he carried it around with him beside the cheap little photograph of them both at Brinton.

Now he could picture her in a background, she seemed to have gone less away from him than that day when the train whisked her off. And as the summer went by, the background she drew in her regular twice-weekly letters became almost as real to him as life at 81 Group.

Even if she'd been at Avonmead, he told himself, he would have been able to see very little of her. The Battle of Hamburg had started with an attack of 741 four-engined bombers. Such a conflagration was produced that it created its own hurricane, literally blowing people into the inferno. All services failed, and thousands of acres were obliterated. Further attacks were made during the end of July, and then things quietened down again.

Gallagher wrote to say he was hoping to get long-overdue leave, and he'd be seeing her in the middle of August. They exchanged excited ecstatic plans of what they would do. And then, just when everything seemed settled, and he was about to go, another crisis started.

A place called Peenemunde, high on the shores of the Baltic, was producing (according to the official hand-out) special night-fighter radar, which would make our bomber losses even heavier than they were. This was a special attack, and had to be carefully prepared, so that Gallagher rang Edwina at her landlady's and explained that his leave would now have to be postponed till the end of the month. But that would positively be the latest. With luck it might be earlier.

On the night of 17/18th August, 577 bombers attacked Peenemunde. Studying the photographs afterwards, Gallagher was somewhat puzzled by a huge concrete emplacement, on which was built what looked like a catapult on rails. But one thing, however, was quite clear: the raid was a success.

A week afterwards, Edwina's usual Tuesday letter did not appear. He was busy at the time, detailing the Peenemunde results, and its non-appearance did no more than make him slightly irritable. When Thursday came and still no letter had come, he rang her landlady's number.

He was told, it was unobtainable.

"What d'you mean . . . *unobtainable*?" he asked the operator furiously. "Try them again till it is!"

Finally, she came up with the information that the number was no longer in service. And for the first time, he felt a twist of fear in his stomach. Regardless of whether he ought to, or ought not to, he told the girl on the switchboard to get him 92 Group. When he finally got 92 Group, he asked for Operations, MF/DF Section.

And when they answered, in a matter-of-fact voice without giving his name, he asked to speak to L.A.C.W. Corrie. And in as matter-of-fact manner, the voice at the other end told him she was dead.

Edwina had been dead for four days before he knew. Gallagher's mind, stunned at first by the news, fastened on that fact as the first terrible whip with which to flay himself. All through that day, while he must have handed over the squadron states and the readiness orders to Aitcheson, while he told the Controller that he was leaving immediately and would not be back at Group until the following afternoon, that fact seemed to clamour at the back of his head until he wondered if he was saying it aloud.

He was appalled that this could have happened to her without any presentiment in him, without an uneasiness at the time, without the slightest feeling of calamity. It seemed to make her death also a desertion, as if in some way she had abandoned him. There was no one he could ever explain that to—except Edwina. She was the only one who, knowing the sometimes telepathic communication they had with one another, would have understood.

Somehow, Ken Ash had got to know about Edwina. It was Ash who put through another call to 92 Group, and who found out a bit more of what had happened. "Because," as he said, "it's better to hear it from a friend than from strangers."

The Sunday before, the house with the elegant address had received a direct hit. Three other girls had been in the house, besides Edwina. They would feel nothing, of course. It had come very quickly.

"Sunday," Gallagher said. "What time?"

"Ten forty-nine. Edwina had just come off watch."

He could see Ken Ash looking at him anxiously, wondering if he was going to break down, if he was going to say "Christ, if only the bloody transport had been late! If only she hadn't worked that shift! If only I hadn't let her be posted!"

"I'll run you to the station," Ash said. "If we hurry . . . you can get the two eight."

He couldn't remember telling Ash that he was going to Stanbridge. Perhaps the man assumed that he must. He didn't know himself until that moment *where* he was going. But the very fact of having somewhere to get to momentarily eased him.

"Just drop me," he said at the station, when Ash made as if to get out of the car and see him off. "I want to be on my own."

He couldn't have anyone else standing with him on this same platform. He paced up and down, hands in his pockets, hoping this time the train wouldn't be late. It wasn't as if he yet felt grief. It was this feeling of emptiness and abandonment.

Before in his life he had glimpsed such a feeling, but at a distance. Flying over the sea on a moonlit night, he could remember experiencing a similar sensation of almost primeval fear. He was caught in some terrifying nothingness, an eternity of emptiness. As if the whole universe was some silent wilderness

. . . nebulous, uncharted, unsupported, without substance, because there was nothing on which it hinged. And again, when he was first learning to fly, he would dream that without warning, the aeroplane fell out of his hands, or he was baling out in a parachute, and the parachute dissolved, or he was climbing a mountain and it disappeared—and then, all support gone, he was falling into unending nothingness.

When the train arrived at the platform, he was glad of something on which to focus his eyes, glad of something to do—even if it was only opening a door, finding an empty compartment, putting himself in it.

At the moment, he was untroubled by any pictures of waving Edwina off from this platform, of Edwina herself staring out of the window as he now stared . . . of seeing (or probably because she had left him) *not* seeing, the countryside moving past the window.

Arriving in Stanbridge, he took a taxi to the address on the top of Edwina's letters. He had at first thought he would go to 92 Group H.Q., but there was nothing that they could tell him, nothing for that matter that anyone could tell him. He just had to see for himself. Speed now seemed to him imperative. He was impatient when they were held up by traffic lights. He was irritated when, arriving at the bombed site, the driver asked him if he was sure he'd got the right address.

He was here. And he breathed a sigh that was almost of relief. The houses on either side of where Edwina had lived were exactly as he had imagined them, gaunt and tall and grey. Their windows had been shattered, their chimney pots were in their gardens, but otherwise they were intact.

Only Edwina's house was missing—simply torn out of the terrace. One neighbour still bore on its wall a fireplace, a flapping piece of blue wallpaper, a length of lead piping. He averted his eyes from the pile of rubble on the ground. It was as if he had arrived the moment it had all happened, and he was afraid of what he would see.

He stood there a long time. Dimly he was aware that passers-by along the busy street stared at him curiously, and noticing his uniform, hurried on. Strangely enough, their faces as they stared seemed to print themselves on his mind, so that weeks later he could recall them in more minute detail than the faces of friends . . . a middle-aged man with glasses, a woman with swimmy blue eyes, a schoolgirl in brown uniform.

After a while, he forced himself to look at the heap of grey stone and slates and kitchen tiles and ordinary household things —a gas-cooker, a water-tank—twisted and made monstrous, a few steps climbing into nothing, a broken bath with its taps catching the sunlight, the headboard of a bed, unscratched. He couldn't picture Edwina here—ever. It was nothing to do with her or him. He could smell the dust of powdered stone, and then there was something that he *could* recognize . . . for in spite of the traffic, the feet and voices of passers-by, there hung silence.

It was then that the stone bulwarks of the houses on either side seemed to touch some chord of memory in him. Gaunt and grey and grim, they reminded him of the grey sea at Brinton, and the windowless eyes of the gunposts staring across at it. He remembered vividly the feeling of being caught between two inhuman adversaries.

Then he had turned to Edwina. Now all that remained was rubble—and silence.

It was in almost conscious flight from that silence, an instinct maybe of mental preservation, that his mind sought for anger and revenge.

While he stood there, a middle-aged woman stopped right in front of him. He couldn't remember what she looked like. He could only remember her mouth, which was large and pale.

"Give it 'em back, eh?" she said, her eyes travelling from the rubble to him, fastening a second on his uniform, and then returning to the rubble again. "Give it 'em back . . . with interest!"

INTERLUDE TWO

THURSDAY lunch time, there was still no news. Reports coming in to North Luddenham were still negative. The conference in the Station Commander's office had continued till almost dawn, and though Ingleby had advised him "to get some shut-eye like I'm going to do", all Henderson had done was to go and lie down, fully clothed on his bed.

He had had Gallagher's Service documents, the lectures and researches he'd done, the papers he'd written, all his private letters, insurance policies and bank-statements brought to his room in the Mess. The man had obviously been something of a hoarder—some people always hang on to these things—and there were six great piles of stuff stacked on the table for him to go through. On the other hand, somewhat in contrast to Bunting's recollections, everything was meticulously neat, sorted out under separate headings in files or on paper clips.

He began looking through them after breakfast, but during the morning he was being continually interrupted by phone calls and messages. The net had now been extended to the Midlands and to Yorkshire. Air Ministry were getting more pressing. Twice he had been asked point-blank what line he was following. He detailed the thoroughness of the search, but admitted that so far he had no theory.

The only slight clue he kept to himself. There were no physical indications whatever as to what had happened. All he had were two opposing ideas of a man's character, which might or might not suggest conflict. As the hours went by, he was giving up hope that the whole incident was an accident. They would be sure to have heard by now. All through his mind when he was trying to rest whirled the other alternatives—but each one seemed to have a complete cast-iron alibi against it. There was no evidence at all of mental disorder. The man was at the top of his job, with a distinguished past and a big future. Hardly the sort to be a traitor.

And yet, as Henderson knew from experience, from some damned hidden reason or other, often they were just the sort.

He had a clear picture of Gallagher's face and physical appearance. Now as he walked round the Mess and the Station, he tried to get inside Gallagher's mind. Gallagher walked down this corridor: Gallagher looked at these pictures: Gallagher drank at this bar. That rocket site was Gallagher's responsibility—how would *he* feel in Gallagher's shoes? Gallagher knew these men— Warrant Officer Boase and the other Console Operators, Squadron Leader Mumford and the technicians. All the time he was interviewing them, Henderson was considering what Gallagher's opinion would be of them.

Gallagher wrote this letter to Group. Gallagher came down like a ton of hot bricks on these characters for carelessness. Gallagher walked down this path. Gallagher saluted that flag. Gallagher ate lunch in this dining-room, as he was doing now . . .

He heard the sound of a chair being moved over the floor. Then Air-Marshal Ingleby's voice said, "Any news?"

"Nothing, I'm afraid, sir."

He passed over the menu card—Brown Windsor soup, mutton, bread-and-butter pudding. They were alone at the table. Since it was getting on for two o'clock, most of the other officers had left to do the day-to-day administration of the Station. As Ingleby started on his lunch, he said, "I saw Mrs. Gallagher this morning."

"How is she?"

"Upset. Almost hysterical. I didn't stay long."

"I'm going along later today."

"So she said. But there's no help there, I'm afraid."

"Hasn't she any idea of her own?"

"Talked vaguely about accidents, loss of memory——"

"There's nothing in his medical record to suggest that."

"Don't forget that crash in the sea." Ingleby finished off his soup, and wiped his lips with a napkin. "Got badly knocked about, you know. On his head and his left leg. Still walks with a limp."

"Surely . . . in uniform and wearing identity discs . . . he'd have been found?"

"You'd have *thought* so."

"Did Mrs. Gallagher say anything else?"

Ingleby shook his head. "She's too full of how it affects *her*. Not how it affects *us*."

"I'd still like to see her, sir. I can't understand why she didn't give the alarm."

"She thought he'd be over at the rocket site."

"All night?"

"The exigencies of the Service . . ."

"Wouldn't a wife have expected him to phone?"

Ingleby started in on his mutton and roast potatoes. "Mmm . . . depends on . . . well, their domestic arrangements."

"Sir, this is a delicate question . . . but d'you think the marriage was happy?"

"Seemed so. She's a pretty little thing."

"Ninety times out of a hundred . . . when aircraftmen disappear . . . they go off to some woman. I don't see why we should exclude the possibility of Group Captains doing the same thing."

"Gallagher . . . a woman? He did once get . . . well, most unsuitably involved. But that was a long time ago. Can't dismiss it completely, of course . . . but I wouldn't have thought he'd do the same thing again . . ."

THE BLUE-EYED-BOY

I

IT was unlikely that Air Vice-Marshal Ingleby would have yielded to Gallagher's repeated and insistent requests for an operational squadron posting, had it not been for a switch in R.A.F. policy, in which Ingleby insisted 81 Group be involved.

Gallagher did not dwell upon the fact that his posting was achieved less by his own very real desire for revenge, than by the A.O.C.'s knack of getting his Group into the limelight. And having done that, his flair for choosing the right men for the right jobs, and bringing them together, regardless.

Since Edwina's death, everything around him at 81 Group—his office, his job, his conferences, the countryside he walked along, even sometimes the Ashes themselves had become memory-laden and unbearable. During those two miserable months, there had been several squadron vacancies which Gallagher had asked to be posted to. Without success. "You're more use here," Ingleby would say. "Hang on a while. Things are building up. Wait and see!"

Of the five or six pilots resting between tours at 81 Group, Gallagher and Ash had done the longest ground service. And there wasn't one of them who wasn't conscious that the war was moving to a climax. For in the last half of 1943, Bomber Command was operating at full spate and at maximum efficiency. Duisberg, Dortmund, Hamburg—the industrial towns of Germany ticker-taped through as targets for tonight.

But in October of that year, a new target had begun to emerge. A Directorate had been formed to co-ordinate all information on the peculiar catapults that had puzzled Gallagher in the Peenemunde photographs. It was now known that the aircrews on that trip had been purposely misinformed—partly to make them keener to attack, partly because the target was then so secret. Those curious emplacements had nothing to do with night-fighter radar. They were in fact the launching platforms for pilotless missiles.

Hidden in orchards and fir forests, over seventy of these earth-and-concrete emplacements had now been built in an arc between Dunkirk and Abbeville. All aimed at London or southern ports, they would cause immense destruction and chaos behind our lines, menacing all allied plans for invasion. The danger was immediately recognized. A top secret meeting of politicians and Chiefs of Staff was hurriedly convened. The total destruction of all rocket sites was called for, and the Operation was code-named *Crossbow*.

Coming back from that conference, Ingleby wore the shine and flush of victory in his face. Since the saturation bombing technique could not be used in friendly countries, it had been planned to give the task to American Fortresses and the Tactical Air Force to do in daylight. But Ingleby very quickly pointed out 81 Group's excellent record for low-level pinpoint bombing, and on arrival at Avonmead, he lost no time in sending for Gallagher.

Skipping the trivialities of greeting he said, "Well now, I think I've managed to get you what you want."

Gallagher was not deceived by the implication that his Air Officer Commanding had spent a portion of this highly urgent conference trying to get Gallagher airborne. It was all part of what Ingleby would call the personal touch, the oiling of the creaking wheels of war.

"It's a plum of a job. Right up your street."

"Flying, sir?"

"But of course. Wouldn't dare to give it you unless." He twinkled at Gallagher. "Now sit down, Gavin. No, better still . . . come over here! Let me put you in the picture."

He walked across to the huge wall-map of Europe, and with his forefinger he ringed the Pas de Calais area. "The battle-ground of Operation *Crossbow*. That's where we're going to smash the German Vengeance weapons!"

As Gallagher listened to what Ingleby had to say, it became more and more apparent that these missiles were in every sense a terror weapon. No one knew their range, their explosive capability, their accuracy. They were more likely to cause panic—killing non-combatants—than to destroy military targets. There was at present no known defence against them, except obliteration at their breeding grounds. Each site, regardless of day, night or weather could send off two hundred of these destroying machines every twenty-four hours. Each site was equipped with its own road and railway. Each site was heavily defended.

Vengeance Weapons, Gallagher thought to himself. So that's what they were called. And he was to take part in their destruction. He smiled. For the first time in months, he felt a spasm of pure unallayed pleasure. A pilotless machine of indiscriminate destruction. A murder weapon inhuman and unpitiable. A hand-made custom-designed symbol for Gallagher's own ache for that self-same vengeance.

Since Edwina died, if ever there had been a man without a star, Gallagher had been he. Now he had been given one. The void was filled. Dimly, and not without some consciousness of irony, he felt the possibility of recovery.

"We're forming 777 Squadron, concentrating on low-level night-bombing. Hertfords with first-class aircrews." He paused "Gavin . . . you're to command it."

Ingleby's finger jumped across the Channel and landed on a spot some twenty miles from Avonmead. "There, Gavin. Hutton-le-Wold. Well, now . . . take a good look at it. That's your new stamping ground. Two good pubs. One, they tell me, has an excellent cellar. The church runs a dance in the village hall once a week. Good for that limp . . ."

He went on at some length putting Gallagher in the Hutton-le-Wold picture . . . peace-time Mess . . . good long runways . . .

But this time Gallagher wasn't listening. He would find all that out for himself. His mind was already seeing those launching pads with an almost obsessive fascination. Already sums were forming in his head; concrete thickness ratioed to bombweight, estimated flak, possible patterns of attack.

Tactics formed like beautiful visions in his imagination. The hideous mechanical form of this missile weapon, its absence of crew, absolved him from any need of pity—underground workers protected like wasps in their grey chambers became inhuman, Valkyrie-like, expendable.

He became aware that Ingleby was dismissing him. "Well, Gavin, we must throw a party before you walk out on us. Drinks on me. I insist! We must wet that new command of yours!"

Gallagher hoped he managed a thank you and a suitably grateful smile. He couldn't remember. Already 81 Group and Ingleby were moving away and behind him, like countryside passed in a train. The day-to-day present doings at Avonmead were ceasing to concern him.

The first thing he did when he left the A.O.C. was to go and see Fairbairn in Group Intelligence, a clued-up type if ever there was one who knew something about rockets. He gave Gallagher all he had on the subject. As far back as 1914, the British had been experimenting on rocket-missiles. In 1917, Professor A. M. Low had taken out a patent on them. However, the British Military minds were engaged for the next twelve years on the bitter battle of horse *versus* tank: and it was the Germans who took on the researching. It was known that a rocket had been fired from a submerged U-boat. Lying on his bed, reading through Intelligence reports that evening, Gallagher began to glimpse the long-range dangers of this new weapon. There were diagrams of launching sites, showing ski-shaped buildings, firing ramps, assembly sheds. He became so absorbed that he forgot he had been invited to the Ashes for supper.

"It's all right . . . we understood," Ken said in the bar next evening. "Bad news travels fast. We'd heard you were leaving us. Damn and blast! And I thought I'd be the one to get posted first."

"Don't be in too much of a hurry. You're all right as you are."

There was a pause. Ken looked down at his tankard. "Actually . . . Rosalie and I were talking about Hutton-le-Wold. Sounds all right."

"Not bad."

"Good long runways."

"So I believe."

"I hear they're making up a new squadron. Short of a pilot or three."

Gallagher started to say, "How the hell *do* these things get around?" when he noticed the expression on Ken's face, and began to understand. "Well . . . what is it?"

"I'd like to be one of the lucky bods, that's all," Ash said quietly. "I was wondering if you could put in a word to the wise, as it were?" He finished with an embarrassed little laugh, and added, "If you want me, that is."

And that was the hell of it. Just as suddenly as he'd noticed

184

Ken's face, now belatedly he realized that he didn't want Ash on the squadron at all. Partly because the Ashes, like 81 Group, carried too many memories of a past that he wanted to forget. Partly because already, instinctively, he wanted younger men.

"I'll see what I can do," Gallagher said vaguely.

Ash smiled. "Thanks. And I'll see if I can pull any strings on my own."

On his way up to his room, Gallagher made a mental note not to talk any more about his plans to Ash—or to anyone else for that matter. There were a number of pilots he'd noticed on his rounds of the Stations who had struck him as press-on types. Those were the people he wanted. He also had in mind a king-pin navigator and a thoroughly genned-up bombing leader.

During the days that remained to him at Group, Ash's request went unregarded and largely forgotten in so many other ideas, plans and things he had to do. He got himself up to Air Ministry for his medical, and with little difficulty managed to talk his way through it. Detachment to a Heavy Conversion Unit on to Hertfords came in five days later. And he was in the process of loosening his bonds with Avonmead, when Ash button-holed him in the corridor of the Mess, that Saturday evening just before six.

"Don't be too busy for a drink before you go. Drop in this evening. Any time will do."

Gallagher was both surprised and relieved by the casualness of the invitation. Once or twice, a horrid thought had crossed his mind that the Ashes might make a big do of his going . . . throw a cocktail party or lay on a big dinner.

"Thanks," he said, momentarily noticing that old Ken's grin was somewhat wider than usual. "I'd love to. Round about nine?"

"It's a deal."

Congratulating himself on the neatness of his arrangements, prepared gently to sever this last bond, Gallagher presented himself at the yellow-painted flat door. Rosalie was, of course, dressed up for the occasion.

"Come in," she said. "Ken's getting the drinks. Who's going to sing Auld Lang Syne?"

She was looking very beautiful, and stagily sad. Ken produced the drinks in silence. Conversation when it began was somewhat stilted. Perhaps because he was so glad to get away, Gallagher rather overdid his expressions of regret. Occasionally Ken Ash looked at him wryly. He said very little. Gallagher said they must drive down for a meal on him one night. He'd heard there was a good pub.

Suddenly Rosalie choked into her drink. "I can't bear it any longer!" Gallagher had the embarrassed fear that she was crying. She dabbed her eyes. "Ken, darling, you've *got* to tell him. It's *fiendishly* cruel!"

But even before Ken began, with some uncanny instinct Gallagher knew. He almost said it aloud *for* him. Ken Ash's posting had come in that afternoon. It was to Hutton-le-Wold. To 777 Squadron.

"Hold on to your hat, Gavin! Fasten your belt! You can't back out. The Ashes are coming, too!"

Close to the French coast, haze hung over the sea and Gallagher had to take them up to five hundred feet to get over it. On either side of him, the Hertfords seemed stationary, moving gently up and down, up and down, like big black boats in harbour.

Seven of them—the best number for these low-level attacks on rocket-sites. More, and they got in each other's way. Less, and there was risk of failure. This was the ninth raid 777 Squadron had made, after four weeks' low flying navigational exercises, finding pin-point targets on the Norfolk fens. When he had first joined them just on the New Year, Gallagher's reception had been cool. He still walked with a slight limp. He had more than a year's gap in his flying log-book. All the four-engined experience he had was his fortnight's conversion course on Hertfords. His pilots were a tough and battle-hardened bunch, complete with scruffy uniforms and decorations. His rigid training programme had not been popular. Not all the attacks had been successful, and they had lost three aircraft. Only when it was apparent that the new Wing Commander intended to lead every raid himself did the atmosphere completely thaw out.

"Estimating Sangatte in six minutes, Skipper," his navigator said. "At seventeen thirty-one."

"Roger. I'll let you know if I see it."

Jenkins had previously been a schoolmaster. Navigation—

especially with such latest aids as Oboe and radar—was to him no more than a mathematical exercise. Come flak or fighters, he remained as unruffled in front of his charts as in front of a blackboard, oblivious of the fact that the whole formation depended on his accuracy.

"New course . . . 145."

Gallagher adjusted the grid-ring on the compass. "145."

The compass needle now lay like a luminous brooch between the parallel lubberlines. He looked up and turned his head to the right, saw S, K and L lying a little behind him, stretched out in the path of a yellowish setting sun. How slowly, he thought, their propellers turn: you can almost see each individual blade, like silver porpoises leaping and diving. Then he glanced over to port.

All present and correct. J and B, and far out on the left wing, Ken Ash in F for Freddie.

The Ashes had arrived in the middle of January. Rosalie had said she wasn't going to be left on her own in the flat, and they had taken a room in the *Falconers' Arms* in Hutton main square, where 777 Squadron often did their drinking. Gallagher spent a good deal of what spare time he got down there with them. And they had, in fact, all three had tea in the little oak-panelled lounge, before Ken and he had walked up to the aerodrome together through the winter sunshine.

"Increase speed to 155, please."

It was essential to arrive neither too early nor too late. He inched open the throttles, "Increasing."

Then he pulled back the side window. The steady burr of the engine noise increased as the cool air rushed in to flow over his face. He pushed his helmet a little further back, and rubbed the sweat off his forehead with the flat of his hand. Outside now, further evidence of evening, blue bubbles of flame formed and burst and broke on the exhausts: but the sun was still strong enough to send on the mist a grey ghost tagging behind each aircraft and to ring that shadow round with the rainbow skin of red, green and violet that is known as "glory".

"Land ahead!"

From the prone bomb-aiming position in the nose, Parry called the warning over the intercom, and seconds later, Gallagher saw it, a dark flat stain just below the haze.

"Sangatte," Jenkins identified it laconically. "Watch out for the welcome!"

Gallagher ached to go down to the deck, under the coverage of the German radar, fanning out from the coast. Now he tried it, dipping his nose down, but immediately the stuff came up like grey surf, foaming round the front guns.

"Three minutes to go before the coast."

Gallagher acknowledged his navigator briefly, and then as though to excuse his height. "At least this mist'll be good camouflage for us."

"So long as it doesn't cover the target."

"It'll peter out away from the water."

"Hope so."

"Like to bet on it?"

The bet was never made. Out of the haze came sudden smoke-puffs, coloured mustard-and-black. Caught close on top of one, O Orange lurched to the right, and Gallagher heard the ripping noise of fragmentary metal tearing through the fuselage.

"Christ!" the front gunner called out. "Shore batteries! What do they think we are? The Navy?"

"Bastards have hit us, too!"

Gallagher said, "Only centre section skin. Parry . . . have a look-see what's happened. You all right, rear gunner?"

"I'm all right, sir."

Gallagher's eyes went first port and then starboard. Still seven. The heavy flak got more erratic, then faded altogether as the formation slid over the sands. Parry reported a bloody great hole the size of a football in the port fuselage, but nothing to worry about. Now that surprise no longer entered into it, Gallagher said over the R/T microphone strapped on his helmet. "Come on now! Close in tight . . . and watch for fighters!"

Obediently, they came nearer to O Orange.

"Closer . . . for God's sake! Closer!"

Now he had them all comfortably tucked up, hugging the air around him. Gradually, the sea mist began to dissolve. He could see houses, railway lines, roads, even the faces of people looking up as he led them right down, just above the tops of the trees. Long shadows slatted the flat fields. From a concrete pill-box ahead, a stream of red tracer came up, only to be met and somehow stopped in mid-air by a fan-shaped pattern from the

188

seven front gunners. A formation of fighters was reported taking off, climbing, formating, following.

"New course . . . one eight one."

They were cutting between the flak belts of Marquise and Guines.

"Me 109s . . . twelve . . . two o'clock . . . high."

"Closer!" Gallagher called out to them. *"Closer!"*

Their wing tips within inches, now it was as though one huge aircraft was roaring just above the ground. The fighters came in. Gallagher felt the whole fuselage of Orange shudder as the rear gunner opened up. Then two dark shapes flashed just above him.

"Hit anything, Bond?"

"No, skipper."

Low like this made it difficult for fighters. The Messerschmidts wheeled above them to come in again.

"Estimate Clercourt rocket site . . . six minutes time, skipper."

Dead ahead, a curtain of flak rose up to meet them. Again the front gunners replied—and then they were through it.

Still seven.

A steeple showed up, a small town ringed by chimneys came rocketing towards them. Now darkness was beginning to creep over everything: the sun had melted into a blaze of red and gold. Second by second, things were getting more difficult to see. A high electric pylon materialized out of the dusk, and Gallagher pulled up just in time.

Finding and identifying the target was now on his mind. Another burst of light guns came spluttering up, but at least the fighters had been shaken off. Time began to drag endlessly. He had visions of going on and on through France—leading the formation like a Pied Piper on and on until . . .

"The Liane."

The river flashed past, thick and grey. They were very close now. Below them were the tops of fir trees, massed like regiments of soldiers.

Standing beside him, his engineer said, "There, skipper! Dead ahead!"

The concrete showed up like a white scar on the ground. The long ski-slope launching ramp, the huts and the redoubts, he could see them all quite clearly. And beyond, the railway line going through the woods, and the huge trucks, one after the other, each with its horizontal rocket.

"O.K., everybody!" he said over the R/T. "Break formation and circle to port!"

They circled, to begin dropping their incendiaries, while Gallagher flew forward.

"Bomb doors open!"

He heard the whine of the hydraulics. The front turret had opened up. He screwed up his eyes, and now he picked out against the backcloth of the ramp figures moving, the long silver shape of a horizontal flying bomb. Low down now, he checked his height, as he had learned to do, with the sides of his eyes, on the just visible horizon.

"Left ... left ... stead-y-y!"

A moment like this lasted for ever. He could feel the blood hammering through his veins. The dry mouth, the sticky feel of the control column in his hands, all around the phosphorescent green glimmer of the instruments. Bombing was a physical experience—yet it exploded afterwards in an emotional satisfaction. No wonder some people had to return again and again for the thrill of the injection. It was like a high-powered drug. Never could they get a lift so high without it—the breathless dizzy tightrope between killing and being killed.

"Marker gone!"

Rear gunner reported, "Dead on target!"

All around them now, the fir trees were alight, and as he turned, there behind them now was a great green glow. The whole atmosphere was like being inside a lighted lamp. In the illumination, the shapes of the Hertfords could be seen like giant moths round a flame. Circuiting all the same way in such brightness, careful to maintain a safe height, they could avoid each other easily. Like the spokes of a wheel, tracer poured from their guns.

Gallagher spoke into his microphone. "O.K., Baker ... go on in."

"Baker turning and running up."

Abruptly, the firing from the other aircraft stopped. Gallagher watched, his eyes alternating between the instruments and the view outside. The form was to lob the bomb into the concrete non-magnetic building, in line with the firing ramp and a hundred yards away from it. The compass was housed there, and the steering system. Suddenly he saw the luminous green core of the target indicator turn magnesium white.

"Bloody good, Baker!" He paused. "Now McCallister . . . your turn!"

"S Sugar turning . . ."

That one was to port. "S Sugar," someone shouted, "you need glasses!"

"L . . . London," Gallagher said. "Quickly now!"

"London turning."

Firing from the ground started up sporadically. A searchlight flickered a sudden dazzling addition to the whole weird scene. Momentarily, it glowed on O Orange's cockpit before Bond in the rear turret finally extinguished it.

L's aim was better—bang on the firing hut. In rapid succession came J and K. The whole centre of the target seemed to be molten fire, as though it was an erupting volcano. As the fir trees blazed below, he saw Smith, his engineer, standing beside him, saw the yellow flames reflected on his face, watched him catch his eye and smile with excitement, so that he knew his own face must also show that same exhilaration. He had throttled the engines back, and in the cockpit he could smell the smoke that was now drifting in great clouds all over the ground, lurid with reflections of the flames.

Some people bomb from sheer scientific interest, some for the joy of it, some because they've got to. And to a few—a very few in the R.A.F.—every white explosion was a balm to some soreness. As Gallagher looked down now at the blazing ruins below, more than any other emotion, it was satisfaction he felt. Another of them gone. Another inhuman monster stamped out. He did not consider the possibility of men being down there. It was the machine he was destroying. Pushed forward in operational flying by guilt, now he was obsessively propelled by the desire for revenge.

He spoke into his microphone again. "Now F for Freddie."

There was no reply. Just for a moment, his heart lurched. Louder than he intended, he called out, "Ken?"

"Okay . . . okay," an unruffled voice came back over the air to him.

"Where are you?"

"Turning on target."

There was another blinding flash.

"Nice work!" Gallagher watched the fantastic scene below him: the silhouettes of the Hertfords stamped against a smoky cauldron of markers, fires, blazing fir woods, every now and then spattered with illuminated dots, as an airgunner let go a last sporadic burst.

"Right . . . everybody O.K.? Thwaite?"

"Thwaite here."

"McCallister?"

"McCallister still mobile."

He went through the lot quickly, like a schoolmaster calling the roll. They all answered. Nobody damaged except for a few bullet-holes. He felt the relief flow through him. "Now scarper back home . . . everybody! Get that bloody barman out of bed . . . and we'll continue the party in the bar!"

They left, going back independently. Now Gallagher made his own run, dropped his bomb and climbed. There was no opposition. No evidence of any life whatever. Sudden *whoofs* of explosions were still going on, tiny bursts of added brilliance in the centre of the furnace.

Gallagher said, "There's one rocket commander who's out of a job! Now let's go home!"

There was a sudden blare of power as he pushed the throttles hard against the stops. Light now, the aircraft's speed shot up, the needle on the airspeed indicator flickering round the numbers 160-170-180 on the dial, as the Hertford roared northwards.

The mist had cleared. There was not a cloud in the sky. Orion glittered in the south, and now in the east a full orange moon was rising. To emulate the stationary frozen fireworks show above came a few tinkles of light flak from the ground. There was no other opposition. The trip over the Channel was a ride on the gravy train. As the dark coast of England showed up again, Gallagher began to climb.

He still felt the exhilaration pulsating through him. Throughout the aircraft there was chattering, excitement, congratulation. Outside, the engines muttered sweetly, and Gallagher felt in this flying—in the cool dark air, in the silvery path of the moon on the sea, in coming back, knowing everyone was safe—a relaxed contentment he knew he could get from nothing else.

They coast-crawled round East Anglia, then crossed the Lincolnshire coast just above Boston. The crew started packing up. Parry shared out the orange juice and the chocolate from the uneaten rations. Jenkins said, "Gee fix ten miles east of the aerodrome. Can you see Hutton now, Skipper?"

"Yep . . . dead ahead. Landing positions . . . everybody!"

There was the flarepath—the usual string of pearls. But this time beside it was a bright bonfire, as though a fragment of what they had left at Clercourt had come back here.

Nobody said anything. They were given permission to land. As usual, Smith stood beside him, putting down his gear and flaps.

Slowly lower, they descended on the approach—over the boundary, level with the runway. All the time, Gallagher was conscious of the fire glowing bigger and brighter.

"Throttles right back!"

There was a pause of sudden quietness. Then a bump, and they were down. Gradually, the tail dropped.

They were already just crawling along when they came to the flames. Bright yellow edged with red, then a pillar of smoke that towered dark against the moonwashed sky. Well off the runway were figures and fire engines. There were sparks and the sound of jumping jacks as the gun ammunition exploded. In the centre of it all was the black double fin of a Hertford.

Smith said, "Poor bastard!"

He saw in Smith's face momentarily as they passed the blazing aircraft just the same vivid greasepaint effect that had been there over the holocaust of Clercourt. But the expression was different, and knowing that, now as then, the engineer was reflecting his own emotions, normal human emotions, saw instead of excited exhilaration . . . pity, fear, and apprehension.

He turned off the runway, feeling suddenly sick and immensely tired. A lorry was waiting for him at dispersal. Nobody said much as they humped their parachutes into it. A hush fell as he walked into Operations. A W.A.A.F. officer poured rum out of a stone jar into seven mugs and gave them one each. Gallagher drank, and then wiped his mouth. "Which was it?"

"F."

"What happened?"

"Swung."

"Anybody get out?"

"Nobody."

Gallagher went through the debriefing automatically. There was a subdued atmosphere throughout the Control Room. When he said that the rocket station was knocked out, the Intelligence Officer murmured something about it being a good show—but apart from that, nobody spoke. When it was over, Jenkins said, "The lorry for the Mess is outside, sir."

"Tell it to go off without me."

He had a cigarette, then went off to the locker-room, took off his flying clothes and put on his hat and greatcoat. He walked down past S.H.Q. out of the main gate, then turned left towards the village.

It was one o'clock in the morning.

He had the curious impression that this was a completely different life he was living. It bore no relation whatever to the one only a few hours ago, when he had sauntered up from Hutton-le-Wold with Ken Ash towards the sunlit aerodrome.

Not another soul moved. Not a glimmer of light showed from any of the windows. His own footsteps clanged against the grey stone walls and were echoed back at him, sounding twice as loud. He passed the shuttered shops, the silent church, the forlorn garage with its solitary pump. He reached the square, passed the bandstand, and saw opposite him as though waiting all the time, the snow-cemmed front of the *Falconers' Arms*.

Suddenly, he had the most curiously strong feeling that he was being watched. There was a greeny tinge to the bright moonlight, and his own shadow moved in and out of the stationary shadows of the leafless lime trees. He looked up at the windows of the inn, coming rapidly closer and larger.

But there was no sign there: no crack in the blackout: no light: nobody waiting: no sign of any eyes.

And yet he *knew*.

Subconsciously he had slowed his pace, trying to steel himself up to what he had to do. Already his hands were tightly clenched, and they moved stiffly by his sides. Now he quickened his step purposely, intent on not giving away to those watching eyes anything at all.

He used the side door. It was unlocked specially for Ken Ash's return. He walked into the hall of the inn. As he turned to go up the dark stairs, a light suddenly went on, and he saw Rosalie's face staring down at him from the landing.

2

It rained the day of the funeral. Ken was buried with three of his crew in the particular corner of Hutton churchyard reserved for airmen. Gallagher was one of the pallbearers.

He hated the funeral, and he was pretty sure Ken Ash would have hated it, too—what with Rosalie in a black suit and a black hat, standing at a distance, weeping uncontrollably, the sound underlining the wail of the Last Post.

But once it was over, he promptly forgot about it.

For the next four days, if he wasn't flying on ops, he was planning, doing the Squadron bumph, briefing, examining photographs, going over intelligence Reports, or swearing on the blower to Group. Back in the drinks-all-round-for-the-poor-sod-who-bought-it mentality of operational flying, he found that Ash's death impinged on him hardly at all.

Now and again in the midst of all this, Rosalie Ash kept cropping up in his mind: he must go along and find out how she was making out, when she was leaving and where she was going. But there was no specific moment when he could actually find the time to do so.

All the same, when he arrived in the Mess at lunch time on Saturday, after a conference on aerodrome defence with the G.C., he felt a pang of guilt when he saw a telephone message-slip for him on the letter board. He knew it was from Rosalie before he opened it.

Please, *please* if he wasn't flying that evening would he come and see her? But *early*.

It was because he felt he was incapable of really being a comfort to anyone, with the possible exception of Edwina, that Gallagher wished he could in all honesty say they were on readiness. But he couldn't, and dreading the sight of her grief-stricken face, he got away as soon as he could from the squadron offices.

195

He walked down to the village, arriving at the *Falconers' Arms* just after six.

Rosalie was waiting for him in the bar. To his immense relief, she was both dry-eyed and smiling. She had obviously taken trouble to dress herself nicely and her golden hair looked as though it had been freshly washed and set. Naïvely, he felt reassured, and somewhat clumsily, as if not sure it was the proper thing to do in the circumstances, he complimented her on her appearance.

"Thank you," she said. "Since you haven't seen me for so long, you might have found me changed." She patted his hand to show him that she didn't mean it.

But her smiling appearance of composure didn't last. They were sitting in the corner at a table by the window, drinking martinis, when Rosalie told him why she'd asked him to come.

"I wouldn't have asked you otherwise," she said, her mouth trembling. "After all, if you'd *wanted* to come, you'd have come." And waving aside his protests, "It's just that I'd like to carry out . . ." her voice shook ". . . Ken's wishes."

Gallagher covered her hand then, and she held on tightly to his as if to some lifeline.

"First of all, he always wanted you to have . . ." her voice exploded in a terrible hysterical burst that was neither laughter nor tears ". . . that dreadful old car."

"Oh, I *couldn't* do that, Rosalie!" He felt outraged, almost as if something had been demanded of him, instead of given.

"But he *wanted* you to. Truly! Honestly! Ken would never let *me* drive in case . . ." that awful sound exploded again ". . . I hurt myself. Me . . . I ask you! I hurt *myself*. And he *loved* that car . . . I used to tell him so . . almost as much as he loved me."

Her voice went on and on. When at last it stopped, just to prevent any more argument or exposition, he said "Thank you, Rosalie. That's sweet of you. I'll take good care of it, I promise."

He tried then to get the subject away from Ken and on to her plans for the future. Already the thought of having to take Ken's car weighed on his mood, in some disproportionate gloom. The car seemed to bring with it almost human responsibilities, a hand on his arm to prevent him forgetting someone else.

"Plans! The future!" Rosalie repeated his last three words.

"Yes, I *have* thought of them. Often! I've lain awake at night. Oh, Mummy wants me home, of course. *And* Ken's family. *They* want me to go and stay." She sipped her drink, and then put it down on the table in front of her, stirring it thoughtfully with her cocktail stick. "But right now, I *can't* do any of those things. And," she shrugged, "I can't go on staying here, either."

"How about taking a job?" Gallagher suggested vaguely, but she just murmured wryly, "As *what*?" and went back to the contemplation of her martini. "No," she sighed. "There is only one thing I really want to do . . . one thing I really *must* do. Go back."

"To what?"

She turned to him then, her eyes wide and smiling. "The flat, of course. The flat at Avonmead."

"I see."

Knowing it was inadequate, it was still all he could think of to say. He sat beside her stolidly, waiting for her next move, and longing, if he dared to admit it, for her to let him go. Unable to express sympathy, he felt a discomfort and wretchedness that was almost physical. Although not real hell as he had known it, sitting here with Rosalie and seeing her suffer was as near to it as you could get with anyone you didn't actually love.

Then suddenly she was standing up. "Gavin!" she said impulsively. "Take me there *now! In the car! Will you*? Oh, I'll come back to pack. But right now I just want . . . well . . . to see the dear old place again. And I've got lots of petrol coupons."

His immediate reaction was anything rather than sitting here. Avonmead was only twenty-odd miles away. They could be there in less than an hour. In fact, before he had even thought about it, he stood up beside her, and began to say, "Good idea!"

Then he hesitated.

"What's the matter? You've not suddenly remembered a date with a girl have you?"

"No, nothing like that."

"Well?"

In fact he couldn't explain a feeling of inexplicable uneasiness. That feeling somehow deepened as Rosalie, smiling as if she'd made her point said, "Come on then! Let's go!"

She held the keys of the car up in front of him, twirling them gently as someone might hold up something glittering and bright for a child to reach out to.

But once they were started, the feeling lessened. He could dismiss it as a constitutional hatred of any plans, however small, being sprung upon him without notice. It was a fine March evening, and the sky had that pale cloudless tranquillity that only seemed to favour these flat eastern counties. They followed the winding road through the village, and headed straight on to the B67 for Avonmead.

The sight of the town itself, coming to life under the dimmed car lights, struck him as suddenly and with as destructive an effect as enemy flak, twisting his inside with vivid fragmentary memories of himself and Edwina. He glanced at Rosalie to see if she was similarly wrung by memories of Ken. She was staring straight ahead, her face expressionless.

Just for a moment as they passed through the square and came up to the house, pity quenched any irritation. He took one hand from the wheel and covered hers.

She held on to it for a moment. And then, as if by doing that, he had actually *given* her something, she released his hand, and said in a cheerful matter-of-fact voice, "You might as well turn here and then park in the usual place."

Involuntarily, as he walked up the path, he glanced up at the large windows of the flat. Involuntarily, he slowed his pace. At the yellow painted door, Rosalie handed him the key. "Open up, Gavin dear. I can't really bear to."

When he stood back to let her go in, she smiled up at him gratefully. He had expected the flat to have the musty smell of any once lived-in place, long kept locked up. But Rosalie's help had agreed to keep it aired, and the sweet slightly-scented atmosphere that he had always known remained as if mummified. It carried him back more weirdly to the past than anything else could possibly have done.

He watched Rosalie turn on the lights and then cross the lounge, walking slowly and beautifully, spreading her arms wide on either side of her as if gathering the flat to her.

"Silly of me!" she said. "But it *does* seem to welcome us."

At the window, she turned round and smiled. Retracing her steps, she walked towards him. Her outstretched hands came to rest on his shoulders. She stood on tiptoe, and her eyes stared into his. "We *did* have fun, didn't we all . . . us . . . us *four*, Gavin?"

He nodded.

"Us four," she repeated sadly, shaking her head. "Now . . . now *we're* the only two left." Her eyes left his face a moment to travel the room. Looking at him again, smiling sadly, her lips parted, she added slowly. "We must be *very* good to one another . . . *we two*."

Night after night, 777 Squadron joined in the Tactical Air Force's assault on the rocket sites, while during the day Fighter Command and high-level American Fortresses took over. Almost as soon as the sites were completed, they were destroyed. Sixty-seven out of ninety-two built in the Pas de Calais area were obliterated. The Germans tried dispersal, deeper concrete shelters, temporary sites—but so far, no rocket had yet made the trip across the Channel.

As the Germans got used to their dusk technique, Gallagher varied it—sometimes going over to attack at dawn, sometimes against heavily fortified sites bombing with the new 12,000 lb. bomb from 20,000 feet. During the course of these attacks, twice he had an engine knocked out. Once, near Rheims, Gallagher was jumped by night fighters, but he managed to evade them in cloud. Coned in the searchlights in an attack on Evranches, repeatedly his Hertford was hit by heavy flak. When he returned with six hundred holes in the fuselage, the Station Commander at Hutton took him on one side and suggested kindly enough that the time had come when he was stretching things too far, and he should give himself a rest.

But that was the last thing he wanted. Now over the black flanks of O Orange was a rash of dope patches like measles: but under the pilot's window were neat rows of yellow-painted bombs, one for every raid he had made. And on a good percentage of these, a rocket-site was wiped from the face of the earth.

Of death itself, he had seen too much to think about it. After losses, there was always a party: everybody drank a lot of beer, got a good night's sleep, and forgot. According to statistics, Gallagher himself was already living on borrowed time: but the squadron casualty rate of 4% was well below the average for Command, so he was not concerned. What did trouble him were the accidents on return. Again and again, especially with the replacement intake, a Hertford would be lost through some flying error. It was the waste that got him. More R.A.F. aircraft were lost in flying accidents than were shot down. His own flying had settled down to that of an average pilot—with some rather unorthodox techniques, but steady and safe. That was because he watched himself, he disciplined himself, and never allowed himself to get into a position from which he wouldn't know how to get out.

But the youngsters on the squadron oscillated between overconfidence and under-confidence. They would do the most careless things. Towards the end of March, a Hertford on a training exercise to Wales simply disappeared over the North Sea—the opposite direction. The twenty-year-old pilot had obviously put red on blue: set the north end of the compass needle against the south marking on the grid ring. Investigating further, Gallagher found this sort of accident was common. The route to the Middle East lay down the Portuguese coast, then turning *left* to Gibraltar. Yet some aircraft had turned *right*, to vanish completely over the Atlantic. Many pilots, briefed to turn *starboard* after take off to avoid a hill, promptly turned *port* and hit it. He was stimulated enough to write a paper on the subject, in which he explained that though some people were more liable to make such mistakes than others, as with any other bad habit, by discipline and self-watchfulness such a tendency could be completely eradicated. He also pointed out that the answer lay in the Double Check, and recommended that as there was only one pilot on Hertfords, the engineer should be given a short pilot-navigator's course so as to act as a check against such errors.

He wrote other papers, too—one on tactics against rocket sites, and one on the proper use of r.p.m. and boost to get maximum fuel consumption. He had a clear economical style—by-product of his Oxford tutor's dislike of wordy exuberance—and the papers attracted attention, not only in 81 Group but throughout Bomber Command.

In April, no more rocket sites were attacked, and the whole of Bomber Command was put at the disposal of General Eisenhower. The invasion was close—speculation ran high on where it would be. 777 Squadron bombed targets all the day down the coast of Northern France, but Gallagher noticed again and again they were brought back to the ten heavy guns covering Seine Bay.

When the troops finally did beach at Arromanches on June 6th, none of those guns were firing.

During the rest of June, there was a comparative lull. A number of decorations came through for 81 Group, and Gallagher was named for the D.F.C. He didn't tell Rosalie, nor did he do anything more about it—but she must have heard from one of the types at a Ladies' night. For one Saturday, he went over to the Avonmead flat for lunch and lazed on the warm sweet-smelling grass at the back in his shirt-sleeves during the afternoon. Just before he returned to Hutton, as Rosalie helped him on with his tunic, he saw a purple striped addition under his wings. She had bought the ribbon and sewn it on.

"Well," she said, as he smilingly protested, "I wasn't going to have you going about improperly dressed!"

Relieved of the attentions of the allied air forces, Operation Rumpelkammer began on June 13th with the arrival in England of the first flying bomb. From then, they came continuously, but nothing for the time being was allowed to interfere with Overlord, and Bomber Command was kept pounding at railway junctions and tank parks to help the advancing armies.

The trips themselves were short, and by now the bombing "marker" technique had been so buttoned up that 777 Squadron needed no more training—it was all routine. The pilots infinitely preferred these lightly defended targets to the fighters and flak of the Ruhr: losses were correspondingly low, and everybody—including Gallagher—had more time off. In the middle of July, the Officers' Mess held a cocktail party, and since she was the only girl he knew, Gallagher invited Rosalie.

He fetched her, and brought her back. She enjoyed herself and so did he. She was a reminder, the only connection he had left with Edwina, and being so, she acted somehow as some kind of foothold into the past, a confirmation of what happened at Avonmead. It seemed more real because she had been there, too.

It was natural that Rosalie should invite him to supper. And it was characteristic that she should say, "Now no excuses! I know now they've advanced so far there's fewer targets for the heavies. So Q.E.D., darling, more time off for Gallagher!"

He went again in the middle of August. He went again two weeks later. And once a routine was established, it became inevitable for him to continue it. Every Saturday fortnight, provided he wasn't flying and provided he had the petrol coupons, he would go over to the flat for supper. Discounting the affection and friendliness between them, Rosalie was a pretty girl whose company he enjoyed.

Meanwhile, hundreds of flying bombs still continued to arrive over London every day, and though Fighter Command and the anti-aircraft batteries shot down an increasing percentage, civilian casualties and public outcry mounted. But by this time the advancing armies were capturing all the sites, so that by the 7th September, Duncan Sandys could announce that the Battle of the Bombs was won "except possibly for a few last shots".

Next day, arriving long before the noise of its passage, the first of many hundred V2s exploded.

Forty-seven feet long, fuelled by liquid oxygen and alcohol, the 3000 m.p.h. speed of this rocket precluded all possibility of defence against it. 777 Squadron were again brought in to attack the sites in Holland, but these proved almost impossible to find. In spite of considerable casualties to personnel from continual misfirings, the V2s were being launched from roadsides and in the middle of woods, the only real clue to their whereabouts being a huddle of fuelling lorries. Time and again, the Hertfords brought their bombs back: so that they were switched to backing up the advancing armies, and the V2s continued to fall.

During that summer and autumn, Gallagher's only relaxation continued to be Rosalie. The flat at Avonmead was the one place where he could get right away from the war. Though his trips over there were no more frequent, he began to look forward to them as a necessary part of his life.

One evening, after the usual supper and talk, he was on the point of saying it was time he made tracks for base, when Rosalie kicked off her high-heeled shoes and asked, "Would you like to do something for me, Gavin?"

"Of course."

"When Ken and I used to come back late from a do . . . he'd make me a hot drink, and we'd sit by the fire and drink it. The milk's in the fridge, the Ovaltine's in the larder. You know how to light the stove. Or you should by now."

Twenty minutes later, they sat side by side on the sofa, sipping their beakers of hot Ovaltine, like two children. Rosalie had rested her nylon-stockinged foot on the fender, curling her toes in the warmth.

"Gavin," she said, speaking slowly, "I've wonderful news for you. Suddenly I feel really happy. *Utterly* happy again . . . thanks to *you*."

And in a state of drowsy, childish well-being she rested her head on his shoulder, and gave a playful little pout. "Gavin darling, give me my good night kiss *now*."

If it was a longer good night kiss then than usual, that too became standard practice. It became standard practice for her sometimes to demand it some time before he finally went. But she did so in a pretty little-girl manner, as if, were he to quibble, she would laugh and say, "Gavin, I was only teasing! Honestly you've no sense of humour, *have* you?"

The months moved on into winter, and his trips over to Avonmead became rather more frequent than once a fortnight. Sometimes now he arrived sooner, even as early as lunchtime, and not long before Christmas, Rosalie insisted that instead of lazing in the flat one afternoon, he should take her in the car to Lincoln. "I've simply masses of shopping to do. I'll need the car to put it all in. Besides," she added, "the car is like me. It *needs* an outing occasionally."

When Gallagher started the engine, and drove her out, Rosalie let out one of her rather artificial high-pitched laughs. "Gavin . . . I've just realized something! You'll never guess."

"I've forgotten to put on my tie or I've torn my trousers."

"Wrong!" She paused. "You drive the car exactly like Ken did."

"I imagine," Gallagher said, suddenly irritated with her, "that most people drive pretty much the same. There isn't a helluva choice, you know. Unless you prefer I did it standing on my head."

"Now don't be beastly! It's just that first you give her bonnet a couple of half-hearted polishes before you get in. Then, when you're turning a corner, you draw in a *deep* breath, and put all you've got into it . . . as if you were manhandling her around . . ."

Sensing his disapproval, her voice trailed away.

Still irritated, he said, "Well, she's a bit ancient. And she can be a bastard."

"In one thing at least," Rosalie said with shaky dignity, "I *can't* compare you with Ken. He was never rude. *Nor* was he ever unkind."

Trembling on Gallagher's tongue was, "And a helluva lot of good *that* was to him!" But it was only a momentary temptation. He recognized he was behaving childishly. Yet he felt the desire for an open quarrel so strongly that it was a full minute before he could say, "I'm sorry, Rosalie. I'm a bad-tempered bastard. I'll make it up to you. I'll take you to the best shop in town, and I'll buy you your Christmas present."

And though she didn't immediately forgive him, though she frowned and sniffed a little until they were nearly there, the shopping expedition ended as quite a success. Not greedily but prettily, she helped him choose a simple pair of expensive pearl ear-rings.

All the same, he had expected her to cotton on to the fact that he didn't enjoy being compared to Ken. But only the following Saturday, she said, "You carve like Ken," as Gallagher wrestled with the meat ration. "It's beef, darling . . . *not* the Nazi war machine!"

He had let that occasion go by. *And* the time when she pointed out that he, too, always lit two cigarettes and handed her one. But in the New Year, when she was still doing it, he considered it was time to put an end to the habit. The squadron had been hanging around, doing little, grounded by bad weather, which was far more frustrating than regular operating, and that Saturday evening Gallagher was already irritated when he arrived at the flat. Straightaway Rosalie presented him with a pile of his freshly-laundered shirts, which lately she had insisted on doing for him.

"I could imagine I was washing Ken's," she said, "you get them worn and grubby in exactly the same places."

She was wearing a black velvet dress with a wide flared skirt. Her perfume hung heavily sweet over the flat.

Irritation, superstitious dread of being compared with a dead airman, and the fact that Rosalie was altogether too attractive, made him suddenly take hold of her, and kiss her hard and angrily on the mouth. "Now," he said, releasing her. "Tell me how I compare to Ken on *that*."

He expected to make her furious. But coolly she was mistress of the situation. Neatly sidestepping a quarrel, she said with equanimity, "Let's say *you've* probably had more practice."

Somewhat mollified, somewhat ashamed, he sat down to supper.

From then on, if she compared him with Ken, he hardly noticed it. For without ever realizing the exact moment, he slipped into Ken's place around the house. At supper, while Rosalie got the second course from the kitchen, he would stack the meat dishes and remove the condiments.

He got into the habit of buying the drink and always doing the mixing. He would make the coffee and bring it in on a tray, and she would kneel on the footstool in front of the table, as she always used to do. He brought in food to help out with the rationing. Sometimes he even bought her flowers, though he could never bring himself to buy roses.

Once or twice, tentatively she said to him, "It's a pity you've got to rush back to camp at this time of night . . ." But he always made some excuse . . . church parade . . . possible early morning readiness . . . Duty Station Commander . . . an operational conference. And in times of deep depression he would remember her standing there, inviting him to stay, as yet another thing which sooner or later had to be faced up to. And in order to manufacture within himself the right amount of bloody-mindedness, he would tell himself that he wasn't yet ready to see how he measured up to Ken in *that*.

For increasingly, as the war in Europe sped towards Allied victory, increasingly did Gallagher feel empty and bereft. He even reassured himself that after Germany, there was still Japan. With any . . . and he actually thought of it as *luck* . . . the squadron might be sent out East. For by some contrary process, the thought of peace made him feel insecure. Analyse it as he might, try to talk himself out of it, the feeling persisted.

He had completed seventy-nine trips on this tour, which was stretching fate three times as far as he should have done—but he still went off most nights the squadron was operational. Through fearful winter weather, with thick ice coating up the black leading edges of the Hertfords' wings, with electric rain and St. Elmo's fire flickering all over the airframe, with the target so blind that the T.I.s seemed awash, the Hertfords slogged through to bomb

Berlin or the sodium mines in the Hartz mountains where rockets were being stockpiled.

Yet ironically, just as he had not wanted the war to begin, now he did not want it to end. When 777 Squadron were taken off raids for a week, he rang up Ingleby to get other work for his boys to do. Even when towards the end of April, the squadron were given two highly rewarding jobs, still the let-down feeling increased in intensity.

The first was called Operation Manna. Now, instead of 12,000 pounders, the Hertfords' bomb-bays were filled up with 355 food parcels in specially designed slings. Gallagher's crew were as excited as schoolboys on a picnic, as they watched O Orange being bombed up with sacks of flour, yeast, tins of dried milk and eggs, chocolate, canned meat and vegetables.

It was a cold day. April was going out like a wintry lion, and there were snowstorms over the North Sea. But as the bomb-aimer remarked, it all added up to make them feel more like Father Christmas.

Leading the squadron in formation, Gallagher skimmed across the sands at Scheveningen, and flew inland towards the Hague race-course.

And then he saw them: people waving, flags flying, children cheering, a forest of thin arms and half-starved faces turned up towards the aircraft in welcome.

"Bomb doors open."

"Hold her steady, Skipper."

Gallagher straightened up over the green turf for a low run in. Now he could see that the stands were as packed as the streets. The whole of the centre was filled with the giant white letters THANK YOU.

None of the crew said much on the way back. It contrasted oddly with the return from an attack.

The second job was to fly back the prisoners-of-war as the army over-ran the camps. Senior officers were beginning to suffer from a similar attack of anti-climax as Gallagher. Several times it had been suggested, even in the Mess at Hutton-le-Wold, that now was the time to have a crack at the Russians and be done with it. So perhaps to canalize such politically unwise sentiments, great éclat was given to the operation 81 Group nicknamed Turnkey. For the returned prisoners, a buffet was laid on in the hangars. Hot snacks were provided by the ubiquitous W.V.S. There would be an emergency hand-out of clothing, an Advice Centre, the padres of all three denominations would be on hand to talk to the men.

Even Gallagher, more inclined to be bothered about take-offs from small airfields and load-and-trim factors found himself sentimentally moved by the preparations.

And here, too, Rosalie showed herself to extraordinary advantage. Coming over every day from Avonmead, in no time at all she had ousted the homely G.C.'s wife as head of the wives' Mobile Buffet. She was there when Gallagher and the rest of the squadron took off in the morning. And she was still there to serve tea when they returned.

These flights with twenty-two ex-P.O.W.s crammed in the Hertford fuselage affected Gallagher more deeply than a bombing trip. Their laughter, their songs, their cheers as they crossed the English coast, their gratitude, their all-pervading, all-seeing joy in life unsettled him. It was as if they personalized the war for him, and their relief was as moving as grief. *His* war against the Germans had been impersonal. He saw no human effect of his bombing. Perhaps that impersonality in modern war could make men monsters. For suffering had to have eyes to weep and nerves to feel and a voice to cry out—and ears to hear that voice.

Just as the emotional state of the men he had carried had rubbed off on to him, now their obvious admiration of Rosalie did, too. No one could resent the way the poor bastards stared when they arrived at the tea trolley. McIntyre, the Intelligence Officer, a self-acclaimed man for the ladies, had remarked when they were in the thick of preparations, that the sight of Mrs. Ash would do the P.O.W.s far more good than the W.V.S., the Padres and the S.S.A.F.A.* rolled into one.

Throughout that week, of course, Rosalie always looked beautiful. She had a wonderful sense of occasion. The other wives, mindful of the cold wind, were muffled in head-scarves and hand-knitted sweaters. They wore flat shoes, aprons or overalls, and their sleeves were rolled up, showing reddened arms. Not so Rosalie. Her head was uncovered, and her hair was freshly washed and set. She wore her best grey-worsted suit with a fur thrown negligently over her shoulder. Her ear-rings,

* Soldiers Sailors and Air Force Families' Association.

a brooch in her lapel, the bracelets at her wrist, caught the glitter of the sun, and her heels were so high that the standing must have killed her. But throughout, she looked happy, charming, bandbox fresh. She laughed, made jokes, smiled—and if the men held her hand, she pretended not to notice.

By Saturday she was still tireless, still enjoying herself immensely. She had made friends with a number of the wives, she told Gallagher, and had made three dates with them for the following week.

"Only with the wives, I hope," Gallagher said, meaning it to be just something to say. But immediately McIntyre, standing beside her laughed and said, "Jealous, you see!" And oblivious of any reactions of Gallagher's, smiling admiringly at Rosalie and enviously at Gallagher, he followed it up with, "Hey! That reminds me! When are you two getting married?"

That moment seemed to go on for ever. Then, cameoed against the hangar and the clouded sky, Gallagher saw Rosalie's face—young, eager, momentarily abashed. She seemed at that moment not only beautiful, but infinitely desirable. Emotionally taut, unsettled, for the first time he saw her as necessary to him as he was to her.

Gently he said, "I'm waiting for Rosalie to tell me that."

3

Gallagher was married to Rosalie Ash exactly ten days later in the Registry Office at Avonmead. By what Rosalie called an omen of good luck, their wedding day was on May 8th, coinciding with the celebration of Victory in Europe.

They had both agreed that it should be a quiet affair. "Not a church," Rosalie said. "Not that I don't want us two to be blessed. But churches are so sad. And now, we're both so happy."

But Rosalie had gone even further than Gallagher in her desire for quietness. There were no guests at the Registry Office, not even their parents.

"I know it sounds frightfully selfish. But I had a big wedding before. This time, I want you all to myself. We'll get a couple of passers-by for witnesses. We'll just ring up the families, and say . . . guess what, darlings? We're married!"

And though this method of getting married struck Gallagher as perhaps more affected and whimsical than an ordinary church service, he also preferred to have it this way.

In the end however, it seemed to attract as much attention. Rosalie was wearing a creamy silk suit, and an unmistakably nonsense wedding hat. She carried a little posy of flowers in her gloved hands and she teetered along on her high heels, as they both tried to stop two passers-by to come in and be their witnesses. The streets were crammed with people, for V.E. day was fine and warm and a public holiday. There were young boys with wooden rattles, blow-out streamers with feathers on the end that they shot into people's faces.

A band marched up and down the market square, and Gallagher had to shout in people's ears. Looking back, his memory of that day seemed to be a surprised face mooning up at him, and asking, half-belligerently, half-jocularly, as if not sure if this was all part of the V.E. day fun, "Eh? What's that you said, mister?"

In the end, Rosalie pointed, "*That* couple over there! They've such nice faces!" And they cornered an elderly pair who wore red, white and blue favours and who, somewhere between the pavement and the Registry Office told them their only son had been killed at Alamein.

"I suppose," Rosalie remarked to the Registrar, when the brief emotionless ceremony was over, "that I ought to feel frightfully different. But I don't."

"In fact," she whispered to Gallagher as, taking his arm, they emerged from the cool dimness of the office, "All I *do* feel is that I need a drink."

They stood for a moment at the top of the worn steps. "I'm imagining that all this is laid on specially for us," Rosalie said. Someone in the crowd wolf-whistled and Rosalie grinned back. The band, having circled the market square was swinging now down the High Street. Young children marched in step with it. Women waved from upstairs flats, and fluttered flags. The shops were hung with bunting. Momentarily, his eye was caught by the store at which Edwina and he had stared. The baubles had gone, of course. And the window had been filled with a huge portrait of the King and Queen with *God Bless Them*, and laurels round it.

"We ought to have got a taxi," he said to Rosalie as they were jostled along the pavement. A total stranger seeing his uniform thumped Gallagher on the back said, "Well done!" But whether, as Rosalie pointed out over drinks, it was because he was a pilot or because he had obviously just married *her*, no one would ever know.

The only concession over the wedding they had made to other people, was to have a few friends in at six o'clock. A catering firm had done the buffet. The G.C. had kindly sent them a batman to serve the drinks. The guests were all officers from the station and their wives. And being V.E. day, they didn't stay long. As McIntyre pointed out, there'd have to be a goodly number of them up at the Station, in case the airmen burned up the place. Already, one or two bonfires had been started up, and a toilet-roll battle was reported in progress between the barrack blocks.

By nine, the batman had cleared away, been tipped and pushed off. Through the open window of the flat came the sound of distant voices, a procession of feet, the horns of cars trying to clear a way through the gathering crowds, snatches of songs, the band in the square where people were dancing, a snatch of the King's speech from some nearby loudspeaker, gramophones blaring, church bells ringing.

The long twilight was slowly fading into darkness. The spires and the chimneys of the town were held in violet-edged silhouette against the almost cloudless, windless sky behind. Gallagher stared out of the window. For a moment, the town seemed to hold its breath. Then, with what was, after all, only an illusion of unison, lights sprang up everywhere. A firework arced up into the sky like a Very light. It was all somehow unreal, unnatural after the years of darkness, so that he was caught unawares and wanted to shout out at them some warning. Then the whole twilight was shot through with rockets and floodlights and the flicker of bonfires.

And he remembered again that the war in Europe was over.

"How unlucky *they* all are!" Rosalie said, coming to stand beside him. "They're just celebrating because something is over. We, darling . . . we're celebrating because it's just begun!"

He wanted at that moment to ask her just what *had* begun. Instead, he closed the window and kissed her, holding her tightly to him. The flat seemed suddenly very quiet, an unnatural shell of silence within some vast sea of noisy rejoicing.

In the end, they had a kind of honeymoon. But not until the beginning of August, when someone at Command took it into his head to encourage senior officers to use up their back-logs of leave. 777 Squadron were now ferrying troops to the Far East, where the Americans had assembled 5,000 aircraft for the invasion of Japan.

Rosalie had jumped at the idea of leave. She had pored over a map in the flat. She had written to old-established and expensive hotels where she had spent heavenly holidays as a girl. Gallagher had let her choose for them both—only specifying that as it was August, he didn't want the sea.

In the end, they had gone to a small hotel in Somerset. It was a seventeenth-century inn that stood directly on the High Street. Behind was a garden bright with cottage flowers. Rosalie and Gavin were the only guests. They drank beer in the small dark bar, where the filtered sunlight glowed on the polished brasses. They took long walks during the day, and at night, they went early to their rooms. Gallagher read, while Rosalie would go through a slow long ritual of preparation, before sliding her slim silk-clad body in beside him. He was never relaxed with her like this. It was as if she removed herself to a plane a little away from him. So that in the act of love itself, he seemed to be hurrying, searching, straining for someone who had already gone.

But he had no reason to think that Rosalie was anything but happy. Certainly she had never looked more beautiful. Her fine skin had taken on a slight tan, and her hair was lightened around her temples to a pale sparkling gold. So much did she seem to be enjoying herself, that half way through the holiday she suggested he rang up Hutton to tell them he was taking another week. But for himself, part of the pleasure was in the difference from Station life. And the return was as necessary and as looked forward to as the holiday itself.

He was therefore somehow mentally unprepared for the morning of Tuesday, August 7th. It was fine and warm, and Rosalie and he were down early to breakfast. Gallagher remembered vividly that the dining-room windows were open, and Rosalie was identifying the smell of lavender and Sweet William. Usually, the morning papers were folded by their bread plates, but this morning, the proprietor rushed in as they sat there.

Though the man was waving the paper up and down as he came towards them, and was giving a thumbs-up with his free hand, still Gallagher didn't guess. Afterwards, he remembered it vividly. It was the *Daily Echo*, and the whole of the front page was taken up with the giant size letters, *The First Atomic Bomb, Rain of Ruin from the Air, Collapse of Japan Imminent.*

Vaguely, as Gallagher clutched the paper in his hand he heard the landlord talking to Rosalie, showing her another paper (for they all carried banner headlines), "They dropped a marvellous new bomb. Some secret weapon. *Ours* this time. And now it'll be all over . . . just like that!"

All over, just like that . . . those words echoed in Gallagher's mind. It was as if for the past months he had been walking along some well worn path, and though he had heard rumblings he had ignored them. But now at a stroke, the ground had gone, leaving him nothing. The war had ended absurdly quickly, leaving the hideous blank of peace.

Gallagher forced his eyes to read. "President Truman announced from the White House that the first atomic bomb had been dropped sixteen hours before on Hiroshima. It was equal to twenty thousand tons of T.N.T., and the blast was two thousand times that of the largest known bomb.

Now Rosalie was murmuring to the landlord that there had been a chance that her husband's squadron might have been moved out east. "Now," she said, "this is a *reprieve*."

And turning to Gallagher, smiling mistily, "It's the best news we've ever had, isn't it, darling? Peace . . . at last!"

The proprietor's wife came in then, and some of the staff. As an expert, they asked Gallagher if he knew anything about this secret weapon, but he shook his head. There was speculation as to which day the Japs would finally pack it up. Which day would be VJ day, another public holiday. Someone suggested a small sweepstake on it. There were to be free drinks all round in the bar at ten.

Outside, people were gathering in the street. Across the way the church bells were clanging, and the Vicar was hurrying along, his cassock flying behind him. He stopped one or two of the gossipers, gathering them like the Pied Piper across the churchyard and through the church door. A little while afterwards, Gallagher heard the organ playing the National Anthem and *Our God, our help in ages past* as he finished his coffee.

It took him a few minutes before he could make a sensible comment to Rosalie. He felt confounded. It was as if the Air Force had let him down. Had done something drastic which would affect him *personally* without taking him into its confidence. He couldn't explain his feeling to himself, except this way. For years the Air Force had made him prepare himself for fear, danger, frustration, injury, imprisonment, a quick and tidy death. It had never prepared him for this tame survival.

In the end, Gallagher said, lighting a cigarette, "It's all so sudden. It's going to catch a lot of bods on the hop!"

Now that he looked closely at her, Rosalie seemed a little uneasy, too. She asked if he thought he'd be released immediately, and when he shook his head, she seemed relieved.

Over the free drinks in the bar to which half the village came, Gallagher seemed mentally to thaw out. It was the shock, the suddenness, he told himself. He always hated having things sprung upon him. Even, he thought wryly, peace on earth.

All the same, as he explained to Rosalie, he ought to go back and see how this affected things at Hutton. And in her turn, Rosalie made no attempt to prolong their holiday. They returned to Hutton on the Saturday, where Gallagher found a message awaiting him to report to Group on the following Monday.

He seriously expected the summons would have something to do with the sad business of disbanding of the squadron. But when he went into the office, Ingleby came out smiling from behind his desk, his hand outstretched. "Well . . . great news, eh? What a victory!"

The papers that morning had headlined further details on the dropping of the second atomic bomb on Nagasaki, and Japan's offer to surrender. Briefly, Ingleby discussed this new weapon and its future potentialities, and how all this would affect the trooping schedule. "We'll have them all bellyaching for a ride home now, Gavin. 81 Group will be hard at it again."

Then he asked about Gallagher's leave, inquired warmly after Rosalie. And conversation now being on a personal note, said, "Have you thought what's going to happen to *you*?"

It echoed so much the question which Gallagher had these last few days so fruitlessly asked himself, that he could only murmur in reply that no, he hadn't. That like so many aircrew, his sights had been too close, he had lived from day to day, not allowing himself to see how close the end had come.

"Precisely," Ingleby said. "You kept your mind on the *immediate* job. That's why you did so well."

"Of course, I'll be sorry to leave."

"But, Gavin, *do you have to*?" Ingleby paused. "Don't make the mistake of thinking this war's going to end like the last. There's *not going* to be wholesale disarmament *this* time. We can't. We daren't. I have it on good authority . . . there'll be permanent commissions going *for the right type*."

To quieten the immediate leap of something like hope, Gallagher thought wryly, "What's in this for Ingleby?"

"Russia," the A.O.C. went on, "*may* have been our ally. But by God, Gavin, she'll *never* be our friend!"

Ingleby went on expounding the advantages of the peace time Air Force . . . excellent pay, early retiring age, prestige, security, travel, the good life, while Gallagher tried to revive within himself the old arguments against the military machine. But they weren't alive any more. They were worse than dead. They were crumbled and gone.

"You're twenty-five. You've got a high position. You've given your adult life so far to the Air Force. Why throw it away? Reap the benefit. Stay on to protect freedom. Fight for peace, like you fought the war."

Now like the march of an Air Force band, the jingo words caught at his mind, setting it into well-worn and comfortable rhythms.

"I've seen this coming for some time, Gavin. The peace didn't catch *me* napping. I have it worked out. The Air Force *must* expand But its emphasis will change. A lot of the senior officers won't. It'll be a new men's Air Force. With new weapons. Have you thought, Gavin, what those weapons will be?"

"Not really, sir. No."

"Well, I *have*. They'll be all this atomic nonsense, allied to . . ." he grinned. "*Your* speciality."

"Rockets, you mean, sir?"

"Exactly! Rockets with an atomic warhead. The secret weapon of the Germans *plus* the secret weapon of the allies. Powerful medicine!"

Several times that week he tried to discuss the question of his future with Rosalie. Not so much for advice, as for some indication about what she herself would prefer.

"Well, I can't see myself as the wife of a schoolmaster, darling. Though if *that's* what you want, of course, you must do it."

Vaguely, he had thought of the Colonial Service. "But darling, isn't the Empire shrinking?"

Business, then? "But darling, you're so *luminously* honest."

In the end, off he went to Oxford, his lodestar when in doubt, ostensibly to visit the Appointments Board, really to sort himself out and maybe have a natter with Vince.

He had felt that once there, the old arguments would revive. All his youthful hatred of the mass mind (though quite honestly he hadn't found it like that in the Air Force), his insistence on individual freedom (though who was truly free in mind?), the pure search for truth and knowledge for their own sake.

The cross-country train travelled slowly. The sun was shining, and it was hot in the compartment. In that bright light, the approaches to the city, never beautiful, were highlighted in their commercial ugliness. He could see no trace of bombing, no honourable scars. But plenty of broken windows, peeling paint-work, drab curtained houses.

There was, he thought, always something especially lonely in arriving at a familiar place, unwelcomed. A new place was a challenge, one's very anonymity an added excitement. Now to add to that loneliness, his younger memory of Oxford came up to emphasize this new, somehow weather-beaten face. The tall spires might still soar against the sky, now so obligingly blue. But it was as if Gallagher's eyes could not reach so far up. They were drawn down to the people who hurried along streets, or stared in shops, or queued for buses.

No one who had not been in the Services could know how tatty and disorganized a crowd of civilians looked en masse. Especially a British crowd. Especially an Oxford crowd.

Who said morale was compounded of a number of tiny things? Gallagher didn't know. But now his morale was at a new low, drawn down by tired-looking faces, worn-down heels, women in dun-coloured coats, pimply-faced youths, old men on bicycles.

Nowhere was the silent austerity of an Air Force Station—the order, the pattern, the cleanliness, the rhythm, the quiet. Everything seemed noisy, dusty, drab. Outside a fish shop, a long queue waited. He had to step off the kerb to pass it. A shop window was full of shiny brown-topped loaves and unreal cakes, heavily marked with their price and their bread points value. He made his way slowly along the Corn to the University Appointments Board.

They didn't keep him waiting long. But they seemed surprised to see him. The interviewer filled in a long form. He scratched his neck with the sharp end of his pencil when they got as far as "a degree".

"Of course, I could always—" Gallagher knew as he said the words that he couldn't "—come back and get one."

"What exactly had you in mind? To what end, as it were, would you be returning?"

Gallagher could not enlighten him. The interviewer looked somewhat overworked. He riffled through a card-index. The university was going to be very overcrowded, it was going to be all rather difficult. As for openings in industry, the change from war to peace was too recent to know yet which way industry would jump. Much, of course, might be spent on education . . . the interviewer's voice trailed into vague speculation.

Finally, leaning forward at once indignantly and sympathetically, he said, "Tell me . . . is there no further career for you where you are? In the Air Force. After all, you can fly!"

He said it as if, quite properly, there was little else Gallagher *could* do.

"I suppose I might be able to stay in." Gallagher wanted to follow that up by adding that he had never meant to make the Air Force his career, that he had not meant . . . but somehow he couldn't remember how all that went on. He was aware that both of them seemed immensely relieved, and he was out of the office and blinking his way along the sunlit pavements, wondering how long it would take him to find Vince, and wishing that he'd given him some warning of his arrival.

It took him the best part of an hour. Perhaps he didn't try as hard as he might. Perhaps some part of him wanted to postpone this meeting. Perhaps he wanted to walk through the quadrangles and libraries and halls, willing their age-old emanations of wisdom to work some magic upon him. But somehow they weren't given the chance. Wherever he went, young boys' and girls' faces floated up to him, young voices fled past his ear, youthful expressions of unmatured certainty seemed to engulf him. He was the Ancient Mariner himself. He was Old Father Time. He was the blooded warrior trying to return to the old men, the women and the unblooded boys.

In the end, he tracked Vince down to B lab on the third floor of the Experimental Science Block. He was as energetic and ebullient as ever. As soon as Gallagher put his head round the door, Vince shouted, "Gallagher . . . for Christ's sake, come in!"

The scientist shook his hand, looked at him intently. "You look older."

He sent the red-haired lab boy off to make tea. Then, sitting himself on the bench, Vince said, "Haven't heard from you for months. Tell me . . . how's life?"

"Not much to tell." Gallagher kept to platitudes. He showed Vince a snap of Rosalie, and Vince said, "I'd have sworn you never had it in you! What on earth made *her* pick *you*?"

They chatted briefly about the wedding, the house he and Rosalie hoped to get. Then Vince must come up and stay.

"I'd be a fish out of water on an airfield."

"You'd enjoy it. The bods are a good bunch. It's fun, really."

"You'll soon be out, though."

"I suppose I shall eventually." Gallagher fiddled with a brass gas point. "It'll take time."

"Any plans?"

Gallagher shook his head. "Actually . . . I came up today to see the Appointments Board." He told Vince briefly what they'd said. Vince said nothing. He seemed glad when the tea came, and under cover of sipping he studied Gallagher's face. Slowly, Gallagher tried to explain that he'd hoped to get a lead.

But Vince said quickly, "Who from? How? If you don't know what you want to do by now, no one can tell you." And abruptly putting down his cup, he began talking about his own work: at present he was studying radiation in the upper atmosphere in relation to industrial atomic projects. "I'd explain our cyclotron while you're here," he said, "but I have to get permission first. Anyway, I'll show you the rest of the gubbins."

As he followed the scientist around, Gallagher was thinking that, unlike himself, Vince hadn't really aged. He was unmarked, new and enthusiastic and still young. Sure, he seemed less sparked off by Gallagher, less interested in throwing off his philosophical remarks, more directly involved in the job in hand. But he appeared to have no chamber of horrors inside himself. He was a mind skipping through knowledge, while Gallagher was a scarred human being crawling through life.

"This is interesting now." Vince leaned over a cage of white rats. "Afternoon, gentlemen! Poppets, aren't they? Very intelligent, too. We're testing the side effects of radiation. I'm preparing a paper on it. There's every indication that furred creatures are less affected than their pink-skinned brethren. Exciting, eh?"

He watched Gallagher carefully. "Especially should the last six years' madness be repeated."

"Oh, come off it! We *had* to fight," Gallagher said stolidly.

"Did we?"

"Of course."

"And we'll go on having to. Against someone. We'll simply change partners and dance. Find a *new* enemy. Mankind *needs* an enemy. The Turks, the French, the Germans, the Russians, the Devil."

"You need one, too."

"Of course. It's inside. Fear, Gallagher. Fear. Of what? Of death."

Hotly, Gallagher said, "Some of the bods made a pretty good show of conquering that fear. Only *they* aren't around to shoot their bloody mouths off about it."

"Nor are the people they dropped their bombs on."

"We had to."

"And now you're going to do it by mass-production."

"I don't know what you mean."

"This!" Vince's face had become alight with wrath. He fumbled in the pocket of his jacket, and brought a clipping out of his wallet. "The uninvolved view. The unbiased opinion. Go on . . . read it!"

It was a cutting from the *Times* of August 10th, quoting the Swedish newspaper *Aftonbladet*. "Although Germany began bomb warfare against open towns and civilian populations, all records in the field have been beaten by the Anglo-Saxons. At all events, the so-called rules of warfare, which were hailed in 1939, must hold the bombing of Hiroshima as a first-class war-crime."

Gallagher handed it back without comment. Conditioned to saturation bombing, the atom bomb varied only in degree.

"History will condemn the Germans for the way they started the war perhaps," Vince said. "But by God, it'll condemn us for the way we finished it!"

For a while, neither of them attempted to bridge the angry gap between them. Then Gallagher said, "What about you? You're doing nuclear work, aren't you?"

"Purely for peaceful purposes. There's vast possibilities in this business, you know, for human good."

"Odd that a wartime Government should finance it."

"I don't go in for murder."

Gallagher said stiffly, "War *is* violent. Violence can only be met by violence."

Vince merely pursed his lips.

"Come over here," he said, as if to change the subject. "This isn't my department, but it's interesting." He took Gallagher to another cage full of white rats. "You won't have heard of Douthwaite," he said. "But he's doing experiments on conditioned reflexes. A bit further on from Pavlov."

There was something in Vince's manner. Some angry excitement that warned Gallagher that whatever was coming had some special import for him.

"Watch this," Vince said. "Watch carefully!" He motioned Gallagher to stand at the opposite side of the cage from him. "These rats have been kept in captivity for many months. Brought to a point by conditioning . . . so that, Gallagher . . . you're not watching . . . I'm lifting the door, Gallagher . . . wide open, Gallagher . . . and look, Gallagher . . . watch carefully . . . they're *free* now . . . free as air . . . free to go into the world . . . but look, Gallagher . . . though the door's wide open . . . they *can't let themselves come out* . . ."

INTERLUDE THREE

FROM the start, Henderson found her difficult to question. She was vague. She didn't know. She had forgotten. When she did speak, tears welled up in her large eyes. She interrupted herself to say to him, "*Is* this necessary? Do you *have* to ask *me* all this?"

She was a good-looking woman, all right. She had once been beautiful. Now she was smart, elegant, and despite the tears and their implied reproach, *hard*. Her face was carefully made up, and she was wearing a smart dark-green dress of fine wool. Henderson noticed that the brooch she wore, the bracelet she fiddled with, were the real thing. Her shoes were those a younger girl would wear. She sat in the most becoming light, half turned from the long lounge window.

In the centre of this large room where good antique pieces mixed discreetly with Air Force issue furniture, was a black cloisonné table. On it, a shallow silver bowl of flowers. Because it was four o'clock, Rosalie Gallagher had insisted that the batman should bring in tea. Henderson's efforts to find the truth were coloured with the scent of flowers and the clink of china.

"On Tuesday night then, your husband seemed just the same as usual?"

"Yes, exactly the same."

"There had, I understand, been a big exercise the night before. Was he tired?"

"He didn't say so."

"Mrs. Gallagher, your husband's job must have been a great strain."

"To me, d'you mean?"

"To both of you. Did he have any relaxations? Hobbies?"

"His *work* was his hobby. Certainly it absorbed a great deal of his time. But," she shrugged, "he *did* relax. He read. We entertained."

"Did he play any sports?"

"Golf, sometimes. Squash occasionally. He wasn't very fond of sports."

"Any other interest?"

"I don't *think* so. Except in America . . . ages ago . . . he skied a little in winter . . . sailed in summer. You could do that sort of thing over there . . . you could lead a *fuller* life. Gavin said sailing was like flying."

"Did you go with him?"

"No. It didn't appeal to me. I watched him once at a competition on the Lakeshore, that was all. He won a cup."

"He was quite an expert then?"

"He usually made himself good when he made up his mind."

"Did he sail *ocean*-going yachts?"

"Oh, yes. All sorts."

"Did he do any ski-ing here?"

"He talked of going up to the Cairngorms maybe next winter. Switzerland *if* we were lucky."

"Any sailing?"

She smiled scornfully. "In the English winter! Aren't the boathouses shut till the spring season starts?"

Henderson put his empty cup back on the table. "You were in America . . . how long, Mrs. Gallagher?"

"Three years. Perhaps a little over."

"And in Australia before that . . . at Woomera I believe?"

"Yes . . . we moved around. It was impossible, of course, to establish a home."

"Before that, the Group Captain was at Air Ministry on Weapons Requirements?"

"You know it all I see, Wing Commander. You'll know, too, that my husband was in on the ground floor as it were, of missile development."

"In fact he hasn't been flying since he was Wing Commander of a transport squadron . . . a good many years ago."

"Not regularly. But where does *that* get us?"

"Did he miss it?"

"Why should he? He was tied up with his present job. He had no *time* to miss *anything*."

"And what posting did *you* enjoy most, Mrs. Gallagher?"

"Oh, *I'm* not important. But I enjoyed America. We had a delightful time over there."

"And then coming to North Luddenham. It must have been quite a change. Did you *want* to come here?"

"I did."

"And d'you like it?"

"I make the best of wherever we are."

"Mrs. Gallagher . . . the Group Captain I believe is your second husband?"

"He is."

"Are you happily married?"

"Very."

"Did you ever have disagreements?"

"We may," she said slowly, "have differed over certain small things. Never at all over anything *fundamental*."

Henderson paused. "There's no question of another woman?"

"None. Nor has there ever been."

"Mrs. Gallagher, your husband didn't warn you he would be out all night?"

"No. Why should he? I've been a Service wife long enough."

"Is it his practice to stay out all night?"

"I knew he went to the rocket site. I presumed he was still there."

"Wouldn't he have phoned you?"

"Most frequently he didn't. His mind would be on the job. Not on me."

"Didn't you expect him to breakfast?"

"He often ate at the Mess. I don't get up for breakfast. It was simpler for him to eat over there."

"Mrs. Gallagher . . . this is a personal question . . . but I must ask it."

"Haven't they *all* been *personal*?"

"Did you and your husband have a quarrel on Tuesday night?"

Momentarily, her jaw tightened. Her eyes widened with a curious angry light. She glanced away, and Henderson thought she was going to tell him to leave at once. Instead she said simply, "No, Wing Commander. We did *not*."

Henderson got up and took his hat off the cloisonné table and said, "Thank you for seeing me, Mrs. Gallagher. And thank you for the tea."

In the hall, as she held open the door for him, almost as though he'd forgotten about it, he said, "Oh, by the way . . . I've been going through your husband's papers, Mrs.

Gallagher. I see he was the friend of a scientist called Peter Vince."

"A long time ago," she said quickly. "At Oxford."

"Your husband still wrote to him though?"

"Only occasionally."

"He hasn't seen him recently?"

"No. Not for years."

"Has he stayed with you, Mrs. Gallagher?"

"Once. Twelve or thirteen years ago."

"On an R.A.F. Station?"

"Yes." He saw the tight-lipped look on her face. "I know exactly what you're thinking, Wing Commander. I saw that piece in the paper. So did my husband. You'll probably know a good deal more in your department about Mr. Vince and his activities than *I* do. But as far as my husband is concerned . . . you're *completely* wrong! Your questions have been on the wrong track . . . all this afternoon. My first husband was killed in an accident, Wing Commander. It was a terrible blow. Now something like that's happened to Gavin. Just you see."

It was getting dark outside. Henderson walked slowly away from Gallagher's house, along the road on which Gallagher was last seen. When he arrived at the Mess, he put in a call to the police.

"The river Hume . . . it's only four miles from North Luddenham, isn't it? Are there any boathouses and anchorages there? Farther down you say? Well, I want them all checked. Yes, I know it's winter and they're probably all shut up. I want to see if there's a boat missing . . . that's all. *Any* boat . . ."

ECHOES ALONG AN EMPTY RUNWAY

I

"Home!" Rosalie said, and sighed. She let her hand rest on Gallagher's, as freeing itself of the dusty cluttered suburbs of Highgate and Holloway, the R.A.F. staff car gathered speed and headed north.

The clock on the dashboard to the left of the L.A.C. driver's shoulder said three minutes past ten. Automatically Gallagher checked it with his watch. Quite correct. He made a brief calculation that they had lost less than ten minutes with the traffic jams they had encountered after leaving Air Ministry. They should still arrive ahead of schedule. Satisfied, he laid his gloves, his cap rimmed with gold-leaf on the seat beside him, and with an almost conscious effort, relaxed.

Through his half-closed lids, he watched the small lime trees of Hertfordshire displace the grey roads and houses. How green even the shallow winter hills were after America, how small the fields! How naturally the cottages, the houses, the villages and towns, emerged and filled the landscape! Like a well-established marriage, someone had once said.

Deliberately, as if he had one more duty yet to do before he allowed his mind to wander over the pleasure of return, Gallagher glanced sideways at Rosalie's profile. How was *she* going to take this return to life in England, after three years in America where at least to begin with she had been a truly remarkable success? Feeling her eyes on him, he turned. Her face, shaded under the smart felt hat, was smiling and still at a distance, beautiful. "It'll be fun," she said firmly, "settling in on an R.A.F. Station. Especially with *you* in command. And such an important posting. I feel, darling, that somehow we've *arrived*."

He patted her hand and put it back in her lap again. He had no intention of allowing the driver to see them holding hands in the driving mirror. Especially as Rosalie, who was cool and undemonstrative in private, had a habit of being bewilderingly over-affectionate in public, and in front of other-ranks. All the same he was pleased that *she* was pleased. For himself, the command of the new Zeus rocket site could be nothing less than gratifying. But he sometimes thought that life for Rosalie might really be, as she cried in her moments of desolation, most terribly unfair.

By and large, he had learned through their years of marriage that he could be happy if she was. Sometimes, however, on the occasions when Rosalie manifestly was upset or ill or felt herself slighted, it did not perhaps disturb and trouble him as profoundly as it ought. For in this marriage, maybe he did, as she said, have everything. And she had nothing.

He had his career, success, honours, respect. He had a way of life, and a purpose in that life. A long time ago he had read a psychological definition of happiness—that one's feelings and thoughts should be harmonized within. And that one's aspirations and ambitions should be stretched towards some point beyond oneself. He remembered vividly on the Staff College course a lecturer on psychological warfare pointing out something similar in the Communist doctrine. It gave its adherents just that. A coherent way of life, an end to strive for. That was its strength. But, that too, on a far more *ethical* basis, was the strength of Gallagher's own life and *his* career.

He believed in the Western Way of life, in the role of the R.A.F. And he believed without sentimentality that he had a duty to protect freedom.

They were streaming along the Great North Road now. Speed always soothed and stimulated him. Pointed poplars fled past their window. The R.A.F. pennant stretched out proudly, starched with the wind of their speed. South-bound lorries passed them at regular intervals so that their *whum-whum-whum* beat a curiously exciting rhythm. He might have been rushing down some long, long runway. And almost his body tensed itself for that moment of lift.

Instead, the car slowed down past an aircraft factory. A few workers were crossing a compound towards the canteen. The offices were full, like a glass beehive, of anonymous figures. Outside, people waited for a bus—women with shopping baskets, men in overalls. Suburban houses stared peacefully out across the road.

This, oddly enough, was *his* lift. The fact that without himself and Ingleby and others like them, who both mastered and controlled the Great Deterrent, these people could never go about their ordinary, peaceful daily lives.

This was not a thought that he often luxuriated in. Nevertheless, rather like the Christian belief in heaven, it was there at the back of his mind. He had once tried to explain this to Rosalie when she had said that life was pointless.

"Oh," she had screamed at him, "that doesn't mean a damned thing to me! I don't give a hoot for your Great Deterrent! I don't want to play with stupid goddamned rockets!"

She had wept then, crossly, uncontrollably, and lapsed as she sometimes did when frustrated into an incoherent destructiveness. "They're only an excuse . . . *an excuse* . . ."

But for what she didn't know.

And he had left it like that. As he had left so many of their quarrels. Because at the back of his mind, he acknowledged that her life *was* empty. While a man could look forward to increasing success and unflagging interest, year by year, the sands of a woman's life ran out.

Sometimes he knew that Rosalie hung on to her beauty with angry despair. He noticed her ceasing to raise her brows in the act of so doing, then smoothing her fingers over her forehead. He was aware, as if a bubble had appeared over her head, of the one word, "Wrinkles!" She only smiled now in a certain *un*wrinkling way. Constantly she held her head high, jerked her pointed chin in the air to preserve the tautness of her jawline.

On his posting to the rocket range at Woomera, she had refused to appear out in the Australian sun. While he was in Paris with NATO in '54, she had taken up eurythmics. When he was stationed in Washington, she had tried a two weeks rejuvenating course at a farmhouse in New England. In New York and London, she had tried out new hair-dressing salons, new couturiers, new milliners. In short, as she had once gaily remarked, she had in the course of his R.A.F. career, collected clothes and beauty hints, while he had collected medals, majesty and seniority.

Gallagher noticed all these things, but said nothing. He understood her well—but at a distance. He satisfied himself that he had never been deliberately unkind to her, never unfaithful, never unreasonable, denied her nothing. Except, of course, the devoted love she had had from Ken Ash. But only a little while after their marriage, he had realized that neither of them could give the other that. And he had realized it, astonishingly enough, not with any sense of deprivation, but with real relief.

"Stevenage." Gallagher broke through his own daydream to point it out to Rosalie. Obediently, as if it were a reminder to *him*, the driver dropped down to thirty, so that they ambled through the streets, past a cinema, past a wide square that once had tolerable Georgian houses. "Came here once on detachment . . . but it's changed. Not much I can remember."

Which was the odd thing—he could dig out nothing *personal* in this journey. Aboard the *Queen Mary* last week, he had looked forward with an almost boyish zest to this long ride to his new station. Stevenage faded, the signpost hurried them on to Biggleswade. Soon they would be in Huntingdonshire. But still the journey lacked some special anticipated emotional warmth. Perhaps emotion needed a person. If they had, say, parents, family, children eagerly waiting, mentally hurrying them homeward, their homecoming would be warmer, involved, more real. But Rosalie's parents had moved to South Africa. Gallagher's father had died in '56 . . . when Gallagher was in Weapons Requirements at Air Ministry. And his mother had died three months later.

Even now, Gallagher couldn't honestly say that he mourned not having children. He would have had them if Rosalie had wanted to, of course. Always supposing that they *could* have done. He couldn't exactly remember when Rosalie had ceased to be *afraid* of being pregnant, and had demanded hysterically that they have babies. "Lots of them, darling! What fun it would be! A house *filled* with jolly Gallagher babies!"

But they hadn't. Maybe they'd left it too late. Or maybe all along Rosalie had been right, and she was too delicately made. And now Rosalie was over forty. "Middle-aged," she would say. "You don't know how *barren* that sounds to a woman."

Yet by some sad metamorphosis, she got mentally younger, year by year. More the little girl, while in contrast—partly by her needs, and partly by his career in life—he acquired the role of an almost infallible father.

They had friends who would welcome them, of course. But they were mostly *Service* friends. So that in a way, they were impersonal, inured to the ebb and flow of Service life, keeping some inner part of themselves to themselves. As ready to adapt themselves to new people as they were to new houses, issue furniture, a different Station that was yet somehow the same.

There was, of course, still Vince. In spite of their disagreement, very occasionally he still wrote. The last time he heard, the scientist was still at Oxford, now doing research on some apparatus provided under a NATO grant, over which Gallagher had permitted himself a wry smile, while at the same time feeling disappointed. Vince ought never to have agreed to that. He should go on for ever, independent of everybody, changing his ideas maybe as rapidly as he ought to have changed his socks. But still having them—his *own* ideas, disagreeing with the herd, whether it was Eastern or Western, sometimes leaving the Gallaghers to take the consequences.

After receiving that letter, he had had a curious dream. He could still remember it vividly. Vince and he were trying to find their way through some involved underground caverns—deep and dark like the dispersal chambers for the old-type nuclear warheads. Vince swore he knew the way out. They stumbled around in circles. Gallagher kept imagining he saw a chink of light, but close to it always vanished. After a while, Vince gave up. He sat down on a pile of rubble. Gallagher felt the stuffiness of the air, the lack of oxygen, the claustrophobia, the feeling of being buried alive. Yet Vince only laughed, the noise echoing round the empty vaults. "We're lost," he kept laughing. "Quite lost!" The laugh kept coming back in waves like the sound of the sea. Desperately rummaging in his pockets, Gallagher produced a match and struck it. Then he saw that, in fact, Vince was blind.

"Eleven-forty," Rosalie said looking at her diamond wristwatch. "Is there time for coffee?"

But Gallagher shook his head, partly because it made difficulties for the driver, and partly because he wanted to keep themselves well ahead of schedule. So Rosalie lit a cigarette, rested her head on the upholstery, and stared up dreamily at the drifting smoke. "Will they like me?" she would be asking it. "Will I like *them*?"

Just outside Grantham, the driver missed the A153 and

headed towards Lincoln. "You're off track." Gallagher leaned forward. "Stop. Get out your map. And check up."

He watched, while red-necked and clumsy-fingered, the driver had found the road they should have been on. Gallagher felt not the slightest sympathy. Long ago, he had diagnosed and conquered the tendencies which had made him a slow-learning pilot. Like a religious convert, he had espoused the efficiency which nature had denied him. But it had only been in recent years that he had realized that as the R.A.F. grew year by year more technical and swift, the margin for error had grown smaller. No doubt Vince in the old days might have unearthed some deep psychological reason, but Gallagher found himself these days more able to tolerate actual moral lapses, than he could genuine mistakes.

"Keep your mind on the job next time," he said, as the airman turned back on to the right road.

From here it was easy going. A pale yellow sun managed to disperse some of the whitish grey clouds that had hung over the sky all morning. This flat fenland was familiar to them both. Always of course, even in this October sunlight, it had a curious quality of melancholy dignity. Here were the stretches of black soil where they grew tulip bulbs. Here were the windmills, the churches, the chapels. Here the horizon melted into blue-grey as the low countryside merged with the distant sea. Over there a row of houses stood by a still and swollen river, as if it were their highway. And dimly a long way from his conscious mind, some ineffable and unidentified sadness stirred.

NORTH LUDDENHAM 3 miles.

They both saw the signpost at the same time. Briefly they smiled at one another, suddenly united in their pleasure. In loose and perhaps at times unhappy harness, they had struggled up some hill. Now, the pinnacle awaited them.

The command of the newest, most powerful rocket station in the world. The only British Zeus Squadron yet in existence. Three Zeus rockets, each of thirty megaton capacity, each packing more punch than all the bombs dropped in the war put together.

They were about to arrive.

Already on the horizon, he could see a water-tower, blackened with age. Soon they were passing the disused sites, the old W.A.A.F. camp, a gun-post green with moss. North Luddenham had once been in Five Group: sixteen years ago, Lancasters had operated here. Turning to the right, the car crossed an old aircraft dispersal, its tarmac potholed and overgrown. Now they were on a new white arrow of a road, and the remnants of the old airfield slipped away.

Ahead was the main entrance.

The driver let out a gasp, then jammed on full brake. Rosalie and Gallagher pitched forward. The Humber came to a squealing stop a good ten yards before the first of them.

It took Gallagher a whole minute before he could properly take in the scene in front of him.

It was perhaps the silence that lent it all this nightmare quality of unreality. No one spoke, no one said anything. Yet despite the cold, all along the newly laid concrete, all along the clay of the newly dug drains, were people. Civilians, untidy in duffle-coats and headscarves. Young people, some with children, some hardly more than children themselves, saying nothing, doing nothing, just obstructing, lying prone in the path of his car. While at intervals, carried by some unblooded boy or some sexless girl were the anti-nuclear banners, the white flags (how right they were to take the emblem of cowardice!) with the black meaningless sign.

Always sensitive, Rosalie said, "Is it us they're against, Gavin?"

As if afraid that in some way he would be the object of Gallagher's wrath, the driver let out a bleat on the car's horn. Mournful, urgent, pleading. But as if they were corpses on some battlefield, no one moved.

Gallagher felt sick with rage and impotent anger. For a moment he glanced scornfully at the pitiful immature faces. While all the while he seemed unaware of the pleading of the Humber's horn . . . let us in. Let us in.

Yet almost at once outrage gave way to the necessity for action. Through his mind, Gallagher marshalled his arguments. If these demonstrators wanted to hear the R.A.F.'s side, or for that matter they didn't, *he* had it ready. Yes, they could bring their children to demonstrate, but by God he'd like to know who was defending their children right now, and who had fought in the past to give them this very freedom to make bloody nuisances of themselves.

"What are you going to do?" Rosalie said, as with his hand on the door handle, Gallagher prepared to get out and speak to them.

Before he had time to answer, a sudden mass wail went up from the demonstrators. A spurt of water skidded off the Humber, momentarily blanked out the windscreen as if they were moving through storm. When it cleared, Gallagher saw that Station Security had ordered up the Station fire engines. With specially pressurized hoses, they were literally hurling the demonstrators to either side of the roadway. Gallagher had a momentary vision of a child with its black hair plastered to its head like a Japanese doll, lying face downwards in the yellow mud, a woman in clinging clothes running before the force of the water. A young boy blubbering as a jet caught the side of his face. To either side, the demonstrators scattered like chaff in the wind.

Then the Humber was moving forward again, its tyres sizzling, its pennant limp, down the long wet road to the raised main gate.

It stopped at the Guard Room. Gallagher got out and produced his special pass. The road was awash with ochre-coloured water, and he had to pick his way through the puddles. The Security Officer rushed forward to apologize about the disturbance. The Wing Commander Admin shook his hand. The Service Police saluted.

But all these happenings were somehow one degree removed from Gallagher's immediate awareness. His eyes were caught by a large stain of toffee-brown mud over his sock which continued up his left trouser leg. That stain seemed to slide through some chink of memory, to produce like some curious coin a picture bright and clear as a lantern slide.

A fifth of a century ago. The fight in the High, Britons against Britons, the bloodstain on his sock.

And briefly with the fragmentary communication of a shared revulsion, the Gallagher of then looked at the Gallagher of now.

There was no reason to doubt Mumford. Gallagher could tell at a glance his worthy character. Long white face, black brushed-back hair, honest brown eyes. He was on the tall side and had a slight stoop. Gallagher met him for the first time not in the bar, as he had met most of his officers, but conscientiously on the job in the Control caravan.

"Good morning, sir." A stiff salute. "Mumford. Senior Launch Control Officer."

"Morning, Mumford." Gallagher put out his hand. The man had a rather limp handshake which did nothing to increase his confidence. During his career, Gallagher had developed a definite ability to assess people, and whether or not he could get on with them. He knew perfectly well that there was a kind of chemical reaction between two human beings that either brought them together or opposed them, and you couldn't put the blame on one individual of a pair. Gallagher looked for warmth, enthusiasm and efficiency—like the qualities Ingleby possessed—and all he was conscious of receiving from Mumford was an aura of damp bad breath. That first afternoon, as Mumford escorted him over the installations, the Senior Launch Control Officer did his best to be both friendly and respectful, and somehow even those conscientious attempts, talking about his service career, the house he had got for his wife and child, irritated Gallagher even further.

"You'll want to see everything, sir?"

"Everything."

Like all rocket stations, North Luddenham was built on the site of a wartime aerodrome. The runways were still there: so was the Control Tower: so were the hangars. Only the main hangar was in use, and that had been converted into a Repair, Inspection and Maintenance building, with full air-conditioning, dust-proof floors, overhead cranes and all the necessary high-pressure systems and machinery to do the delicate checks on the missiles. Farther north, the bomb-dump was still in use for housing the Zeus warheads, immensely powerful nuclear weapons capable on their own of obliterating over two hundred square miles of enemy territory.

In the centre of the aerodrome, surrounded by a rectangle of high barbed wire and floodlit at night by neon lights, was the Control Caravan, the three launching pads, the three Zeus rockets lying horizontal under their blue-steel hangars.

"Efficiency," Gallagher said, after he had made a careful survey of everything from the savage security-patrol dogs to the three red fire engines, their crews completely encased in special suits with windows for their eyes. "Efficiency *and* safety. We've reached a stage where mistakes simply *cannot* exist. The smallest, most harmless mistake, Mumford . . . and straightaway we must clamp down hard!"

"I'll show you," said Ingleby one week later with that same sense of showmanship that the years could never dim, "what's going to happen at the Moment of Truth."

This Operations Room was top secret. Circular in shape, the whole of the wall was one vast map. The ceiling was a dome of light, and on the linoleum floor were a number of plotting tables, briefing desks and chairs. No one else was present. It appeared to Gallagher, as he stood beside the A.O.C., Rocket Group, that the two of them were poised on the hub of the world. During the course of the years, he had often been in close contact with Ingleby at Air Ministry and Woomera, but this was the first time since the war that he had been again under his command. Their speciality was the same, but where Gallagher had concentrated on ballistic missiles at a technical level, it was in the highest political and military circles that Ingleby had fought sceptic, fool and Doubting Thomas in his battle to prove that the rocket had superseded the bomber.

Now he leaned over a small steel control panel. He pushed a red button. There was a slight whirring noise. The maps——just ordinary Bonne projections dotted with airfields, squadrons, rocket sites, routine training areas—slowly began to slide down, showing they were just a blind for what lay beneath.

"The War Map," Ingleby said. "That's what the world'll look like . . . just before the balloon goes up."

Gallagher raised his eyes. High over the Baltic, he saw four squadrons of V-bombers, poised for the dive on Leningrad, Moscow and Minsk. Six more squadrons were patrolling the Black Sea. Fifty aircraft were airborne from Turkey and Persia. All round the underbelly of Russia were aircraft with the nuclear capability already on their way to their targets. The position of forty flying tankers were shown. Sixteen white winking lights represented the Thor complexes, and the larger red steady was the Zeus site at North Luddenham.

"What strikes you straightaway, Gavin?"

"Too many bombers . . . not enough rockets."

"Exactly!" Ingleby walked closer to the wall. "This map's out of date. Obsolete. *I* know that and *you* know that . . . and one day soon, *Air Ministry* will know it, too. God knows, I've hammered hard enough . . . and at last we're making headway. Not long now, all being well, that picture will be completely different. The other way round. All these manned aircraft—" he began walking along, tracing with his finger the eastern and southern boundaries of Russia "—will be replaced by I.C.B.M.s. We'll have rocket complexes everywhere. We'll have them on rails. We'll have them underground. Rocket Group will mount the Great Deterrent."

Like all Air Force officers, Gallagher had no illusions that his country was at peace. He knew that the Cold War presented an even greater peril than the hot one. He and Ingleby and all the others were defenders of peace, the protectors of mankind. The whole point of the Deterrent was that it should deter. Nemo me impune lacessit—you'll get as good as you give . . . *or more*.

"Manned aircraft," Ingleby was saying. "Expensive . . . slow . . . inefficient . . . subject to weather . . . liable to human error . . . easily shot down . . . incapable of packing the punch that Zeus can. Our point's already proved. Stares you in the face." He swivelled right round on his heels and stared, bright-amber-eyed, across the room at Gallagher. "If it wasn't for those sixteen minutes." With his forefinger and thumb he measured a minute portion of air. "Just a fraction of time . . . that much! If we could manage to get round those sixteen minutes!"

That fraction of time, Gallagher well knew, was the Achilles' heel of the liquid-fuel rocket. It was a theme continually harped on by the advocates of manned aircraft. At conferences and political meetings, Bomber Command would continually emphasize that during international tension the greater part of its force would already be airborne. Mobile, they could be directed anywhere in the world, virtually untouchable till they were on the borders of enemy territory. While the present rockets, due to technical and fuelling difficulties, took sixteen minutes to be launched from cold. A great improvement on their grandfather, the V2, which took six hours—but still not good enough. For the 12,000 m.p.h. Russian missiles that were certainly zeroed on them took only four minutes to arrive, and even politicians' arithmetic could work out that the rockets would be destroyed on their concrete ramps long before they could be fired. As Ingleby had often pointed out, the West's declaration never to fire first put its commanders at the gravest strategical disadvantage.

Those sixteen minutes were a sore spot with Ingleby. One pro-V-bomber Air Marshal had once said that the rockets were the scarecrows of the Western Deterrent. Apparently good-humouredly, Ingleby had promised, "I'll make you eat those words." It was a promise he had not forgotten, and which he had every intention—for the safety of the country, of course, not for his career—of soon fulfilling.

"Reactionary lot . . . politicians. Won't move with the times. Still cling to the manned bomber like they did to the horse."

"They won't think."

"We'll *make* them think. And once they belong to the con-verted . . . then we'll get Zeus on mass-production." Ingleby returned to the control panel and again pressed the button. Up came the mundane maps to cover up. "And on the 6th of November, Gavin . . . we'll have our chance. A mass exercise. V-bombers and rockets. *Operation Sabretooth* it's called. That's the time we've got to show them! That's our opportunity to win!"

"Sixth of November, did you say, sir! I'll get everyone on the top line."

"Knew I could rely on you." Ingleby smiled. "Cigarette?"

"Thank you, sir." Gallagher produced a lighter and lit first Ingleby's cigarette and then his own. Puffing companionably, they began walking across the linoleum to the door, their feet in perfect step.

"Good to be back in harness beside you, Gavin. Asked for you specially."

"So they told me, sir. Thank you."

"Been following your career with interest. Put the odd word in the right ear! All the way along."

"Thank you."

Ingleby smiled. "We did it last time . . . the dazzle-painted ship and all that—— Haven't the least doubt we'll do it again. The old firm, eh? Quite like old times!"

They had reached the heavy oak door. As Ingleby began turning off the light switches, Gallagher said slowly, "Of course, sir . . . this sixteen minutes' business . . . there *is* one way we might——"

Ingleby had opened the door. "Yes . . . yes. I was thinking along the same lines myself, Gavin." He smiled that same white flashing smile. "Great minds think alike."

Now they were out in the corridor, and away from the holy of holies, by a well-disciplined reflex both of them stopped talking secrets. Ingleby began making inquiries about America, reminiscing over Woomera, had he settled in to North Luddenham yet, how long had it taken him to drive down to Air Ministry that morning, how did his wife like it.

"It's a nice big house. After so many hotel rooms and digs . . . Rosalie's all for it. We get a bit of privacy."

"Good . . . good! Give her my regards."

"Will do."

"And what about the personnel . . . your technicians . . . satisfied?"

"From what I've seen . . . a good bunch."

"And your launch teams?" They started to go up the stairs to ground level, where Gallagher's staff car was waiting to take him home. "Who's your Senior Launch Control Officer?"

"Squadron Leader Mumford."

"Mumford? Oh yes . . . tall, rather pale face?"

"That's the chap."

"How d'you find him? All right?"

For a moment Gallagher hesitated, because when talking personalities to senior officers, one had to be quite fair.

"Oh, I think so . . . yes," he said.

On the morning after he returned from seeing Ingleby at Air Ministry, Gallagher did his daily inspection of the camp as usual, and found Mumford conscientiously fussing round the Control Caravan. He was not officially on duty—a junior was. But that was another somewhat grating thing about him: whether he had no idea what else to do, or whether he didn't trust his subordinates, Mumford *always* seemed to be there. The three Warrant Officer Console Operators sat in front of their Control desks with nothing to do except stare at the five Phase push-buttons, and the PEACE—NEUTRAL—WAR keyhole above them, and listen to Mumford tapping the myriad dials and gauges which signified the serviceability of the missiles.

"Check and double-check . . . that's my motto, sir."

"Quite right."

"All three serviceable. Missile 190 will be returning to R.I.M. for routine inspection tomorrow. To be replaced by Missile 186."

Gallagher saw that strung round the Senior Launch Control Officer's neck on a string was the firing key. When the five phases of checking, erecting and refuelling had been completed in the inevitable sixteen minutes, all that would remain was to insert the key into each keyhole, turn anti-clockwise from NEUTRAL to WAR—and the missile would be on its way.

Perhaps the reason why Mumford always seemed to be around the pads was that he had a kind of inverted power complex. Those insignificant characters often had. Couldn't bear to give up the key to anybody else. Wore it as a kind of emblem : perhaps it made him feel like God.

Rather more brusquely than he intended, Gallagher said, "Mumford . . . I'd like a word with you outside."

Down the caravan steps they went together, Mumford looking a little apprehensive, and they walked over to the central launching pad. They stopped beside the silver liquid-oxygen tank, and Gallagher said, "You know I was at Air Ministry yesterday?"

"Yes, sir."

"We're having a big exercise on November 6th. V-bombers and Rockets. *Operation Sabretooth.* I want everything on the top line."

"It will be, sir."

"I also had a word with the A.O.C. Rocket Group. About those sixteen minutes."

"The sixteen minutes' preparation time before firing . . . you mean, sir?"

"Exactly! Since four minutes warning is all *we'll* get . . . we *must* cut that time down!"

"I couldn't agree more, sir."

"Now how long does Phase One take?"

"The electronic check under the hangars? Four minutes, thirty seconds."

"And Phase Two?"

"Three minutes for the hangars to move back . . . and the missiles to come up vertical to the firing position."

"Now the big bugbear . . . fuelling. Kerosene and liquid oxygen."

"It's not the kerosene in Phase Three, sir. The liquid oxygen's the trouble."

"How long though?"

"Six minutes for Three and Four."

"Final check-out in Phase Five?"

"Two and a half minutes."

"Then there's only inserting the key in each keyhole . . . turning . . . and we'll have fired all three."

Gallagher paused to look around the site. Then slowly and deliberately he said, "Can you suggest a way of getting those sixteen minutes down?"

"Well, sir . . . we have regular dry countdowns, as you know. For speed and efficiency. We *have* got it lower."

"How *much* lower?"

"Fourteen seconds."

"That's no damned good! I'm thinking in terms of fourteen *minutes*."

"You mean keeping them at Phase Five, sir?"

"Yes, I do. I mean just that."

He looked towards Mumford. Now was the time for the Launch Control Officer to bring up all the undoubted difficulties and problems. Gallagher would have wished a subordinate, especially in a job like this, to point out this and that: to remind him of the *real* difficulty, the *real* reason why the rockets were not already maintained at instant readiness.

For the main fuel of the Zeus was liquid oxygen, which was not only expensive and highly inflammable, but evaporated fast. While erect in the firing position, the missile fuel tank had to be continually topped up through pipes leading from the big site tanks themselves, right up to the very last minute before blast off. Special cooling devices had been installed in the Zeus to keep the liquid oxygen evaporation to a minimum. But this excessive coldness was inevitably transmitted, and eventually affected the workings of the rocket parts—especially the metal components of the guidance system, known as "the brain". This snag, combined with the rocket's thirst, necessitated that after a number of hours, the Zeus had to be lowered for a thorough inspection and to have the main liquid oxygen tanks replenished.

There was a silence between them for a while. Then Mumford saw he was apparently expected to say something.

"Sir . . . and why not?"

It was Gallagher himself who had to skim through the difficulties. "Expensive . . . but no more than keeping V-bombers airborne. Lox evaporation and cooling problems . . . well, we'll eventually get round those. Safety . . . we've got every safety device there is. What we must aim at in the Rocket Group, Mumford, is that watchword . . . Instant Readiness!"

"Sir . . . exactly! I couldn't agree more!"

Any feelings he might have had about Mumford, Gallagher put beneath the disciplined blinkers with which the Service had equipped his mind. The man's personal record was undistinguished, but blameless: he had once been a Stores officer, afterwards armaments, then taken an electrical course. He had only recently completed a long technical training on rockets. Mumford and he, Gallagher decided, were just different sorts of people. They were, after all, both brother officers, dedicated to the Service, doing what the Service told them. You couldn't expect to like everybody in the R.A.F. Nor could you be expected to.

That problem out of the way, with his usual energy he got cracking on the management of his new command. Space age though it might be, North Luddenham was nevertheless organized on conventional R.A.F. lines, with three wings: Operations, Technical and Administration. He had 612 men and 42 officers under him, the ability of whom he had to assess. There was a great deal to do, and he looked forward to doing it. During the last fifteen years it was in work that Gallagher had found his peace of mind.

Peace in a daily ritual: peace in raising the flag at 9 a.m.: peace in dealing with letters and orders: peace in his extremely tidy desk, his immaculate uniform: peace in inspecting the

Station Operations Room, the R.I.M. building, the Control Caravan, the rocket-pads: peace in parades: peace in organizing entertainments, cinema shows, football matches: peace in ringing up Group and Air Ministry and playing hell that there wasn't enough sports equipment: peace even in having the capless defaulters marched into his office for punishment.

". . . left, right . . . left, right . . . prisoner and escort, atten*tion*!"

"What's the charge?"

"Sir . . . on the sixteenth of October, when carrying out routine inspection, cleaning and replacement on the launching pad fire hoses . . . did fit connection stores number 16/22 instead of connection 22/16."

"So it wouldn't fit the hydrant?"

"That is correct, sir."

"What d'you have to say?"

"Sir . . . it was a mistake."

"Why didn't you check?"

"Sir . . . I meant to."

"And if there'd been a fire on the rocket site?" Gallagher paused. "On a nuclear missile station, a mistake cannot be tolerated. Especially a mistake like this, which menaces the safety of everyone. Carelessness, laziness, thoughtlessness. Twenty-eight days detention is all I can give you . . . and that's not enough. Case referred to higher authority. All relevant papers to be sent to Group."

". . . prisoner and escort, left turn! Quick march! Left, right . . . left, right . . . left, right . . ."

Gallagher soon became known as a tough character, who came down like a ton of bricks on the least technical error. He explained his philosophy to Kendrew, the grey-haired Wing Commander Administration, with whom, unlike Mumford, he had a great deal in common. "If you get it into their heads a mistake *can't* exist . . . it *won't* exist." And when Kendrew had agreed so long as you had safety precautions all along the line to back it up, he asked, "Safety precautions? We've got dozens of safety precautions! What other safety precautions can you possibly suggest?"

Safety—he was just as keen on safety precautions as he was on mistakes, for the two were closely related. In his inspections of the warheads in the bomb-site, daily he made sure himself that the weapon was inert—not capable of electrically triggering its nuclear component. Trailers took the warheads to the rocket site, and immense precautions were taken on that short journey. The fitting of the warheads under the hangars was done by a number of skilled technicians, each of them checking and re-checking each other's work. He had all relevant information on missile accidents cut out of the newspapers and Service publications, and displayed prominently on notice boards throughout the Station. When an American air-to-air missile was accidentally let off, shooting down an American bomber, he put up the photograph of the debris with the caption underneath in large red-ink capitals: MAKE SURE IT CAN'T HAPPEN HERE.

Nor could it. Check after check after check from dozens of technicians had to be carried out before the rocket rose with its shattering roar two hundred miles up into space, to fall in a curve controlled by its gyro-electronic "brain", to burn up to nothing on re-entering the atmosphere, catapulting only its nuclear warhead on to the pre-set Russian target below. At present, the three Zeus lay under their hangars—unseen to the world, heavily guarded, unapproachable except by specially screened and authorized personnel.

Nor did Gallagher forget the psychological side. It was because of the forced inactivity of a rocket station that he had insisted on all possible sports and entertainments for his men. Not only that, he wrote a paper for Group, pointing out that always being in attendance on something that was never let off induced a form of tension that grew month by month. Camps should be organized on the new rocket-range on South Uist so that launch crews could fire off at least one rocket a year. And this idea, in spite of the expense involved, had been received sympathetically.

Within four weeks, he had got the Station into first-class operational shape. His officers and technicians were first-class, for even though he still could not like Mumford, the man never put a foot wrong. As for Kendrew, he began to rely more and more on him for general administration. His imminent retirement was unfortunate, of course, but Gallacher had been promised a first-class replacement.

So that all in all, he had reason to be satisfied. He walked over his five hundred acres now with confidence and knowledge. He had an excellent home of his own. Ingleby was pleased. Gallagher's future horizon looked rosy.

And yet there was one thing both he and Rosalie noticed—each in a different way. One night, towards the end of October, he was walking home in the kind of green afterglow that the everlasting neons round the Zeus site shed over the whole Station, when suddenly he was conscious of how quiet it was.

Not a sound.

On a normal aerodrome, there would have been night-flying, the sound of aircraft in the sky, the roaring of engines. Here there was just . . . waiting. And all at once, nostalgically, he yearned to get up in the air again. What was that bit someone had once said, he thought to himself . . . the heart of an aircraft is its engine, but its soul is the pilot.

After dinner that same night, when they were sitting at either end of the long refectory table, Rosalie suddenly held her finger to her lips and said, "Listen!"

Disciplined to use his ears for sounds of failures, breakdowns, saboteurs, he got up to walk to the window.

Dramatically, she waved at him. "Sssh!"

He stopped.

"I can't hear anything, Rosalie. Not a sound anywhere."

"No." She whispered her words at him. "That's just it. Neither can I. Nothing . . . nothing . . . nothing! Except . . . silence."

3

Yet this silence, as Gallagher sometimes reminded Rosalie, did *not*, as it did in the outside world, get worse on Sundays. Quite the reverse. Sunday was a day which Rosalie enjoyed, and which Gallagher had no feeling about whatever.

Certainly she frequently remarked to him that it was something like the old-fashioned type of village Sunday. For although there were no compulsory church parades, the rocket base possessed its own little corrugated-iron church, and its own squadron leader padre. And it was an Air Ministry Directive that as many airmen as possible should be encouraged to attend.

It was obligatory, therefore, for Gallagher and the rest of the officers to set a good example. And from ten-thirty onwards the empty roadways were busy with cars filled with officers' families and groups of other ranks, wending their way towards the church, to the sound of its little iron-clappered bell.

Most of the officers and airmen got down to entertaining each other that day—buffet-lunches, tea parties, drinks, evening get-togethers or record sessions. And to set further good example, Rosalie always invited five or six of the officers and their wives for pre-lunch cocktails, immediately after service.

As always, when they opened the front door, Gallagher had a quick feeling of relief that soon other people would be joining them, that the onus of pleasing, of being amusing, would be on *them*. And as quickly, he was ashamed of the disloyalty of his thought.

That Sunday, the last in October, they had invited Kendrew with his wife, because he was retiring at the end of the month and Gallagher wanted to get him in a corner and tell him exactly how he had come to rely upon him, and how much he would be missed.

The fact that he did so earned him one or two *you're-not-helping-me-with-the-entertaining-one-little-bit* glances from Rosalie. But all in all, she obviously enjoyed herself very much as usual.

After that, it was standard practice to have a roast beef lunch. Then for Rosalie to take a nap upstairs, and for Gallagher to sit in his study, catching up with the news in the Sunday papers.

At first when he saw it, he thought he had dozed off. It was only a small item down near the bottom of the international page. And it leapt out at him with the clarity and prescience of knowledge in a nightmare. "British Scientist," it said, "in Eastern Germany." And then staring at him from the smaller printed text, the name *Professor Peter Vince*.

Gallagher read it three times. From the start . . . *Berlin, Saturday* through to the on-good-authority report that Vince was now conducting similar experiments in East Berlin to work he had done in Oxford under a NATO grant. This research had later proved valuable in the new tritium bomb, but the Foreign Office denied that they had ever considered confiscating his passport, or that Professor Vince had access to secret information.

Gallagher stared down, frowning. Vince. Vince, the liberal-minded man. Vince, the ideas man. Vince, the detached man. Vince, the hater of the mass mind. Vince, who had chided him for staying inside the Air Force like a rat in a trap.

Gallagher had a sudden pitying vision of Vince striding along, his coat-tails flapping, crossing that sorry, sordid frontier, trying to pluck ideas out of the barren Communist air.

Yet Gallagher's main feeling was tremendous outrage. He felt as outraged as if the padre this morning had recited the Creed backwards, performed the Black Mass, or run stark naked down the aisle. Vince's action made the world momentarily turn upside down.

Gallagher sat for a long time staring into space, trying to rationalize Vince over the years. Was this a gesture? Showing off? Guilt that his nuclear research work had, after all, been used for defensive purposes? The desire not to fit in, or alternatively the desire for the very authority he despised?

But Gallagher didn't know. His machinery for understanding Vince had long since rusted. Besides, Gallagher had his own way of life now. Carefully, he dismissed thought-wasting speculation about Vince. Methodically, he folded up the papers and put them back in the rack.

Then as a harassed man might turn to the sanity of a mathematical problem, he concentrated his mind on the details for the forthcoming *Operation Sabretooth*.

On the night of *Operation Sabretooth*, knowing he would get very little sleep, Gallagher went to bed soon after supper. He had not troubled to undress, but had just taken off his shoes and his tunic, and lain down as he was. Tired by the day, he had not heard Rosalie come in. One moment he seemed to be closing his eyes and letting his head sink into the pillow—and the next, there was a whirring sound going round his brain, and starting up, he saw the round phosphorescent face of the little alarm clock juggling up and down on the table beside their bed.

Eleven o'clock.

He put out his hand and silenced it. Then he lay back for just a little while longer, counting the seconds in his mind because that way they seemed longer, allowing himself ninety.

244

Then carefully he laid aside the bedclothes, and got up and walked over to the window.

He saw the glisten of rain falling on the darkness outside.

"Gavin."

When he turned, she had put on the bedside lamp, and was lying back on the pillow, blinking her eyes at him sleepily. The light caught the golden tints in her hair, making her face by contrast even whiter. "Close your eyes," he said. "Lie down. Go back to sleep."

"I thought I heard it raining."

"It is. Just a bit."

"Not a thunderstorm? On the news, they said something about thunderstorms."

He looked out of the window again and saw the slight silver shading round the boiling top of a cumulo-nimbus. "No," he said, shouldering into his tunic. "Starry. I can see stars."

He had a wash, more to freshen up than anything, and brushed his hair. By the time he put his shoes on, she was asleep. She lay with her head on one side, her hair covering the left-hand side of her cheek. Before switching off the bedside lamp, he drew up the bedclothes around her. Then he went downstairs, leaving the hall light on, because she always liked to have some light on when she was alone in the house. He got his car out of the garage, and drove down to Operations.

He went first to the Met Office, screwing up his eyes against the harsh glare of the lights. He would always wonder why Met offices were such closed cells, glowing with false sunlight, hardly a window to them: all the information about the elements outside fed in electronically.

"Well," he said, indicating the machines busy chattering away. "What's their verdict tonight?"

"Not too good, sir."

The forecaster indicated a thick purple line that curved over Norfolk and Lincolnshire like a rainbow. "It's this occlusion."

"Stormy?"

"Yes, sir . . . I'm afraid so. A little electrical disturbance."

"And the icing index?"

"High."

"Any word from Group about curtailing the exercise?"

"None, sir. The V-bombers are already airborne."

Gallagher put his elbow on the chart table, and cupped his chin in his hands. He had not really expected there would be any change of plan. Too much was involved. Too much preparation had been made. The planning alone was a fantastic operation, as he had seen in the Group conference earlier that day. This was the first time rockets and bombers had been used together. Because of the vast difference in speeds—600 against 12,000 m.p.h.—great care had to be taken, so that all targets should be saturated simultaneously. Take off and firing times had to be regulated to the second. The three Zeus were scheduled for blast off at 00.32.26 precisely.

After he had studied the weather, Gallagher checked his watch with the time-piece in the Controller's glass cage, satisfied himself that the telephones to Group and the Zeus caravan were serviceable, and leaving Operations, walked down the four concrete steps to his car.

He noticed how warm it was—unnaturally warm for a November night. There was no wind, and the air seemed heavy with unshed moisture. Drizzle only was falling, but as he drove round the disused perimeter track, steadily the rain increased till, as the illuminated complex approached, it was coming down in sheets. Whirls of water on the windscreen caught the glitter of the neons and spun like catherine wheels. The barbed wire gate swung open for him.

He saw the Control Caravan, the missile hangars with their searchlights on, the waiting fire-engines, the silver liquid-oxygen tanks, the dead-white concrete pads as though through a curtain of crystal beads.

And there, out in the pouring rain, his face luminous under the dripping peak of his cap—Mumford.

A wave of irritation came over Gallagher. Why didn't the man wait inside the caravan, like any normal person would have done? Why this rigid adherence to good form in spite of the elements? He left his car and made a dash for it, catching Mumford in the act of a thundering salute and shouting, "Come on, man! Inside! Before we're both drowned!"

Inside the caravan, at least it was warm and dry. The three Console Operators sat waiting at their controls. "Well," Gallagher said to Warrant Officer Boase, in charge of the phase sequences for Missile 191, "how'd you like to be up in a V-bomber now?"

Boase was a plump little man, with a black tooth-brush moustache. "Rather them than me, sir. Not Warrant Officer's weather tonight!"

"Nor Group Captain's." He walked over to the wide window and saw the safety crews and the missile technicians standing against the blast-walls, all heavily covered in oil-skins and protective suits. "Not too pleasant for those characters, either." He looked at his watch. "Time check . . . everybody! Zero zero one one and six seconds . . . eight seconds . . . ten seconds . . ."

There was another five minutes before commencement of count-down. The Emplacement Safety Officer, responsible for safety within the fall-back area, came in. "Water hoses connected! Fire engines standing by!"

The Chief Missile Technician reported. "Pipes, propellant complexes and missiles checked for leaks, sir!"

Mumford was moving round the caravan, checking the dials for serviceability of the gyro directional mechanisms, the hydraulic and electrical circuits. A little officiously, as though throughout he was conscious of his C.O.'s eyes upon him, he was fussing round each Console, tapping instruments, putting his hand on the red EMERGENCY HOLD bar, sited just above each keyhole, the final safety precaution that would stop everything, whispering a final brief message into each Operator's ear. Again Gallagher noticed that he had undone the same two buttons of his shirt, so that through the gap could be seen the key on its string, silhouetted against the white of his singlet.

"Attention . . . attention!"

Mumford had taken his place by the Tannoy, and his voice sounded out over the sodden site. The men outside were running now, taking up their positions. Above the electrical hum in the caravan, Gallagher could hear the revving up of the fire engines.

"Zero hour minus two minutes!"

The Console Operators bent over their controls, concentrating on the clock-like centre of their instruments: the Phase Timer. Already each of them had their thumbs poised over the first button below.

"Zero hour minus one minute! States of missile readiness?"

Back into the caravan echoed the answering voices of the technicians.

"Missile 191 . . . ready!"

"Missile 199 . . . ready!"

"Missile 186 . . . ready!"

The rain was pouring down now—no longer in lines of drops, but like a waterfall, an illuminated, greenish-white waterfall that came down like a torrent, splashing up on the blast-walls and sending rivers and lakes of reflected neon-light washing this way and that over the emplacement.

"Zero hour minus thirty seconds!"

From where Gallagher was standing, he could see the missile hangars, their outlines furred and muzzy in the rain. Then what he had been expecting all this time happened. A deep roll of thunder reverberated throughout the caravan, and seconds later, the whole sky was alight with lightning.

"Zero hour minus twenty seconds. This is the Chief Launch Control Office. On my mark, the terminal launch countdown will begin." Mumford raised his hand. "5-4-3-2-1 . . . MARK!"

"Phase One," the Console Operators murmured, pushing their buttons. The needle on the Phase Timer began to rotate. Gauges flickered, as still hidden under their sheds the Zeus were given a completely automatic check out.

A critical period, this. A loose connection, one faulty part out of its 37,000, and there would be a buzzing noise, a red light would go on—and that would be one Zeus less: a third of the armoury gone: a black against the Station: a frown on Ingleby's face.

But gradually Gallagher saw all the needles steady-up. A battery of white lights came on. There were whirring noises that started and stopped, so that the whole effect was as though they were inside some giant pin-table.

All right so far—but now the weather was worrying him. Half his attention was on the dials, half on the storm outside. There! That was another one! A deep rumble of thunder, followed once again by a split-second of zigzag lightning. He felt his mouth go dry. His breathing was harder and quicker. But he kept his arms folded across his chest, his chin out a little, his face giving no sign of what he felt. All round him, everybody was too busy, too obsessed to be at all concerned. Mumford's face—he took a glance sideways at it now—was a model of efficient concentration on the job.

"Four minutes, twenty-five seconds . . . thirty seconds . . ." In a choir of three, the Console Operators were chanting out the readings from their Phase Timers.

"Phase Two!"

The Operators pushed the second of their buttons. A klaxon sounded, shrill against the rumble of thunder. As though this was the opening movement of some strange water-ballet, under the glittering neons and the streaming rain, exactly in time, all three blue-coloured missile shelters began to move—noiselessly farther and farther back on rails, slowly revealing the three white Zeus lying horizontal on their transporter-erectors.

Very slowly, up and up and up, the three Zeus rockets rose. Vertical now, they stopped and stayed still—each stamped with the R.A.F. roundel, each glistening in its anti-radiation paint, each towering a hundred and eighty feet into the blackness of the night. They were three pinnacles of some modernistic cathedral, triple-spired: three symbols of the soaring urge in Man, aimed at the stars.

"Phase Three!"

The most dangerous part of the launching now began. From the tanks beside each missile-pad, thirteen thousand gallons of liquid oxygen and kerosene were being fuelled into each rocket. As the lox entered the Zeus tanks, immediately it began boiling and evaporating. Plumes of smoky vapour drifted out of the vents under the nose cones.

This scene, it momentarily crossed Gallagher's mind, had all the colour and luminosity of an oil painting. The white rockets stretching out of the neon-glow: the dark shadows of the huts and shelters. And then from above, like the shafts of sunshine that slant through Rembrandt's paintings, came the intense magnesium illumination of the electric storm: bringing up for a background the deserted runways, the tumble-down Flying Control tower, the skeleton of a nearby Nissen hangar.

Nobody moved inside the caravan. Their eyes were watching the needles on the fuel gauges.

But Gallagher kept his eyes on the tips of the rockets, conscious now of the sweat on his forehead. He began fidgeting, tapping his feet on the steel floor of the caravan. Would the

fuelling never be over? Was there a block in the lines or something? Why the hell didn't Mumford . . .

"Phase Four."

He breathed out again. Anyway, that was over. Not much
longer now. It wasn't a nuclear explosion he was worried about
—that was impossible. It was the thin steel skin—1/20th of an
inch thick—that he was thinking of. If one of them got struck,
the rocket would be ripped to ribbons. Fire was almost a certainty—but they could cope with that. A fizzle of radio-active
material from the nose cone—that was the real danger, oozing
down like lava on to the technicians and safety teams below.

Tritium, the most deadly poison known to man.

How many men down there now went in risk of their lives?
Nobody could tell, of course: nobody could yet calculate the
elements: nobody could say where or when lightning would
strike. No point in letting that thought revolve round his mind.

Half out loud, he began counting seconds, trying to concentrate his mind on that.

Tick, tock—should he, shouldn't he? The decision itself
shuttled to and fro like a pendulum. Should he apply a hold?
Should he stop the exercise? Should he bring those three Zeus
down? Should he put them safely under their hangars?

Another flash of lightning lit up the rocket site like day, paling
the neons and the search-lights into nothing.

He was going to. He would have to. He would tell Mumford
now. He had even opened his mouth—but again he hesitated.

What showing would the rocket force make? What would
Ingleby say? That quotation—what was it again? The one about
safety and the nettle, danger? This was the Cold War. Certain
risks inevitably had to be taken. The V-bombers accepted certain
risks. He had to accept risks too. An important exercise like this
couldn't be turned into a fiasco. Britain was showing her war-
preparedness. He couldn't shut up shop because it happened to
be raining. Determinedly, he began to regulate his mind, discip-
lining it into a proper way of thinking.

"Phase Five!"

As though from far away, he heard Mumford's voice. Taking
his eyes away from the nose cones, he saw Mumford's smile of
self-congratulation.

"All three Zeus ready for firing, sir! And dead on time!"

Now all that remained connecting the rocket with the earth was the pipe known as "the umbilical cord", through which fuel and electrical power were fed to the Zeus till the very last moment: the turn of Mumford's key which would sever it, ignited the firing mixture at the same time.

"Holding at Phase Five and reporting, sir!"

Mumford hadn't been worried. The storm outside had meant nothing to Mumford. Mumford's mind had remained static throughout.

Now there was an air of jubilation in the Control caravan. Mumford began congratulating the Console Operators on a good countdown. Everybody had done their job well. Everybody was smiling. The missile technicians came in, quite oblivious of how wet they were, and got slapped on the back for a damned good show.

The feeling was infectious. Gallagher began to feel less conscious of the storm still outside, the rattle of rain on the steel caravan roof. The exercise had been successful. All the delicate mechanisms inside the Zeus were in full working order—a considerable technical achievement. None of the missiles had been struck. In a short time now, Group would be ringing up to tell them to lower the three Zeus. They had played their part in *Operation Sabretooth* to the letter.

Every minute, the rain was lessening. The thunder seemed farther away. He'd been worrying unnecessarily, Gallagher thought to himself. When the telephone rang, he said cheerfully, "That'll be Group. I'll take it," and lifted the receiver.

It was Ingleby. "That you, Gavin? A magnificent performance! Congratulations!"

"Thank you, sir. How did the exercise go?"

"Well . . . four V-bombers returned early. Two crashes . . . unfortunately."

"I'm sorry, sir."

"Yes . . . most tragic. The weather, of course. Still we all have to take risks. You did."

"The thunderstorm . . . you mean?"

"I *do* mean. I knew all about that thunder and lightning. You must have been biting your nails a bit, eh?"

"There *was* a faint possibility of a fizzle, sir." After it was over, it was never so bad. "But I felt we had to press on."

"Gavin . . . you were *absolutely* right. Not a scrub, not a failure throughout the Rocket Group. A hundred per cent show. The C. in C. was every impressed."

"I'm glad, sir." Gallagher paused. "And now . . . can we put them to bed?"

"Ah, that's just it!" There was a pause, rich with satisfaction. "No. We're to keep them up. At Phase Five. Trial period . . . but Gavin, it's the beginning of the R.A.F. rocket age. We're winning the battle of those sixteen minutes. Now it's seconds . . . a turn of the key only."

"That's good news, sir."

Cordially, they said good night to each other. When he put the receiver down, smiling broadly, Gallagher told that particular good news to Mumford, the Console Operators and the technicians. The jubilation increased. This was the beginning of the rocket ascendancy—naturally they were pleased. Things looked much brighter all round. Outside, it had stopped raining. All trace of cumulo-nimbus had gone. Now there was just a light film over the sky, through which Gallagher could see the stars.

The atmosphere in the Control Caravan was almost like a party. Warrant Officer Boase handed round mugs of hot tea. Gallagher produced a packet of cigarettes. Mumford dived into his battle-dress pocket for some matches.

With everybody waiting with cigarettes in their mouths, Mumford got hold of the box in his right hand. Then he took out a match and struck it with his left.

The flickering match waited and waited under the tip of Gallagher's cigarette.

There were dozens of reasons, Gallagher was telling himself, why an action like that meant nothing at all. The tension, the excitement, the exhilaration, the need for haste, the desire to please—all sorts of better reasons than inherent hidden tendencies. Nobody else noticed anything odd.

"Mumford." Gallagher's cigarette was alight now. "Are you left handed?"

"No, sir. Why?"

"You struck that match with your left hand."

"*Did* I, sir? Why yes, sir . . . so I did!"

4

Gallagher woke at exactly twenty-eight minutes past six. The alarm had not yet gone off, but with the automatic prescience of long habit, frequently he woke those few minutes before. He pressed the button of the alarm so as not unnecessarily to wake Rosalie, and lay back, his arms folded across his chest, staring up at the dark ceiling. A light breeze blew in through the open top of the centre window. It was from the east. Soft with mist, lightly touched with the tang of the sea. From a quarter of a mile away came the shout of a Sergeant S.P. But the voice only underlined the dark morning quiet, contained it in a hard harsh shell of sound.

Now, Gallagher thought, *now*. Now he waited for exaltation and triumph to flood his mind. No real road, he had once read, leads nowhere. No one should embark on any undertaking without the desire to reach its ultimate goal. Last night, he had achieved a summit that years ago he had set out to attain. Though not by any means the ultimate of what the Air Force and he had still to offer one another, nevertheless it was in itself an ambition—smooth, complete, shapely as the rocket itself.

Yet gratification eluded him. Perhaps he had gone to bed too late, too tired, too full of this new responsibility. But his short sleep had been heavy with fragments of half-remembered dreams. And now the only fact that his mind could fasten on was the picture of Mumford. Mumford with the box of matches in his hand. Now instead of the triumphant sound of Ingleby's voice in his ears, all he could hear was the rattle of the matches in the box. Instead of the majestic sight of the rockets fully armed and immediately operational, rising like ghostly cathedrals to the night sky, Gallagher's memory was filled with that rather nervous hand. Up there on the ceiling he could see the clean short nails, ridged and ugly, the spatulate fingertips.

Absurdly into his mind floated a jingle of song . . . *I may not know my left from my right, but I do know right from wrong* . . . thin smiling voice accompanying the strumming of a banjo. Who was it? . . . where had he heard it? He tried to concentrate on that to drag his mind away from the matches. And immediately some pigeon hole of his memory came back with the information . . . George Formby. A film his mother had taken him to.

And released, back went his mind to the matches.

Yet the discipline of Service life allowed no undue time for either attempted self-congratulation or self-analysis. His body rather than his mind made Gallagher rise at his usual time of six forty-five. As he padded across the bedroom floor towards their bathroom, he heard the batman open their backdoor, and clatter across the concrete yard to fill up the coke hod. Rhythmically, distantly, no more obtrusive than the ticking of a clock, came the marching of feet.

It surprised Gallagher that he should be in the mood to be soothed by these minor reassurances that all was well with his particular world.

God's in his heaven, all's right with the world—— Browning in his ignorance. Gallagher's in his heaven, all's right with the world. Some alien tired fragment of his brain, some microscopic Vince-like creature juggled behind his eyes. Doesn't scan, he said into the shaving mirror. Rockets in heaven, all's safe with the world . . . that's more like it. With the lather all round his face, he was surprised how young he looked. Well, he was still younger than the President of the United States whom they called a youngster. Now, in his own way, he had almost as much responsibility.

With one cheek scraped, he examined his face. At a distance, he still looked a little like the Gallagher who had never heard of the Air Force. A pitying smile briefly illuminated Gallagher's face. Did other people, he wondered, remember their early days with the sort of pity that one usually reserved for a sad but distant relative?

He turned on the shower. It was possible, he thought, soaping himself down, that Ingleby would put him up for another decoration. Or wouldn't he, Gallagher thought, prefer to wait till as Ingleby put it "he could get his K". Rosalie would like that. Lady Gallagher. He could imagine her. No, send the order, would you? Who to? *Lady* Gallagher.

He had a shower, then vigorously towelled himself down. Excitement was beginning to come through. Like the blood through his veins, it seemed to fill all his being. Not so much with the almost spiritual elevation of pure success, but with a feeling that was physical. He kept looking at his own arms as he rubbed them dry, his own hands and feeling like some primitive god. In these hands . . . In Thy hands . . . I am in *your* hands. In his youth, he remembered he had always had a thing about hands. Well, God knew, *he* knew, *they* knew that with those rockets at readiness, he had the power of God.

He padded into his dressing-room and put on his uniform. At seven-thirty sharp, he was downstairs, and unfolding his napkin. Pouring his coffee, the batman remarked that after the storm, today looked like being fine. There'd been a factory chimney struck at Spalding. And an oak had been split in two just beyond the perimeter of the old field. He'd seen it as he came up on his cycle.

Gallagher's sole comment was, "Take Mrs. Gallagher her tea at eight-fifteen."

That gave him time to sit on her bed and have a natter, before taking the salute at the raising of the flag at nine. Perhaps his own mood communicated itself to her, for she was restless and uneasy.

"What shall I *do* today, Gavin?" She sipped her tea. "Can't you suggest something?"

Shopping in Boston? Early closing, silly! A matinée? But where? Having some of the wives to tea? Darling, they're as bored and boring as I am! She finally settled for taking the car and giving herself a nice lunch somewhere.

"See you for dinner then! Sure you don't mind lunching in the Mess?"

He shook his head, gave her a kiss, and walked downstairs. It was three hundred yards to the flagpole. Gallagher walked briskly, unconsciously marching. Left, right, left, right . . .

"A . . . a . . . *tenshun!*"

Twelve pairs of feet snapped smartly together. The trumpeter raised his trumpet.

Launched on the first notes of the General Salute, the blue Air Force flag shivered up the pole.

Gallagher stood at the salute. Distantly, beyond the hangars and the intervening huts, he could see the tips of the rockets. Ready, poised, beautifully still, wonderfully powerful. The flag reached the top. The last drop of music faded. In the stillness, Gallagher felt an enormous and terrible pride.

By nine-fifteen, he was in his office at Station Headquarters ready to hear the morning's charges. There was nothing in any of them to worry about. An L.A.C. cook flogging the Sergeants' Mess bacon in the village. An airman with a dirty rifle on guard duty. Another who was A.W.O.L. for eight hours.

At ten Gallagher signed leave passes. At ten-thirty, he talked with his Adjutant about the doings of the day. Briefly, Gallagher informed him of the successful part played by North Luddenham in *Operation Sabretooth*.

"A satisfactory job all round, sir?"

Gallagher smiled. "Very."

Now that the curious uneasiness of the dark had been cast off, now that he was in the healthy rhythm of an Air Force day, he was beginning to feel the much desired gratification warming his being like alcohol in his blood.

The clerk G.D. brought in the morning tea.

"By the way, sir," said the Adjutant as they drank it, "to get down to more mundane matters . . . Wing Commander Kendrew's replacement's in."

He thumbed through the signals and produced one of the flimsies. Gallagher held out his hand for it.

When he had read it, he gave a slow surface smile.

"D'you *know* him, sir?"

And vaguely, reaching out his hand for the rest of the morning's mail, Gallagher said, "I *did*. I knew Bunting at Oxford. And in my early flying days. But that was a long time ago. He'll have changed . . . *too*."

All that morning, concentrate as he might, Gallagher couldn't get the name of Bunting out of his mind. He'd known that he was around, of course. That he'd survived the war. That he was still in the Air Force. But these last years he doubted if he had ever given him a single thought. Now as if to make up for it, the name *Bunting, Derek* danced over the mail he was reading, over a signal, tucked itself in at the bottom of a letter. Derek Bunting. First the name. Then the face. The good-looking face, the fair hair. Inconsequentially in the midst of reading a directive about airmen's Savings Certificates, Gallagher wondered if he still wore it carefully in a slick.

And thinking that, he had a sudden vivid image of the two of them at Oxford, that day on the river. He could smell the water, see the dappled shadows, hear the ripple of the paddles. He could almost have reached out over the years and touched himself.

He wondered, as alone he walked over to the Mess for lunch, if Bunting would mention Vince. Neither of them these days would be exactly proud to claim his acquaintance. Yet oddly, now Gallagher found himself mentally defending Vince to Bunting. Then he was talking *Mumford* over with Vince. Vince was the only one who'd understand. Vince might have a theory.

Gallagher had to break in the middle of his reminiscing to listen to something the Chief Technical Officer was saying about liquid oxygen storage.

Vince's theory got muddled. Genes, heredity, left-and-right, the mass military mind, the robot mind, a weapon on the stage must be fired before the end of Act Three . . . dear boy, ask *any* dramatist. Vince had slipped that last bit in.

But Gallagher's Air Force training was ready. It clamped on that. It produced facts like stabilizers. The deterrent power is stronger than the nuclear power. Staff College—Air Marshal Marshbanks who had a mole on his nose. Gallagher's mind regained its equilibrium.

Instead of inventing conversations with Vince and Bunting he found himself staring at the flying pictures that lined the Mess walls. His eye, as it often did on the infrequent times he ate in the Mess, rested on the picture of a Blenheim diving through flak to attack a ship. True to life, tense, accurate, good sombre colouring. Now it suddenly struck him, that's where it all began. And succeeding that illogicality (for *where* did *what* begin?) he thought sentimentally, as if he was thinking of someone who was already dead . . . I owe a lot to Vince.

He was late back from work that evening, and Rosalie was in the hall to meet him. She was wearing an off-the-shoulder dress of some amber shining silk. Her hair had been nicely set. She had been out to lunch, of course. Now he remembered. But all he could think of was that if he hadn't been slow, he could have come home early and had the house to himself. Instead, all day he had this curious ambivalence . . . that time had stood still, that every second *counted*.

Aloud he said, "Hello, darling. You're looking very beautiful tonight. Who's it for?"

257

"You."

He took off his cap and kissed her. "I'm flattered."

"I'll mix the martinis while you change."

"I'm not changing. I'm going up to the site after dinner."

"Oh?" Rosalie asked. "Why?"

"Just checking." She wouldn't understand, even if he told her. When the main liquid oxygen tanks were empty, the Zeus had to be lowered for inspection and refuelling. That meant the key had had to be turned clockwise before the Phasing Sequence was reversed from Five to One. Tonight, anyway—he had already come to that decision during the day—he intended to assume Mumford's responsibility for him. "But I'll go up and have a wash."

"Shall I just have to sit in here all evening?" she called after him. And turning, he noticed she was wearing the pearl earrings.

It was the first time he noticed something was wrong.

As he washed, he tried to go over in his mind the times Rosalie had worn those earrings. He couldn't identify all of them over the years. But since that day he had bought them in Lincoln years ago, they had been the certain prelude to trouble.

He noticed the second thing when he joined her in the dining-room. The table was set for an occasion. Lace mats on the polished wood. Candles. And the centre-piece was a bowl of red roses.

"Heavenly, aren't they?" she said leaning over the table so that the candlelight wavered as the air moved about her. It might have been all those years ago. And almost as if he was trembled back in time, he could hear her finish, "Ken always brings me them. Every sixteenth of the month. The day we were married."

"Is it a day," Gallagher said clumsily, "that I ought to remember?"

She swivelled herself away from the hand he put out to her. "No. I just thought it was time we made an effort. We were getting in a rut."

Then she rang the bell for the batman, and they sat in silence while he served the soup.

It was an uncomfortable meal. He asked her if she'd had a nice day.

Yes, very.

Did she take herself out to lunch?

No. As a matter of fact, she didn't go out till close on one. Gavin would never believe it, but she'd been bitten by a work-bug. She'd had a sudden desire to spring-clean.

"Silly, wasn't it?" she said, waiting till the batman had brought in the pudding, and then smiling till he had closed the door shut. "The wives at Hutton used to say it was a sign they were pregnant." She laughed. "But I can't be, can I?"

He said nothing.

"I'm too old, aren't I?"

"I don't know. I'm not a doctor."

"But you're everything else, aren't you? Doesn't it frighten you?" Still she smiled as if she was only teasing. "You're almost God, aren't you? I the ivy, you the oak." She finished her coffee and pushed the cup away. "But sometimes, the ivy's stronger than the oak, you know. Have you ever thought that you're not nearly so strong as you think you are? That you're hard on other people . . . oh, don't deny it . . . you *are* hard . . . because you're afraid of the same things in yourself."

"Rosalie," he interrupted her sharply. "I don't know what's got into you. But cut it out! I've had a tiring day. I don't feel like being badgered."

"And I don't feel like being fobbed off. *I've* had a *miserable* day."

"You said you enjoyed it."

"Then I was lying."

"Don't."

"Why not? I was lying like you do. To make *you* feel happier."

Patiently, he said, "When do I lie to you?" And he felt at once that his foot had encountered a soft surface that was about to give way.

"When you say that you love me."

He got up then and came round and put his hand on her shoulder. With relief, he felt it shake and heard her begin to cry. Another crisis was going to pass. He glanced at the clock on the mantelpiece and saw that it was close on eight.

"Of course, I love you," he said over and over again, stroking her head till her sobbing subsided.

"Promise?"

"I promise."

"And swear that you've always loved me."

Like a litany. "Always, I swear."

"More than you have ever loved anyone else?"

He didn't hesitate. It was only the setting for tonight's dinner, only the fatigued state of his mind that brought back the faraway thought of Edwina. Marriage to her would probably have been very much like marriage to Rosalie. It was he who was the difficult bastard to live with.

"More than I have ever loved anyone else."

"Swear. Cross your heart and hope to die."

"I swear."

She heaved a long sigh, and seemed almost satisfied. She dried her eyes, and looked in the mirror. "I'm sorry." She brought a compact out of her satin reticule. "I was silly. I get worked up sometimes. You know . . . it's the quiet . . . the boredom . . . having you all tensed up . . . let's talk about something else . . . what did you do today . . . oh, no you can't tell me, sorry, sweet. Well, then . . . what did I do?"

"You spring-cleaned," he said. It was nearly half-past eight now. His thoughts had resolved themselves into getting himself up to the site by nine, to supervise the lowering of the Zeus.

"Oh, so I did! That reminds me." She laughed. "I came across a lot of your old junk."

"Did you?"

"You're a hoarder, my love! Do you mind if I get rid of it? It attracts the moth."

"Of course not. Go ahead."

"You don't want to look it over first?"

"Why should I?"

"Just because this—" She went across to her small writing-desk, and opened the top drawer, "—is one of the things I'm throwing out."

She advanced towards him, smiling broadly. And absorbed with thoughts of Mumford, vaguely recognizing that he ought to be smiling at some joke or other, Gallagher smiled back.

"Isn't it too ridiculous for words?"

She held it then right under his face. There, out of the background—the roses, the candles, the polished table—that might have been the Ashs' flat in Avonmead, he saw their faces. His and Edwina's. Staring at it, he wondered that he could ever have thought he had forgotten.

He stood there, too stunned to say anything. And as he made no movement, very slowly and deliberately Rosalie tore the photograph into small fragments, and then with a wide gesture, flung the pieces into the fire.

The only thought that Gallagher could fasten on, as he shut the front door behind him, was that till then he had no idea that Rosalie hated him so much. Yet he recognized it as a simple fact, without emotion. He felt neither angry nor offended nor bereft. Yet he knew also, and again as a fact that only his mind recognized, that some injury had been done him. Further than that his mind refused to explore. He had been hit. Eventually he would have to examine the wound, deal with it.

But not yet.

Usually, he took the car to the site, but now it seemed imperative that he walk. There was feeble moonlight. A faint melon-coloured light filtered down through the thin overcast. There were not many night sounds in this part of Lincolnshire. No bats, no owls, no nightjars. Just occasionally, the scuffle of an animal in the grass verge. A rabbit or a rat or maybe a mouse. A furry animal. Furry animals had more chance of survival in intense radiation.

Why had he suddenly remembered that remark of Vince's? Abruptly he quickened his pace. Through layers of his mind, fragmented and colourful with shattered memories, Gallagher searched for what he was doing—at this moment, now, walking along here.

Mumford, of course. He was going to supervise Mumford. Mumford. Mumford and the matches. His mind worked slowly, moving from one stepping-stone of association to the other. Mumford and the matches and his *left* hand. Left-right tendency. Peace-war tendency. The phrases bubbled, spawned out of one another.

He hurried on faster and faster, till his own footfall sounded like the beating of a giant heart, the ticking of a giant metronome. Left, right, left, right, right, left, right, left . . .

Marching along like this, he had a sudden feeling of wisdom

and elevation. He knew all the answers. No longer did he feel tired, no longer tethered. He had a rocket's-eye-view. He seemed to be floating over the countryside, detached from it. He was a giant. God. And he looked on it and it was Good. Or was it Bad? He said . . . let there be Life. And there was Life. Let there be Death. And there was Death. At the turn of a switch. Just like that. Turn left. Or was it right? Quick as God.

Now straight ahead lay the glowing, beaded lights that outlined the site. Above towered the three white rockets into the sky.

Let there be rockets with a nuclear capability of thirty megatons. And lo, there *were* rockets with a nuclear capability of thirty megatons. Gallagher's feet crunched over the gravel. It had a loose temporary surface: it was not permanent enough under his feet. Tomorrow he would insist that Works and Bricks put down a hard concrete pathway.

He thumped up the steps of the caravan. It was much easier, walking now without a caliper. He opened the door.

The quick light blinked his eyes. He saw Mumford turn sharply, go pink with embarrassment and the desire to please. The Console operators did not turn their heads.

Gallagher said, "Good evening. Fine night. Better than last night, eh?"

He felt full of an easy charm. He felt as he had felt the first time he was drunk. He could convince anyone he was sober.

"O.K. Mumford. I just thought I'd look in for the first lowering. It's Missile 191 . . . isn't it?"

Reassured, Mumford smiled. Warmed by Gallagher's apparent good humour. "That's right, sir. We're doing 199 tomorrow at ten, 186 four hours later. To get a proper balance of time between all three."

"Good! When are we starting?"

Mumford looked at the clock. "It's zero hour minus five minutes, sir."

Easily and pleasantly, Gallagher said, "Five and three quarters to be precise."

"Yes, sir."

They both smiled.

Actually it wasn't like being drunk. It was as if Gallagher had divided in half like a worm that had been chopped by a garden spade. He didn't suppose the worm felt any pain either. And he could watch himself. He was doing very nicely. At three minutes to zero, the Console operators began to give signs of tension. Wriggling their uniformed shoulders. Adjusting their head sets. Coughing. They'd have given many more signs if they'd known about Mumford. A latent left-right tendency. In three minutes from now, gentlemen, S/Ldr Mumford will turn the Peace-War key.

Which way?

At two minutes to, he saw Mumford put his hand inside his shirt and pull out his necklace with the key. Gallagher had worn a necklace like that in the war. It had two name tokens on it. To identify the body. One red. One green. One proof against Water. The other proof against Fire. Fire, water. Peace, War. Green, red. Left, right. Right, wrong. How they loved alternatives, to pretend things were opposite!

"Zero hour minus one minute."

He held out his hand. "*I'll* have the key, Mumford. *I'll* do the lowering tonight."

Mumford began to stammer. "But sir . . . it's laid down——"

"I'll do it . . . I tell you," Gallagher said pleasantly, not raising his voice, still smiling. "I want you outside. I want a visual report on the lowering. I want the key."

He could feel it already in his hand. He heard the caravan door open. Mumford's feet going down the steps.

Saved! He'd got it! Done it! Mumford was saved from Mumford. They were *all* saved.

"Zero minus thirty seconds," said Warrant Officer Boase, the Console Operator on Missile 191.

Gallagher took the two paces over and stood behind him. On the Console, above the Phase Timer was the War-Neutral-Peace keyhole. Anti-clockwise for War. Clockwise for Peace. He drew a deep breath. Which hand d'you take? Eeny-meenie-miney-mo, catch old Mumford by the toe. If he hollers——

"Zero minus twenty."

In twenty seconds, Mumford would have sent that rocket high over the North Sea to its pre-set target in Russia. Then over to you! In *your* court! My service. Vantage to North Luddenham. A rocket back. Deuce!

263

"Zero minus ten."

He'd have turned it right instead of left. Left instead of right. He'd done it before. Flying. At Cirencester. Put on full right rudder, Mumford did.

"Zero."

Gallagher put the key into the keyhole. Left, right, left, right, Mumford had had to ink it on his thumbs. He'd put on full right rudder when it should have been left. Sent the Henley into an upside down spin. Tordoff was livid. But he'd lied his way out of it, Mumford had. Left. He'd turned the key left. Mumford . . . Mumford . . . it *wasn't* Mumford . . .

Christ, it was Gallagher!

His name seemed to be shrieked throughout the Caravan. *Gallagher,* you've turned it *left!* Damn and blast you! You've sent the balloon up! This is what Ingleby called the Moment of Truth! Look out! *Look out!*

The noise in his ears was a tumult. His eyes were blinded with kaleidoscopic fragments. Through them all, he saw only the red Emergency Hold bar just above the Phase Timer. He grabbed it, pulled it, hung on to it with the strength of a dying man.

Nothing happened. It wouldn't pull. It wouldn't give.

Then abruptly, the feel of the cold metal, and the vigorous straining of his arm cleared his mind. He became aware of his surroundings. Missile 191 had not gone off. He would have heard it, as he had done so many times at Woomera and Cape Canaveral. He was still pulling the Emergency Hold, but still it wouldn't work. So the key had not been turned.

Nor had it. There it was, still upright in the neutral position.

He took a quick glance down at the Console Operator. But Boase's eyes were still on his Phase buttons and dials.

Gallagher turned the key—clockwise.

"Phase Five," said Boase, immediately pressing his button. And shortly afterwards, "Phase Four . . . Phase Three. Lowering about to commence, sir . . . Phase Two!"

Gallagher saw the tall white middle pinnacle slowly descend —lower and lower, till once more it was horizontal, and like a coverlet its blue missile shelter came silently over it.

"Lowering complete, sir!"

Gallagher turned the key back to Neutral, then withdrew it. Still with the string necklace in his hand, he walked to the door, and joined Mumford outside.

"Everything was quite normal visually." The Launch Control Operator spoke a little stiffly. "No hesitations."

"Good."

There was a silence. Mumford was waiting for something.

"After inspection and refuelling, Mumford . . . erect 191 again. Go up to Phase Five."

"Will do, sir."

The man was still waiting.

"However . . . *I* shall keep the key."

"But, sir——"

"Should it be wanted you can phone me at home."

"Sir, in the event of an emergency——"

"I'll be over fast enough." He fastened the string necklace round his own neck. "Good night, Mumford."

"Good night, sir."

He walked away, down the gravel path, out of the rocket site. Overhead the thin cloud had cleared, and the sky was luminous with light. The winter trees stood out in ice-clear tracery. He heard the curious dead sound of a dry leaf scraping the tarmac, as he turned on to the old perimeter track. Now he seemed to notice everything about him with the kind of heightened perception that was supposed to be the hall mark of young love. His head felt clear as the sky above. The tumult of his thoughts subsided. Yet physically he seemed tired and weak as if he had been ill, or had fought a long struggle.

He had the distinct impression that he had been suffocating in a million fragmented thoughts, the metabolism of a life-time's mental processes, a dark pit, a deep sea. And that suddenly he had swum upwards towards a chink of light. He knew what it felt like to be that first amoeba that had swum up out of the slime. He knew what it was like to be the first creature to struggle out of the water.

He leaned against what had once been a blast wall to protect aircraft. He seemed to see every blade of grass, every branch of every tree, every patch of field and hedge and roadway, every iridescent particle of moonlight held in some warm and loving radiance. After a long while, he opened his shirt and took out

265

the key and held it in the hollow of his hand. The key that he could not trust to himself—or to anyone else.

The key.

As he turned it over in his hand, it glittered. Just a key. It seemed as if the moonlight were a long succession of mirrors reflecting other keys. Keys to open the garage at home, his locker at school, his room at Oxford, the Bibury bus key, Edwina's morse key, Ash's car key, the key to Rosalie's flat.

All his life, a key turned, a door opened, And through he went. Except now. This key that he held opened nothing.

Was it a hundred years since he'd walked down this same perimeter track towards the Zeus site? Seventy years, anyway. Three score years and ten. A lifetime. Something had happened. Some rhythmic pattern of this day's doings, like the hypnotic blink of light or the beat of sound, had sent him hurling back upon himself. Through himself. He had struggled for and found something.

But what?

He turned the key round in his hand, willing it to hypnotize the truth out of him.

That he could be wrong? Wrong as, *more* wrong than Mumford? That *anyone* could be wrong? That humanity was poised on the rocket tip, awaiting the inevitable human error, accidental or deliberate made little difference? The recognition that he was a fighter, not a press-button mass exterminator? That nothing was so wholly true that you had to murder to justify it? That no civilization which allowed itself to be so defended had anything of value to preserve?

Coolly, his mind examined them. There was in his thoughts perhaps something of all of them. Yet only one clear fact remained, simple as truth and as unassailable. He, Gavin Gallagher, could never in his true and right and human mind turn that key to War.

It was as if he had lived all his life to know that one truth. As if he had been briefly mad, to know that single sanity. All his life, he had been turning in ever-decreasing, ever-tightening circles of compromise. A cliché here, a lie there, a half-truth everywhere. Till he was faced with that one simple question. Could he? Or could he not?

He had read a remark by a famous scientist author: if the

ultimate act is simple, human beings can forget, can absolve themselves of the horror that it brings. Now he knew that *he* could not.

Yet he could not renounce the Air Force either. He had grown up in the Air Force. Its struggles had been his struggles. You couldn't renounce your left leg, your arm, an eye, one lung, and half your heart. He *was* the Air Force, the Air Force *was* him. Bone of his bone. Flesh of his flesh. But he was conscious neither of division nor choice. He was conscious only of illumination. Of a sense of elevation. Of a one-ness with the earth and the night.

Now he began walking briskly towards his home. Glowing squares patterned the sides of the airmen's barrack-blocks. Dark figures moved behind the uncurtained windows. An airman passed him on a cycle. At the main gate, the S.P. saluted.

Two hundred yards down, was the entrance to his drive. He did not turn in. He continued to walk along the straight road. He picked out a star low in the bright blanched sky. He could smell the winter grass, and the damp earth.

As he walked, he left behind the remnants of the old airfield, the dispersed Nissen sites, the rusted hangars, the broken fences. Ahead lay the dark countryside patched with shadow and moonlight. And beyond, the thin pale glimmer that was the sea.

EPILOGUE

At eleven o'clock on Friday morning, Henderson was in the Station Commander's office, questioning Mumford and the Console Operators again, when the police phoned.

A boat had been discovered missing from a river anchorage, four miles from North Luddenham. They had instituted an immediate search over all waterways and Broads.

Henderson asked, "Is there an outlet to the sea?"

"There is." The police inspector's voice sounded doubtful. "But in a small sailing dinghy——"

"Still search the sea," Henderson said. "And all along the shore. With every man you've got."

He put down the receiver, and began to make a note on the paper beside him. Already drawn there were lines and shapes as well as words, so that the whole impression was more a pattern rather than a page of writing. Here was another piece, and now he fitted it in—but still there were blank spaces. If only the Zeus crew had not been such a worthy bunch, they might have helped fill them. If only they had not kept their eyes so dutifully on their dials and switches, they might have seen what was happening around them. Since yesterday, he had been sure that something had happened in the Control Caravan. Now he was surer than ever. He looked into Mumford's righteous eyes and for the third time asked. "You can think of absolutely no reason whatever why the Group Captain insisted on keeping the key?"

"None."

"Everything proceeded smoothly on Operation Sabretooth?"

"Apart from the weather . . . quite normal."

"Thank you, Mumford. Now Mr. Boase——" Henderson turned to the Warrant Officer Console Operator "——you were nearest to the Group Captain when the Zeus was lowered for refuelling?"

"Yes, sir."

"He operated the key, I believe?"

"Yes, sir."

"Clockwise, isn't it?"

"Yes, sir."

"Did you notice anything out of the ordinary?"

"No, sir. Of course, I was busy with my Console——"

"Yes . . . yes, we know that. But think, Mr. Boase . . . try to remember!"

"I am, sir."

"Would you have known if Group Captain Gallagher had inadvertently turned the key *anti*-clockwise?"

"I'd have known." Boase gave a kind of grunt. "We'd all have known."

"I mean momentarily . . . and then switched it back?"

"He didn't."

"You're sure?"

"*Quite* sure."

"Oh." Henderson sat back, and picking up a pencil began turning it in his fingers. There was a long silence, and he seemed just on the point of letting them go, when Boase said, "There was one thing . . . but it isn't important——"

"Tell me."

"The Group Captain did put his hand on the Emergency Hold."

Henderson put down the pencil quickly, and leaned across the desk. "Why would he do that?"

"I thought he was just testing it. He gave it one or two good old pulls."

"It isn't the usual drill?"

"No . . . no. But it's the sort of thing you *could* do."

"There's no need to do it?"

"No need . . . but it wouldn't do any harm."

"Nothing would happen I take it?"

"It couldn't come into operation . . . no. The Emergency Hold is for *after* the key has been turned."

"A safety device, in fact?"

"Yes, sir . . . the last safety device."

Henderson said slowly, "Do you think it's possible the Group Captain *thought* he'd turned the key the wrong way?"

Boase looked back at him stolidly. "I don't know what the Group Captain thought, sir."

"Why d'you think he grasped the Emergency Hold then?"

269

"People do touch things, sir. Take hold of them. Make sure they're there."

"But he *might* have thought he'd turned it the wrong way?"

"He *might* have done, sir. I don't know."

"Thank you, Boase," Henderson said, and looked round at the others. "Well, gentlemen . . . that's all."

When they had gone, the Provost Marshal's man got up and putting his hands in his pockets began a short walk round the office, looking at the pictures on the walls. Drawings of aircraft, illuminated squadron records, prints of bombers coming back in moonlight, caught in searchlights. He stopped for a while at a photograph of a Blenheim.

Then he returned to where he started off from, and picking up the files, the papers, the photographs and log books of Group Captain Gallagher, one after the other he made a neat pile of them on the top of the desk.

They found the boat and the body at almost the same time—not long after dawn on Saturday. The boat was fifty miles off the coast, bobbing up and down quite empty in a light easterly, and the launch brought her back unharmed to harbour.

Gallagher they found on a sandy beach, close to a small headland. As soon as he heard, Henderson rang up Bunting, and they drove down to the sea together in the same Humber that had brought them up from the station, three days before.

It was a twelve mile drive, but they said little to each other. The fens and dykes slipped silently behind them, till they reached some sand-dunes where the driver parked the car. The two of them got out and began to walk towards a little knot of people at the water's edge.

He was lying there as he had been found—quietly on his back, his arms outstretched. The sea at least had been kind to him. What change there was between life and death could not be seen here. His hair was still wet, and was pressed damply over his forehead—but otherwise it was the same face as Henderson had seen on all those photographs, the eyes wide-open, but quite calm and natural. They had unloosed his tunic and shirt and pulled down his tie—Henderson thought in a belated effort to revive him, until he saw the string round his neck.

"Well, the key's here," Bunting said. "We've got the key back."

"Yes."

"And now I suppose," Bunting said, "the Air Ministry are going to say it was an accident? That's what they'll want to say, isn't it . . . to hush the whole thing up? That's what you'll recommend in your report, I expect?"

"I expect so, Bunting."

"But what do you really think, Henderson?"

"What do I really think?" Henderson knelt down on the sand and closed the dead man's eyes. "I think he was . . . *murdered.*"